PIER PRESSURE

Deadlights Cove, Book 4

B. PERKINS

AIMEE VANCE

Revel Books

Revel Books
ISBN: 979-8-9863649-8-8

www.aimeevancebooks.com

Be like Stevie Nicks:
Go your own way.

Playlist

As any true musician would, Lys mentions a lot of songs in this book. Enjoy!

Paralyzer - Finger Eleven
Heartache Tonight - The Eagles
The Chain - Fleetwood Mac
All Along the Watchtower - The Jimi Hendrix Experience
Dreams - Fleetwood Mac
(Sittin' On) The Dock of the Bay - Otis Redding
Don't Stop Believin' - Journey
Bye Bye Bye - *NSYNC
Everybody (Backstreet's Back) - Backstreet Boys
Layla - Eric Clapton/Derek & The Dominos
Iris - The Goo Goo Dolls
Gimme All Your Lovin' - ZZ Top
I Love Rock 'N Roll - Joan Jett & the Blackhearts
Paradise City - Guns N' Roses

Chapter One

MAISIE

I STARED AT MY FATHER, trying to process the words he'd just said. I understood each word individually, of course, but *together*?

Surely I had heard him wrong. That had to be it. My hearing was going, which was a little unlikely for a 28-year-old supernatural sea nymph, but not impossible. Or maybe I still had water in my ears. More likely. Ronan had called me to his study straight from a swim, after all. I'd only had time to shift from my mer form back to human, pull on dry clothes, and walk from my end of our family home through the glass-domed tunnel to his office.

I tilted my head, trying to shake and knock the water out, but nothing happened.

"Could you repeat that?" I asked, proud of how calm my voice sounded despite my heart thudding wildly in my chest. I was *totally* calm. He was going to repeat it, and it was going to sound nothing like —

"You're going to marry Owen Kincaid."

Ah, crap. That was what it had sounded like the first time.

"Marry."

Ronan nodded slowly.

"Owen… Kincaid."

Another nod.

I opened my mouth, closed it again. Words were lost to me as I sat there gaping like a goldfish, wishing I had the same memory span and could forget this whole conversation. His brow furrowed slightly, like he could read my mind.

"Okay, this is probably a silly question." I gave a little laugh as my fingers gripped the armrest of the chair I sat in like it was my last hope to hold onto my sanity, but my father didn't even blink. "But, *who* is Owen Kincaid?"

"He's a demon from Scotland," Ronan explained slowly, like I was a child, not the almost thirty-year-old heir to his kingdom. "An old acquaintance of your mother's, and you've met him several times before."

"And," I started, trying to get my mind to catch up after this shocking news, "*why* would I marry Owen Kinkaid?"

Ronan leaned back in his chair with a sigh. That caught my attention — my father was more prone to barking orders than sighing. Dread settled in as I forced my fingers to pry off the armrest, half expecting to have ripped it off in my death grip. Just from that one small exhale, I knew whatever Ronan said next would make all of this feel real, not like the elaborate joke I'd hoped it was.

"The supernatural leaders have been convening, discussing an old legend about linking powers between species. For so long, we've each held ourselves separate with only a basic understanding how the other species' powers work, but apparently, that wasn't always the case, or so the legend says. Everyone wants to be better prepared after the recent chain of catastrophes abovewater in Deadlights Cove, so it may be time to band together. Errakal is behind bars for now, but none of us are foolish enough to believe the chaos will stop with him."

"That makes sense. It never hurts to be prepared." I bobbed my head, still not seeing how this led to my arranged marriage. Our people were left vulnerable when Errakal, a powerful demon-witch, had messed with the ley lines a few months ago. And it hadn't ended there. But I'd never heard of linking powers before.

Hearing my words as the approval he wanted, even though that was *far* from my intent, Ronan went on. "I reached out to your mother's people, and it turns out that Owen has been leading a research study regarding linking magics — the very same thing that everyone here has been discussing. Owen found documentation of an ancient witch Coven that was formed by a witch and a demon linking powers. Not only were they able to pass on their diluted powers to their children, but they also were able to share in *each other's* powers. A witch with demon magic, and vice versa. Owen has been searching for information on the ceremony to join magics between species, offering the potential to increase the power of each partner substantially. All of the evidence he's been able to find of successful linkings were married partners, so there must be some element of proximity required to maintain the magic."

"Okay." I drew the word out, focusing heavily on the desk in front of me so I didn't have to meet my father's eyes. While I'd always known my parents' marriage had been arranged for a political alliance, not once had anyone spoken to me of needing to do the same. Would Owen and I even get along? How much time would we have to get to know each other before we would be expected to share the rest of our lives together — lives that were significantly longer than typical human lives? Would he come live here, in our underwater city, or was Ronan shipping me off to Scotland? What kind of expectations did Owen have for this arrangement? Demons were practically immortal — just how old *was* Owen?

Not sensing my internal distress as I watched any plans for future romantic entanglements — not that I had any — flush down the drain with a sad wave, Ronan continued. "After some negotiation, we came to an agreement. You'll marry Owen, and then link your magic. The next time some jumped-up demon-witch decides to pull power from our nexus, you'll have enough power as both a sea nymph *and* a demon to defend our people, as is your responsibility as heir."

I blinked once. Twice. Nausea rolled in my stomach as I thought through his words.

As much as I didn't want it to, what he said *did* make sense.

Erakkal had caused significant problems for our people over the last year, pointing out our weaknesses in a way that had my father continually on edge. Most recently, my youngest sister, Corissa, was rendered unconscious for days as our magic failed to restore itself after each use. Fortunately, Errakal was caught, the magic he'd been harnessing released again, and she was able to replenish her power enough to wake up. But those days she'd lain in a sleep state, stuck in her mer form, and unable to replenish her magic haunted all of us. We could have lost Corissa if she'd been without her magic much longer.

Just the thought of that had my eyes burning. Not at all because of this new responsibility laid at my feet.

But it wasn't just our magic replenishing that had been a problem lately. Our underwater city had suffered damages during the attacks last fall, an issue we were still trying to recover from. Normally, my family's magic was enough to sustain the many spells that both held our underwater city together and hid us beneath the waves from the humans above, but whatever magic Errakal and his following had used on our city had caused damages that didn't want to heal. Not permanently, anyway.

My head tipped back as I tried to stay calm, blinking back any and all emotion. Ronan, ironically, never reacted well to big shows of emotion, so a freak-out from me wouldn't stop this. No, only *he* was allowed to have a temper, not any of his genetic offspring he'd handed pieces of his personality to. Like the crack in the glass ceiling above me, my heart fractured at the thought of marrying a stranger.

Besides, no matter how I wanted to fight back, I knew Ronan was right. From what he'd just shared about linking magics, I understood the benefits it would offer me. On land, sea nymphs were nearly powerless, practically human except for some enhanced senses, hence why it was all but forbidden for us to be abovewater for long stretches of time.

Owen was a demon, though. And I knew my father — Owen must be a demon of immense power, or Ronan wouldn't have agreed to this. If I went through this — bile rose in my throat at the thought, but I choked it down —

and linked magic with him, I could lead by example. I could show my people that it was safe, and something we could *all* potentially do, so all of our magic would extend far past the sea.

If linking powers *was* possible, then we needed it. As heir to the royal family for the sea nymphs of the northwest Atlantic, it was my responsibility to be the protector of our people, of our way of life, of our city. They deserved a leader with access to more power, and that was what the magical linking offered. I could see that.

But, *Owen Kinkaid?* Some random demon I had zero memory of ever meeting? If my mother knew him, then that meant he was from Scotland, and I hadn't been to Scotland since I was ten, so even if I'd met the male, it was well over a decade ago.

There was a whole town of powerful supernaturals just a few minutes away in Deadlights Cove, some of whom I knew pretty well from my bartending job at Scallywags, though my father didn't know about that part of my life. His own issues with the local supes aside, surely one of them would be able to offer the type of magical power needed to help protect our people too, right? Maybe I could find someone on my own to marry, to join powers with.

A school of fish swam by on the other side of the glass walls of Ronan's office, seemingly unbothered even though my future was sinking faster than a ship taking on water. I cast my eyes around his office, looking at the driftwood desk, the nets hanging on the glass walls, the dark water beyond… anywhere but at my father as panic took over.

Poseidon, I wanted to fan myself, feeling sweat pool in every crevice of my body as I fought to remain calm with each passing second. I leaned forward. "Is there maybe another —"

My father rubbed his temples, and suddenly, he looked… not *old*, exactly, but older than I'd ever seen him look. Like all seven of his daughters, Ronan had shining blond hair, though his was more golden whereas mine was platinum. He looked like he belonged surfing waves off the coast of California more than governing an underwater city off the coast of central Maine, his skin permanently suntanned, tattoos scattered across his nearly always bare shoulders. Sea nymphs were constantly popping outside to swim around the city — much faster than walking — so clothing could become cumbersome to keep track of. I couldn't say the last time I'd seen him put on a shirt, and I was fairly sure Ronan didn't own shoes.

"We need this, Maisie," he said at last, his dark blue eyes boring holes in my head as I fought back a whimper that wanted to escape. "Believe me, I've considered other options, but we need demon magic on our side, and you know how hard it is to find one of them willing to comply with… well, *anything*. Owen's a good male; I think you'll even like him. His family has been close with the Douglasses for centuries. He wants to help us out with this." An emotion I didn't understand flitted over my father's face, but was gone before I could decipher it. His eyes dropped, focusing on his hands, jaw tense. "If you were dating anyone, I wouldn't ask this of you, but seeing as you've never shown an interest in any of your suitors…"

My ears pricked up at that, though I tried not to let it show. *If I was dating someone*, I could get out of this.

"I know you'll do what's best for our family." He smiled,

but it didn't quite meet his eyes. I fought my facial muscles into submission to match it. "You always do, my Pearl."

I hardly heard the rest of what he said, even as my mind recognized my dismissal and I left his office, walking aimlessly through the tunnels that connected the many glass bubbles that made up our city.

Knowing my father, even if I managed to find someone to date, he'd just move on from me to my sister, Saoirse, the second oldest. Something I absolutely wouldn't allow. She was the ultimate rule follower and would never argue back against Ronan, willing to live a life he chose to appease him. I could put my fist through one of the glass walls at the thought of her eternal misery, locked in a relationship with a demon she hated.

I, on the other hand, wasn't afraid to fight back against Ronan. To outright defy him, if need be. But I also wasn't stupid enough to try without some sort of a plan.

To truly get out of this arranged marriage, I had to make my own match with someone who could offer my people the same measure of protection as Owen could.

If I chose a match for myself, it wouldn't be with a demon. A few notable exceptions aside, they were unpredictable and flighty, on the whole. I needed someone with roots in Deadlights Cove, because no *way* was I leaving my sisters behind, and my responsibility was here, to my people in Crunamar City, the heart of our kingdom.

In order to convince my father, it needed to be someone with a decent amount of power, so that ruled out shifters. Angels were a bit too fastidious, and besides, there were so few of them around, it'd be hard to find one and convince them of this scheme. I wasn't even sure I'd ever seen an angel date *anyone*.

That left witches. I needed a witch, fairly high up in their Coven to appease my father. Someone with connections. Someone with enough breadth of training and skill that they could compete with a demon when I had to convince dear old Dad to give up on Owen. Maybe a little charm wouldn't hurt, then, either.

Certainly, they had to be a decent actor.

A seal glided by outside the tunnel beside me, and I locked eyes with it for a moment while I ran through all the witches I knew.

Then my thoughts snagged on someone, and a nervous laugh bubbled out of me. I gave the seal an exasperated look before it pushed off the glass, gliding away into the dark.

The witch I had in mind was not someone I would pick for myself, if I was actually trying to date. Okay, maybe I'd had a crush on him for... the past couple years or so, but only superficially. Objectively, he was sexy, but he was also a total player and absolutely *not* bring-home-to-Ronan material, not if I wanted him to leave that meeting alive, anyway. But I had to admit he had the training, the magical ability, the acting ability, and maybe even — I grimaced — the *charm* to make this work.

If I could convince him to go along with it. And actually work up the courage to ask him in the first place. *Not likely*, the voice inside my head that loved playing my social failures on repeat every night scoffed at me.

"Great," I muttered to myself, turning down the next offshoot tunnel to head back to my room.

I pushed open the door, almost slamming it into Kymari's face where she stood just inside my bedroom.

"Whoa," I said, jumping back in surprise. "Didn't realize you'd be here so fast."

"Well, you texted it was an emergency, and as your guard, that means I need to be quick." Her head cocked to the side, long dark braids shifting as the seashells tied into the ends clinked together. Kymari's family had been part of our royal guard for as long as I'd been alive, her ancestors the guardians over our southern boundaries in the Caribbean, and she bore the brown skin of their line. Her dark eyes scanned my body for any injury, taking in the mom-jeans and hoodie I wore. "Didn't realize you meant *fashion* emergency. I thought I burned that hoodie."

I rolled my eyes, stepping inside and slamming the door shut behind me as I threw myself onto my bed with a sigh.

Despite the fact I was heir to the throne, my room was simple, and I liked it that way. All my textiles were creams and teals, with accents of coral and seafoam green, the furniture an aged wood that resembled driftwood. The main feature in my room, like most rooms in our city, was the wall of curved floor-to-ceiling windows revealing our ocean just beyond, like a living aquarium on all sides. The only true decor I had was the shelf above my bed, where a row of pristine shells rested. They were from travels with my sisters; whenever we went to a new sea, a new beach together, we found the best one and brought it back.

When I didn't even react to her usual prod at my horrid

taste in clothes, Kymari sat on the edge of the bed next to me.

"Your father?"

I turned my head to stare at her, blinking slowly.

Kymari scrunched her nose. "What happened?"

"He's arranged a marriage for me."

She raised a jewel-studded brow and plucked at my jeans. "Will you get a new wardrobe beforehand?"

I rolled my eyes. "I'm serious. To *Owen Kinkaid.*"

"*Kinkaid?* Like, the Scottish Kinkaids?"

"Yes?"

"Maisie, that's a big deal. And not that surprising since they're loyal to your mother's family."

I threw my hand over my eyes, a whimper leaving me without permission. "I don't even *know* him, though." I sat up, gripping my friend's shoulders tightly as I stared into her eyes. "I need a distraction, so you're going to help me. I can't deal with this today."

Kymari chewed on her lip, her dark eyes squinting. "You want me to sneak you out again, don't you?"

A slow, innocent smile spread across my face as I lifted my shoulders, shooting for the cherub look, but probably hitting somewhere more along the line of an awkward turtle. "At least I'm asking you to go with me this time, right? That's safer."

Kymari sighed. "You know how much I hate breaking the rules."

"Just think, someday *I'll* be the one making the rules."

My friend shuddered. "No offense, but that is a truly terrifying thought. You'll probably insist we all wear the ugliest uniforms. Baggy sweatshirts that hide the fact that we have any shape at all in boring colors like *beige*."

I chuckled, nudging her in the arm. Fashion was not my thing, but Kymari *lived* for it. Though she knew as well as I did there was a very good reason for my abovewater wardrobe choices. "What if I let you pick out my outfit? You can even take my hoodie away from me again."

"The whole month of June, I'm choosing your outfits, or it's no deal," Kymari said, leaping off the bed. "And I want the other two hoodies I know you own that are nearly identical to this one, too. You're far too old for a security blanket, and that's exactly what this thing is for you. Take it off."

"Okay, rude," I said, but pulled the hoodie over my head when she waved her hand impatiently.

Kymari tugged me to my feet and towards my closet. She threw me a pair of flare jeans, a tee she took a pair of scissors to and chopped the bottom half off, and then a crochet duster she'd made me for my last birthday.

"Turn around. I'm taking your braid out."

I did as she said, a plan forming in my mind.

It was time to go find a rockstar.

Chapter Two

LYSANDER

LEANING my forearms across the bar, I glanced at the text that had just come in from my mother — no, sorry, not a text, a *calendar invite* — and clenched my phone a little too tightly before sliding it back in my pocket. I'd deal with her later.

"Ready, man?" Dillon spoke over the music thudding through the bar and clapped a hand to my shoulder, a look of concern flitting across his face. He jerked his head behind the counter at the shelves of liquor, his blond curls swaying with the motion. "You need a shot?"

I pushed down my parental issues and flashed him a grin. "Saving my beer goggles for *after* the show when I'm free to make questionable decisions."

"Your strong suit."

"Practically an expert. Do they offer certificates in questionable decision making? You know how Ostara loves to dote on my long list of accolades."

Dillon laughed, downing the last of the beer in his hand.

"I'll steal one from Natalie, and just cross out the *Canine Good-Citizen* title. Or maybe not."

I shook my head. I didn't care if the others drank before a show — as long as someone was sober enough to keep an eye on Bodhi — but I never did.

Despite my attempt to focus on the here and now per my usual M.O., my mind's eye replayed Ostara's message.

Meeting, Home Office, 9 A.M. Tomorrow, Discussion of your Future.

What future? The woman held such a tight grip over my entire life, it wasn't like I had a say in the matter, whatever she had in mind. So why did we need a meeting to discuss it? Like always, she'd just tell me what to do.

My teeth ground together as I fought to keep my temper from flaring, but, right now, she didn't control me. Music was *my* arena, and it was the one thing she couldn't take from me. I wouldn't let her.

"You know what?" I said as I raised my hand to flag down the bartender. "I've changed my mind. Change that title from Expert to Master."

Dillon smiled as he slapped my shoulder, raising his hand for a shot as well.

I was going to regret this later, but fuck it. We tossed back the tequila and I turned toward the stage before Dillon could ask what had caused the shift in my normal routine.

"Get Bodhi," I called over my shoulder as I went for my guitar. Our bassist was probably outside smoking, if we were lucky. If we weren't… Well, his location was anyone's guess.

Dillon went to track down Bodhi right as Natalie, our rhythm guitarist, emerged from backstage and took up her space beside me, setting a beer down on the stool next to her mic. She swept long, honey brown hair over her shoulder as she picked up her guitar. Natalie was a wolf-shifter, from Deadlights Cove like Dillon and I, and supplemented her band income with a fairly lucrative side-hustle as a dog-trainer for humans in the surrounding areas.

"Bodhi?" she asked, and I rolled my eyes.

A minute later, Dillon stomped on stage, taking position at his drums, and shrugged at Natalie's and my questioning glance. "He's on his way."

I knew my band well enough to know that probably meant Dillon had caught him in the bathroom, not alone.

Right on cue, Bodhi leapt up on stage, whipping his chin length dark hair out of his eyes as he reached for his bass, his Ramones t-shirt slightly disheveled. Though, to be fair, as a demon, the male normally looked slightly disheveled.

My phone buzzed again in my pocket, but I ignored it. I had a pretty good idea what it would say, and I wasn't interested. Not tonight. Instead, I walked up the mic to get us started, and the sound of loud cheers immediately relieved all of the pressure I'd felt mere moments ago. I grinned, and the cries grew louder.

This.

This is where I felt the most *me*.

Not caught up in Coven bullshit, worried about political gain and increased power. I didn't want any of that. Not right now, at least.

I wanted *this*.

I leaned into the mic, swinging my guitar behind me momentarily. "How are we doing tonight?"

My eyes scanned the audience as I smiled at our fans. Sure, Maine wasn't exactly Nashville or LA, but our band, the Lost Talisman, was booked solid year-round playing a mix of cover songs and originals I wrote for us.

The high-pitched squeals of women lining the stage drew my eyes down, and that was when I saw her.

Standing a bit back from the stage was a girl I'd seen several times at our shows before — the ever illusive boho blonde bombshell. Tonight she wore a cropped tee over flare jeans, showing off a toned and pale stomach. Her nearly waist-length blonde hair was in loose beach waves, and she was so effortlessly gorgeous it hurt. Every time I'd seen her, she was never alone, shadowed by a tall woman with dark braids, no less stunning, but with a formidable frown, and they were always gone by the time I was off-stage.

Mystery Girl.

Thoughts of my mother dissipated immediately as her sea green eyes locked on mine. I flashed her a cocky grin, raising an eyebrow, and leaned into the mic. "This one is for you."

Quickly turning to my band, I mouthed, "Change of plans. Starting with *Paralyzer.*"

No one questioned me, and I strummed my guitar as Natalie leaned in, humming the opening. Dillon stomped on the bass drum, and off we went.

Instantly, everyone near the stage sang and danced along. Energy hummed in my veins, the feeling nearly identical to the magic I used daily. Knowing that I brought joy to everyone here, that I controlled the atmosphere, the feelings in this room, was a high I perpetually chased.

That is, I brought joy to *nearly* everyone here.

Mystery Girl stood stock-still towards the back of the

room, her eyes squinted and locked on me. Seemed it wasn't only me that was paralyzed.

The more I sang directly to her, growling the words of the song into the microphone, I couldn't stop a slow smirk from spreading across my lips.

A movement I noticed she tracked.

And that, infuriatingly, she returned with a series of unreadable blinks and then a coughing fit before turning her back on the stage and making her way to the bar.

Not the usual reaction I got from women.

I stumbled over the lyrics momentarily, and Natalie shot me a confused stare before I caught back up. I frowned, but the show must go on. Hypnotized by the crowd, I finally swung my eyes away from Mystery Girl's retreating back and wrapped up the song to loud applause.

After the show, I settled my guitar back in its case as my phone buzzed incessantly. A call, this time.

I slid it open, not bothering to try to remove myself from the noise of the bar. If she didn't like it, she didn't have to call.

"Lysander." My mother's austere tone clipped my name into three sharp syllables, *Lee-San-Der*. "Did you not receive my notifications? You didn't reply to confirm."

"All 27 of them." I tucked the phone between my ear and shoulder so I could keep packing up.

"Enough with the attitude. You aren't a child any longer."

I shut the case a little too aggressively and Dillon looked

over with a raised brow. Rolling my eyes, I pointed at the phone, which was more than enough for him to figure out what was going on.

"Funny that you keep treating me like one then."

"Are you in another club? Lysander, I can barely hear you," Ostara chided.

"Sorry, got to go." I let the phone drop into my hand and clicked it off, rolling my neck.

"Ostara?" Dillon guessed, crossing his arms as he came to stand beside me.

"Tomorrow's problem." I tucked the phone away and straightened my shirt. "Beer goggles, engage."

I scanned the room after we got our drinks, wondering if Mystery Girl was still here.

A handful of other girls came and went, trying to chat us up, and, while I was charming and polite with all of them, I encouraged them to move on. With the stress of everything happening in Deadlights Cove, the rift between my supernatural life and this very human bar scene felt like a chasm, and I hadn't hooked up with any girls from a show in months.

"Don't feel like you have to turn anyone down on my account," I called over to Dillon after the latest group moved on.

He shrugged, leaning on the bar with one elbow so he could look around the room. "It's fine. I'm tired anyway."

Liar. But I appreciated the moral support. Dillon knew me better than anyone, had been my closest friend since middle school, and was the only other witch in our band. As such, he was also the only one who knew, in detail, the shit I went through with my mother.

Natalie had some awareness of Coven matters, there was only so much we could discuss in front of her. Bodhi didn't even live in the Cove — last we checked, he technically lived in Montreal, and just flickered back and forth as needed for practice and shows. From what I understood, it took a fair amount of energy to flicker that far, but seeing the amount of energy he still had when he showed up, maybe it wasn't far enough.

Dillon started going off on his latest *Game of Thrones* theories — dude was getting into the series about a decade too late, and none of us had the heart to tell him about the last season — when a petite brunette sidled up to me, inserting herself between us and completely ignoring Dillon.

"Hey, sexy." Her low-cut tank top left little to the imagination as she leaned forward, trailing a finger up my forearm.

"Hey." I grinned at her, flicking my gaze to Dillon with a *What can you do?* look that had him throwing a hand up in defeat and marching away.

"Lysander," the woman's tone turned petulant as she lowered her lashes to look up at me. "You don't remember me?" A small hand landed on my chest as she took a step closer. She raised up onto her tiptoes and I leaned down obligingly so she could whisper in my ear, "The Philly show, last fall? We had a lot of fun afterwards."

"Oh yeah?" I ran through my memories, trying to place her as she stepped back so I could look at her again. But nope, nothing. "And you came all the way up to Maine to see me again?" I flashed her a grin. "Must have been some kind of fun."

"Definitely worth repeating."

I was about to step forward, brush her hair over her shoulder, when I caught sight of long, platinum blonde curls out of the corner of my eye.

"You know what, baby, tonight's not the night. Thanks for coming to our show, though." I stalked after that hair, ignoring Brunette's calls after me, moving through the crowd and the darkness and flashing lights of the club.

Mystery Girl was leaning up against the bar when I reached her, and I slid in next to her, noticing she was taller than I'd anticipated. Only a few inches shorter than my 6-feet, but I liked a tall girl. Especially this one.

"Hey, beautiful."

She started turning towards me, but her knee twisted as she began to crumple to the floor. I shot out a hand to steady her, lifting her back up, a light scent of coconut and peaches reaching me.

"Easy there. You okay?"

Mystery Girl's cheeks flamed pink as she bent over, ripping the wedge sandals off her feet. "Damn shoes. I hate heels."

I fought back a laugh, glad to see it was just a wardrobe malfunction and not a drunken stumble. Consent was a real thing in my book, and I had high hopes for an evening with this woman.

With a sigh, she looked up and I grinned as she gave me a not-so-subtle once over. Women usually liked what they saw. I was tall, toned, tattooed, and tan, the last part thanks to my half-Black heritage.

"Buy you a drink?"

Her seaglass eyes found mine again — such an unusual color, somewhere between a green and a blue — and she tilted her head.

Her hands fiddled with the straps of the shoes dangling from her fingers as she chewed on her bottom lip, drawing all of my attention there. Indecision warred on her expression, and silence stretched between us so long, even *I* felt the need to fidget. Hell, I wanted to straighten my shirt or something. This was uncomfortable. But I wouldn't push — I'd asked, she had every right to say no, and I'd walk away. I wasn't a total jerk.

Before she answered, she raised her eyebrows, looking at something behind me. "You know what, Lys? I can't do this."

I startled at the nickname — I played here often enough that I supposed she could have easily found out my name, but *Lys* was more of a *friends-only* moniker. Did we know each other?

Confusion pinched my brows as I tried to catch up to the conversation. Her eyes locked on something behind me, and I turned to see what had caught her gaze. Brunette stood behind me, waiting her turn for my attention. Twisting back around to Mystery Girl, I waved a vague hand in her direction.

Leaning in to be heard over the music, I said, "I'm not interested in her tonight."

"Asshole," Brunette said from behind me, not-so-subtly ramming my shoulder as she stomped by.

Mystery Girl watched Brunette's retreat with wide eyes, a nervous giggle escaping her as she smiled. It was entirely too toothy, and obviously forced, but my mind couldn't move on from this girl, despite her awkwardness.

She waved the bartender down and ordered a paloma for herself, leaning an elbow against the bar. Brushing her blonde waves behind her shoulder, the forced smile disappeared as her eyes narrowed to something more calculating.

"I'm Maisie Douglass," she offered at last, hand outstretched for a shake. I glanced down at her delicate hand, not sure how often I had shaken hands and used last names in a bar, but she was stunning enough that I dismissed the quirk, gripping her hand in return.

"Seems you already know my name. What else do you know about me?"

"I know you're desperate to break the hold your mother has over your life," Maisie answered as she lifted her paloma to her ruby-red lips.

I nearly choked on my tongue as I searched her face, trying to find even an inkling of recognition. Unlike Brunette, who I'd obviously gotten to know *with* beer goggles, this was information I'd never share with anyone in a drunken ramble. "How do you know me?"

Maisie laughed, a full head-thrown-back *laugh*, and once again, this girl had me feeling off-kilter. "I know *all* about you. And that's why I'm here."

I shook my head, confused by her words and regretting the tequila I'd already had. "And why is that?"

Maisie grinned, white teeth flashing. "I have a proposition for you."

Chapter Three

MAISIE

THE MORE TIME I'd had to stew over my father's command, the more I was sure that I couldn't go through with it. This was the twenty-first century, for Poseidon's sake. I didn't want this marriage to *Owen Kinkaid*.

But the thing about arguing with Ronan, King of the Sea Nymphs, was that you didn't. He commanded, we obeyed. That was all there was to it.

Hell, I didn't even know of any other supernatural royal families outside of sea nymphs. The tradition was so old and out of style, but we clung to our ancient ways, and my father sure wasn't walking away from the power trip anytime soon. And that meant the responsibility to keep our people safe would one day fall to me.

But was it worth the potential protection linking our magics could offer if it meant my eternal entrapment to someone I didn't love? Could I sacrifice my own happiness for my people?

Not today.

Not yet anyway.

Kymari had informed the guards on duty that she was accompanying me on a night swim, and luckily, no one had questioned her. Sneaking our clothes and makeup into a dry-bag, we'd left the underwater city, swimming for Spring Harbor. After a quick change under the pier, we were dressed and ready, heading for the Purple Dragon.

It wasn't the first time we'd snuck out to this bar, but I'd chosen it tonight on purpose. The Lost Talisman was playing.

The band was fun, but that wasn't the point. Or, at least, not all of it. Kymari knew I'd had a crush on Lysander for years, so she didn't bat an eye when I'd told her where I wanted to go. She did, however, shake her head with an exaggerated eye roll, muttering something about me being too chicken to even talk to him. Up until tonight, that was a true statement. I'd never once gotten up the courage to talk to Lysander, not in town or at a show.

But tonight was different. Before I pulled the trigger on my plan, I needed to see for myself what type of person he was. I'd seen him around town from time to time — and, okay, yes, maybe *lightly* stalked his band because, let's face it, the guy was gorgeous and his voice was incredible. But having a crush on a guy from afar was completely different — I'd never taken the time to consider him in this way, to try to get an actual read on him as a person like this, not just as a front-man piece of eye-candy.

The minute Lysander's eyes locked with mine, I almost abandoned my plan entirely. Up there, on stage, with women practically throwing themselves at him, he seemed untouchable, especially for a floundering weirdo like myself.

And that song? Sure, he might have looked sexy up

there, but seeing him croon to *Paralyzer* was like a flashing neon-sign warning *Self-Absorbed*. For years, I'd been right under his nose in town, and yet I was positive he didn't recognize me. Sure, he didn't visit Scallywags while I was on shift *that* often — I tended to work day-shifts so I could be home at night and not arouse suspicions at home — but I'd seen him enough that I'd hoped he'd know who I was.

No such luck.

Looking around the small, dark bar, there were easily half a dozen women who would have been happy to go home with him, and I'd been to enough of his shows over the years — okay, maybe *medium* stalking — to know he was equally happy to oblige them most of the time.

Then again, I reminded myself, maybe that was exactly why this hare-brained plan could work.

The fact that my insides had done a backflip when his full lips had pulled back in that smirk when he saw me was neither here nor there.

We were incredibly different. He lived for the spotlight, while I spent my time abovewater trying to stay out of it. The oversized hoodies I loved so much were more than just comfortable; they were a disguise. Nymphs had a certain allure, especially for other supernaturals, and I needed to maintain a low profile. Legends of sirens luring their captives to their deaths weren't based on nothing.

No one underwater, not even Kymari, knew that I had a job on the mainland, and my father would freak out if he caught wind of it. Ronan was slightly overprotective.

Slightly being a generous term.

Even considering this plan seemed desperate, but caught between that or marrying Owen Kinkaid, sight-unseen, I couldn't help but feel a little desperate. And that gave me an extra boost of courage.

Heading up to the bar to grab another round for me and Kymari after the show, I felt the moment Lysander's gaze finally found me, felt every step he took in my direction across the crowded space.

Needing a moment to settle the nervous thoughts rattling around in my brain, I looked him up and down, not hiding my perusal, which seemed to amuse him. Of course it did. He was used to women assessing him in his favor.

I'd have been lying if I said he didn't look good, though. This male had been the star of every dirty dream I'd had for the last ten years, and dammit, I wished the real thing didn't live up to those expectations. But, despite my worries earlier today, I wasn't deaf.

I heard the way the women at his shows talked about him, the way our town gossiped. Lysander Theroux was reportedly a god among men in the bedroom, and as he moved closer and his citrus and vetiver scent hit my heightened senses, my body was ready to be the next sacrifice.

Tonight he wore dark ripped jeans and a black v-neck t-shirt that showed off the tattoos I knew covered most of his medium brown skin from the waist up. He'd let his black coils grow out a bit recently, though they were still short with a fresh fade on the sides, and then there were his eyes. His light green eyes had always drawn me in, even just in passing around town, mesmerizing in the way they were unexpected with his complexion.

I was *almost* tempted to let him buy me a drink, but then I saw that groupie over his shoulder and any confidence I'd felt went down the drain, remembering who I was talking to. Didn't help that I'd almost tripped the moment he walked over to me — hell of a first impression. Way to go, Maisie.

When he turned back to me, completely dismissing the other woman, my tentative plan turned into something a little bit firmer, and I tried to shore up my courage even as my heart fluttered like a school of minnows.

"I'm still confused as to how you know so much about me," he said, not even addressing the whole proposition thing. Hell of a word choice I'd picked, but my mouth was uncooperative when Lys was around.

"You know who I am, too." I raised a brow, smirking at his confused look, hoping it was a sexy smirk and not a, *my upper lip got stuck on a tooth*, smirk. "I'm Ronan's oldest daughter."

His eyes widened, and I sipped my drink, downing the liquid courage, as I let him have a moment to process that.

"But you're," — his face scrunched as he worked through it — "on *land?*"

"You've seen my father on land." I pointed out calmly. This was a typical reaction to meeting one of our kind abovewater since we so rarely ventured out of our sea. Well, most of us, anyway.

"No, I mean, yeah, I know." He shook his head, and I couldn't help but feel a little powerful as this gorgeous man stumbled over his words in my presence. He almost sounded like *me*. "I mean, Ronan let you come on land?"

"Well." I traced a finger around the top of my glass, clinging to any bit of confidence I could muster. I had to, if

I wanted this plan to work. "I'm not sure *let* is the right term. Actually, that's the exact opposite of the term I would use. Let's hope to Poseidon for both our sakes that he never finds out about this, or any of the other times I've seen your band, because I'm not sure if you know this, but Ronan has a bit of a pesky temper. Have you ever seen White Sharks fighting over a tuna head? Probably not, I guess — why would you, or any sane person? Anyway, they've got nothing on Ronan, *believe me.* But that's neither here nor there, witch boy."

He huffed out a laugh, his confusion at my rambling giving way back to his usual charm. "No?"

"No. I know Ostara controls you, too."

"Too?" He edged closer. "Your father?"

I blinked. To assume Ronan was controlling required not even a little bit of a stretch of the imagination. "An arranged marriage this time. An alliance with a *demon.* Even if he's Scottish and has a sexy accent, can you imagine? Not that I'm species-ist, or anything," I added hurriedly, because it *did* sound like that. And was I? I didn't think I was. I didn't *want* to be. "It's just, demons are generally unpredictable, you know? I like safety. Security. Comfortable. Demons are none of that. I mean, I know *some* great demons, but on the whole? And that's not even the main problem — I've never even *met* Owen Kinkaid." I shuddered, and Lys's eyes widened, which I took as an encouraging sign. "You understand my dilemma. But Ronan wants more magic for me. For us, our people."

"Okay." Lys drew out the word, probably wondering where he fit into this.

"Look, I'll level with you." I turned to face him straight on, heart racing as I fought every instinct to run screaming before I revealed just how stupid my plan was. Lys's head cocked as he tracked the motion, hand slightly outstretched as if he expected me to topple over again, which thankfully, I didn't. "My father made a lot of arguments for why this arranged marriage shouldn't be a problem for me," — I rolled my eyes at the memory, as if being shackled to an impulsive, unreliable *demon* who I'd *never even met* wasn't bad enough on its own — "but he unintentionally gave me an out when he said, 'It's not as if you're dating anyone else, Maisie.'" I lowered my tone in my best imitation of my imposing father, and Lys chuckled at my attempt before his amusement dropped.

"Wait —"

"This is what I propose." I held up a hand to stop his objections. Could he see how sweaty my palm was? Crap, I hoped not. "I don't entirely understand the history between my father and your mother, but, whatever it is, it isn't friendly. Wouldn't you love the opportunity to give them back even an *ounce* of their own medicine and take control of your own life?" Lys raised his brows, but didn't interrupt, so I went on before I lost my nerve, trying to subtly wipe my palm on my jeans. "So, I think we should date. You stick it to your mom, I get out of my arranged marriage." He opened his mouth, and a laugh bubbled out of me before I could stop it at how that sounded. "I mean, just *pretend* to date. Just until I figure something else out to boost my magic and you get your mom to back off planning your entire life out for you."

He sighed, flagged down a shot of tequila for himself,

and leveled a patronizing look my way that still somehow flushed my cheeks.

"Ronan will see right through it. You do know that, right?" He threw back the shot and I watched the way his throat worked as he swallowed, Adam's apple bobbing in a way that shouldn't have been sexy but totally was. "Not to mention Ostara's never going to get off my back about controlling my entire life until I take over the Coven, which I don't see happening anytime soon. And she'll never believe I'm dating someone seriously."

He gestured vaguely at our surroundings, at the groups of women eyeing him and giggling behind their hands to each other, at his lifestyle in general.

"Isn't that a good reason to do this, then? To convince her you *can* be serious? You can be all, *Look Ma, No groupies!*"

I grinned as he scraped his shot glass across the bartop, signaling for another and considering my offer. Hopefully.

Impatient as ever, I pressed on before I lost the last tiny scrap of nerve I still clung to. "Are those your only objections? Because the solution to both of them is the same."

"Yeah? What's that then?"

"We'll just have to be undeniably convincing."

He laughed again, shaking his head, and threw back the second shot, nodding at my glass for me to take a drink as well. I obliged him with a sip, smiling as I lowered my lashes, hoping for sexy and mysterious, not desperate and nervous. Why hadn't my father included seductive glances in my long list of studies? Surely that was something a 28-year-old princess should have down pat, right along with the signature princess waive, but I was pretty sure I looked like I was on the verge of a mild heart attack. Which, from the state of my racing heart, I was.

Lys's eyes were focused on me as I glanced back up, searching his face for even the barest hint of what he thought about all of this. He had to admit it wouldn't be *that* bad to fake-date me. While I was as awkward as awkward came, I did think I was more than mildly attractive, as most sea nymphs were. And that mattered to a guy like Lys.

Suddenly, his fingers circled my wrist, my skin zinging at the connection and my heart skipping a beat. His pale green eyes darkened as they moved from my hand, to my neck, to my lips, then met my gaze again.

"When do we start?" His mouth twisted up into a smirk, and my thoughts stuttered. My brain short-circuited as his fingers moved to my upper arm, pulling me into him. His lips were at my ear. Oh, my God, *Lysander Theroux's lips were at my ear!* I prayed on my mother's watery grave that the squeal that rang inside my head did *not* sound outside it. "Because I say we should start now."

My breath hitched, his nearness overwhelming me, the heat of his body so close. When was the last time I'd been this close to a male? I could hardly remember, and it had never been like *this*. Had never been so intoxicating.

No, intoxicating was certainly not the word I would use for my encounters with Drew, my first, last, and only entanglement. I couldn't even call it a relationship, really, as I didn't think either of us cared about the other. Those had been more along the lines of *bland*. Transactional. A means to an often rather disappointing end, that usually left me finishing the job myself, so to speak.

From the heat of Lysander's body alone, the way he

pressed into me here, I could already tell Lys was a male who would *not* leave me disappointed.

Not that it mattered, because this was all for show.

I totally knew that.

I could hear the smile in his voice as he clocked my reaction to him, his lips skimming just behind my ear. "There are several supes here tonight to see us, to be witnesses for us. My band has seen you at our shows dozens of times. They'll vouch for us."

I sucked in a breath at his words. Maybe he hadn't noticed me around town, but he *had* noticed me at his shows. That fact sent a riot of minnows loose in my chest.

Pulling back just enough to make eye contact, he traced my bottom lip with his thumb, eyes transfixed. Poseidon, he was so *physical.* I hadn't anticipated that, though maybe I should have. And if I were being honest with myself, it didn't take much for someone to be more comfortable with physical affection than I was. Especially *public* affection, for which I'd had exactly zero practice. "What do you say, Maisie?"

Getting him to agree to this seemed almost too easy. Was he just messing with me right now? Doubt clouded my mind as I tried to remind myself he was a *player.* Used to women fawning all over him. Lys was sin personified, from his breathtaking looks to the smooth way he carried himself. I would *not* be one of the many to fall for him, even if I thought he was the most beautiful male I'd ever seen. My crush ended there. I could keep my feelings separate. Probably.

The cheeky smirk he wore was impossible to read. Was he really willing to do this, or was he just jerking me around before he'd inevitably laugh off my plan and headed back to his friends and a groupie or three?

Dark fingers tangled in my pale hair, twining it around them, tugging gently. He was waiting for my answer.

"Fine, yes, we can start now." That was what I wanted, the whole reason I'd come here. Excellent, okay. So this was happening. Success! I nodded, half to myself.

When his smirk spread into a full grin, a dimple appearing on his left cheek, I felt the rug ripped out from under me.

A hand circled the back of my neck, pulling me to him and tilting my head up, and before I knew it, lips pressed against mine that tasted of the tequila he'd just downed. Another hand was on my hip, hauling me closer as his entire body pressed against mine, solid and strong and demanding. My body ignited in his touch, my mind gone blank and hazy as my pulse quickened. When he spoke, his lips brushed against mine.

"Relax, Maze." A soft chuckle came with the words and my breath caught at the nickname. Why was that hot? "We're dating now, remember? Make it look good. Open up for me. Or will you choose the demon after all?"

I knew he was baiting me, but heat pooled low in my abdomen at his words anyway, my knees practically buckling at his melodic voice, low and sultry and aimed at *me*.

"You want to be *undeniably convincing* or not?" One brow raised, in challenge, as he repeated my own words back to me.

I raised my slightly shaking hand to his jaw, feeling the short stubble he always had, and he leaned into my hope-fully-not-too-sweaty palm, that infuriating smirk still in place. I was tall — all nymphs were — and even without my heels, he only had a handful of inches on me.

A quick glance around the room informed me that both Kymari and Dillon had spotted us, were watching and probably wondering what was happening. Unfortunately, for this to work, they were the ones we had to fool the most. The ones who knew us best.

I leaned in closer, trying to muster up the confidence to do this.

I *could* do this.

I *had* to.

Lys's lips grazed across my jaw, his hand dropping to grip my ass, and I froze, body tensing as I pulled back.

"Too bad," Lys said as his hands dropped from me, light green eyes glittering in amusement. "Could've been a fun game, but I don't think you can sell it, so it's not worth the risk. I don't need an angry Ronan out for me when you inevitably can't pull it off."

"Wait," I said, hand shooting out to grab onto him before he could leave. But he slipped into the crowd, waving as he turned back to the stage and his band.

Chapter Four

LYSANDER

WELL, that was not how I'd seen *that* interaction going. For the number of times I'd pictured kissing Mystery Girl, the feel of her lips on mine was beyond my wildest dreams. Fuck, she'd tasted good. And I wanted another.

But she wasn't asking for a night with me. She was asking for a *commitment*, even if it was a fake one. And that was a bit much for my brain to take in.

Did I want to rebel against my mother and her *future plans?* Hell yeah, I did.

And Maisie had a point — would being in a serious relationship, even if it was fake, show my mother that I wasn't as irresponsible as she thought I was?

Maybe.

Maisie was certainly not the type of girl my mom would expect me to be with, especially as Ronan's daughter. This would be seen as a borderline smart decision in her eyes, which I couldn't decide if that made it better or worse. But was this really how I wanted to stand up to her?

I brushed a hand over my hair, rubbing at my neck as I

walked away, refusing to look back at where I'd left Maisie standing slack-jawed at the bar.

"What was that about?" Dillon asked as I jumped onto the stage, heading to where we'd left our gear to the side.

"Nothing," I said, shrugging it off.

"Yeah, *looked* like nothing." Dillon laughed, his eyes sparkling with amusement. "Mystery Girl coming to the after party?"

I shook my head. As much as I'd been dreaming of Mystery Girl, Maisie was very real, with real problems. And I didn't need to get myself tangled in her fake dating plans.

I had enough drama to deal with in my own life.

"Nah." I picked up my guitar case, and moved towards the door, dropping it in the van Natalie drove. "Why would I need her when I have my hetero life mate right here? Just you and me, buddy."

"Don't try and snuggle me again."

"It only happened once, and that hotel had the worst mattresses I've ever slept on. I still say yours was more comfortable. You can't blame me for choosing to spoon you instead of laying on the rocks in my own bed."

"Changing your name to Princess and the Pea in my phone for good."

My head pounded the next morning, regret for one or five tequila shots weighing on me as I tried to focus on my mother's house in front of me.

I hadn't done myself any favors by ignoring the chain of texts she'd sent this morning after I blew off her 9 a.m.

meeting request. It was already noon, but she should be glad I showed up at all. Despite her controlling nature, this level of urgency was out of character, even for her.

Still, I'd pulled on the cleanest clothes I had, so maybe that would appease her slightly. Pulling myself up the steps of the old Victorian house I'd grown up in, I took in the familiar sight. Everything here was dark and foreboding, but with a Southern elegance that showed my mother's family ties to New Orleans. Antiques were placed around the foyer, all dark wood ornately carved, and a crystal and bronze chandelier hung overhead. Black candles lined the entryway table, ivy curling around their gold holders and a series of gilded ceremonial raven skulls on an onyx plinth. Everything about the house screamed *witch*. But a classy witch, to be sure.

"Hey, Henri." I waved to the butler that had worked here for as long as I'd been alive. For all of Ostara's many faults, she treated her staff excellently, and most had been lifelong employees. "Can you let her know I'm here?"

"Of course, Lysander." Henri smiled, handing me a bottle of water with a knowing look. I took it with a thank you, then moved towards Ostara's office. Our family's grimoire sat on a large book stand behind her desk, a full wall of books and trinkets behind it. Someday, this office, this house, these responsibilities for the Coven would pass to me, and I'd be ready for it. But today was not that day, and I was determined to live my life to the fullest until responsibility came knocking.

Several minutes after I dropped into the red velvet armchair in front of my mother's desk, she turned the corner.

"Lysander, at last." Ostara came into the office, heeled boots clicking, and shut the door behind her. Apparently, this was a *private* conversation. She moved around her desk and took a seat behind it, placing a hand with ruby red nail polish to match her blazer on the glossy wood surface. The red against the deep brown of her skin and her black hair streaked with white was a bold statement, but everything my mother did was bold. She had a way of making every movement look calculated, severe, and elegant.

"At last? I've been here for ten minutes. Where were you, chatting with your magic mirror again?"

She shot me a sharp look, her lips pursed tight. "How charming, your favorite joke. Yes, I'm the Evil Queen, of course."

"We both know it said I'm prettier than you." I stretched my legs out, crossing them at the ankles. "What's this about? We're leaving for a show in Boston in the morning, and we need to switch out some of our gear."

Her dark gaze hardened, as it always did, at the mention of my band, but this time she ignored it.

"You are aware that now, more than ever, it is of the utmost importance for our Coven to have access to the strongest magic we can," she began, and I nodded. I was well aware of the events that had taken place in the Cove and in other supernatural towns over the past ten months. "You've heard the rumors surfacing about the potential of linking powers, yes?" She raised a brow in question, but didn't wait for me to respond. "The heads of the other species and I all believe that linking powers across species will lead to greater power for both parties, and is something to be explored."

Again, this wasn't news to me, so I nodded. My mother had spent my entire life sending me to the best tutors to learn anything and everything I could to expand my powers. For some reason, I have a deeper well for my magic than most witches, and she exploited that at every turn.

She tapped her nails on the desk, her eyes narrowing as she continued. "Therefore, I've arranged a match for you." My brow furrowed. "A powerful bear shifter female, Clara, from upstate Vermont. You'll marry her, then perform the ceremony to join your magic. Together, you'll set an example and be able to offer our Coven power like we've never experienced before." She leaned forward over her desk, dark eyes twinkling with the promise of more power. "A witch with the power to heal as a shifter can, with their keen senses and increased strength. Can you imagine how this would help us, Lysander? This will be only the beginning; once you lead the way, we can encourage others to do the same, and bring even more magic into our fold."

I stared at her for a long minute. Several minutes. Then I laughed. "No."

Her jaw tightened, but I pushed on, shaking my head before she could start seething at me.

"No, even *you* wouldn't make me marry some girl I've never met. For power?" I scoffed. "You've made me train in every expertise for decades, ensuring I'm *plenty* powerful enough as is." I splayed my hands, hoping she would see reason. This was *insane*.

Though, if I pushed through the tequila haze from last night, I realized it did sound familiar. Wasn't this what Maisie said Ronan had told her, too? That he was setting her up with some demon?

"Not if every other Coven and pack and horde start linking their magic with other species, too," she said, sitting back once more. "And they will. As soon as that ceremony is figured out, every head of every supernatural group in this country and around the world will be working on how to link powers and increase their own. We have to stay ahead of them, Lysander. We have to stay competitive so our Coven and our town will stay strong, protected."

"What, so leaders everywhere are just going to start forcing their people to marry whoever they choose for them?" I shook my head. "I don't see that going over well with demons, or a lot of the more independent shifters. Shit, even witches have minds of their own, you know."

She raised an austere brow. "It *will* start to happen. More and more. And you will be our first. It's better to get our first pick *before* the frenzy begins than to wait until everyone else has paired up, don't you think?"

I leaned forward in my chair, elbows dropping onto my knees as anger coursed through me, so I let loose the low-blow I knew would make her furious. "And why not you, Mother? Why aren't you signing up for an arranged marriage, to stay the all-powerful Coven leader? Or are you still stuck on my father? The one whose name you've never even mentioned to me?"

"Do *not* question me," Ostara shot back, eyes blazing with cold fury like they did anytime I brought up the subject of my dad. I knew nothing about him other than he'd been from New Orleans, and was the reason my mother had left.

Whatever. I didn't have time for this. "You know what? I just remembered I'm busy that weekend."

"Lysander, I didn't even tell you the date yet."

"Listen, this has been a great chat, as always, but I have to run." I stood, moving around behind the chair and bracing my hands on the back of it. "Good luck with that whole marriage thing. Maybe Castor is willing, if Clara has a brother."

"Lysander, you *will* be doing this." Ostara stood too, her eyes nearly level with mine from across the desk. Waving a hand in the air, she added, "It's time for you to step into your responsibilities. I've been plenty patient while you've spent years hooking up with random *human* girls after your little shows. It's not like you're dating anyone. I know you, you've never been serious about anyone in your life."

That was when it clicked.

"But I am."

Her eyes shot to mine, disbelief on her features as she let out a short laugh. "Please, Lysander. Of course you're not. And you and this shifter female can make whatever sort of arrangement works for the both of you, once the power ceremony is performed. Who knows? Maybe she'll even let you keep your little human infatuations."

"So romantic." I rolled my eyes. Of course Ostara wouldn't even care if the girl and I were faithful to each other, as long as *she* got her power. It's not like she prioritized romance in her own life, either. Not once in my 36 years had she ever dated *anyone.* "But, I am dating someone. It's pretty serious, so I'm afraid this won't work out at all."

"Oh really." She leaned forward over her desk. "Who?"

"Maisie Douglass," I said, grinning at the shock on her face. "You know, Ronan's daughter?"

Something flared in Ostara's eyes at that, her hand

chopping through the air decisively. "No, absolutely not. I forbid it."

I shrugged, sliding my hands into my pockets as I stood and took a step back. In for a penny. "Too late. We're in love."

Leaving my mother seething in her office, I turned and left, chuckling as I saw myself out of her pristine house, satisfaction coursing through me at having left a little disarray behind.

Maisie was right. It *did* feel good to give her a taste of her own medicine for once.

Now I just had to figure out how to find Maisie again.

Chapter Five

MAISIE

"SO," Kymari nudged me in the shoulder as I sat on the edge of my bed, pulling at the hem of the crop top she'd picked for me the morning after our abovewater excursion. She insisted that this was all the rage fashion-wise, but I couldn't help but fidget in the fabric. At least she'd made concessions to allow for soft fabrics, and her teal, coral, and band tee choices showed she chose them with me in mind. Even though I loved my best friend immensely, I needed her to leave so I could slip out of my room, and make my way towards shore, this time, without her. "Want to talk about that kiss last night?"

"Kiss?" Saoirse said as she pushed open the door. Wearing a swingy floral top and straight-leg baby blue pants with coordinating ballet flats, my sister, only a year younger at 27, was far more put together than me. As the second in line to the throne, Saoirse was saddled with the majority of the political relations between the other sea nymph kingdoms and traveled often, rarely home for more than a few days at a time. "What kiss?"

"I didn't know you were back," I said in surprise as I hugged my sister. Although we both sported shades of Ronan's blonde hair, that was where our similarities in looks stopped. She was shorter than me by several inches, her curvy, feminine frame opposite my lanky limbs.

"I got in last night," she said as she dropped down on my bed. "Wrapped up business early with the Indian Ocean sea nymphs. But don't think I'm letting you shift the conversation. *What* kiss?"

"Nothing to say, really." I shrugged, hating that I couldn't confide more in them. How could I have been stupid enough to believe I could convince *Lysander Theroux* to fake-date me? Of course he didn't want to be involved with me, in any capacity. As if being Ronan's daughter wasn't enough to push anyone away, I'd tripped over my own feet in front of him and filled our conversation with more awkward silences than even I knew what to do with. Poseidon, I felt like an idiot in the light of day. I flopped back on the bed, my hair falling around me in a halo as I threw my hands over my eyes, admitting defeat.

When the bed sank beneath me, I moved my hands, glancing over at my friend and sister.

"Didn't look like nothing," Kymari laughed. "I didn't even know you *knew* Lysander."

Saoirse gasped, eyes wide. "*Lysander?* As in *the* Lysander? *Ostara's* Lysander? The one you've had a crush on ever since we bought his first album a decade ago and you'd pretend to make out with his photo on the cover?"

I could feel the heat of my cheeks flushing bright red, but I refused to meet my sister's questioning stare. "Okay, that never happened."

"Maybe not in front of us," Saoirse added under her breath.

"Not sure I know many other Lysanders," Kymari answered for me, cutting off my sister's perhaps-too-accurate deductions. I both loved and hated her for it.

I laughed, trying to sound casual but hearing the strain even in my own voice. "What is there to know? He's cocky. He sings adequately decent music. He's a player, and he kissed me."

"Right." Kymari's eyes held a tinge of mischief as she studied me. "So that's why you drag me out to his shows, sneaking out for a night on the town. Because he's *adequately decent.*"

"Maisie," Saoirse said, and her voice took on the serious tone she used in business meetings. Here came the lecture to follow.

I slapped my hand out, smacking my sister in the side as I shook my head, pushing up to sitting. "I wish I had more time to hang out, but duty calls."

Saoirse's brow dropped, but Kymari groaned. "Even on Sunday? Don't you usually have the day off?" I shrugged noncommittally, willing my face to remain neutral. "You're always busy these days. Half the time, I don't even know where you are, and that's literally my *job.*"

My pulse quickened at her words, hoping she didn't follow that line of thought. While I trusted Saoirse and Kymari with my life, both of them were loyal to our kingdom and my father's rules. "Working, same as you. Ronan has me overseeing all of the repairs, so I'm never in the same place for long." Changing the subject, I asked, "Is your dad still making you run through training drills every day? Xuma working you to the bone?"

That did it. Kymari sighed heavily, rising to her feet and moving towards the door. "Yes. Though he did let me practice with a trident last week, so that was fun."

Like I was heir to the sea nymph kingdom, Kymari was heir to her father Xuma's legacy. One day, when I became queen, Kymari would serve at my side: my Second, and my shield.

So as much as I wanted to share my secrets, to tell her about how I spent my days when she wasn't looking… I couldn't. Like me, her duty was to the crown, and if Kymari knew I led a double-life, risking my safety every time I went abovewater, she'd tell her father, who would tell mine. Even if she wouldn't want to, I never wanted to put her in the position to have to make that choice.

"Saoirse, are you here for a while, or headed back out?"

My sister studied me, but I fought hard not to meet her gaze, afraid of what I'd unintentionally give away. "Ronan had some meetings he wanted me here for this week, but I'm needed in Australia by Saturday. There's a lot to get done before the Summit."

I nodded, used to my sister's short visits, but then processed the rest of her words. "Summit?"

Saoirse took a deep breath, fingers flexing at her side as she gave me the deadpan stare she had perfected somewhere in her tween years. "Do you not read a single email I send you?"

I puckered my lips, afraid to say the honest *no* and be on the receiving end of her wrath, so I smiled. "I'm *kidding* Of course I know about the Summit. Big deal."

"That's putting it lightly," Saoirse said, eyes squinting at me.

Before she could confirm that I had no idea what she was talking about, I pushed them both towards the door. "See you both tonight?"

"What's tonight?" Saoirse asked, eyes shifting between Kymari and me.

It was my turn to deadpan. "It's Sunday. Girls night. Sisters, and Kymari, only. Whatever else you agreed to, cancel it right now."

Saoirse sighed, glancing down at her phone before meeting my gaze again. "Tonight."

Sunday was my weekend. When I'd stepped into my role as heir, accepting more and more responsibility for the underwater city, Ronan had insisted that I have one day off, a day away from everyone else's problems. I'd picked Sunday so I could end it with my sisters, my favorite night of the week.

But Ronan was more right than he even knew. I *did* need a day off from the problems of our people, distance from the weight of my crown. Which was how I had ended up on the shores of Deadlights Cove two years ago, watching from the pier as the town convened in Scallywags. Laughter had burst through the door every time it opened, and the sound was as mesmerizing as a siren's call. Before I knew it, I'd entered the bar, falling under Blaze's spell as he wove happiness and mirth into the air. By the time I'd left later that night, I'd applied for a part-time position, and crafted a plan to make a double-life work.

After saying goodbye to my sister and Kymari, I threw my clothes into my waterproof bag, rolled and sealed it, and pulled on a robe. Magic-infused glass encased our city, showing the ocean beyond as I walked through the hallways to the closest exit, braiding my long hair to the side.

There were three ways to leave our underwater city. The first and most convenient were the dozens of strategically placed exits out into the ocean — landing pad areas encased in a bubble of magic that we could push through, then shift into a magic form and swim. That was the fastest way, and was used often as sea nymphs did jobs outside of the city itself. But since it required shifting, it also meant you had to carry a waterproof bag of clothes for when you made it to the surface and shifted back.

The second way was an elevator that led to a tiny island — a rock, really — that used concealment magic to keep any humans or even other shifters away. Several dinghies were buoyed there if you needed to get to the mainland.

The last way had been under repair since the demon-witch attacks last fall and winter, and was the way that, if necessary, outsiders would be brought into the city. It was a portal from the edge of our city to the Deadlights Cove pier, created by some containment of demon flickering magic.

For the sake of time and anonymity, I'd been using option A lately. The elevator was too obvious and dealing with the dinghies was a pain, not to mention could lead to questions if they kept being found out of place.

Unlike other shifters, who only had one form they could change into, sea nymphs had several, as changeable as the water that was the main source of our power. A favorite, of course, was the mer, or siren, form. Our legs joined together to make a tail, scales covering us from our tailfin up to just across our collarbones, a few lines of scales sprinkled across our temples, but our arms and heads were kept otherwise human. It was generally accepted by supernatural society that sirens were a myth, and as part of our secretive culture, we never corrected anyone. But the truth was that, as sea nymphs aged, our powers grew, and a mature sea nymph *could* exert siren powers — luring people in with our beauty and voices, even compelling them to do our bidding.

The most powerful sea nymphs could also adopt other forms most humans thought were only mythology — my father, for example, could take kraken form if he wished, though I'd only seen it once. It had taken a level of rage and despair that I never wanted to see in Ronan again, both for his sake, and our people's.

We could also shift into a number of regular marine predators, too, including seals, which is where selkie lore came from, or sharks, whales, and dolphins, though those were more complex forms to hold.

While I frequently went as a harbor seal to blend in along the coast, my mer form was my favorite. Iridescent teal scales shimmered in the late-May sunlight glinting through the water as I took off towards the Cove.

Ten minutes later, I pulled myself out of the ocean just down the beach from downtown. Along the north side was a set of sheer rock faces, hiding me from view in a little nook as I shifted, pulled the water off myself with my magic, and dressed. Then, with a little nimble bouldering, I made it to the top of the rock face and took off towards town, meeting up with Ocean Avenue across from Blaze's cottage, just down the street from work.

Val and Caedmon sat in beach chairs facing the ocean as I neared downtown, turquoise coffee van behind them, seemingly forgotten as they both lounged in their chairs in matching Hawaiian shirts and fedoras.

"Morning!" Val called, lifting his hand slightly in a wave, but didn't bother to get up. I glanced down at my watch, noticing it was five minutes to noon, so he wasn't *technically* wrong, but it was hard to believe it had only been hours since the bar last night. "You on shift tonight? We were going to stop by and play charades later."

"Sorry, guys, day shift today," I said as I flipped the Scallywags hoodie I'd hidden from Kymari's violent intentions up over my head and pushed open the door to the bar.

The bells jingled above me as I entered. "Sorry I'm late, Blaze. Couldn't get —"

I stopped in my tracks when I saw Blaze standing behind the bar, a wrinkle in his brow. He wore his typical white tee, contrasting against his olive skin and intentionally messy dark hair. In front of him stood Lysander, leaning across the bar, eyes focused on me until a lightbulb went off and a slow smile spread.

"Maia," Blaze said as he threw the towel he'd been wiping the bartop with over his shoulder. "No problem. Hey," he pointed at Lysander, "Leesey Piecey here was just asking me if I knew Maisie, Ronan's daughter. He was trying to figure out how to contact her. Is there some sort of sea nymph directory? Do you use *shell* phones?" Blaze snorted at his own joke, but I didn't react.

Panic seized me as I stared wide-eyed at Blaze, then Lys, then Blaze again. But before I could find the words to go on, Lys pushed off the counter, crossing the room towards me.

50

"What are you —" I began as Lys stood just in front of me, his hands lacing around my back as he dipped me, kissing me hard on the mouth. I hardly had time for my mind to catch up what the hell was happening before he righted me, but didn't remove his hands from my waist. My head still spun with the sudden shift, hand shooting out to grab the back of one of the stools. Not at all from the kiss itself.

"Couldn't stop thinking about you all night," Lys said, his voice laced with heat and sincerity, so convincing even I believed it. "I couldn't wait to kiss you again, babe."

Blaze choked behind us, spluttering a cough turned laugh. "Did *not* see this coming, Maia. But man, do I love a good plot twist."

"Maia?" Lys whispered in my ear now that my hoodie had fallen back, my blonde braid spilling across my shoulder. "So, which is it?"

"Sweet nothings," Blaze said, his chin resting on his hands as he leaned his elbows on the counter, black eyes watching us intently. *"So cute."* Then he stood upright, shaking himself visibly, dark hair mussing just so, the way it always did on my demon-witch boss. "Excuse me. I think I've been spending too much time with Mo lately."

The fact that my eyes didn't fall out of my head was shocking, my mind reeling to catch back up to where we were.

"You okay, Maze?" Lys whispered, noticing the way my mouth kept opening and closing. "Act natural, or I'll kiss you again to wipe that expression off your face."

That did it. My mouth snapped shut, eyes squinting as I

stared up at Lys. His green eyes danced with amusement as he smirked, noticing the change.

"Mind if I use the office for a quick chat with —"

"Her boyfriend," Lys cut in, wrapping an arm around my shoulder and kissing my temple. I fought not to shove my hands into his side, whether I intended on pushing him away from me or yanking him down for another kiss — undecided. Instead, my fingers ended up tangled in the fabric of his grey henley, feeling across the muscles cording his waist and back.

"No sex on my desk," Blaze said, finger pointed at Lys, then at me and my cheeks flared bright red as I blinked rapidly.

"Got it," Lys nodded, cool as a cucumber as he laced his fingers through mine and tugged me towards the office. "We'll just use the wall."

Chapter Six

LYSANDER

"WHAT THE HELL WAS THAT?!" Maisie whisper-shouted the second the door clicked shut behind us. "I thought you said no last night because you didn't think I could pull it off!"

"And clearly I was right. That was horrendous," I said, leaning back against the door as I studied *Maisie* in front of me. "So, which is it? Maisie or Maia?"

"Both." She sighed, her hand rising to rub at her temples as she slumped back to perch on the edge of Blaze's desk. "Technically, it's Maisie Arabella Bridget Douglass Crunamar, princess of both the Northeastern and North-western Atlantic Sea Nymphs, and heir to the Northwestern throne. A mouthful, I know. My mom always called me Maia though, and my sisters call me M. Shit, I was *so* not prepared for this today."

I chuckled, getting some level of satisfaction out of Maisie's floundering. "How were you expecting this to go, then? Fake dating was *your* idea, was it not?"

Her hands dropped down to her side, and she looked up

at me. Last night, Maisie had been gorgeous in her boho outfit and neutral makeup, but today, free of makeup, in a pair of ripped jeans and an oversized hoodie with her hair in a braid? Equally as stunning. Suddenly, I wondered if the legends of sirens were true as I couldn't look away.

"Yes, this was my idea *yesterday*," she said, and I fought hard to keep my eyes on her face, not letting them wander back down her body. Her Scallywags hoodie was unzipped, and the barest sliver of pale skin showed between her high-rise jeans and teal crop-top, just enough to draw my attention even as she rambled. "But then you said no, and I thought this was off the table. Don't worry, I already went through the fake-denial and fake-sadness and fake-eating-ice-cream-in-bed stages and got over the whole idea. Now, I'm deeply regretting proposing it at all. It turns out I may not have thought this all the way through. I was absolutely *not* prepared for having my two lives collide like this, and having you kiss me *in front of my boss* all before noon."

"It's 12:15."

Her seaglass green eyes cut to me, her full lips forming a flat line. The fact that I kept my own from tipping up into a smug grin must have been some divine intervention from the Goddess herself. Why was needling her so fun? I didn't even know her yet.

"What made you magically change your mind?" she asked, head tilted as she studied me.

"Believe me, you'll know my *magic* when you feel it." Her cheeks flushed pink at the insinuation, just as I'd wanted them to. "And my change of heart certainly wasn't due to your acting skills." I slipped my hands into my pockets, crossing one leg over the other as I leaned back against the door. "That was like kissing a dead fish."

She gave a long, controlled exhale of irritation.

"Sorry." I licked my lips. "Bad joke for a sea nymph."

"Okay," Maisie said as she pushed away from the desk and began pacing the small office space. "First of all, no one," she paused, shooting me a pointed look as she pulled off her hoodie and began fanning herself, "and I mean *no one,*" then resumed her pacing, "knows that I lead a double-life here. In town, I'm Maia, the sea nymph bartender at Scallywags who mostly keeps to herself and has been known to occasionally drop a glass or walk into door frames. At home, I'm Maisie, heir to the sea nymph throne, and full of more responsibilities than you could possibly imagine. My life is a far cry from your little barfly-lead-singer-playboy lifestyle."

"I mean, I can *kind of* imagine," I muttered, slightly insulted at the assumptions she was making about me — even more insulted given the amount of truth within them — but she didn't slow down her pacing enough to hear my comment.

"You really want to do this?" she asked as she tripped over an invisible wrinkle in the carpet, catching her balance at the last minute. Apparently, sea legs were a real problem — or land legs, as it were. With a muttered curse, she righted herself and breathed in a deep inhale. "I wish I could say you're pairing yourself with a graceful mermaid princess who will make all of your dreams come true, but that's more my sister Saoirse's style, not mine. Most days I'm more like a bumbling giraffe just trying to take its first steps on this Earth." Her voice dropped to a whisper as she mumbled, "That analogy is a little *too* accurate."

I pushed off the wall, wrapped my hands around her shoulders, and held her in place. Her eyes snapped up to mine, wide with shock. I'd noticed this reaction the other night, the way she seemed to freeze at physical touch — was it possible this gorgeous woman wasn't used to it, or was it just *my* touch that caught her off guard? I didn't miss the way her mouth parted slightly, or the way she leaned forward into my hold just a little, expecting another kiss. As much as I wanted to oblige, to taste her again, this was a business arrangement. Contrary to her assessment of my character, I *did* know how to take things seriously.

"Yeah. I'm sure. And you're a catch." An exasperated, slow blink. I was killing it with these fish jokes. Dropping my hands from her shoulders, I continued, "It turns out Mother Dearest had the same idea as Ronan. I've been matched with a *bear*-shifter from Vermont, and no way in hell am I going through with it. I'll take a bumbling giraffe mermaid princess with ten names instead."

"Five."

"What?"

"Five names. Not ten."

"Right." I waved her off. "Point stands."

Maisie's nose scrunched as she winced on my behalf. "You already told Ostara no?" I nodded. "What exactly did you say, then?"

"I might have said we're dating." Maisie laughed, the sound high and airy and slightly manic as her face tipped up towards the ceiling, exposing her neck. As close as we stood, I couldn't help but follow the long column down to the soft swell of her breasts in her tight crop-top. Shit, she was beautiful. "And that we're in love."

Her gaze snapped back down, eyes bulging wide once again. "We're *what?*"

I shrugged, forcibly pulling my eyes up from the dip of her waist just above her jeans. "If we're going to sell this, it can't be a fling. This has to be serious, or neither one of them will buy it."

Maisie raked her teeth over her bottom lip as she considered that, drawing my eyes straight to her mouth. "Did Ostara buy it?"

I blinked my gaze away, studying the wall behind the desk. Every square inch was covered in Sandra Bullock movie posters, overlapping as they layered together to paint a collage of obsession. You'd think this might be what comes from growing up with a bubbly mother like Morgaine, but as I knew that witch would probably watch *Rambo* over *Miss Congeniality* any day, I could only assume this was all Blaze's doing. "I didn't give her time to tell me whether she bought it or not. Dropping your name was enough to shock her, and I left before she had time to respond. My phone's been blowing up since I stormed out of her house, but I've muted it for now."

"So, this is really happening then," Maisie said the words slowly, as if forcing her own mind to catch up to the conversation, hands flapping as she fanned herself violently.

"Yeah, Maze." I slid my hands from her shoulders down to her waist as I let my magic send a cool blast of air over her. I wished I could say I didn't notice the way she reacted when it hit her skin, faint goosebumps rising that my fingers tingled to soothe, but I absolutely did. "This is really happening."

A nervous giggle was my only answer, but I smiled, hoping I could give her some of my fake-confidence that this wouldn't go up in flames for both of us.

We emerged from the office a few minutes later with a tentative plan to meet once the band was back from Boston in a few days. She'd meet me at the house I rented just down the street from Mo, a block over from downtown. My mother had bought the old little Cape-style house when I was in my early twenties, and rented it out to me and Dillon. While I hated being indebted to her, the location couldn't be beat, and at least it got me out from her old Victorian.

Blaze whipped his wrist in front of his face as though checking the time, even though he didn't own a watch, and then gave me a disappointed shake of his head. "I think I'm going to start calling you the Minute Man. Is that any way to treat a lady, Lysander?" I rolled my eyes, not rising to his bait, but Blaze rarely required a response to keep a conversation going. "So how long have you two been hiding this little tryst?" Blaze asked as I settled onto a stool at the bar. My eyes shot to where Maisie stood, back ramrod straight as she dusted the bottles on the shelf.

"Three months," I said, counting backwards in my head as to when that meant that we'd met. "March. Right, *Maia?*"

"Yep!" she said, not bothering to turn to look at me. "Couldn't believe it when I saw Lysander standing in front of me at the Rare Coins Convention in Portland. All this time spent here in the same city, I never knew there was another sunken treasure aficionado right here."

Blaze's dark brows drew down as he glanced sideways at me, but Maisie steamrolled us both as she continued on with the entirely too detailed fabricated meet-cute.

"There we were, standing over the same table, admiring the coins collected from the Castine Hoard, right here in Maine. Local coins are extra special to me, and apparently Lys, too. At first I didn't realize it was him, distracted by the giant mustard stain in the shape of a penis on his shirt, dripping off the corndog he was practically deepthroating. Everyone there was watching. If they'd sold tickets to *that* show, it probably would have outsold the coin convention itself. Downright scandalous."

Blaze laughed, glancing my way as I tried to hide my horror, heat rising in my face at the image she painted. I immediately regretted not having this conversation before we left the office, but there was nothing I could do to stop her as Maisie barrelled on like a runaway train.

"Anyway, I felt kind of bad for him, considering he wasn't aware of the utter spectacle he was putting on for the patrons of the show as he eyed the coins. Which, I mean, I get it. It's really exciting when you find such rare gems. One time I found a silver shilling from the 1600s and nearly flooded the lobby with my water magic."

"So you told him about the stain?" Blaze said, and I started to nod, hoping to put a stopper in this story, but Maisie went on.

"Oh, no." She shook her head. "He started choking on the corndog. You should have seen it. Standing there, gasping for air with those pretty green eyes of his blown wide. Hot dogs are the number one cause of choking in children, did you know? That and grapes. Deadly. Luckily, I know the Heimlich, so I rushed behind him, tugging on his torso."

"Wow," Blaze said, seeming to be as surprised as I was, and I prayed to the Goddess that she'd reached the end of storytime. "So naturally you needed to take your savior out on a date."

"Well, when the hot dog came flying out, unfortunately so did everything else he ate. Projectile vomit sprayed across the coins, covering everything in hotdog and mustard sludge. It. Was. Disgusting."

"I can imagine," Blaze said, wrinkling his nose as he surely imagined the same scene I was from this terrible picture she was painting. I eyed her cautiously, wondering what sort of crazy I'd just shackled myself with.

"He apologized profusely, of course," Maisie said. "Offered to buy the whole table to make up for his little accident, but didn't have enough money, what with his measly band salary and all."

"A shame," Blaze said, leaning on his elbow as he listened to her story with rapt attention. Meanwhile, I wanted to fall through a hole in the floor, never to be seen or heard from again with every word that came out of her mouth.

"So embarrassing. I couldn't stand to see him standing there with his mustard dick, puke in his five-o'clock shadow, for even a minute longer, so I bought the coins for him."

"And then she gave me her number so I could pay her back immediately, after I got home and showered," I cut in, needing this story to end before she had time to come up with another humiliating twist to throw in. "We met up the next day so I could give her the money I had *plenty* of, just not with me at the convention. Overpaid her by several hundred dollars for what the coins were actually worth. I won her over with my charm quickly enough, and the rest is history."

"Yep!" Maisie smiled, that same toothy, forced grin from the bar last night, and I blinked rapidly, trying to catch up with the conversation. "Turns out he's only an *amateur* numismatist."

I hadn't the faintest idea what a *numismatist* was, but I decided not to risk another story tangent by asking. "You're worth far more than any rare coin. I stand by my decision."

Maisie's cheeks flamed red as she spun towards me, and I momentarily forgot my own deep-seated embarrassment as I stared at her. I couldn't help but notice how *cute* she was. Not normally my go-to adjective for potential flings, but this wasn't a fling, was it?

"It's all been a bit of a blur, really," Maisie said, trying to regain her composure. "We've been keeping it a secret for a while."

"Didn't think it would go over well with the parents," I added as my mind finally caught up to the conversation. "But we're tired of hiding our love, right babe?"

"Right."

"Huh," Blaze said, rising up to resume cleaning the bar. "Can't say I ever saw this coming, but I like it. Do I need to give you the protective big brother speech, Lys? I can't say I'm not a little nervous for my favorite bartender, knowing your reputation."

I shifted in my seat, my skin feeling itchy as I considered Blaze's words and my past behaviors he referred to.

"I'm your *only* bartender. And not necessary, Blaze," Maisie answered for me, sliding a glass of iced tea with lemon across the bar. I looked up, noticing the way she studied me, and fought not to shift in my seat again. Her eyes softened slightly as she said, "He's not like that with me."

"Good." Blaze nodded. "Be good to my girl. Or else."

"You should leave the threats to Devanna." I forced a smile, aiming for the cocky lothario I was apparently seen as, even as his words stung. I had no intention of hurting Maisie, or any of the girls I'd ever been with, but had I? "She's much better at it than you."

"Don't I know it," Blaze muttered, grabbing several empty wine bottles from under the counter and carrying them into the kitchen.

Maisie's eyes met mine as she wiped down the counter, and I took a tentative sip of my iced tea, wondering if I'd soon regret agreeing to this fake relationship. Too late now.

Chapter Seven

LYSANDER

AFTER A QUICK GOODBYE, I pushed through the doors, headed towards Mo's house on the other side of the square. A line had formed outside the fudge and popcorn store, Pop Nox, but that wasn't what caught my attention. To my right, someone stood on scaffolding, two stories high, as they pulled boards from the windows of the old abandoned church at the back of the cemetery. I squinted, sure I recognized their frame. The next time they turned to toss down a board, I realized it was none other than Devanna.

More than a little curious what the hell she was doing up there all by herself, I hopped the cemetery fence and cut through the tombstones until I stood at the edge of the scaffolding. With a loud whack, her hammer slammed down on the wood, and it flew through the air, crashing down on a stone cross below.

"Sorry, Morty!" she called down, not turning around to see if her hammer had murdered anyone.

"Who's Morty?"

Devanna spun around and peered down at me. Her blue

hair was piled high on her head in a messy bun, brown skin sheened with sweat as she worked.

"No one, and everyone. I've been calling all of my graveyard neighbors Morty for lack of a better term. What would you call them?"

I glanced around the cemetery, most of the dates on the tombstones reading between 1600 and 1800. "Dead?"

Even though I couldn't see her face as she resumed her work, sans-hammer, I could *feel* Devanna's eye roll. "Did you need something, or are you just stopping to annoy me? Make yourself useful while you're at it and toss me my hammer back."

"Isn't that reason enough to stop?" I asked, and Devanna chucked a board directly at my head.

"Oops. It slipped."

"Hate when that happens." I chuckled as I kicked the board aside, then retrieved her hammer and chucked it up to her. Devanna had spent summers in Deadlights Cove when she was younger, becoming a permanent resident and member of our Coven when she was in her tween years, and I'd always thought of her as a younger sister. A wildly annoying, angry younger sister. "Should I even ask what you're doing? Or why you're doing it all alone and tempting fate?"

"Haven't you ever heard of DIY projects?" she said as she pried another board loose, rusted hundred-year-old nails raining down like a plague of tetanus on any passersby below.

"Sure, but usually that's in reference to an ugly clay pot, or maybe a dilapidated bird house. What does that have to do with the church?"

"I bought it."

I frowned at her, then the property in confusion. "You…
you bought the church?"

"Yep. And the graveyard. Meet my roommates! Morty,
Morty Jr, Morty the Third…"

I shook my head in disbelief. "You're going to *live* here?
You're just asking to get smote. Smited?"

She snorted. "Please."

"It's *definitely* haunted."

"Counting on it. Everyone else is settling down, planting
roots, falling in love. Since I'd rather join Morty under-
ground than get married, I figured it was time for some
roots of my own. Just you and me at the singles table now,
Sandy. At least I can say I bought a house. You still live in
your Mommy's house."

"Her *rent* house. Not *her* house. Big difference."

Dev shrugged. "If you say so."

"I hate to break it to you, but it's just you at the singles
table now, Hay-Bailey."

Dev's hammer stopped midswing as she slowly turned
towards me. "I would say that's a terrible joke, but you're
not laughing, and you always laugh at your own jokes."

"What can I say? I'm funny. Handsome. Charming.
Talented. The whole package. And now I'm off the
market."

"Sure," Dev said as she swung again, taking her excessive aggression out on the rotten boards covering the broken
windows. "Who's dumb enough to tie themselves to you?"

"Maia is far from dumb," I said, the jab hitting me a
little too closely yet again. Was I really that bad? "A little
quirky, but never dumb."

"*Maia?*" Dev said as she pried another board loose, leaving a gaping hole in the side of the church.

"Are you supposed to be making the church look better or worse?" I asked rather than answering. "It's definitely looking worse."

"Orion put me on the city-wide improvement team, giving us three weeks to get the town in shape before the Summit arrives. His mistake if he left *improvement* up to interpretations."

"Summit?" I asked. "What Summit?"

Dev *tsk*ed in disapproval. "Sounds like someone has been avoiding Mommy again. You didn't see the blast this morning to the whole town?"

I pulled my phone from my pocket, finally scrolling through the missed messages I'd ignored all morning. At the top was one that read:

Citizens,

The Paranormal Relations and Interspecies Council has called a Summit to discuss the state of the supernatural world in regards to activity in Deadlights Cove, Maine. The Summit will be held in Deadlights Cove beginning June 17. Please see the attachment for assigned responsibilities to prepare our town for this event.

- *Mayor Orion*

"What did Lucifer assign you?" Dev asked as I finished

reading. I held up a finger as I clicked the attachment, scrolling until I saw my name written under —

"Landscaping?"

"Maybe he meant *man*scaping. I feel like you're a manscaper, aren't you? The ladies probably love it," Dev said as she made exaggerated retching noises. "Oh Goddess, now I'm picturing your junk."

"You're sick, you know that?"

"Well aware." She retched again. "My mind is a terrifying place."

"I believe it." I shook my head, staring down at the screen again. "Why would he assign me to landscaping when there's an entertainment category? Who the hell is he putting in charge of entertainment?"

Dev climbed down the scaffolding, dropping the last few feet at my side as she peered over my arm to look at the phone, right as I saw the list. "Hold up. The *Ladies* are in charge of entertainment? Peg, sure, maybe. She seems like she was fun 300 years ago, but I'm sorry, I can't imagine Eva Watford knowing a good time if it slapped her with a lace doily in the face."

"Simmer down now, Sandy," Dev patted my arm, and I shrugged out of her touch, unable to help wondering if my assignment had been meant as an insult. "Maybe Orion is trying to bore everyone as quickly as possible so they all turn tail and leave. Should be an easy task with him and Eva at the helm."

I hummed in agreement as I scanned the categories again, trying to understand Orion's reasoning, but nothing came to me.

"Time for you to go trim some hedges, then?" Dev asked as she bent to examine the pressure washer at her feet.

"You're really going to do this manually rather than a renewal spell?"

"Have you ever used a pressure washer?" Dev said as she put her booted foot up on the machine, yanking hard on the starter cord, the ear-splitting roar of the engine shaking the windows of the buildings on either side. Without waiting for an answer, Dev flipped down her overly large sunglasses and pulled the trigger, water shooting out as it peeled layers of paint from the side of the building. With a shake of my head, I waved to her, turning around and crossing the street back towards Mo's house.

By the time I turned the corner at Immortali-Tea, I glanced back over my shoulder to the church, noticing that Dev was using the power washer to write letters. It didn't take a wild stretch of the imagination to understand how she intended to finish the rest of the *FUC—* message she'd begun.

She and Orion had been at each other's throats for nearly a decade, and while I didn't understand the reasoning behind it, I had Dev's back every day of the week, no matter how much I loved giving her shit.

As I hopped up the steps to Mo's magenta and turquoise house, hand raised to knock on the yellow door, a loud crash sounded from within.

"I'm so sorry," a young female voice said, before Mo answered in a low tone I couldn't make out.

I knocked twice before opening the door, not waiting for a response. Mo had texted me earlier that morning, asking if I had time to stop by and help her with a problem the young witch, Ruby, was having, and I was happy to help. Even though she and my mother had never gotten along, I had always liked Mo.

As I closed the door, Mo's bright white hair and large pink glasses magnifying her eyes to a startling size peered around the corner at the end of the hall.

"Oh good. You're here!" Mo said with a bright smile. "Fashionably late, as always. Never expect a Theroux to make anything less than a dramatic entrance. Surprised you don't have a billowing cape and a top hat."

"Left them at my mother's." I walked down the hallway towards her. "Remind me and I'll wear them next week. I could even bring a voodoo doll with me."

Mo's eyes widened, excitement shining through as I met her where she stood in the doorway to her living room wearing a chevron-striped black and white kimono over pink polka-dot pants. "For *whom?*"

"Mo, I was kidding. You know we don't mess with dark magic."

"Right." Mo waved me off, grabbing my wrist and pulling me into her overly floral living room. As in, all of it. Wallpaper, rugs, couches, all clashing patterns and colors, and all floral, like a botanic garden had thrown up on every surface of the room. Everything in Mo's house was overwhelming, but so was the witch herself, so it suited her. "You're the *boring* kind of Cajun witch. Momentary lapse on my part. I always get your parents' families confused."

"Wait." I stalled in the hallway, not sure if I'd heard her correctly. "Mo. Did you know my father?"

Mo opened her mouth to answer, then snapped it shut, her back snapping straight as she mechanically walked into the living room. Both were so out of character for her I realized she *did* know, and someone had cast a spell on her to maintain their secret.

Magic hummed in my veins as I let it seep out of me and into the room, feeling the lingering spell that hovered over Mo's usually purple aura, casting it in an odd, blurry shadow. But before I had time to inspect the spellwork, a blazing bright wave of magic flared from the other hall. I blinked rapidly, clearing my vision as I stared at the young witch framed in the doorway.

"Hey Lysander," Ruby said with a little wave. Before she lowered her hand, a vase exploded on the shelf where it sat to her right. I winced at the sudden noise, and Ruby burst into tears, her tan hands coming over her face as she hid behind her black hair, dyed red on the ends. With a dramatic flare only seen in teenagers, she fell to the floor, her long black skirt pooling around her.

"It's getting *worse*," Ruby said between hiccuping sobs. "I don't know how to stop it."

"Well, that's why Lysander is here, sweetie," Mo said as she dropped to the ground next to the young witch. Without Ruby understanding what was happening, Mo placed her fingers around Ruby's wrist, pushing calm into her aura. I watched in awe as Ruby breathed evenly, her tears drying in an instant as Mo rubbed a soothing hand over her back.

While I was the most talented witch in our Coven aside from my mother, I had never seen power like Mo's before.

The instant access she had to her magic was unnatural for our kind, pooling in her fingertips, ready to use. I'd asked her about it once, and Mo had cocked her head to the side, lips pursed as she studied me.

"Old magic worked differently, dear boy," she'd said. *"Witches like us are rarer than the most precious gemstones. But you and I are the same, aren't we?"*

Eighteen years had passed since that conversation, but I'd never looked at Mo the same after that. Because she was right. We *were* different. And I'd never told anyone how easily my magic came to me.

"So, what exactly is the issue you are having, Ruby?" I asked as I sat on one of the floral wingback chairs. Mo helped Ruby to her feet, and together they sat on the couch across from me.

"She came into her powers a little unusually." Mo patted Ruby's leg, still letting the calming aura seep from her hands and into the girl at her side. "But that's a story for another time. Right now, Ruby seems to have some sort of a hex on her powers causing all of this misfiring magic without her permission."

"A hex?" I tilted my head, focusing my attention on Ruby.

"That's the best I can figure," Mo said. "I called you, wondering if you might notice anything different."

I shared a long look with Mo, reading between the lines. Neither of us had broached the subject of our similar powers since that day, and she'd never asked me for anything like this, so my curiosity was piqued. With a breath, I summoned my powers, letting the magic show me what I'd never heard of another witch being able to do before.

My magic flowed out over Ruby's, her power alternating between a bright red and the darkest blue, the red threaded with black wisps that indicated a hex. While two-toned auras weren't unheard of, if rare, I'd never seen one in such contrasting colors before, but that wasn't what caught my attention. In several spots, her power seemed to disappear, floating into the in-between, the insubstantial place through which demons could flicker and from which they pulled their powers.

Something her witch magic absolutely should not be doing.

I sat back, scrubbing my hand over my face as I thought through everything I knew about witch powers. Ruby clutched Mo's hand in her lap as the girl bit her short, red nails, looking anywhere but at me.

The way Mo's smile didn't meet her eyes, I knew there was more to Ruby's story than she could share, but that wasn't my immediate concern.

"I do see a hex on you," I said as I dropped my hands to my knees, standing from the chair. Ruby exhaled, seeming relieved and anxious at the same time, and I couldn't help but feel for the girl. "Let's see if I can untangle that part, yeah? Then you and Mo can resume your magical lessons."

Placing my hands on either side of Ruby's head, I looked to Mo one last time before I murmured, *"Recifere."*

Ruby gasped, her shoulders rising as I lifted the hex, feeling the dark magic seep out of her and into the air where I dispelled it into a nearby crystal. The power transfer singed the table underneath the crystal, leaving a black ring as it glowed the darkest black before settling into a smoky grey color. I sat back, dropping my hands to my side. "Don't touch that stone."

Mo and Ruby nodded, and I allowed my magic to focus once more. I looked back at Ruby's tangled web of contrasting red and blue, now free of the black wisps, but still seeping in and out of the in-between.

Mo hopped up from the couch, wrapping me in a tight hug. I could feel the happiness radiating off her, and for some reason, my mind seemed to think this whole ordeal was more about Mo's curiosity about *my* magic than fixing Ruby's. Mo was plenty powerful — she could have easily lifted that simple hex herself. "Thank you, dear boy. It's always a delight to watch you work your magic. And I hear congratulations are in order." Her eyes sparkled. "A sea nymph and a witch, who'd have thought!"

"How —"

"Oh, Blaze told me. Well, told *everyone*, I suppose. Cove text chain. He must have forgotten to include you on this *particular* message. Demon magic can be so specific, you know. I could hardly *believe* the story of how you two met. How fortunate for you that sweet sea nymph was there to save you!"

Mortification settled in that *everyone* now knew Maisie's elaborate story. Then my mind snagged on one thought, my nerves ratcheting up. "Do you have any idea who else is on that chain?" Please, not Ronan. I was rather attached to my head.

"Relax, dear. The nymph king never turns his phone on, if that's your concern."

Wait, she knew about Maisie? I was under the impression that Maisie's identity as the sea nymph princess was a secret only she — and now I — knew. I narrowed my eyes at her.

"How is it you know everything that goes on in this town, Mo?"

Mo tittered a laugh, waving an airy hand. "When you've lived as long as I have, dear, you get a sense for these things."

She pushed me towards the door before I could ask any more questions, dumping me on the front doorstep with a peck on the cheek. I wiped at my face, hand coming away coated in hot pink lipstick as the door slammed behind me.

Even for this quirky town, that entire exchange was *weird*.

My phone dinged as I turned towards my house, a text from an unknown number showing. I swiped on it, pulling up a message.

UNKNOWN

It would be weird not to have your girlfriend's number in your phone, so save this number.

It's Maisie, by the way.

I got your number from Blaze. Had to tell him I dropped my phone in the ocean and had to get a new one.

A low chuckle slipped free as I saved the number under "Maze," shaking my head in amusement at how she could ramble awkwardly even through text, and walked towards my house, mind already shifting to my to-do list before we could leave for Boston in the morning.

Chapter Eight

MAISIE

THE REST of my shift at Scallywags flew by after Lys left, but it could have been because my mind was anywhere but here. Regret coursed through me as Blaze told every patron who entered the bar that I'd been in a secret relationship with Lys for the last three months, hiding it from all of them.

I smiled and nodded, hood pulled up over my head like I wore it here as he asked me to retell our meet-cute over and over. I'd never regretted my own rambling train of thought as much as I did now, trying to keep straight all the random details I'd thrown into my story.

Why hadn't I just said we'd met at one of his shows?

Panic. That was why.

I was *not* good under pressure.

"It's good to see Lysander settling down," Eva Watford said as she patted my arm. One-half of the ancient witch duo who ran the Historical Society in town, her short white hair bobbed as she fluffed it, as if a single strand on her head would ever dare to step out of line. "We've been watching that boy burn hot and bright for years, wondering when he'd slow down enough to step into his responsibilities in the Coven. We've all been patient with him."

My brow scrunched, but I kept my thoughts to myself. Because, really? As much as I thought of Lys as cavalier, nothing about Ostara screamed *patient,* but I didn't know much about Coven politics. Maybe Eva was right. Still, the knee-jerk reaction to defend him surfaced, and I couldn't help myself.

"He's not as wild as you think he is," I said, not even sure I believed my own words. "Lys is a good guy."

"Just took the right woman to tame him, dear?" Peg Fernsby said with an eyebrow waggle as she sidled up to the bar. Unlike Eva, Peg's hair was light purple, either accidentally or on purpose, I could never decide.

I shrugged, brushing off their comments, but hating the way my insides churned. In all honesty, I didn't know Lys well, but I *did* know what it felt like to be forced into a life you didn't choose. Like me, he'd never been given a say in the matter. Lys was born to a powerful witch who led a Coven, and someday, that yoke would fall to him. Sounded familiar.

While I'd never been asked if I wanted to be the heir to my father's kingdom, I did love my people. Up until yesterday, I'd even have gone so far as to say I'd do anything for them. But apparently, I'd found my limit.

I couldn't marry Owen Kinkaid.

I wouldn't.

Resolve settled in my bones as I pushed away my lingering doubts over this fake-dating plan, determination to make it work taking up residence instead.

"I'm in love with him," I blurted, and everyone at the bar turned to stare at me. "Madly in love. Deeply. Truly. Never felt like this before. On cloud nine — *ten*, even. We couldn't be happier. So, *so* happy together."

Blaze patted me on the back, amusement lighting his dark eyes. "Glad to hear it, Maia."

"Young love is so sweet," Val said, leaning his head on Caedmon's shoulder. "Remember when we were two young lads, sneaking around, nuzzling each other's necks in darkened alleys as we whispered about what outfits we'd wear the next day?"

"Remember that navy doublet you used to have?"

"If I recall, *someone* tore its buttons clean off."

I fought back a laugh as the attention was shifted off me and to the eccentric coffee van guys instead. Punching my time card at the end of my shift, I waved to Blaze and made my way down to the beach.

Thoughts swirled in my brain as I walked down the boardwalk, enjoying the cool breeze as the sun began to set. I hardly noticed anything as I tried to figure out my next steps.

I needed to tell Ronan. My father was bound to be angry — I knew him well enough to realize that. But he also wasn't a terrible male. As protective and controlling as he was, I knew he loved me, and only wanted what was best for me. So, how could I convince him that *I* knew what was best for me, and it wasn't Owen Kinkaid?

Best case: he held true to his word and let me out of the arranged marriage with Owen, if I could convince him I was happily in a relationship with Lys. *Big if.*

Worst case: Ronan banished me from our city,

denounced me as his heir, and refused to let me see or speak to my family ever again. I'd be forced to be a lone nymph, or return to my mother's people in Scotland, where I'd then have to face an angry and disappointed Kinkaid family, knowing the reason I was there to begin with was because I'd turned down Owen for a witch. The thought of never seeing my sisters again stopped me in my tracks on the beach, doubling over as I shoved my head between my knees.

Breaths heaved in and out of me as I tried to calm my mind, tried to reassure myself that that wasn't what would happen. Clawing at my clothes, I didn't even bother to make it behind the rocks as I shed my jeans and hoodie, leaving them on the beach behind me as I dove into the biting cold water and shifted.

Instantly, the water calmed my roiling thoughts as I dipped below the waves, returning to my comfort zone. The moment Crunamar City came into view, my breathing evened. Hundreds of glass domes merged together, forming a reef-like structure that encased the city inside. The royal household was in the center, with homes and buildings dotting the outer rings. Several hundred sea nymphs called this city home — the capital of the Northwestern Atlantic sea nymph kingdom. Cities just like this one, although smaller, were spread along the coastline between here and the Caribbean. Soft light glowed from within, calling me home like a lighthouse on the shore.

To think that all of this was invisible to the rest of the world was astounding. That no one else could witness the beauty of such an amazing display of engineering and magic mixed in one was a shame. This was my home, and I loved it here.

I slipped back into our city unseen, into my room, and threw on pajamas before I could think any further on my problems. Emotional exhaustion rode me hard, but I forced a smile on my face and followed the scent of popcorn to the family room down the hall.

Before I even turned the corner, I could hear bickering. "Who chooses a *documentary* for a girls night? Can't we watch a rom-com?" Saoirse said. Coming into the living room, I found all my sisters already assembled, some of the tension leaving my shoulders just at the sight of them. Saoirse was seated at one end of the giant seafoam green sectional, her legs tucked underneath her, as she shook her head at the TV screen.

"Me," McKenna answered from a pink bean bag across the room. Third-youngest, her dirty blonde hair was streaked with platinum highlights and thrown in a messy ponytail. She crossed her arms and stared Saoirse down as she continued, "In case you haven't noticed, we females don't have to subscribe to the picture-perfect image of womanly grace, and it's my week to pick the movie. Broaden your horizons. Humans are destroying the ecosystem of the ocean at an alarming rate, and as the ruling family, it's our duty to stop it. We need to see what they're saying."

"Anything is better than Isla making us watch *Les Misérables* for the 90th time," Blaire said as she tossed a piece of popcorn in the air, legs dangled over the edge of her chair.

"It's beautiful and tragic. I can't think of anything better," Isla answered as she tossed a pillow at Blaire. Despite being twins, Isla and Blaire looked almost nothing alike, something Blaire reinforced by keeping her hair dyed all sorts of unnatural shades — currently, deep green.

"You just want to watch Samantha Barks," McKenna chucked an M&M at Isla, who bit her lip and shrugged.

"We're not watching this," I said, grabbing the remote from McKenna's hand even as her jaw dropped open. "Dad would choose it, and I just can't, in good conscience, allow that. As the heir to the throne, what I say goes, and I won't hear any arguments."

"Sure," Saoirse scoffed from her seat at the end of the sofa. "*Now* you're interested in your title."

I eyed her, sensing the bitterness in her words, but before I could respond, my Second had my back.

"Not tonight, Tiger," Kymari shot at Saoirse, whose favorite form to take was a tiger shark, as she came into the living room, plopping down on the aqua bean bag beside McKenna.

"Well, if we're skipping McKenna, then it's my turn." Riona sat up a little straighter, already looking too hopeful. "And I say we watc" — there was a chorus of *No*s at the same moment as Riona finished — "*Pride and Prejudice.*"

Riona furrowed her brows behind her clear-frame glasses. "But it's a classic."

"You make us watch that *every time* it's your turn, Ri." Blaire rolled her eyes.

"I think Cory should pick if we're skipping Mac," Isla piped up, for which she got another M&M pelted at her.

"You're just saying that because you know she'll choose whatever you want —"

"I will not!" my twelve-year-old baby sister Corissa squeaked.

I sighed as the arguing continued like it did every week, until the sound of my phone receiving a text brought silence down around us immediately, seven heads turning my way.

"Who was that?"

I winced. "No one?"

"Why do you even have your phone on?"

McKenna pretended to count how many of us were in the room right now, as though trying to see who was missing and could possibly be texting me.

Corissa's eyes were wide. "Is it a boy?"

Crap.

"Kymari probably knows, don't you, Kymari?" McKenna said as she leaned towards my guard.

My Second shoveled a handful of popcorn in her mouth and shrugged, but the look was far from nonchalant. "I know nothing."

"But *I* do," Saoirse said with a sinister smile that matched her nickname.

My jaw dropped as all of our sisters spun on Saoirse, eyes bouncing from me to her. Unfortunately, despite the fact that we were Irish twins, Saoirse did not understand the not-so-subtle eye daggers I shot at her. Or, maybe she did, but was enjoying being the center of attention for the few moments she got to spend with us.

"I bet it's Lysander," Saoirse said as she sat back on the sofa, crossing her legs, the epitome of casual despite her business attire even now. "Ten bucks says I'm right."

"Wait —" But it was too late. Like sharks at a feeding frenzy, my sisters were on me in a flash, half of them distracting me and holding me down, the other half grappling for my phone. "Hey, I'm your future queen, you piranhas!"

"Got it!" Blaire held up my phone, wiggling it tauntingly as she raised a black-dyed eyebrow. She cleared her throat dramatically as she clicked on the screen. "*My dearest and most radiantly striped angelfish—*"

Corissa giggled and I scowled at Blaire.

"It does *not* say that." I stood, walking over to her, but Blaire merely backed up and kept "reading."

"*Would that I were an anemone, and you a clownfish, so that we might form a most symbiotic —*"

I reached out for my phone, but right before I grabbed it, Blaire tossed it to McKenna across the room, who picked up right where Blaire left off.

"*— Symbiotic and pleasurable of relationships. You are the increasingly rare vibrant coral in an ocean of dying polyps —*"

"For the love of Poseidon," I grumbled as I wrestled my phone back from McKenna and my sisters all burst into laughter.

Checking my screen, my insides did a little flip-flop when I saw it was a message from Lys. But it was far from what my sisters had read aloud.

Lys: *Got it. Let me know how your talk with Ronan goes. Can't wait to see you Thursday.*

I didn't realize I was smiling until Isla and Corissa's childish "*Oooooh*"s sounded through the room. Ignoring them, I typed back a quick, *Haven't seen him yet — girls' night,* before clicking my phone off and sliding it back in my pocket.

"That better be on silent now," Saoirse chided, a French-manicured finger pointed at me accusingly.

"Okay, well, since none of you want to pick," — Kymari was interrupted by both McKenna's and Riona's indignant splutters, which she ignored — "then I'm putting on *Clueless* and whoever disagrees can fight me on it." She raised her eyebrows in challenge, pointedly meeting everyone's eyes with a bared-teeth smile. None of us moved a muscle, knowing just how powerful Kymari was, even without a weapon. "I didn't think so. Pass the candy."

Despite the low wave of grumbles that swept through the room, we settled down to watch the movie. I ended up on the far end of the sofa, Riona's feet over my legs as I stretched out. Blaire got up and turned off the lights as the opening credits started, and McKenna wordlessly passed over her bag of M&Ms to share.

My phone buzzed in my pocket, but I ignored it, refusing to give my sisters even an ounce more ammo about Lys texting me.

This was the only place I wanted to be, bickering sisters and all.

Chapter Nine

LYSANDER

LYS

Miss me yet?

MAZE

Hardly. You've been gone for two days.

LYS

That's plenty of time to miss me. There's a lot to miss, you know.

MAZE

Is that supposed to be an innuendo?

LYS

… You said it, not me.

MAZE

I just rolled my eyes so hard, they got stuck in the back of my head for a minute there. That would be a hard one to explain to my sisters.

LYS

Not when you're dating me, it isn't. I can
make your eyes roll, Maze.

MAZE

I feel like that's another innuendo, but I
refuse to acknowledge it.

Aren't you supposed to be starting your set
right now?

LYS

Keeping tabs on me? That's cute. I knew
you missed me.

MAZE

Keep telling yourself that.

And break a leg.

Actually, don't. That would be bad.

Could you heal yourself though?

I'm shutting up now.

LYS

LOL. Thank you for your concern. I will only
metaphorically break a leg, in your honor.

MAZE

See you tomorrow.

LYS

I'll be ready to make your eyes roll.

I'D NEVER BEEN this distracted during a show. We'd played back to back nights at a bar in Boston, but by the second night, my heart wasn't in it. Going through the motions with our set, my mind reeled over what Maisie and I would need to do to make our little ruse convincing, and how long it might last before our parents were off our backs with their crazy plans. I wasn't sure what had driven me to text her earlier today, acting like a true boyfriend, but I couldn't get my mind off her.

Several women approached me after, but I dismissed them all with polite words. Fake-relationship with Maisie aside, I couldn't shake the comments about my life that I'd heard over the past few days. First, Maisie, then my mother, and even Blaze and Devanna. As much as I wanted to annoy Ostara and fight this arranged marriage, I was also coming to an uncomfortable realization that in my effort to push back against my mother's many demands and constraints, I'd made a name for myself as an irresponsible asshole. And I didn't like it.

"You doing okay, man?" Dillon said as we packed our gear into Natalie's dog-walking van that doubled as band transport.

"Hmm?" I said, jogged back to the present from my wandering thoughts. "Yeah, just a lot on my mind tonight."

"Is Ostara still on your case?"

A bitter laugh escaped me before I could stop it. "More than you know."

Dillon didn't push me on it, closing the door to the back and climbing in the passenger seat. By the time we hit the interstate, I decided I had to tell him. Not everything — obviously he couldn't be in on the whole *fake* part of the dating thing — but at least about what Ostara had tried to make me do. Natalie had fallen asleep in the back already, and Bodhi had his earbuds in. Even though, as a demon he could just flicker home, teleporting himself instantly through the in-between, I thought sometimes he just liked the company.

"Goddess, an arranged marriage." Dillon shook his head from the passenger seat as I wrapped up my story. "What century is this again?"

I shrugged, my hand hanging over the steering wheel lazily. The best part about driving home at four in the morning was no traffic. "She says all the supe leaders are going to start doing it." I nodded at him. "She's probably got plans for you and anyone else unattached in the Coven."

"How are you going to get out of it?"

"She backed off when I told her I've been seeing someone and it's serious."

Dillon laughed. And laughed. Then he must have realized I wasn't joking. "And she *believed* that?"

"We've been keeping it under the radar," I said, not liking to lie to him, but he *had* to believe it. I was sure Ostara would corner him at the next Coven meeting for an interrogation and Dillon was a notoriously terrible liar. "But you remember Mystery Girl?"

"Damn." He whistled. "Gotta say, it did *not* look like you guys were dating when you kissed in Spring Harbor. She looked pretty shell-shocked."

"Yeah, well," I smirked, "Maia's not used to PDA yet. That was the night we decided to stop hiding it." Fortunately, I'd remembered to use the name she used in the

Cove in case Dillon knew her from Scallywags, rather than how she'd introduced herself to me.

"Wait." Dillon turned towards me in his seat. "That was *Maia?* Mystery Girl is Maia from Scallywags, the ever-elusive sea nymph bartender? And you've been keeping this a secret for *how long?*"

My fingers tightened on the steering wheel. Had I been the only one who had never noticed Maisie at Scallywags before? And fuck, *how* had I never noticed her? Even with her hoodie hiding most of her appearance, Maisie was stunning. I had a strict no-locals policy for the women I slept with, but I wasn't blind. Or, at least, I didn't think I was. "Three months. We met up in Portland." I conveniently left out the whole coins-convention bit of the story Maisie had spun, knowing my friend would never believe it. How *anyone* believed it was beyond me.

Dillon laughed again, his hand resting on his forehead. "You're shitting me. How have I missed this? Where have you guys been hooking up?" His eyes lit with excitement. "Wait. Have you been to Atlantis?"

I shook my head with a chuckle. "Dude. It's not Atlantis."

"Well, what else am I supposed to call a hidden underwater magical city that no one I know has ever been to?"

Needing to change the subject, because I knew nothing more than he did about the nymph city, I said, "You *are* aware that your drums are making you go deaf rather quickly, right?"

"Ugh, I didn't think I was that bad yet. Maybe I need to get some new earplugs."

Glad he'd shifted directions with me, I nodded. "Take

extra from our split from tonight and buy yourself some new ones. Call it a business expense."

Dillon punched me in the arm with a *"Thanks, man,"* and fortunately, dropped the subject, drumming the beat of the song on the radio on his legs.

I leaned forward, turning the knob up as The Eagles' *Heartache Tonight* came over the radio, letting the music carry me away from my problems, just for a few more hours.

Jogging up the steps to the Town Hall that afternoon after a few hours of sleep, I waved at Julian, Second in the local wolf shifter pack and something like a police deputy, on his way out and headed straight into the administrative offices wing of the building. I had several things I needed to take care of before Maisie came over later today, but the first order of business was getting out of landscaping duty.

As I neared the mayor's office, I heard a shatter and then a grumbled curse that had my steps slowing.

Orion sounded… perturbed.

I rounded the edge of his door and raised my hand to knock, but halted with my fist in the air, my mouth dropping open.

Like most angels, Orion was meticulously clean and organized at all times. Most days he wore full business attire, dressing down in jeans and a polo or button-down a handful of times in my memory. His pale skin was freshly shaved but deep creases were forming between his grey eyes, his expression frustrated. Normally, his silver hair was neatly combed, but it looked like he'd run his hands through it, leaving it slightly disheveled. If that wasn't enough to tell me something was off with the male, the sight of his office in complete disarray and his tie pulled loose around his neck would do it.

"Um." I cleared my throat to announce my presence. "Is this a bad time?"

The angel looked up from his desk, seeming to look right through me for a minute before he blinked and sighed. His desk was strewn with stacks of papers, several old coffee cups, and a wrapper that looked like it came from a to-go sandwich. I spotted shards of ceramic on the floor next to the desk and raised an eyebrow.

"Dropped a plate."

"I see that."

A feather twitched irritably. "I didn't throw it."

I huffed a laugh. "Didn't think you had." Well, *now* I kind of did. I stepped into his office. "What's that?" Leaning over his desk, I tilted my head to read what he was working on.

"It's the seating chart for the preliminary dinner for the Summit meeting, and it's a disaster," he said, pinching the bridge of his nose. "Everyone will be arriving soon, and I've spent so much time renovating the Last Resort that I haven't had time to dedicate to the welcome party. I can't sit Ronan next to your mother, because God forbid they ever have to have a civil conversation, but Ezra, the Council Chancellor, can't be near Ronan either or I'm pretty sure this will end in a blood bath. Really, Ezra can't be next to *anyone* or he might not leave here alive. Not exactly friendly, that angel. Pascar, fuck if I know. I don't even know why she's coming. West and Tulok I can put anywhere, but if I seat them favorably, then the other shifters will see it as a slight. Blaze, well, obviously you can't put him *anywhere* safely, so that's another minefield. I could put Ezra next to Winona, but what has she ever done to deserve that? And then there's Malachi. I'm not even sure he's going to show, but if I *don't* have a seat for the Premier angel, and he does show, that would be catastrophic."

I nodded sympathetically, even though I had no idea who half the people were he mentioned.

"You seem pretty stressed out," I started, helping myself to one of the chairs in front of his desk. "Why don't you let me take over the entertainment section of your duties list, and we can give landscaping to—"

Orion snapped to attention at my words, narrowing his eyes. "No."

His abrupt answer pulled me up short, but I was determined to get out of landscaping, so I pushed on.

"I just wasn't sure if you actually meant to give me landscaping? It's not something I have a lot of experience with, so maybe —"

"Look, the PRICs are breathing down my neck." Orion sat back in his chair, leveling his gaze on me. I bit my cheeks to not react to the abbreviation he used for the Council. Sure, *we* all called them the PRICs, but I'd never heard an angel use that term. Orion really *was* flustered. "They are looking — well, *Ezra* is looking for any reason, any little thing, to strip me of my position here and send me back for re-credentialing. There is basically no one I trust to oversee appropriate entertainment in this town, but Eva Watford might have the most tact, so she will be helping me out. *Everyone* needs to pitch in. I think you can handle mowing the grass in the square. Make the flowers around the gazebo bloom. You're talented. You can make it happen."

Without waiting for a response, Orion looked back down at his seating chart, scratched out a name, and penned in another one as he muttered under his breath.

I pushed up from the chair, hovering for a moment while I waited to see if he'd spare me a glance, but Orion was so focused, I wasn't sure he knew I was still here.

With a frustrated sigh, I turned and walked back down the hall to head outside. Apparently I was the new town yard boy. I was so lost in my thoughts about whether I should run to a garden center or just look up horticultural spells that I nearly ran smack into a male who was just entering the lobby.

"Whoa, there, sorry about that," the other guy said in a thick Scottish accent as we both stepped back. The entry way door clicked shut behind him the same moment a semi-hazy lightbulb went off in my head.

Scottish. Why did that ring a bell?

I took the newcomer in, from his polished leather Oxfords, cuffed tan chinos, and white collared shirt under a forest green *cardigan*, sleeves rolled up his forearms. His dirty blond hair was shaved close around his ears and longer on top, swept back fashionably, his whole look dripping *Oxbridge*, but that wasn't what snagged my attention most. His irises were black.

A Scottish demon. Shit, this was —

"I wonder if you could point me towards the library?" He adjusted the strap of the satchel slung over his shoulder as he tilted his head.

"Are you Owen Kinkaid?" I blurted before I even realized I was speaking. He blinked at my outburst and I shook my head. "Sorry, I mean. Hello, I'm Lysander Theroux, Second in our local Coven." I couldn't help standing a little taller as I spoke, though Owen still had a few inches on me. Fucking demon. "I heard you were joining us for the Summit." There, that was smoother. *Nicer.* Could he see me gritting my teeth?

"Ah, Lysander!" Owen sounded genuinely pleased to meet me, and I felt like an asshole for already hating his guts. This was the dickwad that was supposed to marry Maisie against her wishes. *That* was why I didn't like him, naturally — why would he agree to that? — not any other reason. "Of course, my apologies. I've met your mother on occasion, I should have recognized you! You have her particular, er," — he stuttered over his words for a moment, and I wondered what he wasn't saying before he finished smoothly — "aura of great power."

I snorted, even as my curiosity was peaked. "Can you see auras?"

"Ah, no, not as Aura witches can, I'm afraid. But I can get a general sense of power."

"Right. Well, the library is right through there. Kai, our librarian, can help you with whatever you need." I pointed towards the right hall off the entryway, which had *Library* written over the frame. Could he not read? That might make me feel better. Why did I need to be made to feel better?

"Ah, grand! Oh, where are my manners?" He held his hand out to shake mine, and I obliged, though it was a near thing. "And yes, I'm Owen Kinkaid, as you astutely deduced. I wonder," — I dropped my hand, though Owen only stepped in closer — "do you know Ronan Crunamar's daughter Maisie?"

On the one hand, I could lie and say no. On the other hand, I could… "Oh, Maze?" I clocked the slight flare of surprise in his eyes at my casual nickname for her, and it soothed something in me. "Sure. Great girl."

"Oh." He swallowed. "You know her well, then, do you?" He tried for an offhand laugh and utterly failed.

I slid my hands in my pockets, running my tongue over my teeth. "She's a fan. Of my band, you know? She comes to a lot of our shows. We hang out sometimes." I smirked, letting him read into that.

Black eyes raked over me, and I could tell he was trying to assess if I was a threat to his little agreement with Ronan. But it seemed he had too much tact to press the issue right then, and only took another step back, giving me a polite smile.

"Well, I'm sure I'll be seeing you around town, Lysander." He gave me a little salute. "Cheers — for the directions."

I might have glared at his back as he made for the library.

Chapter Ten

MAISIE

NIGHTMARES OF SWIMMING ALONE in a sea devoid of any other life plagued me, and I woke dripping in sweat. Now that this was really happening with Lys, I had to tell Ronan. My stomach clenched just imagining it. This was not about to be a fun conversation, but it had to be done, and waiting any longer would only make it worse.

Luckily, today I was due to review the status of the repairs to our underwater city with my father.

Before I lost my nerve, I stepped into the hall towards the closest landing pad, dropped my pajamas, and shifted into my mer form as I pushed through the bubble that protected our city.

Iridescent teal scales covered my body instantly as I took off for the pier, where Ronan and I were to meet to discuss the portal. I was glad he was out in the blue for this conversation; it'd be easier than facing him in his office.

Zipping around small islands and sand shoals, I made my way over, passing schools of fish and a couple seals along the way. Our many lobster traps dotted the seafloor, chains connecting to buoys floating overhead, the main source of income for my people. The pier was several hundred yards in front of me, but I noted the tell-tale signs of Ronan's presence off to my left, as there would be for any large predator in the water — suddenly, the small groups of fish disappeared, the silence in the water growing as I swam closer.

Rounding a large boulder, I spotted him. Ronan was a giant in his mer form, easily twice my size, his navy blue scales glittering as he swam circles around a rock outcropping, inspecting it with a furrowed brow but slowing as he spotted my approach.

Is something wrong? I spoke to him mind-to-mind, the way all sea nymphs communicated in any of our shifted forms.

He gestured around and above the outcropping, and a shimmer of magic appeared, but it didn't look right.

Our glamour is fractured here. Every time I think I've found the last of the damage that demon and his witch spells did to our city, I find another. I can't lift this hex on my own though, he responded, and I glided closer, spotting the fissures in the semi-reflective sheen of magic.

The region around our city held a glamour to hide us from any humans who might venture into the area by boat or, occasionally, swimming and scuba diving. It would not only urge them to turn back and find another area, but on the off chance they still made it through, would convince them anything they saw was something more ordinary. Instead of a mer, they'd see a large swordfish, or a shark, go on their way, and we could stay hidden.

If we had a crack in the glamour...

I reached out, tracing the line with my hand to get a

better feel of its shape and size, tilting my head as I directed at Ronan, *Has this had any side-effects?*

Corporal Williams swam through here unknowingly earlier today, and it nearly made him shift all the way back to human. He had to surface immediately.

My eyes widened, but I tried not to show any other reaction. Ronan had no idea that Drew and I had ever been anything more than... well, heir and guard, and it was better for both of us if he never found out. We'd known each other since we were children, and somewhere along the way, our friendship had morphed into friends-with-benefits, though I could never bring myself to make it more than just a hookup. While easy on the eyes, Drew was just... not for me.

Besides, the fact that this fracture had almost forced a shift on one of us was far more important than some non-existent relationship.

Owen will be here in two and a half weeks for the Summit. Once we gain his magic, we should be able to fix this quickly.

Ronan's words jolted me back to the real reason I'd sought him out this morning, so I let myself drift closer to him. Also, I *really* needed to check my emails more often because I had no idea what this Summit was about.

About that. I waited until his dark blue eyes found mine before I went on. *You said the other day you wouldn't make me marry Owen if I was seeing someone, right? Well, I haven't known how to tell you this, but I am.*

Ronan's eyebrows shot up, but I pushed on before he could interrupt.

We've been keeping it secret because we weren't sure how you — his eyes narrowed, so I hastily added, *— or his mother would* *react. But we've been together for about three months. I'm sorry I didn't tell you sooner.*

Even in the constant eddies of the ocean currents, Ronan went eerily still. *Who?*

I didn't blink even though I was tempted to shrink down to the size of a shrimp and swim away. *Lysander Theroux.*

His jaw tightened even before I'd finished the name, and I sensed the order that was about to come my way, the one to break up with him immediately and never talk to a Theroux again. *Lysander Theroux only cares about his little band and the women that come with it. He's irresponsible and immature. Care to inform me how you've even met the witch? You haven't been sneaking out again, have you?*

My mind stuttered, realizing just how much I had to reveal to explain this. Man, that shrimp form sounded appealing right now. Maybe a squid. I could send out a jolt of ink and disappear before he saw which direction I went. Bob and weave. But no. I wanted to *not* marry Owen more than I wanted to get away from my father, and I wasn't ready to give up my life abovewater yet. So I told a half-truth.

I did. I rushed on before he could say anything, *But, I promise, I didn't go alone this time. I just wanted to go to a show, pretend to be* normal *where everyone didn't know me as the future queen. You, more than anyone, know how much pressure there constantly is on me. I feel like even the way I* breathe *is judged in our city. I'm far more pufferfish than anyone cares to see in a royal.*

Waves thrashed around him as his temper flared. *Do I even want to know who went with you? Or how many times this has happened? How often are you seeing this male, breaking my rules by spending time ashore? The last time you snuck out, Corissa tried to follow you, and look how* that *ended for her. Do you not see the example you're setting?*

I flinched. As much as I wanted not to blame myself for Corissa's near fatal accident, he was right. My heart sank, but I dug my heels in, determined that I also needed to set an example for my sisters to stand up for what made them happy. That mattered, too. So I said nothing.

Ronan's eyes shut, corded muscles in his chest flexing as he fought to control himself, but I stopped him before he could say anything else.

Lysander could help us with this. I gestured at the magic, at the obvious crack, hoping I could appeal to Ronan's desperate need to protect his people and our world. *He's an extremely powerful witch, and this is both witch and demon magic, right? He could help us* now, *before it has time to get any worse. We don't need to wait on Owen when Lysander is right here in town. I could call him tonight.*

Theroux's don't help us, he scoffed. *They only care about themselves.*

Ronan's tone was so full of bitter resentment, I couldn't help but wonder what the backstory was between Ostara and Ronan, but he'd never answer me. With a gentle flick of my tail, I drifted closer until I could touch his arm. *Lys isn't his mother. He loves me. He'd help us. He tried to help Corissa, didn't he?*

This isn't a discussion, Maisie. His voice boomed in my mind, his blue eyes flaring. *I will never allow* witch *magic in my sea. You will break it off with Lysander, and never mention his name to me again.*

Now, I blinked, pulling my hand off him and drifting further away. I'd known Ronan would be upset at my deceit, but I'd hoped I'd be able to sway him by saying Lys loved me, or at least get Ronan to allow it in favor of the power for our family. But any hope I held that I could convince him this was good for us shattered with his steely expression.

Return home, check on your sisters, and don't leave again until I get back and can think of an appropriate consequence for three months of lies from my heir. And I will not have you continuing to set this example for your sisters, so the next time you sneak out, be prepared to leave your life here behind.

With a powerful flick of his tail, he shot away, leaving me in a whirlwind of bubbles and indecision.

Chapter Eleven

MAISIE

I COULD HEAR music the minute I turned onto the street. I'd had a vague idea which house was Lys's before, but the sound of drums as I passed Immortali-Tea made it unmistakeable.

The house was a simple cedar-shingle with an attached garage, which was where the music was coming from. Despite our flirtatious texts yesterday, panic rose in me as I walked up the driveway, wanting to turn around and flee when I saw Dillon at the drumset, blond hair bobbing. He nodded at me and stopped playing for a minute to jerk his head at the interior garage door.

"Hey, Maia. Not sneaking in this time? Lys is inside somewhere." He smiled at me, and went back to playing.

Lys must have had a conversation with him, then. Not knowing how much Dillon knew, I gave him a little wave and let myself into the house. The door near the garage opened into a small, outdated kitchen that overlooked a cramped living room, stuffed with two mismatched couches, a recliner, several amps, an empty guitar case, and a coffee table littered with guitar picks and cables.

"Uh, Lys?" I called out, not exactly wanting to wander around to find him.

I heard a muffled call in return from somewhere down the hall, and had to assume that was for me.

"All right then."

The original intention of our *date* today was to iron out all the finer details of this arrangement, but after speaking with Ronan, I was having second thoughts about the whole thing. Making my way down the hall, I passed a bathroom, then a messy, empty bedroom that must have been Dillon's, before coming to a half-open door at the end.

I barely raised my hand to knock when it pulled open, and Lys smiled down at me.

"Hey, come on in." He stepped back to let me into his bedroom.

Apparently, we were talking in here. I was about to walk into Lysander Theroux's bedroom. No big deal, I was totally cool with that. Cool as a cuttlefish.

Lys gestured for me to take a seat on his bed — his *bed!* I perched on the edge, casual as all get-out, as I tried not to become intoxicated at his citrus and vetiver scent that pervaded the space and glanced around his room.

It wasn't snooping if he invited me in.

The walls were painted a dark grey, almost black color, and all of the available wall space was covered in multi-colored guitars. Some acoustic, some electric, but all meticulously cared for and clearly prized possessions. After the outdated view of the kitchen when I'd entered, I had low expectations of this bachelor pad, but was pleasantly surprised to see a wrought-iron headboard, and a light grey comforter, pulled tight over the king-size bed.

Lysander Theroux was a bed-maker.

I couldn't decide if that was just for me, knowing I was coming over, or if it was a normal thing for him. Either way, I couldn't help but admire the tidiness of the space. My fingers itched to run across the fabric, knowing that Lys slept here, but I refrained, feeling like that was edging toward *intense* stalking.

"So." I brought my focus back to Lys where he stood next to the wall as I tugged on the hem of the cropped grey Pink Floyd tee Kymari had forced on me for today. My eyes roved his body, admiring the tattoos peeking out from the edge of the sleeve of his olive green t-shirt, the fabric perfectly taut over his chest and shoulders. How was it fair that one man could be this gorgeous? My fingers itched to reach out and touch him, but recognized that would be exceedingly weird at this moment. Before those thoughts could slip out, I said, "You told Dillon?"

"Just that we're dating."

"Right."

"Well, and that we've been hanging out here without him noticing for three months."

My eyebrows shot skyward. "He bought that?"

Lys lifted a shoulder. "I told him he's going deaf." He laughed. "It's not even a lie. Dude can barely hear himself talk."

I narrowed my eyes slightly. "You seem pretty relaxed about this whole thing."

Another shrug. What was with that?

"Should I not be? We'll pretend to date. Ostara's already backed off a bit. Is King Triton giving you a hard time?"

A laugh bubbled out of me before I could stop it as I processed his reference

Lys grinned, and I couldn't help but notice the way it lit up his entire face. "I mean, he's a shirtless, angry merman. You can't tell me you've never made that comparison before. Does that make you Ariel, the naughty daughter who steals away to be with the humans? Please tell me you brush your hair with a fork."

I shook my head, but didn't bother responding to that. We *did* need to talk about Ronan. Of its own accord, my leg started jostling, drawing Lys's eyes to it with a frown.

"Um, about this whole thing." I cleared my throat. Sweat beaded on my skin as anxiety took over, and all I could think about was the tirade I would launch at Kymari later for choosing a *grey* tee today. I was well on my way to pit stains if I wasn't there already. Only dark colors or sleeveless tops for abovewater days from now on. "Ronan has ordered me to break up with you immediately or he'll banish me from his sea. *The* sea. Or lock me up. I'm not sure he's decided one way or the other yet, to be honest. But either way would be terrible."

Concern entered Lys's green eyes as he opened his mouth. "I don't think he'd really —"

I laughed. A sharp, manic sound that I tried to bring into a more normal register, but my voice broke. "Oh, no, he would. He totally would. Probably lock me up, if I had to guess, since I'm sure he still wants the whole demon-marriage thing to go forward. Maybe in my room, if I'm lucky, which wouldn't be as bad, but still. I'd be trapped, and

I hate being —" My voice wavered as I tried to slow my words, feeling the sweat drip down between my boobs, only making my anxiety that much worse. "Poseidon, I *hate* sweating. This is the worst part about being abovewater."

My sudden shift in topic caught Lys off-guard, a chuckle rising out of him as he reached a hand behind him, rubbing his neck. "Shoes. Sweating. Being trapped."

My brow drew down in confusion. "What?"

"Just cataloging the things you *don't* like," Lys smiled, an easy expression even amidst my panic attack. "Figure it might come in handy, since I'm not letting you break up with me. These all seem like things a good boyfriend would know."

"That," I paused, not sure how to answer him, but Lys stood with one shoulder propped against the wall, confident as ever. It was rude of him to be so calm, collected, and downright sexy while I floundered like a fish out of water. "That's not how breakups work."

"Should I add gravity to the list? You seem to be not too fond of it either."

I couldn't help but chuckle as I shook my head, but his easygoing attitude somehow eased the weight of my own worries.

"We can't do this, Lys." I got us back on track with a sigh as I looked down at my hands in my lap. "I'm sorry about this, and now you'll have to tell your mother, and it's all a mess. This was a stupid idea."

"Hey," Lys said, pushing off the wall and standing in front of me. "This isn't over yet. I told you, I'm not accepting this breakup. You're not marrying that Scottish —" he cut himself off, shaking his head, before pressing on.

"We can still make this work, I promise. Thanks for the, *it's not you, it's me,* bit though."

I looked up at him, his green eyes searching my face. "You don't understand."

Lys's hand came up, resting lightly on my shoulder, then moving to the side of my neck as he leaned down. My breath caught in my throat as his eyes flicked down to my lips for only a second, then back up, face looming mere inches from mine. "I understand perfectly. We're both grown adults whose parents still treat us as children, and it's time we take a stand. So I'm not giving up on you, or this plan, because you need this taste of freedom, too."

I wanted to disagree with him. I wanted to get up and leave. I wanted to explain the weight of my responsibilities to my people. I wanted to do those things, but I didn't.

Because Lys was right.

I did want a taste of freedom. Desperately. And he needed this just as much as I did.

"But. Ronan."

Lys dropped his hand, and I was both relieved and sad at the same time. "What are his hangups with me? What were his reasons for saying no?"

I stared wide-eyed at him, thinking through the many reasons my father had launched at me, none of which *anyone* would like to hear about themselves. As I puckered my lips in thought, Lys winced.

"That bad, huh?"

"I mean, it wasn't *good.*"

Lys heaved a deep sigh, waving a dismissive hand in the air. "Okay, well, let's think this through. I'm extremely powerful for a witch —"

"And humble."

"Aw, you noticed." Lys grinned, and a thousand inner Maisie voices sighed in a chorus in my head. "But what I was *going* to say is that maybe actions speak louder than words. What is there that I can do for you," — Lys stopped, clearing his throat — "for *Ronan* that would show I'm not who he thinks I am?"

That made me pause. Maybe Lys was right. After all, I did think my father was being short-sighted as far as Lys went. His problem with Ostara shouldn't automatically extend to Lys. That wasn't fair. So what *could* Lys do that would make Ronan see him differently?

"There's a weakness in our glamour," I said before I could stop the words from spilling out of my mouth. "He wants Owen to fix it when he gets here, but maybe you could do it first."

Lys shifted on his feet, clearing his throat as he looked anywhere but me. That was weird. Almost, dare I say, awkward? Something I would have done?

"What are you not telling me?" I said through squinted eyes. "You're fidgeting, avoiding eye contact, and your sweat glands are working in overdrive. I happen to know these are three tell-tale signs that someone is lying. Or uncomfortable. Or lying. I think you're lying."

Lys not-so-subtly lifted his arms as he tried not to sniff his own armpits. Something I was *also* trying to avoid. Two self-conscious peas in a pod. "You sure don't trust easily do you?"

"Understatement." My eyes were still narrowed, inspecting his entirely-too-handsome body for other signs of deception. "Spill it."

Another throat clearing. Then — "I don't know if my powers will work underwater. I've never tried it."

He still wasn't making eye contact with me, but his shoulders dropped slightly as I glared at him, trying to feel if that was the truth. But, as far as I knew, Lys had never admitted there was *anything* he couldn't do, so maybe.

"Worth a try, right? Let's do it," Lys said, then beamed a wicked smile at me.

My nostrils flared under his appraisal, and Poseidon, I hated how *weird* I was around this male. Could I not function *normally?* Apparently not.

Lys met my gaze, and I did my best to rein in my overactive nostrils, feeling as his eyes fell to them. Wait. No. Maybe he was looking at… Was he looking at my lips?

"But before we go for a swim," Lys said, his voice suddenly deeper, and sexier, and now *I* was the one fidgeting, sweating, and avoiding eye contact. "We need to get to know each other."

"Mmhmm," I mumbled as I fought to control my racing heart.

"And you can't be flipping out like you currently are every time we sit next to each other."

"Who, me? The picture of elegant composure you see before you? Flipping out?" My voice came out about two octaves too high and I cleared my throat. Lys laughed, but it was a warm laugh, a chuckle I wished I could put my hand on his chest to feel. "Right." I nodded far too aggressively. "Totally. Yes. We should work on that."

Lys pursed his lips in thought. "We should go on a date. Scallywags, probably. Somewhere people will see us."

I nodded mechanically. "Yes. We should do that. Definitely." Trying to get myself to focus on the task at hand, I pulled the papers I'd brought just in case out of my back pocket, unfolding them in my lap.

Lys dragged a chair over from the corner, flipping it around to straddle it backwards as he leaned on the back. "What's that?"

"This?" I held up the paper as panic rose in my chest. Why had I thought this was a good idea? "Well, two things. The first is a general contract for our agreement so we can understand the rules for this arrangement. Then I also brought a list of questions I thought we might need to know about each other. Things I should know three months in."

"A contract?"

"If we're doing this, then I'm taking this arrangement seriously," I said, gripping the paper tightly in my fist.

"Is that supposed to imply I'm not?"

I hesitated for a moment before answering, choosing my words carefully. Truthfully, I wasn't sure Lys took much seriously, but the way he studied me now said that would be the wrong answer, and I didn't want to hurt his feelings. "To be determined."

"That's fair, I guess," Lys said, tilting his chin towards the paper. "Have you already drafted it?"

"Just some preliminary things, but we can change or add anything you think I missed."

"Read it to me."

"Okay," I said, my voice wavering slightly as I looked down at the words I'd typed out earlier, which all sounded stupid now that I sat here with him. Sensing my hesitation, he leaned forward and lifted the paper from my hands, flipping it around to read it.

"Rule #1. Monogamy." Lys's eyes lifted to mine, but I didn't budge, even though my heart pounded in my chest wildly as he continued to read. "During the stated term dates of this contract, both parties agree to forgo relations of any kind with anyone other than the listed parties in order to maintain the image of monogamy in the relationship."

I nodded, confident in my choice of wording.

"Done," Lys said, agreeing more easily than I would have thought to those terms. "Rule—"

"You realize that means no sex for the next month, right?" I interrupted, making sure he understood what he just agreed to. "If Ronan thinks you cheated on me, he might kill you. You have to at least *appear* to be loyal to me."

Lys glanced down at the paper, then back at me, his eyes full of mischief. "It says *other than the listed parties*. So I could have sex with you, Maze. That's not breaking the rules."

My cheeks heated as I stared wide-eyed at my hands in my lap, unable to meet his gaze. Why hadn't I thought of that when I'd written it that way? "Save your energy. That will not be happening."

"Well then, that still leaves one listed party, and it's a good thing my right hand gets nothing but rave reviews."

Dear sweet baby Poseidon, was he talking about jerking off? He was, and I was dying. Several beats of silence went by while I continued to stare at my hands, regretting all of my life choices that had led me to this moment.

"Rule #2. Physical Contact," Lys continued, and I wanted to bury myself in his blankets, maybe crawl under the bed in my embarrassment. "Physical contact between parties will be limited to public appearances only. Acceptable contact can include, but is not limited to, hand-holding, hugging, and the occasional kiss to the forehead or cheek, if necessary." Lys set the paper on his lap. "No can do on this one, Maze. I'm a snuggler. I'm gonna need more than this."

"Like what?" I asked incredulously.

"Sitting on my lap, maybe. I'll probably put my arm around you if you're next to me. Kiss you if I feel like it's necessary to sell the ruse. I don't know. Nothing that will make you uncomfortable but more than *hand-holding and hugging*. How you got anyone to buy the coin collecting story is beyond me, but it will come off as downright odd if I'm not touching my beautiful girlfriend any chance I can get."

My heart came to a screeching halt in my chest at his words, imagining Lys casually touching me like he was talking about. And… had he just called me beautiful?

Grabbing a pen from his nightstand, he scratched several words on the paper, adding to the list before he moved on. "Rule #3. Secrecy. No one, outside of listed parties, can know about this arrangement." Lys nodded, then kept reading. "Rule #4. Both parties will agree to be seen in public together no less than two times a week during the terms of this contract. These terms extend one month from today, May 31, or until both party's arranged marriages have been called off."

Without even rereading the paperwork, Lys signed it, handing it back to me like it was nothing. I gripped the paper, eyes unable to focus on the words.

What had we just agreed to?

Chapter Twelve

MAISIE

BEFORE I HAD time to recover from the fact that Lys had just agreed to all of my terms, he snatched the second paper out of my hand, skimming the questions I'd printed ahead of time to get to know each other better. "Why do you need to know my blood type?"

Forcing my mind to rejoin the conversation, I took a page out of Lys's book, I shrugged. "Better safe than sorry. What if an emergency happens?"

"Maze. You can't be serious." He crumpled the paper, tossing it over his shoulder, and I had to force myself not to get up and fetch it. "*I* don't even know my blood type."

"How is that even possible?"

"Easy." He scoffed. "I'm a witch. I can heal myself magically. I've never had a reason to go get my blood drawn, let alone ask what blood type I have."

"But," I stuttered, "what if we're in a car crash, roll off the highway, and you're left in a ditch with glass shards in your skin, bleeding out, need a transfusion, and you're taken to a human hospital? They'll ask me what your blood type is and I'll have no answer. The jig would be up."

"I assume they'd be able to figure out my blood type, in that very precise situation." Lys studied me, eyes roving my body. "Is that a specific example you're using? Did that happen to you?"

"Oh." I chuckled. "No. I've never been in a car. But you can never be too prepared, right?"

"You've never been in a car." He said it like a statement, not a question, and stared at me for a long minute before shaking his head and moving on. "Favorite band?" he asked, apparently done with my worst-case-scenario conversations and practical questions like, *Who should I call in case of emergency?*

"Fleetwood Mac."

Lys perked up, eyebrows raising as he leaned back and grabbed an acoustic guitar off a stand in the corner, slinging the strap over his shoulder. "Now we're getting somewhere," he said, right as he strummed the opening chords to *The Chain.* "Stevie Nicks?"

"Yeah." I nodded, somehow more at ease in his presence and also wound tight as I watched his fingers move across the strings. "Exactly."

"Can't really blame you. She's an icon." He strummed the chorus, the muscles in his tan, tattooed forearms working overtime as he played, and I clenched my jaw to keep drool from dripping out of my mouth. Seamlessly, he switched to *All Along the Watchtower.* "Hendrix is my favorite though."

"So this is your passion then?" I asked, suddenly going for the gut-punch question as I waved a hand around his room. That one wasn't even *on* my list. Look at me, flying by the seat of my boho-flare pants. "Music?"

"Yes," he answered immediately. "Without a doubt. Don't get me wrong, I love all of the witchy business. Yesterday I lifted a hex off a young witch whose magic wasn't cooperating. She was so relieved, and I was delighted to be the one to help her. I was raised in the Coven here in town, and I know more about our practice than… well, pretty much anyone else I've ever met. But none of it compares to the feel of the strings under my hand, a song in my head, and the faces of an audience having a good time." He stopped playing and looked at me. "What about you?"

"My family," I said, also not needing to think about it. "My sisters, mainly, but our people."

He nodded, a flicker of something that might have been respect playing across his features before he stood to set the guitar back on the stand.

"So we know each other's passions, then," he said, only he didn't sit back down in the chair. He came and sat next to me on the bed, our knees touching. "We know how we met, which, thank you for that. I've been asked twice now how I came to be at a rare coins convention, and we will never speak of puke-mageddon again. Why did you say that?"

"I panicked and said the first thing that came to mind."

He squinted. "*That* was the first thing you thought of? Do *you* collect coins?"

I laughed entirely too hard. "No. One of my sisters made me watch this documentary about the Hoard a few weeks ago and I was bored to tears. Which, by the way, you should probably know I have six," —my words cut off as his hand landed on my knee, warm even through the denim of my jeans — "sisters."

"Great, six sisters." He chuckled, tapping his thumb on my knee. "See, I think there's something more important we need to work on, and it's this." *Tap, tap.* "No one is going to believe we've been dating for three months, that we're in love, if you close up every time we touch. It was Rule #2. Touching in public. And you're terrible at it."

He had a point there. Even though I was experienced, technically speaking, I'd never been openly in a relationship with anyone. As Ronan's daughter and the heir to the sea nymph kingdom, I couldn't do public displays of affection and casual dating without it becoming everybody's business. That aside, there was something about Lys that kept knocking me off-kilter.

"You're right." I took a breath. "What should we do about that?"

He held my eyes a minute before he grinned, squeezing my knee and standing up again. "Practice."

Ten minutes later, Lys had set up a show on the TV across from his bed, retrieved some snacks and beers from the kitchen, and said we were going to relax, hang out, and *practice.*

Practice touching.

Easy enough.

"Do you like this show?" He nodded at the TV as he popped the caps off the beer bottles, passing me one where I now sat leaning back against his headboard.

"*X-Files*? I've never actually seen it," I took a sip of beer. "I don't have much time for TV."

"No?" He laughed. "Do you guys even get WiFi down there?"

I paused, grip tightening on the neck of the bottle. Sea nymphs weren't allowed to disclose anything about Crunamar City, our underwater world. Anyone from the outside, if they were ever granted access to visit, had to agree to have all memories of the city wiped when they left, and I couldn't think of a time in the last century when an outsider had been invited anyway.

Lys, keen observer that he was, noted my hesitancy almost immediately. "Not allowed to talk about it, are you?"

I gave a sheepish smile. "Not exactly, no."

He pointed at himself with a pretzel. "Not even to the love of your life?"

Honestly, I didn't know how it would work if I were to marry and join magic with an outsider. I had no idea what Ronan had planned with regards to Owen and this whole situation. But I knew it was better to err on the side of caution. Luckily, it didn't seem to bother Lys whatsoever, as he waved it off and moved on.

"I'm going to put my arm around you now."

I didn't know if he was warning me, or asking me, but either way I appreciated the heads-up. His arm settled over my shoulders, hand draping down as he tugged me into his side. Even though I could admit the weight and warmth of his arm felt nice, comforting even, I flinched as my body pressed more firmly into his, and he *tsk*ed me.

"I warned you and everything." His thumb worked small circles over my shoulder where it rested on my cut-off tee, the feeling both relaxing and utterly *not* at the same time. "Put your hand on my chest."

I shot him a confused look, my arm trapped between our two bodies.

"Right hand. Palm flat. On my chest."

Oh. Right. Poseidon, I was bad at this, even though that was exactly what I'd wanted to do not too long ago, and now here he was, giving me permission. I did as I was told, fingers splayed wide as I set it gently on his chest. Warmth radiated through his shirt and into my skin, spreading quickly through my body even with just the minor touch.

"That's not so bad, right?" Lys asked, leaning his head on mine.

"Mmhmm," I mumbled, my heart creeping up my throat.

"You're breathing heavily. Like an anxious cat. Or maybe… a fish out of water?"

I slapped my hand down on his chest as a laugh rumbled through him, the feel of it under my palm exactly how I'd imagined and the sound sultry with my ear pressed against him.

"Okay, so, physical touch you're extremely awkward at, but banter? We can handle banter, right?"

"Better than this, for sure."

"What?" he asked, leaning back to stare at me. "Are you not having a good time being pressed up against a hot musician such as myself? Really, I think you could do a lot worse as far as boyfriends go. At least I'm attractive."

"Ah, there's that humility again. What is this show even about?"

"See, this is lesson number one in dating," Lys said, his

left hand coming up to touch on my chin lightly, lifting my face up to his. "It's not about the show. It's about the intimacy of watching it together. Of holding you close. Of feeling the way your breath hitches when I run my thumb across your lips like this."

His thumb trailed across my bottom lip, and without any thought, my gaze dropped to his own lips, full and parted slightly as a smug smile took up residence.

"I've been wanting to do that again." My breath caught in my chest at his murmured words, spoken so low it was almost like he hadn't meant to say them out loud.

With a pointed cough, Lys spoke again, his voice back to normal. "It's an excuse. A way to pass the time as you get comfortable enough to let me kiss you again."

My heart raced as his hands shifted to my jaw, fingers running lightly over my neck.

"Your heart is pounding." His thumb traced over my pulse, confirming it without me needing to say anything, but I fought to control my reaction. "I haven't even kissed you yet."

"I mean, you did at Scallywags on Sunday."

Lys smiled, his eyes crinkling slightly at the corners. "That was only for show. This, though," — he paused, his thumb tracing over my neck again, sending tingles all the way down my spine — "it has to be real. No one is going to buy it if I don't have my hands all over you. Because, fuck, I want to."

My nostrils flared again, this time scenting the arousal in the room coming from both of us. Even if this was fake, Lys was smooth, and I was undeniably affected by him.

But it was fake. It was *all. Fake.*

Right?

"I'm going to kiss you now," he said, his voice barely above a whisper as his mouth hovered over mine. I froze.

Suddenly, I knew if I felt his lips on mine, here in his bedroom, just the two of us all alone, my brain would find it impossible to know the real from the fake. It would be too hard to separate that this was all a lie, all just practice, all just acting.

I wasn't here to *actually* catch feelings for him. And this feeling, this rush from him, would be way too easy to give into. I pushed hard on his chest, and immediately, Lys pulled away from me. Eyes wide, I threw myself off the bed, tripping over my own feet as I ran into the bathroom, slamming the door behind me.

My chest heaved, sucking air in great gulps as if I was drowning. Maybe I was. Why did I ever think I could pull this off? Lys was too smooth, too confident, too sexy, way out of my league socially. Even though I was well aware that he'd had *plenty* of practice to get him to this position, rightfully earning his title as a player, and the logical side of my brain said he was bad news, my hormones didn't agree.

Shit. I was in *way* over my head.

Chapter Thirteen

LYSANDER

THE DOOR to the bathroom snicked shut as I righted my shirt, evened my breathing, and adjusted my pants. Having her within reach, in my arms, in my *bed*, was intoxicating. I wanted to taste her lips, even if it was all a sham.

When she'd pushed at my shoulders, practically sprinting from my embrace, I knew I'd blown it. And the way I'd let it get physical so fast, wanting her mouth under any pretense I could have it... I scrubbed a hand over my face. Was I just as bad as everyone thought I was?

Shit, with the physical limits she'd written into our contract, I should have known not to push it. I bet *Owen* wouldn't have sent her running out of the room. He'd have probably asked her to afternoon tea, gallantly kissed her hand, and called it a day as he walked away, flexing his fist at his side.

Barf.

I wasn't sure if Maisie was a virgin, but after spending only a half-hour with her, I was confident she was inexperienced and I'd pushed her. In our short time together, I'd lived up to the very low expectations everyone seemed to have of me.

Even the addendum I'd added to the contract with an expanded list of physical touches felt sleazy now. Why was I like this?

Then and there, I decided I'd let her take the lead from now on. I didn't want to be the sex-crazed playboy everyone thought they knew. This was a great opportunity to test my ability to slow myself down, especially since every bone in my body was screaming to pin Maisie to the nearest surface and show her how good I could make her feel in my hands.

Maisie was easily the most beautiful woman I'd ever seen, and the fact that she didn't seem to know just how weak-kneed she made men in her presence made her that much hotter.

Holding myself back from her was going to be one of the hardest things I'd ever done, but I needed to, for both of our sakes.

Switching off the TV, I slid off the bed, and pulled the chair back to the corner next to my guitar. I dropped down to sit and picked up the instrument, beginning to strum. Without a thought, *Dreams* came together, choosing yet another Fleetwood Mac song. Was it to calm Maisie's nerves, to make her comfortable? Or was I trying to show off? The former, surely. Right?

The bathroom door opened a few minutes later, and Maisie reemerged, flared jeans and cut-off tee looking just as relaxed and sexy as they had when she'd arrived earlier.

"Sorry," she said, shoving her hands into her pockets.

I set down the guitar, standing in front of her, but allowing a few feet of space between us so she wouldn't bolt again. "I should be the one to apologize. I went too fast."

Maisie didn't say anything, rocking back on her heels as she glanced between the bed and me. "Do we need to try that again?"

I bit my cheeks to refrain from smiling, but my eyebrows inched towards my hairline. "Do you *want* to try that again?"

"I mean," she sighed. "No way can I sell this. Maybe we should just give up now."

With a shake of my head, I stepped closer, ducking slightly as I forced her to look at me. "No negative talk about yourself."

Her blue-green eyes clouded as emotion surfaced there, and even knowing she was close to tears was enough to break me. I was breaking the promise I'd just made to myself to let her lead physically, but she needed comfort and I knew she'd never ask for it. I hauled her into my chest, wrapping my arms around her as I rested my chin on her head. Slowly, her arms wrapped around my waist, hugging me back.

"Hugging was in the contract, and you need one. We're going to figure this out together, Maze," I said, placing a gentle kiss on her forehead — also on her approved list. "I promise. And we'll fix that glamour so good, King Triton will have no choice but to like me."

"How?" She half-giggled, half-sniffled, but didn't let go of my embrace. That was a start.

"Not every relationship has to be in the fast-lane physically. We slow it down, get to know each other, become friends, and trust me, we can fool anyone."

She nodded slowly, her hands loosening on my waist as I dropped my hands to rest on her upper arms, smiling at her. Maisie's lips tipped up in return as she steeled her nerves, letting go of the emotions that had gripped her moments before.

She lifted her arms, pulled a scrunchie from her wrist, and began braiding her long platinum hair to the side, already seeming to sink into a version of her I wanted to know. Her shirt rose, revealing just the barest sliver of a teal bra beneath the cropped length, and my breath caught in my throat.

This might be fake, but I'd been craving a taste of Mystery Girl for months. Now she was here, very much within reach, but I was starting to realize she deserved so much better than me. It didn't help that she was also caring and funny and sweet, so much more than just a tempting package wrapped in jeans and a vintage band tee. Pink Floyd, to be exact.

Shit. I was in *way* over my head.

Slipping my fingers through hers, I let her take a moment to get used to the simple hold, then tugged her down the hall to where I could hear Dillon settling into the living room, TV blaring.

"Done with the *Phantom Gourmet* and moving on to *Diners, Drive-Ins, and Dives?*" I asked as I dropped Maisie's hand, leaning against the door frame.

"Listen," Dillon said, picking up a cheeseburger, "I can't get enough of this shit. It's not as good as *Phantom,* but he gets so passionate about each restaurant, and how are you not supposed to share that feeling? It's about way more than food."

"Then why do you make me stop at every single location featured along the eastern seaboard if it's not about the food?"

Dillon pointed his cheeseburger at me. "Don't even try to deny that every meal hasn't been *phenomenal.* Maia, have you ever been to one of these restaurants?"

"Can't say I have," Maisie answered, walking in front of me and plopping down on the chair across from Dillon. "What's this one about?"

The two chatted easily about the show while I watched from my perch, struggling to comprehend that this was the same girl who had fled my bedroom minutes before. Just like that, she'd found easy companionship with my best friend, and I couldn't help but love that.

"I still can't believe Lys never mentioned he was dating you," Dillon said on a commercial break. "You're pretty chill, Maia." Then he threw a fry at my head. "I'd have approved, man. You should've said something."

Clutching my heart, I pushed off the doorframe and stopped in front of where Maisie sat in the chair. "If I'd known how offended you'd be, I would have said something. Are you harboring a secret crush on me? Or, on Ma—ze?" I caught myself at the last moment.

"We're to the cutesy nicknames phase already?" Dillon said, tilting his head as he appraised me. With a shake of his head, he dismissed whatever thought had been rolling through his mind. "Whatever, man. I'm happy for you."

Before I had time to respond, Maisie stood, grabbed my hand, and pushed me down into the chair she'd vacated. Once I'd sat down, she shocked me by sitting on the armrest of the chair, legs dangling over my lap. Right as I was about to lay a hand across her legs, gravity got the best of her and she went toppling backwards. It was like watching in slow motion, her arms flailing, eyes blown wide as I tried to grab her ankles to steady her. Then her left sneaker connected with my nose. My head snapped back right as a puff of air escaped her, her back slamming into the wood floors.

"You okay?" I asked as I gripped my nose, head tilted back as I sent a wave of healing over myself to staunch the bleeding.

"Yeah," a pained answer came from the floor next to me. Then she started to laugh. Deep, full, belly laugh.

"That," Dillon paused, popping a fry in his mouth, "was impressive."

This only seemed to make Maisie laugh harder, rolling to her side as she wiped tears from her face. A snort escaped, and she slapped a hand over her mouth attempting to muffle the sound. But we'd already heard it.

"Did you just snort?" Dillon asked, laughing with her.

"I'm so sorry. Lys, add gravity to your list."

Recovering slightly, I stood and grabbed her hand, pulling her to her feet and leading her to the couch between Dillon and me.

"What list?" Dillon asked as we all settled, the laughter ebbing.

"He's keeping a list of all the things I don't like," Maisie answered as she brought a slightly trembling hand down on my thigh. The touch was hardly indecent in its location near my knee, and yet, every nerve in my body lit up like the fourth of July.

I flipped her hand over, lacing my fingers through hers,

and Dillon noticed the move. "I never would have believed it if I wasn't seeing this with my own eyes."

"Just call me Wendy Darling. I've tamed Peter Pan," Maisie said, then smirked at me. I forced myself to match her smile, and her smirk faltered, questions swimming in her eyes. "But no one should be surprised. I'm part-siren."

Dillon slapped his leg, eyes wide. "Should have fucking known."

Maisie laughed, and I couldn't combine the nervous girl in my room to this confident, relaxed one.

"Sirens aren't real, Dill," I said, forcing my eyes away from my *girlfriend* and back to my friend.

Dillon polished off the last of his burger. "That true, Maia?"

She hesitated, body stiffening, but it was my turn to rescue her.

"Can we change the channel? Or are you this into tacos?"

"How can you even *ask* a question like that?" Dillon scoffed, and Maisie chuckled.

The three of us fell into easy conversation as we watched the rest of the show, another hour passing quickly before I knew it. Maisie glanced at her watch — 4:30 — and rose. "I need to get to Scallywags, but it was nice hanging out with you, Dillon."

"You too," he said, leaning over with a closed fist to bump knuckles with Maisie. "Glad to be in on this little secret. I've always liked you. And now that I know you're a Pink Floyd fan, I like you even more."

Maisie grinned, the look more forced than she'd been in the last hour, and I grabbed her hand, pulling her from the room and towards the front door. She opened it, and I followed her outside, standing on the front steps.

"Well, I don't know who *that* girl was," I said as the door closed behind me, "but Dillon bought it, hook, line, and sinker."

"Are you going to make fish jokes constantly?"

I shrugged. "Probably."

"Your nose okay?"

Scrunching it, I wiggled it back and forth. "All good here."

Maisie rolled her eyes, flipping her long braid over her shoulder to cascade down her back. "So Monday, then? Meet me on the pier at sundown, and we'll go check on the barrier magic."

I nodded, hands shoved in my pocket as I forced myself not to notice the way she fidgeted with the end of her braid while she talked. "Monday. I'll be ready."

"Oh, wait," Maisie said, pulling at the bracelet on her wrist. "This is twine my family makes. It's woven with sea nymph power, a protection spell of sorts, but it's tradition for nymphs to give them to their loved ones." She choked, dropping her eyes suddenly at her words, and I couldn't help but smile. "It'll make it seem real if you were wearing mine."

I extended my wrist, letting her tie the teal threads around it, feeling the magic sit against my skin. "I love it."

She nodded several times, then finally lifted her head to

meet my gaze as she drew in a deep breath. "Bye, Lysander. Thank you for this."

"Wait," I said, my hand snaking out to seize her wrist as she turned to leave. "Can't leave without a goodbye kiss, can you?"

Maisie's eyes blew wide once more, and I stepped down off the stairs, pulled her back into a hug, and dropped a kiss to her forehead before she could panic, trying not to think *What Would Owen Do?* "Bye, babe."

MAISIE

MY HEAD WAS SPINNING as I left Lys's house, headed for Scallywags. Unease rippled through me at the thought of outright defying my father — something I'd never done publicly. Ronan had been furious over the news of me dating Lys, so how would he take it when he found out that I'd been lying to him for much longer than three months? That I'd created a whole life for myself abovewater?

I stopped on the beach in front of the gazebo, fighting for air as panic set in. Waves lapped against the shore, an easy rhythm I tried to set my breath to. In. Out. In. Out. In… Out.

It was a foregone conclusion that if I kept this up with Lys, my father would hear about Scallywags, and this whole other life I had. My days as Maia, unknown sea nymph bartender who kept a low profile, were numbered.

But what Lys had said stuck with me. I *did* need this freedom, now more than ever. I needed Scallywags. I needed my life abovewater. I needed to find *myself* outside of my title and responsibilities before this opportunity was all snagged out from under me. I needed this just as much as I needed to link powers, and I had to find a way to make Ronan see that.

Even though he was controlling, I knew how much he loved me and my sisters. Everything he did was for us, for his people.

"You okay?" someone asked from behind me, and I turned to see Orion standing on the sidewalk. His white wings ruffled slightly in the breeze, the only thing setting him apart from a sleek businessman headed to Wall Street.

"Oh, yeah, you know how it is," I said, waving a hand. "Just having my whole life crash down around me, right on the verge of an existential breakdown. A typical Thursday. Nothing a little fresh air and a couple bottles of wine can't fix. Or witness protection."

Orion's eyes widened slightly in alarm, seemingly unable to tell if I was joking. He fell into step beside me and I couldn't help but notice that his hair didn't seem as neat as it normally did. "Are you in trouble?"

"The way you say that sounds like the old fashioned 'in trouble,' like, *pregnant*." I tried to laugh it off, because *that* was ridiculous, but I might have sounded slightly more hysterical than the breezy, *que-sera-sera* vibe I was going for, especially judging by the way Orion's silver brows lowered in concern. But I couldn't even remember when I'd last slept with Drew, so at least that was one concern off the table. "Nothing like that, no."

"Right." Orion slid his hands in his pockets, as though he had any idea what it was like to have the rug pulled out from under you the way I was currently experiencing. I was pretty sure the mayor's idea of a chaotic day was when the Town Hall printer jammed, or he was faced with a particularly stubborn wrinkle in his shirt.

Luckily, the mayor was spared from any further discussion of my lack of a love-life as we entered Scallywags. I gave him a nod as I scurried straight to the back room to drop my stuff and grab an apron, grateful not to run into anyone else on my way.

I didn't typically work night shifts, but it was a normal night — our regulars came and went for dinner or a drink after work keeping us busy, a blessing as it kept my mind from spiraling farther with my own problems. If anyone noticed I was having an off night, they didn't mention it, and for that I was glad.

I was starting the usual end of the day cleaning routines when Petra, Blaze's red-haired very-human girlfriend, slid onto the barstool next to Orion. That in itself wasn't unusual, but it *was* strange that the male immediately turned to her.

"Have you found anything about the linking ritual? I'd like to be ahead of the game before the Summit," Orion said as he swallowed a cheese fry. I blinked at the sight, wondering for a moment if my eyes were deceiving me. I had never seen the male order cheese fries, and *never* seen him talk with food in his mouth.

Then his words sank into my brain, and I froze half-bent over the dishwasher, mid-unloading, certain they couldn't possibly be discussing what I *thought* they were. And was the Summit *about* linking powers? Checking my emails just became my top priority.

Petra was a historian, and had been researching supernaturals with Morgaine's guidance since last fall, but I'd never paid much attention to the books she poured over in her booth when she was here. She held up a large, black, leather-bound book, eyeing the sticky bartop with distrust before her gaze slid to mine.

"Maia, could I borrow a clean towel?"

"Sure." I reached under the counter to grab one from the crate and tossed it over to her.

Unfolding it over the bartop, Petra set the book down on top of it gently, pulled on some thin white gloves, then opened the book to a tabbed page and turned it slightly to face Orion.

Petra glanced over at me while he read the page, and with a little shake of my head, I went back to my routine, desperately trying to hide how hard I was eavesdropping.

The mayor hummed in thought as he finished reading, sitting back in his stool again, and Petra sighed.

"I know. It isn't much to go on."

"And you've checked Rare Collections for anything else?" he asked as he worked the knot on his tie, loosening it.

"Oh, now you're *asking* me to go to Rare Collections?" Petra snorted. "Of course I have. There is one more text I want to check, but after that?" She shrugged. "What about the PRICs? I imagine they've got to have some sort of fancy-shmancy library up there, right?" I looked over just in time to see her blue eyes gleaming with barely-concealed eagerness. "Get me in there."

Orion sighed, pinching the bridge of his nose. "For the last time, it's not heaven. It's not *up there*. And you know there is absolutely no way *you're* getting access anywhere near Headquarters. They don't even know you, a *human*, know about our world, and it's in all of our best interests to keep it that way."

Petra waved a hand and scoffed. "We'll see about that. I remember a time not too many moons ago when a certain *someone* said the same thing about Rare Collections, and look at us now." She raised a red brow. "You're practically begging me to go in there."

Jaw working, Orion crossed his arms over his chest, his wings shifting with the movement. "I've never *begged* in my life."

"Oh, O, we both know that's not true." Blaze, black eyes glittering, emerged from the kitchen, saloon-style doors swinging behind him. "You beg me to shut up on the hour."

The next four days were a whirlwind of activity, overloaded with repairs on the city as my father prepared for the imminent Summit. Ronan had everyone working double shifts as we worked to complete all of the repairs possible, and I was bone tired by the end of every day. But my role as heir extended beyond just my usual responsibilities. I also had to attend *princess lessons*, as my sisters called it.

It was rare that Ronan himself ever deigned to go abovewater for meetings with the other supernatural leaders, but even he couldn't outright defy summons from the PRICs, and they had ordered all heads present.

With the impending date only two weeks away, Ronan was in rare form. He hadn't brought Lysander up again, and I sure as hell wasn't going to volunteer that I hadn't followed instructions when even the slightest transgression seemed to set him off.

I yawned behind my hand, slouched in my chair at the table as I fought to keep my eyes open.

"Fix your posture," Ronan barked, and I jolted back to attention, sitting upright in my chair as I looked around the table at my sisters. Saoirse shot me a look that spoke volumes — *she* wouldn't dare slouch at the table. McKenna, on the other hand, eyed me as she put her elbows on the table, propping her head up sleepily, even as Ronan glared at her.

My father had woken us all up early, insisting we have a family breakfast together to practice our table etiquette. While we regularly ate together, the stuffy dining room we sat in hadn't been used since my mother died 11 years ago other than for visiting guests. Normally we ate at the huge table in the kitchen, seated next to our guards and friends as we chatted freely.

This dining room, however, screamed Royal Household. Twenty high, straight-backed chairs sat around the long table in the center of the circular room. Glass walls rose around us on all sides, making it feel as if we were dining in a bubble underwater. Coral reefs exploded with color and life on all sides, and the view was meant to impress. Gold flatware — way more than necessary for breakfast — was laid out at each place setting along with turquoise China dinnerware. Everything was fancy, and it was all intimidating.

And then there was my family.

Only Saoirse, Isla, and Corissa had dressed up for the occasion, each wearing pretty sundresses in a variety of flattering colors. Blaire, Riona, and I wore jeans and t-shirts, as per usual, and McKenna hadn't bothered to change out of her pajamas. Ronan wasn't much better — his bare chest, bare feet, and wrinkled linen pants contradicted the gold filigree of the chandelier overhead, and I struggled to hold back my smile as I looked at my father, holding a tiny teacup. The idea of a male who was the epitome of a shirtless beach bum requiring etiquette classes was beyond ridiculous.

Xuma, Kymari's dad and my father's Second — our most powerful warrior other than Ronan himself — walked behind the table, a small floral teapot in hand as he poured tea into each of our cups. His coral linen shirt was mostly buttoned against his dark brown skin, and his locks were pulled back in a low ponytail, but I couldn't get over the juxtaposition of these huge, muscled males serving and drinking tea.

"Orion is planning a dinner party the night before the Summit, and I've asked him to reserve a table for all of us to attend," Ronan said. All seven of his daughters, myself included, snapped our heads up.

"Really?" Corissa asked, practically bouncing in her seat as she grinned. "Oh, this is so exciting! I've never been to a party abovewater."

Ronan's gaze was harsh as he looked at Corissa, then me pointedly. No one needed to speak it aloud — the last time Corissa had been abovewater, she'd tried to follow me and nearly died. I stared at my hands in my lap, remembering the day clearly.

"What is the dress code?" Saiorse asked, delicately placing the cloth napkin over her lap next to me.

"Formal," Ronan all but sneered, his nose wrinkled in disgust. "You will all wear dresses fitting for the royal household."

"That's not going to work for me," McKenna said, shaking her head. "I don't do dresses."

Ronan's jaw clenched, his teeth grinding as he stared at my sister, fighting the urge to unleash his short temper on her. He hardly ever yelled at us though, not like I'd seen and heard him do to others.

"Kymari can figure something out," I offered, smiling at McKenna, then my father, before meeting my best friend's eyes where she stood along the outer edge of the room. "We'll handle it."

"Good," Ronan nodded, then lifted his tea cup to sip the hot liquid, pinky extended.

Riona spluttered a laugh, and I bit my cheeks to not follow suit as my phone vibrated on my lap.

LYS

Good morning, gorgeous

I smiled as I peeked at the text, fingers hovering over the keyboard as I thought through how to answer. Lys had texted me every morning and night since I'd last seen him. In between, he asked me questions about myself, and I answered when I could, but the conversation was easy, and I found myself grinning every time my phone vibrated in my pocket. Part of me thought he just liked talking to *anyone*, but he also said he was taking this fake-dating seriously, so maybe that was it.

Even fake, it felt good to have a new friend.

We now knew that we both loved sushi, especially spicy tuna rolls. His favorite color was olive green, and mine was teal. We both loved summer, but for different reasons: outdoor concerts and beach weather, of course. Lys also had an obsession with the Avengers that was borderline obscene, and I had never seen a single movie. This response resulted in 14 gasp GIFs in a row, then a calendar invite for next Wednesday, listing "Avengers and Sushi Date." I'd smiled, shaking my head as I'd hit accept.

With each text, I couldn't help but feel a little better about our fake relationship. The more I found out about Lys... he made it easy to like him, that was for sure. Frequently I reminded myself this was fake, and he didn't *actually* care to get to know me, but already the lines were blurring. My knee-jerk reaction was to run the other way and call the whole thing off, but potential heartbreak over Lys was still better than marrying a stranger.

Hopefully, Lys could fix the barrier magic and Ronan would be so delighted that something was taken off his plate, he'd change his tune towards Lys, letting me out of this arranged marriage. At least, that was what I kept telling myself.

"No phones at the table," Ronan said, hand outstretched as if he expected me to hand my phone over.

"Dad," I deadpanned, sliding the phone back in my pocket. "I'm fully capable of putting it away. Like an adult. Because I *am* an adult. You do not need to confiscate my phone."

As soon as I'd said it, I regretted it. I could feel all of my sister's eyes darting back and forth between my face and my father's, wondering if my defiant words would be the last straw for him this morning.

Leave it to me to piss my dad off before breakfast — it was a talent of mine.

Ronan's nostrils flared, but I refused to back down even as sweat dripped down my back. Why was I doing this? Making this stand?

Lys's words as I'd sat on his bed came back to me, reminding me how much I needed this freedom. I was tired of Ronan treating me like a child, and it was time to stand up for myself, even if I wanted to hyperventilate at the thought of the consequences of my actions.

Giving up on our stare-down, I turned back to the table, picked up what I hoped was the correct fork, and took a bite of the spinach quiche on my plate. "Delicious."

My sisters all dropped their gazes to the food in front of us, and fortunately, the tense moment passed as Saoirse picked up the conversation, discussing what everyone would wear for the Summit dinner.

Monday afternoon came, and Kymari was sprawled across my bed, massaging her arms. "I swear, Xuma was trying to kill us all with the drills today."

"Worse than normal?"

"So. Much. Worse."

"That sucks."

She mumbled an assent, and I glanced down at my watch, checking the time. Lys and I were meeting at sundown, so I had about two more hours to gather everything I needed and sneak back to shore unseen.

"That's it," Kymari said, sitting up. "Spill."

My brow furrowed in question even as my heart sped up under her squinted appraisal. "Spill what?"

"You've checked your watch four times in the last twenty minutes. What has you so distracted? You told me Ronan said you were never to see Lysander again, so I know you don't have a date."

I paused. Then laughed. "Yeah, no. No date. You know me. When do I ever date?"

Kymari stood, closing the distance between us as she lifted my arm, and I did my best to pull it back, but my guard was both bigger and stronger than me.

"You're sweating. A lot."

"I changed to a natural deodorant. I don't smell, but man, do I sweat. Please note this and remove all grey from my closet."

She squinted. "I don't believe you."

"That I pit out every damn shirt you pick?"

"That, I believe," Kymari said as she dropped my arm. "But you're hiding something, and I want to know what it is. Are you sneaking out without me tonight?"

"No?"

"Where are we going?"

"Nowhere?"

"Why is everything you answer punctuated with a question?"

"Is it?"

She glared at me, and I shrugged.

"You know I'm just going to stick to you like a remora to a shark. Out with it."

"I appreciate you making *me* the shark in that scenario."

"You're welcome. Don't get used to it."

"And fine. But as *my guard*, I have to swear you to secrecy. You can't go running off to Xuma or anyone and tell them what I'm up to. Agreed?"

She gave me a wide-eyed look of total innocence. "Of course, Your Highness."

I rolled my eyes, and then explained my plan, putting my trust in my Second to back me up on this.

"A boat?"

Kymari and I stood on the tiny rock outcrop that housed the abovewater portion of the undersea elevator. A few dinghies and one fishing boat were tied up on various buoys to transport people between the island and the mainland.

"Yes, we need a boat."

"Let's just swim."

"Um, hello? He's a witch? Lys can't shift, and even if he was the world's best swimmer, it's a long way to go for an almost-human."

I sat the dive gear down in the far end of the fishing boat, along with the bag of items I'd swiped over the past couple days that I thought might help Lys with whatever spell he might have to work. A net infused with Ronan's magic, an heirloom pearl that had been in our family for centuries, and a tooth from Ronan's signature shifted form, a Great White Shark. Then I clambered in myself and went to untie the ropes.

"You better hope no one else comes up here and notices this is missing," Kymari grumbled, but she got in after me.

"They won't." Probably. Really, there was no reason for anyone else to use the elevator or require a boat after sundown, so we should be good.

Unless someone saw us, but there wasn't much we could do about that.

I cranked the engine, and we took off for the shore.

Chapter Fifteen

LYSANDER

I SAT ON THE PIER, feet dangling above the water as I waited for Maisie and fiddled with the twine bracelet, its magic rising in strength so close to the water. The sun had just set, so while light remained in the sky, the ocean itself was rapidly turning dark. Something I hadn't realized when I'd agreed to do this at night. It wasn't that I was *afraid* of open water, but I did like to be able to see my surroundings. Especially if I was going to be in a completely different element surrounded by the Goddess-only-knew-what kinds of sea predators.

Maisie would be able to ward any of them off, though. At least, that was what I kept telling myself.

Ronan wouldn't drown me if he caught us, right?

Right.

I heard the motor before I saw the boat, and I grabbed my satchel with the few items I'd brought for the spell. I'd done a little research since we'd agreed to try to fix the barrier, and while I wasn't totally sure it would work, I had a few strategies I could try.

"Hey there, witch-boy." Maisie flashed me a bright smile as she docked the boat smoothly alongside the pier like she'd done this thousands of times before. A backwards snapback was thrown over her long blonde braid, draping over one shoulder, and she wore a denim jacket with a plain white crop top, black leggings, and checkered Vans slip-ons. Even dressed this casually, she put every woman I'd ever seen to shame, and I was breathless, fighting myself not to gawk at her.

Only my fear of what we were about to do kept my mind in check. I was somewhat relieved to see the fishing boat had spotlights above the helm, lighting up the water around it.

The same female I'd seen at the bar — tall with dark brown skin and long braids, pulled up into a large bun on the top of her head — hopped off the boat, looping a rope around the cleat.

Maisie tipped her head to the female, then looked back at me. "Kymari, Lys. Lys, Kymari."

"Nice to meet you, Ky," I said as I extended my hand for a shake.

"*Kymari*," she answered, arms crossed over her chest as her eyes scanned me head to toe, nose tipped up like a piece of ripe garbage lived on her upper lip. I didn't miss the way her eyes snagged for a moment on the teal twine on my wrist.

"Sorry, Kymari. Got it." I smiled, dropping my hand back down to my side, feeling like I'd somehow already messed this up. "Is this the part where you lure me to the depths with your siren song?" I said in an attempt to lighten the mood, but Kymari didn't crack. "Because if so, you should know that after living with Dillon for a decade, I always have earplugs on me."

Maisie, at least, had the decency to chuckle with a slight shake of the head.

"Are all sea nymphs so slow to impress?"

"I don't know about all of us," Kymari shot back, "but I'm withholding judgment on you, Lysander. We'll see how tonight goes first."

"Right." I nodded like this was a normal interaction for me, which it most certainly was not. I couldn't remember the last time someone hadn't known, or at least *heard*, how powerful I was as a witch. Let alone, my game with women in general.

These two certainly knew how to keep me on uneasy ground.

"Are you coming or not?" Maisie asked, and I stepped into the boat. Within seconds, Kymari had untied it again, pushed off, and Maisie took the wheel, backing away from the pier.

The moon was full tonight, shining above the rocky cliffs in front of us as we left the cove. Stars peeked out from behind the sparse clouds, glowing brighter as we moved away from shore. Despite living here on the coast, I hadn't been out on the water much. It was unsettling as we moved farther away from shore, feeling my magic's connection to the earth growing fainter.

Maisie picked up speed as we got away from the hundreds of lobster buoys dotting the cove, salty ocean spray sprinkling over us as we cut through the water. Strands of Maisie's blonde hair that had escaped her braid blew in the wind as she stood, one hand on the wheel, the other on the throttle, outlined in moonlight. I did my best not to stare, mindful of Kymari's stone-cold glare watching my every twitch. The spotlights glowed in a bright white circle around the boat, but outside of that area, the sea was black, only the whites of the waves showing.

I swallowed, my stomach churning as I patted my satchel again. Suddenly, thoughts of the kraken everyone in town loved to joke about surfaced, and I looked over the side of the boat, half-expecting to see a giant tentacle rise up and loop around the boat, pulling us to watery depths below. Except only *I* would die. Maisie and Kymari could just shift.

Goddess, I hoped this worked. I was going to look like an idiot if it didn't. But Maisie was determined to try, and I didn't want to let her down.

She turned my way briefly, her smile as bright as the stars in the sky above, here in her element.

"Just ahead," she called over the roaring wind and the rumbling engine.

I merely nodded in return, afraid to open my mouth in case words weren't the only things to come out.

A minute later, she cut the engine, bringing the boat to a slow stop, and Kymari dipped her hands in the water near the end of a lobster line. She swirled her hand and I blinked, letting my vision watch the magic at work. A strand of power tied the boat off to the buoy, serving as a magical anchor, I guessed. The two of them worked seamlessly, readying the boat without words, obvious they'd done this before.

I tried to stand, keeping one hand on the side of the boat to steady myself as Maisie approached me nimbly, her movements so much more graceful here on the sea than I'd ever seen her on land.

"Ready?" she said as she held out a wetsuit.

"As I'll ever be."

Maisie smiled and pulled open a bag, handing me a small metallic device that fit in the palm of my hand, about the size and shape of a harmonica with a little mouthpiece attached. I turned it over, trying to see what it was for, but it didn't offer a lot of clues.

"Hold it between your teeth, then breathe normally. It works about the same as a SCUBA tank, but a lot less bulky, and with no oxygen limit."

"Great." I inspected the tiny device that was the only thing standing between me and a watery grave. "And if it gets knocked out of my mouth or something?"

"Don't let it do that," Kymari offered helpfully, and I grimaced.

"Relax," Maisie said as I changed into the wetsuit, squashing *every* part of me into the skintight mold. Maisie spun a finger, and I turned, right as her cold hands came down on my bare back. I shivered, both from the contact and because it was the first time Maisie had touched me without losing her shit. The zipper slid up, and I turned, my breaths slightly faster, as my eyes met hers in the moonlight.

Before I could say or do anything, a plastic mask launched at my face connected with my temple. "Put that on. We're wasting time," Kymari said as she dropped into the ocean. I looked overboard, and instantly a shark fin surfaced, swimming in circles around the boat.

"That," I swallowed, my throat suddenly *very* dry. "That's Kymari, right?"

Maisie chuckled. "Yes. She's always a thresher shark. Harmless most of the time."

"*Most* of the time?"

"I mean, one time she tried this fasting diet and then shifted too soon after. It didn't end well for her or the surfer she nibbled on. But don't worry. I made her eat a granola bar before we left earlier. She should be fine for *at least* another hour. Probably."

Maisie was kidding. I was *sure* she was kidding. And yet she didn't crack even the barest hint of a smile as she turned her back to me, shed her jacket, and lifted her shirt up over her head. I watched for a beat too long, noticing the way the moonlight made her pale skin and hair glow, looking far too tempting for how damn tight this wetsuit was.

"Flippers are under the bench," she called over her shoulder. In the time it took me to locate them, she dove into the water.

I'd seen in movies how you were supposed to tip yourself over backwards to get into the water when wearing flippers, but that was completely out of the question for me. I pulled them on, then stood for a moment peering into the utter black of the water, trying to convince myself to get in as I nervously pat the bag Maisie had given me for my supplies.

"I am *not* about to die tonight," I muttered to myself, then swung first one and then the other leg over the side of the boat, lowering myself as clumsily as possible into the water.

Hopefully Maisie hadn't seen that.

A tail flick splashed water over my face, which told me that Kymari probably had.

I fitted the breathing device between my teeth, clenching

my jaw around it for dear life, and let myself sink below the surface.

A soft glow lit up a few yards away in the water, and slowly Maisie — or, what *had* been Maisie — swam into view.

I nearly choked and died right then and there.

Holding a glowing bubble of magic, Maisie's mer form was illuminated in the otherwise darkness of the ocean. Iridescent teal scales shimmered down her body as she swam effortlessly around me, her tail's powerful flicks gracefully cutting through the sea.

Her braid had come undone, blonde hair floating around her in a halo, framing her face. Scales that matched her tail shimmered along her forehead in what almost looked like a crown, which was fitting.

Had I known I had a thing for mermaids? No, I most certainly had not. But seeing Maisie like this, suddenly all the stories about sailors lured to their deaths made sense. I had just jumped off a boat into the ocean to follow her to its depths, after all.

A hand on my shoulder made me blink, and suddenly Maisie was right in front of me, patting her chest and then pointing to mine.

Oh, right. Breathing. I had forgotten to do that.

Tentatively, I inhaled, still unconvinced this harmonica-thing would work. When it did, some of the tension in my body eased, and I took another, deeper breath. Maisie nodded, then turned, looking over her shoulder once to make sure I was following.

In the corner of my vision, a dark shadow circled as we descended, and I decided for my own sanity not to try to catch sight of Kymari while we were all submerged together.

Why had I agreed to this? I could have sworn, when I suggested this, that I had said daylight. Or had I just assumed it would be daylight?

It took a few minutes to get the hang of the flippers, but once I did, I was able to follow along behind Maisie at a pace I hoped wasn't slowing her down too much.

Fortunately, she'd stopped the boat not far from our target, and Maisie hovered around the edge of a large rock jutting up from the seabed below.

Her eyes flicked to me, the light in her hands shimmering off the teal scales along her brow. My heart raced for a wide variety of reasons, but galloped even faster when she pointed below her.

I followed her direction, but didn't see anything. Maisie swirled around me, the light going with her as she moved faster than I could track. Panic clawed in my chest as I hovered in the pitch black water, but she was back quickly, followed by Kymari in a mer form as well. Kymari's scales were a pearlescent white, heavily contrasted against her dark skin, and the same color as the shells in the ends of her braids.

Kymari moved her hands, conjuring a glowing orb the same as Maisie's and swam down to where Maisie had gestured before.

Maisie moved, inspecting the same spot over and over, just to the right of the rock, and I was mesmerized by every gentle flick of her tail.

Without a conscious thought, my magic surged, the water around me glowing as it revealed the extent of the magic in use. Maisie glowed with a pale lavender aura of magic, while Kymari was a bright, pulsing green.

As I shifted my attention to the spot Maisie focused on, the shadowy fracture lines of a witch hex became apparent. A witch had broken through the barrier here, and definitely not by accident.

I gripped onto the rock with one hand to anchor myself, and opened the bag I'd brought down with the other. Pulling out crystals, I frowned around the breathing harmonica as I tried to work out how to arrange them underwater, pressing them into the sand beside the rock as best I could.

I wouldn't be able to use any words of magic, but it wasn't always necessary to speak out loud; it was more the intention behind the magic that mattered.

A net, a large pearl, and a huge shark tooth appeared beside me, and instantly I felt the distinctive hum of sea nymph power emanating from them. I pulled them closer to me, turning them over in my hands to get a feel for Ronan's magic.

The absolute strength of his power was incredible, far more than any witch I'd ever felt. Once I learned Ronan's signature in the net, I could feel it in the barrier, even in the water all around me. I swallowed heavily with the knowledge that here, in what I now could truly understand *was* "his" sea, as Ronan always claimed, I would be completely at his mercy.

Maisie and Kymari waited patiently while I worked, holding their lights for me to see by while I first extracted the hex that had crashed through this segment of the barrier, then attempted to heal it. I nudged the power in the net to shift from the woven rope to the barrier instead, hoping that using Ronan's own magic on it would make this patch just as strong as the rest of the barrier.

As the last of the tear sealed over itself, I heard an echoing *boom* from far off in the distance.

Maisie and Kymari instantly went alert, all movements ceased as they locked eyes with each other, whites showing nearly all the way around their irises.

A school of shimmering silver fish shot past us, headed the opposite way from the thunderous sound.

Some communication must have passed between the two females, because the next thing I knew, Maisie grabbed my elbow and dragged me through the water *much* faster than we'd been swimming on the way down, headed back towards the surface.

We didn't make it far before the largest Great White Shark I'd ever seen — not that I'd seen too many, or actually *any* outside of episodes of Shark Week, and never up close in person — cut in front of our path, and Maisie pulled up short to stop from hitting it.

From the furious glint in its steely, black eyes, I had a feeling this wasn't just any wild shark.

Chapter Sixteen

MAISIE

I THREW MY ARMS OUT, shoving Lys behind me as Kymari swam to my side, having shifted back to her own thresher shark.

Dad, stop! I spoke urgently, even as Ronan flashed his rows of teeth at us in a smile that scared even me, and I knew he'd never hurt me.

In a flash, Ronan shifted, taking his mer form, smaller than the Great White Shark, but still far larger than the rest of us.

What is he *doing here?* Ronan shouted into my head, his words clipped and angry. *Explain to me why I felt witch magic in my sea.*

He fixed it, I said in a rush. *I asked him to. It's a weakness for us, and I told you he could fix it now so we didn't have to wait.*

And I believe I told you *to cut all ties and never see him again,* Ronan said, his tone dropping, sinking into a calm that scared me even more than his fiery anger. His eyes shot daggers at the bracelet I'd given Lys, and I swallowed heavily. *I warned you, Maisie.*

I shook my head violently, my heart threatening to break my ribs as it pounded in my chest, remembering his words from earlier, his threat to send me away if I didn't break it off with Lys. *Please don't make me go. Don't make me leave my sisters.*

Don't even begin to blame this on me, Ronan said, resignation dripping from his every word. His deep blue eyes flicked to Kymari at my side as he said, *And since Kymari has proven where her loyalty lies — not to our kingdom and laws — she can join you in exile.*

Please, I swam forward, reaching a hand out to him as I felt tears gather in my eyes even underwater. *I can't leave you. I was trying to help.*

Ronan pulled in a deep breath, his gaze turning away from me and back towards the barrier Lys had repaired. *I'll allow your magic to remain,* his jaw ticked, *and his,* ticked again, *until you get back to the boat. And then you are gone until I decide you've learned your lesson.*

I stared at him, at the hardness of his mouth, the cold in his eyes, and realized he meant it. He was kicking me out of the sea.

My thoughts turned immediately to my sisters, and he seemed to read that in my expression.

You deliberately disobeyed me, not once, but repeatedly. For years. His blue eyes met mine, not the blue of a calm sea today, but the cold grey-blue of churning waves in a storm, and the water began to eddy and bubble around us, a mirror of his anger.

Panic swelled in my chest at his words. He wasn't just talking about Lys. He knew about Scallywags.

You know, then, I said, the words sticking in my throat. *About Scallywags.*

I spoke with some of my contacts, and have had you followed since you mentioned Lysander. If you were escaping our notice so easily, who else was?

Dread pulled on me like an anchor as my chest tightened.

You've put yourself in danger by spending time in your human form. You've been shirking your responsibilities to your people, leaving us unprotected while you avoided your patrol duties to live your life on land. His voice shook with anger, and tears welled in my eyes. *You lied to me, and have been cavorting with terrestrials. What secrets have you told them about us? About your people?*

Horror clawed at me with his insinuation. I would *never* do anything to endanger my sisters, my people, my world. *Nothing! I swear! I kept to myself—*

How can I trust you after this?

I didn't say anything. What was there to say?

You're banished. Ronan wasn't looking at me. He *wouldn't* look at me. Bubbles and sand churned in a storm between us. *Saoirse will be my heir. She will marry Owen and protect her people. She will put our people before her own selfish desires, before pointless curiosity.*

Each word twisted a knife deeper into my gut. I couldn't breathe. My vision was narrowing. It had all been for nothing. All a waste.

Please —

You will leave my sea. Finally his gaze shot to mine, tearing me to shreds with its intensity. *And you will not return.*

I swam blindly, my tears mixing with the saltwater surrounding me, hardly aware of whether Kymari or Lys followed behind me.

He'd banished me.

He'd said he would, and yet — why hadn't I believed him? Why had I thought Ronan might put me first, before his ego, just once?

I might never be able to go back.

I took in a deep, wracking sob, thankful I was unable to drown.

My sisters.

Would he let me see them? Talk to them?

And Saoirse. This wasn't meant to be her burden. It was mine, and I'd fucked everything up. I thought I could have everything I wanted, experience both worlds, above and below, and instead, everything was crumbling, a sandcastle at high tide.

I stopped kicking, stopped swimming, and let myself float. Where was I even trying to go?

I had nowhere.

A hand reached forward, gripping mine tightly, and I swung around to come face to face with Lys. He squeezed my hand, and pointed to the surface, where the oval shadow of our boat awaited us.

Mechanically, I surfaced and climbed up into the boat, shifting quickly and pulling my clothes back on. Lys followed right behind me, climbing up the ladder and moving into the bow of the boat as he occupied himself with removing his flippers, wetsuit and mask. Kymari surfaced a moment later, and Lys, accustomed to being around shifters, respectfully kept his back to us until Kymari gave him the all clear. The moment Kymari passed me to sit in the captain's chair, I crumpled to the floor of the boat, my energy utterly drained, and stared out at the ocean that would no longer be my home.

In the background, I heard Lys asking Kymari what had happened down there, and my Second murmured a rundown of the mind-speak conversation he hadn't been able to hear. But I barely took in their words, my mind elsewhere.

How could so much have changed so quickly?

A cool breeze blew in off the ocean, the moon shining across the rolling waves as I pulled my hat down over my wet hair, sniffling. Even in all the many times I had imagined worst-case scenarios for my actions, I never thought my father would *actually* go through with banishing me. Banishing a sea nymph from the water, leaving us magicless, was as good as a death sentence to our people. Only twice had I ever seen Ronan banish anyone, and the last time was Inessa, the most notorious sea nymph of our time, who had returned the favor by luring my mother to her death.

Surely lying about Scallywags wasn't the same as murder?

Maybe I could still fix this. Maybe I could make it up to Ronan somehow. I could quit Scallywags, agree to marry Owen, agree never to leave the sea again. Whatever it took.

I bit my lip as I sought Kymari's face, her expression worried as she watched me, waiting for me to make a decision. To lead the way, like I was supposed to.

"Let's head back to town," Lys said, his eyes darting between Kymari and me until he sank down next to me. "We can go back to my place and figure out a plan from there. I even have snacks."

The slight bob of my head was all the confirmation Kymari needed, turning on the engine and releasing the magic that anchored us as she steered towards shore.

Lys and I sat for several minutes in silence on the floor of the boat, our backs pressed against the side. I tracked the wake that trailed behind us, wondering if my father would ever let me beneath that glistening surface again. I knew these waters better than I knew anything else. Inhaling deeply, I savored the smell of the surf, of salt and seawater, letting it calm me.

My head pounded, the pressure behind my eyes almost unbearable, but with each second that passed, I became more sure of the decision I had to make.

"We have to stop this," I said, and Lys turned slightly towards me, his head close to mine to be heard over the roaring engine. "If we break this off, if I quit Scallywags, I can go back to Ronan and convince him to let me marry Owen like he wanted and —"

"Hey, no." Lys turned towards me, his hands resting on my shoulders. "Tonight really sucked. *Bad.* And I know you're upset. I would be, too. What Ronan did is devastating and more than a little rash. Maybe he'll change his mind in the morning. You said you didn't want the future he planned for you. We *both* said we were done letting our parents dictate our lives. And we *are*, Maze."

"But I *have* to, Lys. It was stupid of me, selfish of me to —"

"It wasn't. It's *not*." He tipped my face up with a finger under my chin, his green eyes searching mine. "It's *your* life. You deserve to be happy. To have an identity outside of your responsibilities."

"They're my people. That matters more."

He dropped his hand from my face, but gripped my hand instead. "We can figure this out. Okay? You're not alone in this."

I gave a choked laugh, wiping at a stray tear. "We don't have anywhere to go." I gestured to include Kymari. "No clothes, no nothing."

"A ship lost at sea." When I side-eyed him, he winked, squeezing my hand. "Couldn't resist. But that's the easiest part, Maze. You guys can stay with me and Dill, no problem. Don't even worry about that. And the clothes thing? I have a laundry machine, an intense amount of band merch, and internet to order you whatever else you need."

"I couldn't do that to you," I said, but he gave me a look that read *Don't be ridiculous*, squeezing my hand again.

"Hey, you're my girl." He gave me a tilted smile, and my breath hitched, even though I knew he only said it for Kymari's benefit. "I want you there."

I nodded slowly, taking a steadying breath. "Okay."

"You won't turn to sand or something if you don't have access to the ocean, right?"

"No." I managed a weak smile. "We'll be fine."

I nestled down further, trusting Kymari to take the reins to get us to the pier safely and letting myself calm down from my panic attack. Even from this position, where I could no longer see the ocean, I could still hear the waves, hear the bell out in the harbor.

Lys started humming under his breath, muffled by the rumble of the engine, but I gave a half-hearted groan as I recognized the tune to *(Sittin' On) the Dock of the Bay*. He laughed and kept going, switching to singing the lyrics as I elbowed him sharply in the side.

"C'mon, do the whistling part with me," he urged, nudging me right back. "I know you know it. And I guarantee it'll make you feel better. No one can whistle in unison and keep a straight face. I dare you."

He kept singing, and eventually I gave in, trying to whistle with him. But he was right, we got about two bars into it before I couldn't help but laugh with him, even as he kept going.

"See?" He turned to me, our faces inches apart, saltwater spray on his cheek that I had to resist wiping away. "There's nothing we can't figure out together. We got this, Maze."

Would we, though? He was wildly optimistic, but I hoped he was right.

Chapter Seventeen

LYSANDER

THE WAVES LAPPED GENTLY on the shore as we walked through town, and I couldn't help but notice the many changes Orion had already implemented. The sidewalks were freshly power washed, the benches re-stained, the windows on all of the storefronts spot-free. I had yet to deal with the landscaping, and the tall grass stood out against the bright white gazebo in the middle of the square, but that wasn't my biggest concern right now.

Maisie tripped twice over her own feet, and both times, I reached out to catch her. After the second near-fall, I decided I was better off keeping ahold of her hand. Plus, according to the contract, Maisie hadn't told Kymari about our fake dating set-up, so I decided to go with it, lacing my fingers through hers. I couldn't remember the last time I'd ever casually held a woman's hand strolling down the street, but rather than feeling awkward, it felt natural. Maybe it was just that I could feel how close Maisie was to retreating into panic again, but either way, I didn't let go.

I watched as Kymari walked, seemingly unaffected by

gravity the way Maisie was. She moved with that same deadly grace here on land as she had underwater in both mer and shark forms, and I was just as intimidated. She kept a sharp eye on our surroundings, a mixture of shock and wariness in her dark gaze as she took in the sleepy town around us.

"Have you ever been into town before?" I asked, and Kymari pursed her lips.

"It's forbidden," Maisie whispered quietly at my side, sniffling once more. "She's only been abovewater the few times I made her accompany me ashore."

Kymari's expression softened as she looked at her friend. "Don't even think about blaming yourself. I make my own decisions, Maisie. You've never once forced me to come with you. And I'm glad I'm here with you now."

Maisie nodded, but it seemed more in response to what was expected than genuine comprehension. I offered Kymari a slight nod, grateful she hadn't used the same harsh tone with Maisie as she had with me so far.

"I hope you have a decent couch," Kymari muttered as she raised an eyebrow at my house's exterior.

I opened my mouth to say there was plenty of room for both of them, but snapped it back shut just in time. Kymari probably expected Maisie to stay in my room.

Offering up my house as a crash pad for them was a no-brainer at the time, but at the thought of Maisie sleeping in my bed, I was starting to think I might be out of my depth.

Damn. And I couldn't even share that ocean joke with her.

"After you." I unlocked the door and stepped back to let them in.

"Hey, Lys — oh." Dillon's jaw hung open slightly at the sight of Maisie and Kymari with me, his blue eyes raking Kymari from head to toe as he stood from the couch.

I could see Kymari working to hide her judgment on the state of our living room and kitchen, but the way her eyes snagged on the half-open boxes of band shirts, a handful of empty beer bottles on the coffee table, and an unknown stain on the rug said it all.

"Kymari, this is Dillon, my roommate and drummer. Dill, this is Kymari, Maze's friend." I cleared my throat, shooting him a look, and he managed to close his mouth. "They need to crash here for a while."

Snapped out of whatever daze Kymari seemed to have put him in, Dillon jumped up, raked a hand through his hair, and stepped forward.

"Hey, great to meet you, Kymari," he said, flashing her a winning grin, and I hid my eye-roll. "May I show you to your room?" He made an elaborate gesture towards the couch he'd just vacated.

Kymari's expression was immovable, not even a hint of what she thought of Dillon showing on her face. She laid a hand lightly on the back of the couch and tilted her head. "Do you have a clean sheet?"

As Dillon helped Kymari get set up, I nodded towards my room for Maisie to follow me, closing the door behind us.

"Does Kymari know we aren't really dating?" I asked,

flicking my hand towards the door to put a silencing spell in place. "I wasn't sure what you'd told her, so I figured it was easier to act like we'd done this before."

Maisie looked anywhere but at my face, studying the guitars behind me on the wall as she shook her head. "We haven't had much time to discuss. Technically, I haven't told her that we *were* dating, but she saw us kiss at your concert, and knew I'd asked you to help us today. Do we need to keep this ruse up since it's all gone to shit at this point?"

Something tightened in my chest at the idea of giving Maisie up, of letting this fake relationship go, but rather than inspect that, I shook my head. "No. We stick with the plan. The Summit is in two weeks, and Ronan will be there, same as Ostara. We can show them both how wrong they are about us. We can live our lives how *we* choose without sacrificing all of our free will for their end game."

A small crease formed between Maisie's brows, her eyes downturning as if she was about to cry again, and my heart broke for her. Pulling her into my chest, I held her close, hoping I could give her some comfort in the midst of this chaos.

"Tell me what I can do for you," I whispered, and her hands tightened in the fabric of my shirt as she squeezed me back. "Snacks? Toothbrush? Leave you alone? Tell you every bad fish joke I can think of?"

"You seem determined to do the last, no matter what I say."

"Yeah, that probably can't be stopped."

Maisie chuckled, and pulled away from me. "A toothbrush and maybe one of those band tees I saw in the box out in the living room to sleep in."

I cleared my throat, my body coming alive at the thought of Maisie sleeping next to me in my bed wearing nothing but one of my band tees. That was an image I did not need to fixate on about my fake girlfriend, and yet, now that I'd thought of it, I wanted *nothing* more.

"Shirt, check. Easy. And we should probably stick to the story we told Dillon. That it's been three months and you've been over here all the time," I clarified, and she nodded, though with a grimace.

"That might be harder to sell to Kymari, but I guess we don't have a choice." She glanced behind me at the room. My bed. "So, I should sleep in here?"

Be cool, Lys. I slid a hand into my pocket. "I can take the floor." There. Gentleman. Never in my wildest dreams had I ever volunteered to sleep on the floor when a gorgeous woman would be in my bed, and I hoped to never do it again.

"Oh, no, I wouldn't do that. It's your place, you're already doing us a solid just letting us crash here. I can —"

"Don't even think about it. You just had a shitty night, you're not sleeping on the floor on top of all that."

Her seagreen eyes met mine. "Well," — she pursed her lips, mulling it over — "I guess it is a big bed."

Oh, sweet mother Goddess. We were both sleeping in my bed. Together. The two of us. I struggled to keep my expression — and other parts of me that were acting like I'd never had a girl sleep in my bed before — calm and cool. "Yeah. No excuses when your iceberg feet end up on my side then." I smirked as a warm blush crept up her cheeks; had she never shared a bed overnight with a male? I shook my head to force myself not to dwell on that train of thought, and moved around her towards the door. "I'll grab that shirt and toothbrush and make sure Dillon still has all his limbs."

Maisie snorted at my implication of the absolute terror that was her closest friend, and I was relieved to see some of the tension easing out of her stiff muscles.

I inhaled deeply through my nose, then slowly exhaled. Goddess, it was just a girl in a band tee in my bed. Like this exact same scenario hadn't happened hundreds of times before. Why the fuck couldn't I keep it together this time?

Maybe it partially had to do with the way her jaw had gone slack when I'd peeled my shirt off, her eyes trailing over the tattoos on my chest and arms like she wanted to trace them with her tongue. Or had that just been wishful thinking on my part? An assumption based on the reactions of past women in my bed?

I'd said nothing as Maisie built a pillow barrier between us, fine with whatever made her comfortable. My bed was king-sized, so we still had plenty of room, and yet with her soft, even breathing, the hint of coconut from her scent wafting through the room, I could barely think straight. No, I *wasn't* thinking straight.

"Lys?" I pressed my eyes shut at the sound of her voice in the dark, willing myself not to get hard at the sound of my name on her lips.

"Present."

A chuckle, then, more uncertainly, she continued, "Do you really think he'll get over it eventually?"

I turned onto my side, facing her, or I would have been without the pillows in the way. "He loves you. He'll forgive you. Just maybe not right away."

She sighed softly, and I heard her shift around on her side of the bed, trying to get comfortable, maybe. When the sound of sniffling started, something inside me broke, hating how upset she was.

"That's it," I said, grabbing the pillows between us and launching them onto the floor. Maisie turned to look over her shoulder, eyes wide as I reached across the bed and hauled her back into my chest, my arms looping around her waist and under her head.

"What are you doing?" she asked, her voice squeaking out higher pitched than before.

"Adding an Emotional Distress Clause to our contract. You're upset, and it's literally breaking me. I need to hold you to make myself feel better about you being sad."

Her body tensed, core flexing as my hand laid across her stomach, but I willed it not to move. The heat of her skin beneath my palm felt scorching hot, or maybe that was just the tension in the room. Either way, I wasn't sure this was easing distress for either of us.

Several minutes ticked by in silence, not sure if I should fake being asleep and leave her alone, until she spoke. "Where did the name of your band come from?"

"Oh, that." I laughed. "The Lost Talisman is an old witch tale told to all of us as kids. It's said to grant its wearer lifelong peace and happiness."

Silence spread between us again, but I could tell Maisie was still awake, so I began humming.

The bed shook as she chuckled quietly, and I smiled up into the dark.

"Is Journey's greatest ballad your version of a lullaby?"

"Shh. I'm just getting started." I rubbed my hand over her stomach, trying not to groan at the way she wiggled back into me as she settled, waiting for me to begin.

"Just a sea nymph girl, swimming in a lonely sea, she took a midnight boat goin' anywhere," I sang.

Maisie chuckled, then sang back in a voice I should have seen coming with how much she loved music, but caught me off-guard anyway. *"Just a witchy boy, born and raised in Deadlights Cove, he took a midnight boat goin' anywhere."*

I sang the guitar riff, and she laughed, the first one that had sounded genuine all night. Damn, it felt good to make her laugh like this. To bring her joy when she needed it most.

"Goodnight, Maze."

"Night, Lys."

"Oh, and hey." I moved my hand to her hip, not expecting the shirt to have ridden up. When I touched bare skin, my pulse went into a sprint. Willing myself to calm the fuck down, I remembered what I'd intended to say. "Don't stop believing."

A loud electronic hum sounded from the other side of the door followed by an aggressive *slam*, then another, the next morning. I shot up, bleary-eyed as I reoriented myself to the awareness of having Maisie in my bed.

And out in the living room —

"Do you have any idea what time it is?" Dillon's voice shouted over the humming, which then ceased. "Shit, what did you do with all our stuff?"

Maisie stirred beside me, and I locked eyes with her when she opened them with a frown. Suddenly I was glad for the pillow-barrier she'd re-established at some point, because morning Maisie, hair slightly rumpled from sleep, was so drop dead gorgeous I felt like I was back underwater, drowning in need for her. Not trusting myself, I got out of bed and threw on a shirt on my way to the door, then cracked it open to see what was going on.

Dillon stood in his own doorway in a pair of boxers, mouth agape as Kymari, fully dressed, paused with one hand on our vacuum.

"Oh, we've been looking for that." I pointed to the vacuum.

She shot me a look that cut right through my bullshit, and I grinned at her.

Dillon gestured frantically at the living room, indicating for me to notice that Kymari had been busy with more than just the vacuuming.

The room was spotless. The boxes of band merch, gone. Beer bottles recycled and glasses rinsed and drying by the sink. Guitar picks, drum sticks, flyers, amps, cables, all either neatly organized or just plain missing.

"Huh, I forgot the coffee table was supposed to be that color." The thing was gleaming. Had she polished it?

"When was the last time either of you bothered to vacuum in here? I've already emptied the canister once and I haven't left this room yet."

I slipped out of my room, closing the door behind me in

case Maisie didn't want Dillon, or Kymari for that matter, seeing her in bed in just a t-shirt. "Listen, this is very nice of you, Kymari, but you really don't need to —"

"No, *you* listen to me, rocker boy." She held up a hand. "I really, really do. And you," — she pointed a finger at Dillon, who looked over his shoulder to see if she possibly meant someone else — "Go take a shower and be ready to leave in fifteen. There is a serious lack of storage and amenities in this house and we're fixing that today. This is the most intense bachelor pad I've ever seen, and you're in your *thirties*. There is no excuse." She swung back on me, and I resisted the urge to take a step back. Barely. "Ask Maisie what she needs from the store. Dillon and I are doing a run and I'll grab her stuff, too."

I locked eyes with Dillon again, his expression turning from startled amusement, to confusion, to uncertain fear. I jerked my head towards his bathroom and shrugged. He'd better get a move on if he only had fifteen minutes for his beauty routine.

He gave a choked sound of indignation before turning on his heel, slamming his door again. But a minute later, I heard his shower running.

MAISIE

I LISTENED to the conversation taking place in the hallway, sitting up in Lys's bed with the comforter pulled up to my nose. The door cracked open, and Lys crept back in, closing it quietly like there was a possibility my tyrannical best friend hadn't just woken every resident on the street.

He turned, stepping lightly, then jumped when he saw me staring at him.

"I wish I could tell you Kymari will calm down, but that would be a lie," I said, still clutching the comforter like it was the last scrap of dignity I hadn't lost by having a complete meltdown in front of Lys yesterday. "You don't have a label maker, do you?"

"What?"

"Never mind. You will soon."

Lys's green eyes lingered on me for several beats, nostrils flaring slightly, before he shook himself free of whatever thoughts had given him pause. My magic didn't work the same on land, but I could still smell the shift in his scent, the usual citrus and vetiver turning into something spicier.

I fought the urge to sink further under the comforter, feeling wildly insecure in just his band tee in the light of day. Mental, emotional, and physical exhaustion had clouded my decision making last night, and now… well, I didn't *regret* it. His bed was comfortable, and having his arms around me had been more soothing than I'd anticipated. But even the many times I'd had sex with Drew, never once had I spent the night with him. This, the morning after, even though nothing had happened, seemed… different. More. And while I'd known Lys had tattoos, seeing them up close and personal, close enough to touch, to lick — well, that had been something else entirely, and I was disappointed — wait, relieved, that he had a shirt on again now, hiding them.

"Do you have plans today?" he asked, and I gophered my face back above the comforter as I thought through the answer.

"Normally, I'd have my morning meeting with the patrol squad I lead, then lunch with my sisters, followed by my patrol shift in the afternoon, then Scallywags later tonight for my night off."

Lys jerked his head back. "You work at Scallywags as your *night off?*"

"I mean, yeah. It's such a nice change of pace from my normal life. No one bats an eyelash when I trip over nothing, or ramble on for too long, or forget to say anything *at all*. It's always one or the other. There is no happy medium." I threw my hands up in the air, forgetting I was still hanging onto the comforter, and it dropped down to my lap. "See? Rambling."

His eyes tracked the movement, and this time, it wasn't

me that tripped. Lys caught the edge of the bed as he moved to sit on his side of the bed, but recovered much faster than I would have in the same situation. Facing away from me, he grabbed his phone off the nightstand and quickly tapped out a text message then threw it on the end of the bed.

When he spun back around, he put one knee up on the bed, leaning over to pull the comforter back towards his corner of the bed. My breath hitched as the blanket lifted, feeling the cool air hit my bare leg between the comforter still in my lap and the bottom edge of the t-shirt I'd slept in. Lys's gaze snagged on the bare sliver of skin, then shifted quickly up to my face. "You're working the day shift today at Scallywags now."

I subtly pulled the blanket higher on my lap even as my brow scrunched. "I am?"

"I just told Blaze you were occupied tonight, so yes."

A laugh stuttered out of me, a mix of indignation that he thought that was okay and downright shock that he'd *told* Blaze I wasn't working tonight, not even asking me first if that was okay. "You can't just *do* that. Change my plans for me."

"It's called spontaneity." He shrugged. "And since we have our last show for the next two weeks tonight, I thought it would be fun for you to come with us. I can stop and hang out with you at Scallywags for a little bit before we go, so then we can have a public *date* and distract you, all at once."

"What if Blaze says he needs me to work tonight though?"

"I mean this in the nicest way possible, so please don't be offended," Lys said, and immediately, my guard went shooting up, as did the comforter in my hands yet again. "Your schedule is *wide* open now. He can schedule you on another night shift this week to make up for it."

I sank down on the bed, pulling the covers over my head as the reality of my situation settled in. My chest tightened, ears ringing as I curled in on myself.

"Hey," Lys said, the bed sinking slightly as he pulled the covers down, reached across and yanked me into his chest, holding me tight like he had all night. "I'm sorry. I didn't mean to make you upset. I thought maybe it'd be easier if you were occupied today instead of dwelling on everything else. I have Coven things to take care of and Kymari seems intent on giving our house a makeover. But I can text him back and cancel it."

"Then I'll look even *worse*," I said, hating the way my voice trembled as I teetered on the edge of another full meltdown. I was making one hell of an impression on Lys in the few hours he'd spent with me. Everything I'd done so far screamed "mentally stable royal heir," but then again, *Ronan* was the current king, so maybe everyone automatically assumed sea nymphs were all unhinged. Considering how Kymari had handled this morning, maybe that assessment wasn't wrong.

Lys's hand smoothed over my back, rubbing in soothing strokes as he apologized yet again. I breathed a deep sigh, feeling the warmth of his chest against my face.

"It's okay. You're right, I don't want to be stuck alone with my thoughts all day. And I'm kind of curious to see if Dillon can survive a day alone with Kymari. I just don't really like —"

"Changing plans," Lys nodded. "Adding it to the list."

"I feel like this list is getting long. I sound difficult on paper."

"Nah," Lys said. I pulled back slightly, meeting his green gaze, and his hand stopped, hovering over my waist. My heart pounded for a multitude of reasons, one of which was that I was still smashed into Lys's chest, his mouth mere inches from mine. The moment stretched, his eyes locked on mine, then slowly dipped down to my lips before snapping back up. "I think you're pretty perfect. The best fake-girlfriend I've ever had."

"Smooth," I said, my voice a little shaky as heat pooled in my belly at his words. I couldn't look away from his mouth, couldn't *not* notice the way his bottom lip pouted slightly. "So smooth, Lysander."

"Just like the ocean, under the moon." He winked, and I rolled my eyes. "Good news, though. You're getting much better at this physical touch thing. You've panicked for several very valid reasons, but look at you, acting like a natural in my arms."

I chuckled, shaking my head as I threw back the covers, grabbed the hem of the shirt, and pulled it down over my butt as I stood.

"I guess I better get ready for my shift then."

The atmosphere at Scallywags was… unusual.

For the most part, Deadlights Cove was laid back. Once in a while, there was the odd petty squabble between residents, but those were rare. More than half of the town had lived here together for over a century, and they'd gotten used to each other. There was an ease that came with knowing people for so long.

But today, everyone was on edge. The Summit dinner was in 12 days, and our esteemed mayor's nerves were starting to wear on everyone.

"You painted it *black!*"

The door swung shut with a bang as Devanna strode up to the bar, Orion hot on her heels.

"You said it didn't have to be white." Dev slid onto a bar stool, cool as a catshark, not even looking Orion's way as she snagged a bottle of whiskey from across the bartop and poured herself a glass. "If you'll recall, I *specifically* asked that."

"I said it had to be *historical.*" Orion took the seat beside her, pulling her glass away with a tug of his magic. Her eye twitched.

"Oh, so, *black* isn't acceptable for your *Puritanical* history, now?" She raised a brow in challenge. "You want to say that again?"

Orion's eyes narrowed, his fist clenching around her glass. "I provided you a list of paint colors that were pre-approved by the Historical Society as acceptable options for the building given its origination date, purpose, and location."

"Hm." Dev's nails tapped the bar. "I must have misplaced that. But you know what they say. When in doubt, go all out."

Orion pinched the bridge of his nose, letting go of her glass to do so, and she swiped it away from him quickly as he sighed. "That is not what they say."

"Here, O." Blaze emerged from the kitchen and slid a beer to Orion. "Take a breather. I happen to like the black."

"See?"

Orion rolled his eyes.

"Yeah, it makes it look charred." Blaze leaned his elbows on the counter, expression dreamy. "Like someone tried to burn it down, especially when the sun sets and that fiery light streams through the belltower." He knocked knuckles with Devanna and stood again.

I shook my head at the trio, but it wasn't unusual to see Devanna and Orion bicker at the counter. In fact, that was the *only* time the two spoke.

Day shifts had a different cadence to night shifts. At night, people came to stay. To hang out. They set up at a table or a booth for the long haul; drinks, games, friends. During the day, people were usually in and out. Grabbing lunch to go, maybe having a quick meeting, then they were out. But today, as people were coming in, they were sticking around. Like everyone just wanted to be nearby in case something big happened.

I had to admit that running food all day at least kept my mind off my troubles. Orion and the town had a whole host of its own problems to occupy me as well. I hardly even thought about the fact that I'd been shunned from my own element and all of my duties and sisters and life's purpose.

Well, maybe once or twice it crossed my mind.

I cleared a table, my hands full of dishes, and was making my way back to the kitchen when the bell jangled above the door and someone stepped in. I swerved to step around them but caught the non-existent edge of a floor tile, and with a muttered curse, the plates and I all went clattering to the ground.

"Ah, shite. Are you all right, lass? Here."

"I'm fine." Luckily, Blaze's dishes were all shatter proof. I was pretty sure he'd had them spelled a few days after hiring me so he wouldn't have to keep replacing them. A hand appeared in front of my face anyway, and I took it to help pull me to my feet.

"That was on me. I wasn't paying attention to my surroundings," the man said, and I dropped his hand to brush myself off.

Then, with a jolt, realized he had an accent. A *Scottish* accent.

My head jerked up so I could take him in. This male who I presumed with 99% certainty was none other than my potential betrothed, Owen Kinkaid.

With dark blond hair that was longer and thick on top, a short-sleeve button down, cuffed olive chinos, and shiny brown Oxford boots, Owen looked like he'd walked straight off an Ivy League campus. If not for his pitch-black irises, I might not have known he was a demon at all for how put-together and genial he looked. He was handsome in a hot-professor way, and I stared for a beat too long.

Owen probably didn't recognize me — I was a pre-teen the last time I'd been to Scotland, and I didn't remember him at all — so, for now, I decided to keep my mouth shut about my identity.

"Hey, Kilty!" Blaze said, catching Owen's attention from down the bar.

I was more than a little relieved when Owen looked away from me, offering a broad smile to Blaze. "Ach, well, it's a rare day I have the opportunity to don a kilt these days. Sabazios, right?"

Blaze shuddered. "Yes, but don't ever call me that again. The name's Blaze."

Owen chuckled, but pulled back a stool and sat down at the counter. I lingered by the bar, absently wiping tables in an attempt to get a read on him.

Blaze slid him a pint of Tennent's, the lager splashing slightly on the wood top as it came to rest in front of Owen. "I'm sure I'm supposed to impart some sort of *Welcome to our town* and general regulation bullshit as head demon, but I got nothing for you. Big O there," — he flicked a towel at Orion — "is the one in charge of this whole shit show, so see him if you need anything."

"I've found this town to be perfectly charming so far." Owen settled himself onto the stool and took a sip of the lager as Orion shot Blaze a *So there* look of satisfaction. "Damn, but that is an excellently poured pint. Perfectly ice cold." Blaze preened, and offered a basket of rosemary fries on the house. "And you," — Owen turned to Dev, who eyed him skeptically — "are you the witch who runs the shop next door?"

"Depends who's asking."

"You've got the best collection of exotic salts I've ever *seen*," Owen said enthusiastically, and Dev tried to hide a smirk. "I'll have to pick up some of your 1783 Icelandic salt from the Laki volcanic eruption. You'll have to tell me the story of how you got your hands on the stuff. It's practically a myth! In the right circles, anyway. Do you know some historians believe the resulting famine was a catalyst for the French Revolution? The papers are fascinating."

If Dev were capable of it, she might have blushed. "I was in the right place at the right time."

"Oh, I highly doubt that," Owen chuckled. "But perhaps it's a story for another time. Orion, I heard you were giving out duties to prepare the town for visitors? I know technically I'm one of those visitors, but as I'm here early, if there's any way I can help, let me know, aye?"

I made my way to the back, needing a moment to collect myself, and began loading the dishwasher.

Owen seemed *nice*. He was handsome, obviously a committed scholar, polite, thoughtful. Maybe it wouldn't have been so bad if I'd stuck out the whole marriage thing.

Except he was missing… something. Something I couldn't quite put my finger on.

The door from the bar swung open violently as Kymari walked into the kitchen like she owned the place. She paused momentarily to look around before noticing me standing in front of the sink.

"Just when I thought I'd burned the last of your hoodies, you somehow have more." She sighed, then shook her head, seashells in her hair clinking together softly with the motion. "Nevermind. You need to change, and right now. Owen Kinkaid is standing in the bar, and your boyfriend is supposed to be here in the next half-hour. You can't be looking like that."

"Too late," I said, my nose scrunched slightly. "I, literally, bumped into Owen already, though I don't think he recognized me. And Lys has never once commented on my hoodies."

"After a day redecorating their entire house, I am debating whether your boyfriend has any taste at all, so I don't think that's the compliment you think it is." Kymari grabbed my arm, dragged me into the staff bathroom off the kitchen, and closed the door behind us. "Change. Now. Owen might not have recognized you, but Dillon introduced me to everyone as *Maia's* sea nymph friend. I haven't heard anyone call you Maia in a long time, but considering I didn't even know you had a job here, I guess there's a lot you haven't told me." Bitterness crept into her voice, and I hated myself for keeping so many secrets. "Anyway, Owen asked if I knew you, and I did my best not to react, but have you met me? Everyone knows something is up."

With a sigh, I pulled off my hoodie and turned my back to Kymari as she pulled out the hair-tie on my braid.

My stomach fluttered nervously, both in reaction to the fact that I was pretty sure my time as Maia was up, and the fact that I was about to officially meet my so-called betrothed. My lives were about to collide, whether I was ready or not.

Chapter Nineteen

LYSANDER

SLAMMING the door on Natalie's van, I slapped the back, and she turned over the engine, ready to leave for our show tonight. Dillon and I were driving separately with the girls later after Maisie's shift, but, since this was an outdoor concert, Natalie offered to arrive early and get our gear set up with Bodhi.

Luckily, a stroke of genius had struck earlier this morning regarding my *landscaping* duties, and I was proud of the environmentally-friendly solution I'd come up with. I only hoped Orion would agree.

Since I saved myself the hours landscaping duty should have taken with my creative solution, I spent the time alone at the house picking at my guitar and jotting down lyrics that swam through my mind. It wasn't until the timer on my phone went off to remind me to leave time to finish my Coven responsibilities that I came out of the zone, looking over what I'd written.

Seaglass green eyes, ocean waves, those new relationship

butterflies, wanting so badly to win the love of a girl who was out of my league.

I scrubbed a hand over my face, staring wide-eyed at the lyrics, realizing I'd unintentionally written a love song to Maisie. A girl I'd known for a week and a half, but had been admiring from afar for much longer.

It wasn't the fact that I'd written about love that was surprising. I loved women. Loved physical affection. Loved people, in general. And Maisie was so stunning, of course I'd written about her.

This was a more emotional song than I usually wrote. I sat back, letting my head fall against the wall behind me as I remembered how it had felt to fall asleep with my arms around her last night. How desperately I'd wished I could fix all of her problems, and make the things that hurt her go away.

But that wasn't what this arrangement was about, and I needed to get my head on straight. She didn't have feelings for me, and I wasn't boyfriend material, even if I was starting to wish I could be.

I set my guitar down and added the lyrics to the pile on my dresser, forcing my mind back to the present. I had four crystals I needed to charge with healing power and drop off at Mo's for Selene, and then I could see my girl.

My *fake* girl.

Magic was a dull hum in my veins an hour later as I stared at the four crystals on my kitchen table, feeling depleted. Charging four crystals in such a short time required a lot of power — I'd pushed myself to finish as fast as I could, eager to get to Scallywags, and then to our show tonight.

Rubbing at my temples, I picked up the crystals and wrapped them in a protective cloth before placing them in a box to leave at Mo's. Nimue, Mo's adopted daughter and local demon favorite, planned to collect the box tomorrow, then flicker it down to Boston for Selene's medical practice.

Selene was a witch, born and raised in our Coven, just like I was, but had moved to Boston to pursue a human medical degree. I'd helped her this past winter get back in touch with her witch powers, and we'd been experimenting with the use of healing crystals in her holistic medical practice. When she'd asked the Coven for more crystals for her patients, I'd jumped at the offer to help her once again.

I knocked twice on Mo's yellow door ten minutes later, box under my arm, on my way into town.

"Lys!" Ruby said when she opened the door, a blush rising in her tan cheeks. "What's up?"

"Hey Ruby," I smiled, "How's your magic been? Still blowing everything up?"

Ruby laughed, twisting a strand of her red-dyed hair around a finger. "Nope. No explosions for three days, thanks to you."

"I love to hear it. Is Mo here? I have Selene's crystals for her."

Ruby shook her head. "Don't you know it's Tie-Dye and Tequila Tuesday?"

"Is that even a thing?" I frowned. "Who is doing this with her? And, on that note, how much tie-dye does one person *need* to be doing this weekly?"

Ruby chuckled, but took the box from me, setting it on

the table inside the entryway. "I've learned when it comes to Mo, it's best not to ask too many questions."

"Smart girl." I winked, then turned to leave. "Glad you're feeling better, Ruby."

She waved, and I looked at my watch. Band, Coven, and town duties seen to, I decided to track down Maisie at the bar. *Early*. I couldn't think of another time I'd ever been early for anything. I jogged up the steps to the bar, bell jingling over the door as I stepped inside.

My good mood dissipated as I halted right inside the door, spotting *him* over at the bartop.

Owen. Kin. Kaid.

From the looks of things, he was busy conning the whole town into thinking he was charm itself. Smarmy Scottish bastard. Had Maisie seen him yet? She'd know immediately who he was.

From a look around the dining room, I couldn't spot Maisie, so I figured she must be in the kitchen or on her break. I made my way to the bar and slid onto the stool beside Dev, leaning close and lowering my voice. "I see you've met *Owen*."

To my horror, Dev's eyes all but lit up. *Shit*. He'd already gotten to her.

"Owen's been informing Lucifer here that Puritans actually viewed the color black as symbolizing the somber attitude with which everyone should live their God-fearing lives," Dev said, grinning like a cat. "That makes it the *perfect* historical color for a church."

"I'm not having this conversation again." Orion shook his head, turning away from them to gaze out the window instead.

Only, then he jolted to his feet, the stool toppling over behind him, his wings fluttering violently.

"Why the *fuck* is there a herd of goats in the town square?"

We all looked out the window with him, the aforementioned goats happily munching through the grass around the gazebo.

He swung on me, and I lifted a shoulder. "They're mowing the lawn."

A crackle of electricity shot through the air, static swirling all around us and light bulbs flickering, as Orion's face contorted in rage. With a disgusted sound from the back of his throat, he swept from the bar, and I followed in his wake, along with half of the patrons.

"Did you forget to spell these goats not to *also* eat the shrubs" — he pointed to the now nearly-barren foliage — "the flowers, the *gazebo*?"

My jaw hung slack as I surveyed the damage the goats had done in just the few hours since I'd set them up here. Several of the smaller dwarf goats Zaphiel, the only other local angel, used when he taught the goat yoga class hopped around the green, bright pink peonies dangling from their teeth as they happily chewed on anything *but* the grass. The largest goat, Beelzebub, stood in the center of the gazebo, chomping on a board he'd ripped from the closest bench. Unlike the other, smaller goats, Beelzebub was a full-sized goat with horns curling back around his head and black, beady eyes that stared at us as if daring us to stop him. His hoof lifted, smacking into the bench, and broke off another board.

I rubbed my hand over my mouth, taking in the destruction I hadn't anticipated. Zaph hadn't mentioned anything about spelling the goats not to damage property when I'd asked to borrow them this morning. He'd looked at me questioningly when I said Beelzebub could stay as well, but hadn't argued. Now, I understood his hesitation a little better. Beelzebub lowered his horns, glaring at Orion with a look that lived up to his name.

Orion sighed so hard the tree to his left rustled, and then that steel grey gaze swung on me. "Where is Zaphiel?"

"Who?" I cleared my throat, and Orion took a menacing step towards me. "Look, this was all my idea. I asked him to leave them behind after yoga, and I miscalculated. I'll get them out of here."

"You'd better." Orion's voice lowered, icy, and most of the bar patrons started filtering back inside, sensing the drama was wrapping up. "*And* fix all the damage they've done, *better* than it was before. If I see so much as *one* angel feather out there, I'll be bringing Zaphiel in for questioning, too."

"Got it, yup." I held my hands up, and electricity danced over my fingertips, so I quickly brought them down and stuck them in my pockets. Angel-electrocution wasn't on my agenda for today.

With one last scowl, Orion left me to clean up my own mess, and I slid my phone out to call Zaph the minute the door closed behind him.

It took longer than I'd anticipated to wrangle up the goats and by the time I was done, I decided to leave fixing the shrubbery and flowers for another day. I needed to double check a few of the spells I wanted to use — it wasn't every day I worked green magic. That was Mrs. Farrington's specialty.

Tired, sweaty, and unfortunately smelling a bit too much like goat for my liking, I returned to the bar, hoping I could still salvage my night with Maisie.

For fake-dating appearances' sake.

I entered the bar to find Maisie on a stool, sipping something clear and bubbly, her hair let down into loose waves that were long enough to skim the bottom of her —*fuck*, she was wearing a Lost Talisman crop shirt. My band logo. On her —

She laughed, throwing her head back, and as I pulled my eyes away from her to see *who* was making her laugh, my jaw tensed.

"Lysander!" Owen called jovially upon spotting me at the door, so then of course I had no choice but to walk over and grit my teeth into a smile. "Great to see you again."

Shit.

Maisie frowned. "You two know each other?"

"We ran into each other when I first got into town. He pointed me towards the Library. You Americans are so friendly."

I forced a smile, but could feel the way my nose crinkled in distaste. Owen definitely didn't smell like goat in his crisp button-down as he leaned casually on the bar. "Duncan, was it?"

There. Very American. Welcome to New England.

Owen's smile faltered slightly, but he sipped at his pint before answering. "Owen, actually."

Kymari sat down next to Maisie in a matching pink Lost Talisman tee. Where Maisie's was cropped to show her pale stomach above her cut-off jean shorts, Kymari's had the neck ripped out, hanging effortlessly off one shoulder. "I'm redoing your merchandise, Lysander. Maisie and I can work the table tonight, showing off some of the newer designs. The fact that you only sell basic tees is… well, it's pretty damn basic."

My breath caught in my throat as I stared wide-eyed at Maisie, unsure how she'd react to Kymari using her real name here in the bar. And in front of *him.*

Maisie offered a faltering smile, but I saw the strain in her eyes as she tried not to react.

"Wait," Blaze stilled where he was wiping a towel across the counter, a heavy crease between his brow. "You just called Maia *Maisie.* Isn't that who you were—"

My heart raced in my chest, knowing what he was going to say, and I had to stop it. Counting on Maisie's clumsiness, I leaned forward, planting a kiss on her neck as I pulled her back into my chest. She jerked, and the drink in front of her went flying, spilling all across the bar and dripping onto the floor directly where Blaze stood.

"Hey!" he called, jumping back.

Maisie hopped up from her barstool and grabbed the mop from where it was propped in the corner behind the bar. "Shit, I'm so sorry."

"Don't be," Blaze said as he held his damp white shirt away from his chest, moving into the kitchen to change.

The saloon doors swung closed behind him, and relief rushed through me. The last thing we needed was Blaze to realize that when I'd asked about Maisie a week and a half ago, I'd had no idea that Maisie and Maia were the same person.

"So, *Maisie,*" Dev said, an eyebrow arched high above her black frames as she more than likely put together all the clues laid out before her about the town's mysterious bartender. "I'm surprised Ronan has let you work at the bar for so long. You're the sea princess, right?"

Yep. There it was.

Of all the times I'd wanted to strangle Dev, this one took the cake.

Maisie froze where she mopped up her mess, her head down, but I could see the way her chest moved unevenly as all the secrets she'd kept for so long unraveled faster than I could stop them. If there had been even the smallest doubt in Owen's mind that Maisie was *the* Maisie, it was gone now. Panic rose in *my* chest for her, an emotion completely unfamiliar to me. Happiness, sure. Anger, frequently. But *anxiety?* No.

"Maze," I said, my brain moving a million miles an hour as I thought through how to salvage this, get the attention off of her, and offer her an out if she needed it. *Deflect. Deflect. Deflect.* "I smell like goats and bad decisions, which is a new combo even for me. We need to hit the road if I'm going to shower before the show. Kymari? Be ready to leave in 20."

With a flick of my hand, I moved the mop across the floor magically, glad to see it didn't multiply and take over like in *Fantasia.* Moving behind the bar, I grabbed Maisie's now-empty hand and pulled her towards the door with me.

It didn't escape my notice that Owen had paused with his pint halfway to his mouth, eyes roving between us, then to our joined hands. He frowned, but dammit, even I could recognize how practically perfect he was. Just what I needed, a male Mary Poppins as my competition.

The thought came and went before I had time to contemplate why I was concerned about competition for Maisie when this was all fake, but her hand tightened on mine as we pushed through the doors and out into the street.

Chapter Twenty

MAISIE

MY HEART POUNDED as I sucked in huge lungfuls of air. Lys dragged me out of the bar and away from the crumbling lies in our wake.

When Kymari cornered me in the kitchen, I'd forgotten to tell her that no one there knew who I *really* was, even though she'd heard them use my mother's nickname for me. But that ship had sailed.

Poseidon, I was getting as bad as Lys with these boat jokes.

Mind spinning, I hardly noticed Lys still clung onto my hand as I turned abruptly, drawn to the ocean to our left. The wooden boards of the pier creaked under our steps as I got as close to the water as I could, sinking down to sit at the very edge and staring out over the water. Instantly, Lys pulled me into his side, curling his arms around me protectively as I closed my eyes, soaking in his warmth, the smell of the ocean, and the gentle lapping of waves beneath the pier.

"Emotional Distress Clause," Lys said, leaning his cheek on my head and squeezing tighter. "I'm very upset right now."

I smiled, but didn't shrug out of his embrace.

"Well, that went disastrously." Lys loosened his hold just enough to rest his chin on the top of my head. "Want me to hurt Dev for you? She deserves it for the number of times she threatens physical violence on everyone else."

"No," I said, not having the energy to laugh, or cry, or anything, really. And, honestly, I didn't blame Kymari for outing me to the entire bar or Devanna for connecting the dots. I'd made this mess myself long before Kymari ever stepped foot on land. And she was only here because *I'd* gotten us both banished.

"Want me to distract you?" he asked, and I paused, not sure where he was going with that. "I'm taking your silence as a yes. After Lost Talisman started to get some recognition, I felt this pressure to perform on stage. No one likes a lead singer who just stands there, singing. I'm an *entertainer*, not just a musician. Mick Jagger didn't just *stand there*, so I needed to do more."

He paused, and I elbowed him gently. "What happened?"

"I'm an idiot, that's what happened. I'm impulsive, and I love to live in the moment. This also means I don't always think through a lot of my decisions ahead of time. So when the urge to do a high kick on stage during one of our shows while singing *Bye Bye Bye*, I went with it. Split my jeans right down the center, flashing my crotch to the entire stage."

A laugh exploded out of me at the visual, my shoulders shaking as I pictured it. "Stop. You did not."

"Oh, I wish it wasn't true," Lys said, laughing at himself. "Mortifying. Needless to say, I always check my jeans ahead of time now. Practice my dance moves at home first. Trust was broken that night."

"You know, I'm a little surprised you played an *NSYNC song."

A long beat of silence went by as Lys soothed his hand up and down my back. "Please don't tell me you're a Backstreet Boys fan. I was really starting to like you, Maze."

My heart did a little flutter at his words, but I forced myself to dismiss them. "Die hard. Brian Littrell was my first pre-teen wall poster."

Lys gasped, his free hand clutching his heart. "Is this it? Is this why we break up? I don't know if I can forgive this kind of disagreement."

"It was nice knowing you, I guess. I should go ask Owen what his thoughts are on 90s boy bands since I now know this is a dealbreaker."

Lys tensed, and I looked up at him, confused by his lack of response. My shift caused his hand to slip onto the exposed skin between my shirt and shorts, and my mind blanked.

His hand stopped, not daring to move any further south, but he didn't remove it either. Heat soaked from his fingertips into my skin, contrasting to the cool ocean breeze. My ears rang as my skin heated, turning overly sensitive to his touch, unable to focus on anything but Lysander.

I lifted my head, eyes meeting his as our faces hovered mere inches from each other. Without thinking, my gaze slipped to his lips, remembering how they'd felt as he'd kissed my neck in front of Owen. The move had been so territorial, it had caught me off-guard, sending us into the tailspin that had led to this moment.

But right now, seeing the sincerity written in every line of his face as he embarrassed himself to make me feel better, I couldn't find it in me to regret any of it.

"I thought you said we were leaving in 20," Kymari called from the sidewalk behind us, snapping us both back to the moment. "I didn't realize that meant you had time to stare lovingly into each other's eyes."

"Lys and Maisie, sittin' on a dock," Dev sing-songed from where she stood outside Scallywags, a glass of something brown in her hand. "Only need five minutes to ride that—"

"*Oh*-kay," Lys called, jumping to his feet as he nearly knocked me into the water. "Dev, you're cut off. No more day-drinking for you. Also, I hate you."

"False," Dev said as she walked towards us. "To all of that. And this is Coke, jackass. I don't need to be drunk to see the way you two are enamored with each other. Makes me want to vomit." She sipped at her Coke while Kymari laughed at her side. "And I have a lifetime of evidence to know you do not, in fact, hate me. I'd even go so far as to say you love me. I might even be your favorite. Well, maybe second favorite now because no way in hell am I ever riding—"

"Dear Goddess, please stop."

Kymari studied me, surely noticing the way my cheeks matched the red of the lobster buoys tied off the side of the pier. I dropped Lys's hand and moved to my friend's side, looping my arm through hers as we moved through town.

Lys followed behind, arguing with Dev about something, but I couldn't focus.

"You really like him, don't you?" Kymari whispered low enough for only me.

I hummed in agreement, not trusting myself to answer her. Whatever connection I felt building with Lys wasn't real, no matter how it felt to be wrapped safely in his arms.

"How did today go with Dillon?" I asked, trying to change the subject.

Kymari snorted. "Fine. I organized everything and left him to label the new storage bins. He was weirdly excited about it, and, I can't lie, it was hotter than I'd expected."

I leaned forward, staring at my friend to see if she was serious, but I should have known she'd never joke about organization.

"Let's just —" Kymari said with a sigh, her arm squeezing where it was looped through mine. "Let's have fun tonight."

I nodded, leaning my head on her shoulder as we walked the rest of the way to Lys's house, glad to have her by my side even as my world imploded.

When Lys had said they were playing an outdoor venue tonight, I hadn't realized the extent of what he meant. Hundreds of people milled around the stage as the sun set over the trees, waves lapping on the beach behind us. Spring Harbor's Food Festival was a very human affair, vendors lining the sidewalks in an orderly fashion you'd never see in Deadlights Cove.

Lights shone down on the stage as Dillon dropped onto his stool behind the drums, fiddling with his ear protectors. Natalie followed Bodhi onto the stage a few minutes later, annoyance written on her features as she slung her guitar over her shoulder, but the look was gone the moment her fingers touched down on the strings.

The energy in the crowd was buzzing as they let out low whoops, waiting for the main attraction. Because, let's face it. Bodhi and Dillon and Natalie were great, and the band was fun, but the large majority of the people, mostly women, waiting near the stage were here for one thing, and one thing only.

Lysander freakin' Theroux.

He stepped onto the stage, a bottle of water in hand, and took one last swig as the crowd erupted.

"Marry me, Lysander!" the woman in front of me called, bouncing on her heels as she threw her bra on the stage at Lys's feet.

He laughed, bending over to pick it up, before slingshotting it to Dillon behind the drums. "What a proposal," he said with a broad smile aimed directly at the woman who'd thrown it. Then that green gaze slid to me, locked in place as he leaned forward into the mic. "I'm beyond flattered."

My breath hitched as I watched him beam at the crowd, the look so genuinely happy I couldn't help but smile along with him even though the last two days had sucked. "For those of you who don't know me, I'm Lysander Theroux," — the crowd erupted in hoots and hollers, and I shouted right along with them — "and we're the Lost Talisman, from right down the road here in Maine."

Lys laughed, his eyes drifting back to me once more, and

I squirmed under his attention. "I hate to break it to you, though, but I have to politely decline your proposal. Your taste in both men and lingerie is impeccable, miss, but see, my girlfriend is here tonight."

Several people *booed* loudly, but I could hardly hear beyond the blood rushing in my ears at the word *girlfriend*. Lys locked eyes with me, and Kymari squeezed my hand where she stood to my right, her gaze on me, not the stage.

"She's had a shitty few days, and I promised her a hell of a good time tonight. So, what do you say? Should we get this party started?"

Everyone shouted around us, and Lys beamed, grabbed the guitar off the stand behind him, and adjusted the strap so it fell just right over his hips. With a look at Natalie, he said something low, and she nodded. I held my breath, squeezing Kymari's hand tightly as I waited. For what, I didn't know.

With his back still turned to the crowd, Lys strummed the opening notes of *Layla*. Hands rose into the air, clapping along to the beat, but I stood frozen, like I'd done the first night Lys had sung to me and I'd come up with this foolish plan.

Paralyzed.

This time, for an entirely different reason.

Lys sang into the microphone, never breaking eye contact with me, even as he sang about falling helplessly in love with a girl, begging for her attention. He was magnetic, not only to me, but to every single person in the crowd as he fed them his positive energy laced in a silky voice.

But the more I got to know Lys, it was so much more than his overflowing charisma that drew me to him. It was how he so readily helped, never asking for anything in return. How little he judged me, not for a stumble or a meltdown. How shockingly selfless he was, quickly putting me and my problems before his own.

Lysander Theroux wasn't the lazy playboy so many people saw him as. He was so, so much more.

More than once he'd joked that *I* was a siren, but really, it was the other way around. Whether it was fake or not, I was under Lys's spell.

"Lucky bitch," Braless said as she threw an elbow into my side.

The motion caught me off-guard, but, standing at the center of Lys's attention, I couldn't disagree with her. Kymari dropped my hand, standing between me and the rude fan as she leaned over the smaller woman.

"Back the fuck up," Kymari said. Her voice dropped several octaves as magic hummed in the air around us, oozing off Kymari even here on land as her instinct to protect me kicked into overdrive. I gripped her arm, my fingers closing around her elbow as I dragged her away from the woman and back towards the merch table we'd manned earlier, needing distance both from the woman and from my own emotions.

Lys watched us move through the crowd, questions in his eyes as he looked between Braless and me, but I shot him a thumbs-up, finding myself incapable of any further thought.

"It's dangerous here," Kymari said, placing herself in front of me and the crowd.

I couldn't argue, but this felt dangerous for different reasons than what Kymari referred to. With each minute I spent in Lys's orbit, the center of his attention, I found it harder and harder to remember this was all just part of the contract.

I should have seen this coming, but Lys was a far better actor than I'd ever planned on. So much so, *I* was even starting to wonder if it was real.

Chapter Twenty-One

LYSANDER

MAISIE WAS quiet the whole ride home, gripping the door handle like she expected me to veer off the road into the trees. But, then again, this was her second trip in a car *ever* apparently, so maybe that was all that kept her staring out the window, away from me.

"Did you two have fun, Kymari?" I asked as I glanced in my rear view mirror at her, taking the exit for Deadlights Cove.

Kymari didn't look any more relaxed than Maisie, her hand wrapped tightly around Dillon's forearm in a crushing grip. "Do you have to drive so fast? The speed limit sign back there said 55 and I can see your speedometer. 58 is not 55."

Dillon snorted, his eyes meeting mine in the mirror momentarily, but did nothing about her hand on his arm.

"Apologies," I said as I slowed the car marginally, hovering right at the posted 55. Normally, I'd have said something snarky in return, but I couldn't focus on anything other than how Maisie was avoiding me. Had been avoiding me ever since I'd hopped off the stage.

As we entered town, I slowed, pulling around the square and down our street, headlights flashing over the many houses that had the lights out, already asleep for the night at just past midnight. I slowed to a crawl as my house came into view, noticing the lights glaring from the windows inside.

Someone was home, and only one person had the key to our house other than those in the car right now.

"Uh," Dillon said, noticing the same thing. "Did we know Ostara would be here tonight?"

Maisie swung her head towards me, eyes meeting mine as my fingers tightened on the steering wheel. "Your mother is at your house?"

My teeth clenched tightly as I pulled into the drive, seeing her imposing silhouette even now through the open blinds. A deep sigh left me as I parked and threw open the door. At the last second, I remembered to circle the car and open Maisie's door for her, linking my fingers through hers as we moved up the driveway.

"You okay?" she whispered, gaze focused so heavily on me she missed the step up onto the stoop.

I stopped, reaching to steady her as Maisie closed her eyes, sucking in a deep frustrated breath, then let the tension go. "One bumbling giraffe girlfriend, ready to meet your mother," she said with a forced smile. "Maybe I tripped now, and won't embarrass myself in front of her. Though my clumsiness is not limited to only one fall per day, so that's unlikely."

A laugh rose in me, my lips tugging into a smile as I

reached across and kissed her temple. She tensed slightly under my touch, and I couldn't say exactly why I'd done it.

On stage, I'd wanted so desperately to make her feel better, to help her let loose, that I'd said those things effortlessly. I couldn't deny it had felt good to see the way she reacted to my words, my song choice, and to sell our relationship status in a very public manner. It even sounded good — my *girlfriend.*

Well. *Fake* girlfriend.

I had to remember that part.

But everyone there had bought it, so surely my mother would, too.

"Let's dive in, shall we?" I squeezed Maisie's hand, and she rolled her eyes but hid a smile as I popped open the front door, bracing myself for whatever was about to come at us from Ostara.

"Mother, what a sur—" My words caught in my throat as I took in my first view of our house since Kymari's little makeover. "Holy shit."

Our house had a Color Scheme.

She'd decided on a dark teal, and replaced our old area rug with a new one in that color, along with off-white slip covers over the two mismatched couches that now had *throw pillows,* which we'd never had before. She'd installed brand new, shimmering gold curtains over the windows. There was a new storage cupboard under the TV, presumably holding the crap that had littered the room before, and atop it were a handful of decorative knick-knacks — a set of gold candle holders in the shape of treble clefs, a large white conch shell, and framed pictures of the band on stage. Our kitchen had a similar color scheme shown in new hand towels, a mat in front of the sink, and a bowl filled with oranges. Were those for eating, or only part of the design?

However, Kymari wasn't the only one who'd gone to town. Dillon had apparently taken his job as *labeler* seriously. Everything had a new, shiny little white sticker on it.

The pantry was the *Midnight Zone*.

The bowl cabinet was *Cereal Boats*.

The spray bottle on the counter was *All-Porpoise Cleaner*.

I shot him a look, and he flashed me a grin. Kymari read his work with a resigned look on her face.

"I suppose this is my fault for not being clearer in *how* to label everything," she remarked to no one in particular, and Dillon shrugged as my mother waved a hand impatiently.

"Lysander," she snapped, "we need to speak privately. If the rest of you could give us a moment —"

Her words cut off abruptly when she finally noticed Maisie's hand in mine, the teal twine around my wrist, her gaze zeroing in on it as her lips pressed into a thin line.

I caught Dillon's eye and gave a jerk of my head. He wordlessly grabbed Kymari and dragged her into his bedroom, deaf to her startled protest. I had a feeling things were about to get ugly with Ostara, and the fewer witnesses, the better. Dillon knew our relationship well enough to figure that out.

Ostara swept forward, her boots clicking over our hardwood floors as she proffered a hand to Maisie.

"You must be Ronan's daughter," she said, her lips not quite tilted up in a smile. More of a snarl. "My son mentioned something about… *this*."

Maisie, to her credit, only gave a warm smile in return, ignoring the condescension in my mother's tone, and shook her hand. "Maisie Arabella Bridget Douglass Crunamar, princess of the North Atlantic sea nymphs," she said, making her voice soft and refined as might be expected of royalty. I fought to keep my face neutral and not betray how delighted it made me to see her acting her part beautifully even in cutoff shorts and a crop top. "Pleased to finally meet you, Ms. Theroux. Lys talks about you all the time. Such lovely things I've heard. And yes, I also happen to be Ronan's daughter. I believe you two know each other?"

Ostara's eyes narrowed, as though trying to assess whether Maisie's apparent kindness was genuine, and in the lull, Maisie continued.

"And yes, *this*," she wrapped an arm around my waist, and my arm went around her shoulders reflexively. She tilted her head up slightly to meet my eyes. "This has been the best thing to happen to either of us. Isn't that right, babe?"

I grinned as she rose on her toes, pressing her forehead to mine. My breath quickened as her coconut and peaches scent invaded my senses. She laid her palm gently over my chest, and I hoped if she felt the beat of my heart, she thought that was all for show, too.

"Three months, it's been, yes?" Maisie pulled back from me at my mother's words, meeting Ostara's fierce gaze head on. "Seems an awfully long time for Lysander."

Maisie smiled, but the look contained more venom than I knew she was capable of wielding. "That's what happens when you find the right person. The one who completes you. Who makes you a better version of yourself. Who loves you just as you are. The thought of letting them go is unbearable. I suppose you have to experience it to understand that, though."

My breath caught in my throat as my eyes blew wide in shock at Maisie's words. I wasn't sure I'd *ever* heard anyone speak to my mother that way.

Ostara's lip pulled back in a grimace as she glared daggers at Maisie, then cut her eyes to me. "Lysander, I really must insist we speak *alone*." She turned a deathly sweet look on Maisie. "Though it was *lovely* to meet my son's current," — she waved a hand in the air, pretending to search for a word — "*saveur du jour*."

Maisie blinked like Ostara had slapped her, then huffed an indignant laugh that she managed to work into a serene sigh. She raised an eyebrow at me in question, and I gave her a reassuring smile.

"Why don't you go do some more unpacking?" I said, clocking the flare of my mother's eyes in the background. "I'll be in there in a minute."

Maisie gave me a sultry smirk — just for show — and gripped the front of my shirt to pull me closer to her level before whispering in my ear, loud enough for my mother's benefit, "Don't be too long, Lys."

But, Goddess, her soft breath in my ear, whispering my name, should be off-limits. I didn't need to worry about sporting a boner in front of my *mother*.

I cleared my throat as Maisie sauntered from the room, and I leaned back on the new storage cabinet, crossing my arms.

Ostara tilted her head at me as my bedroom door clicked shut. "You two are living together?"

I scoffed, not deigning to offer a response. "What do you really want?"

Ostara *tsk*'d at my abrupt change in tone, but didn't bother to deny she had a motive for being here besides checking up on me. Or her house, which was infinitely more likely.

"You're meeting with Clara on Sunday."

"Who?"

I received a disapproving look, and remembered Clara was the shifter I was supposed to marry. I narrowly resisted the urge to roll my eyes.

"I already told you. I'm not marrying her."

"Lysander, please." Ostara's teeth clenched so tight, I almost worried she'd crack a molar. Her words came out clipped and short as she lowered her voice. "Our world is about to change with this new magic. We *have* to stay in front of it. Before you protest" — she held up a hand as I opened my mouth — "Just meet her. Now, as for the Summit dinner. I expect you in our family colors. Does your suit still fit, or do we need to alter it?"

I scraped a hand over my jaw, and wondered when, if ever, my mother would realize I was a grown man.

What felt like hours later, Ostara finally left. I was only halfway through my sigh of relief as the weight of her overbearing presence lifted before Dillon popped his head out of his room.

"Shots?"

I huffed a laugh and gave him a salute. "Only if you twist my arm."

He grinned and made for our bar cart — even before Kymari's makeover, one of our most organized areas of the room, though she'd replaced our thrifted wooden one with a new metallic gold — to start setting up some drinks.

"I'll fetch the girls," I said, making for my room.

"Leave Kymari for now," he said over his shoulder. "She's taken it upon herself to reorganize my closet and no amount of bribery will stop her, apparently."

I chuckled as I knocked on my door, cracking it open. "She's gone," I called in, and Maisie looked up from her phone.

"Saoirse says if I don't find a way to fix this, she'll drown me herself," Maisie grimaced, tossing her phone on the bed. "Your mother is a delight, as expected."

"Try living with her for eighteen years." I opened the door wider and inclined my head to invite her out. "We're drinking. You in?"

She huffed out a sigh and hopped off the bed. "Definitely."

Just as we re-emerged from my bedroom, Kymari came flying out of Dillon's room, her expression flabbergasted.

"*Dillon*," she admonished him aggressively as she waved something at him, then at all of us. "All of you! Look at this!" The plaid fabric rippled in the air, then she pointed an accusatory finger at me. "Did *you* let him buy these?!"

I held both hands up. "I hold no sway over my drummer's purchases. What he does with his money is between him and the Goddess."

"Hey, I look great in that," Dillon argued, handing me a shot and Maisie a paloma.

Kymari made a screech that reached a decibel only dogs could hear, making for the kitchen garbage.

"Whoa, there, what are you doing —"

"These have *no* place in this decade —"

Dillon set his drink down, grabbing at what I could now see were a pair of madras plaid shorts and a matching blazer.

"What if I go to a dressy-casual summer pool party —"

"— Or *any* decade —"

Kymari twisted around like this was a basketball game, feinting and then skirting Dillon, who wrapped his arms around her waist and lifted her in the air, shouting, "Fashion is cyclical!" as Kymari changed tactics and started shredding the outfit instead.

I shook my head, raising my shot glass to clink with Maisie's glass as our best friends tackled each other in the living room.

"To exciting new times?"

Maisie stifled a yawn as she sipped at her drink, and I downed my tequila, placing a hand on her back. I told myself it was unintentional that my hand landed right on the strip of skin exposed between her crop top and shorts, but my body was keyed up and looking for anything it could get. "Exciting times, indeed."

Chapter Twenty-Two

MAISIE

NATALIE AND BODHI came in a few minutes later carrying a cooler between them. Lys fiddled with the stereo, getting his playlist set up as he cast a silencing bubble around the house. The way he used his magic seemed so effortless, I couldn't help but stare. I'd seen other witches cast small spells here and there, but I'd never seen any work the way he did. Maybe I was just unfamiliar with witch magic, though. Ronan had never included that in any of the many subjects he had us study, and it left me feeling unprepared for the coming Summit.

"Mrs. Farrington doesn't like us to play music past 9 p.m. She says it disturbs her cat, Bagheera," Lys explained as the magic settled around the house, faintly buzzing against my skin. "Really, though, what disturbs Bags is the way she insists on making him wear a raincoat when he goes outside in the spring. I've never seen a cat lose it quite like that one does."

"Well, Mystery Girl, in the flesh at last," Natalie said, popping a beer cap as she joined me on the sofa. She'd pulled her long, honey-brown hair into a ponytail since the show, and if I couldn't tell she was a wolf shifter by scent, her sharp blue eyes would have been a dead give-away. "Lys said this was happening between you two, but I have to admit, it was hard to believe until I saw it with my own eyes. I'm Nat, by the way."

"Do you live in town? I'm surprised I haven't seen you around the bar."

Nat barked a laugh. "I live on pack lands, but I'm not in town much."

Bodhi fell onto the couch next to her, grinning. "Yeah, she's usually traveling the area for work when we're not playing."

"Oh?" I tilted my head, not knowing they had other jobs outside of the band, other than Lys working with the Coven. "What do you do?"

Dillon and Bodhi sniggered as Natalie smirked. "I run a small dog training business. I specialize in the worst of the worst, the untrainable ones about to be put down." She ran her tongue across her teeth that suddenly glinted sharper. "My reviews all say I seem to speak a special language with them; like I have a sixth sense for how to communicate."

"More like they scent a true predator and fall in line faster than their owners can blink," Bodhi said, knocking her shoulder.

"Hey, it gets the job done." She shrugged, smiling. "And it saves them from a pointless death just from bad training and misunderstandings."

"And you're a wolf?" I asked, then self-consciousness slammed into me. "Sorry. Is that rude to ask? Sea nymphs can take several forms, so I'm never quite sure how that works for shifters." I took a sip of my paloma, hearing my words replay in my head. "And also sorry for the fact that I now sound like I'm somehow better than you because I can take multiple forms. Someone please make me shut up."

The non-sea nymphs in the room stared at me, slightly slack-jawed, and Kymari made pointed eye contact.

"You can take multiple forms?" Dillon asked, the beer in his hand absently lowering from his lips.

"More than just mer?" Bodhi leaned forward.

"Oh my God, the kraken!" Natalie slapped a hand over her mouth. "Is that you guys?"

I grimaced, realizing what I'd done. "Okay, that can't ever leave this room. Actually, pretend I never said it."

"Way too late for that, Ariel." Bodhi stood and pushed Natalie out of the way to sit next to me, putting a hand on my shoulder and locking his black eyes on mine. "What other forms can you take?"

I felt a pull of magic, subtle enough that I might not have noticed it if I hadn't been in close contact with a demon at work for the past couple years, and slowly felt my urge to spill all sorts of sea nymph secrets grow stronger. Lys slapped Bodhi's hand on my shoulder and he wrenched it back.

"Knock it off," Lys told him, and flicked his ear. Bodhi covered it with a yelp and traded seats again. "She doesn't have to tell you anything."

"Fine, fine," Bodhi gave in, settling back on the couch to my right, and Dillon and Natalie sat back as well, sensing they weren't going to get any more secrets out of me. Bodhi narrowed his eyes and pointed at Kymari. "But a hundred bucks says *you* like to go as a shark."

Kymari didn't answer, but her lips pulled back in a cold, sharp smile that made Bodhi laugh all the same.

"You aren't going to ask about me?" Bodhi said. "I'm feeling a little left out here."

Lys rolled his eyes as his arm settled over my shoulders. "Bodhi is an arsonist. Fitting for a demon, right?"

I was taken aback for a moment as I stared at the demon. It took no stretch of the imagination to see that as a possibility for the male, but surely that wasn't a job?

"I prefer fire genie," Bodhi said with a wide grin. "I'm actually more Smokey the Bear, *preventing* forest fires. Doesn't hurt that I can control the flames. Can you control water, by the way?"

I shifted uncomfortably in my seat, feeling his magic faintly even without his touch.

"Ignore him," Natalie said, waving a vague hand at Bodhi, who pushed his lip out in an exaggerated pout. She clinked the top of her beer against my glass when I chuckled, then leaned back on the sofa, looking around the room. "Wow boys, I like what you've done to the place. I have to say, I never saw you two as macrame fans, but it adds a certain *je ne sais quoi*."

"Dillon picked it," Kymari said from where she leaned against the wall to my right.

"You did?" Lys asked.

Dillon shrugged, taking a long swig of his beer to avoid answering. His hair was messier than usual after his tussle with Kymari over the madras plaid suit, but I wasn't sure who'd won the final argument.

"Well, I asked him if he wanted to put it back and not get it, and he shrugged, so. Yes. He picked it."

"See?" Bodhi said, pointing his glass at Kymari with a wink. "Shark."

Lys laughed, but didn't say anything else. His fingers trailed lightly over my arm, leaving a path of goosebumps in their wake. I shifted into his side, the old cushions on the couch forcing me to slide into him. He'd held some form of contact with me ever since his mother left, but I assumed it was because this was the first time we'd ever truly had to sell that we were in a committed relationship in front of a group of people. I couldn't say I didn't like it, though.

In fact, it felt so natural, so comfortable, I couldn't help but sink into it. And then I stiffened, realizing what I'd done. Lys tilted his head towards me, sensing the shift, but only tapped my arm again, a silent reminder to keep up the façade. With an effort, I willed myself to sink further into the couch, and tilted my head back to rest on his shoulder, the warmth of his body seeping into mine.

It's not real, I repeated to my stupid heart. To the flutter in my stomach.

Lys's chest rumbled with a laugh under my ear at something Bodhi said, and I took a long sip of my drink.

Too late.

"Put your hands on my shoulders."

"I'm not *that* drunk —" But I lost my balance right as the words left my mouth. Just my usual balance issues on land, though.

Lys bit his lip to stifle a laugh as I did as requested, my hands on his shoulders as he helped pull my shoes off.

We were back in his room, heading to bed after staying up late with the band. Seeing them at ease together — two witches, a demon, and a shifter — I started to wonder what else we missed out on underwater, cordoning ourselves off in our city the way we did. Then Bodhi had started bartending, and suddenly I only cared about joining in with the laughter, having fun in the moment. Not my usual speed, but I had to admit it had been nice, for a change.

"It's your stupid land's fault, not the drinks," I continued, sighing as my feet were finally free of the platform espadrilles Kymari had insisted on what felt like hours earlier. "It doesn't move with you. It's always just *there* and in my way and waiting to be tripped over. My least favorite part about being abovewater. Water moves *with* you. It's so much easier."

"If you say so," he said, tossing my shoes aside.

I fell back onto the bed, suddenly too exhausted to move. Maybe I was *slightly* tipsy.

"What's your favorite part about being abovewater?"

"Huh?" I asked, not following his words.

"Tripping is your least, so what's your favorite part?"

"Oh," I said, thinking momentarily. "The smells. Underwater, smell isn't really a thing. I mean, inside Crunamar City I can smell some things, sure. Our city is inside a magical bubble, but here, everything smells so much stronger. Like you, all citrusy and delicious, and dear sweet Poseidon, I should not have said any of this out loud. Please make me stop. Do you have a spell that can make you forget everything I just said?"

Lys laughed, throwing himself down on the bed next to me. He rolled to his side, arm propped under his head as he looked to where I lay, hands over my face. I peeked through my fingers, hiding my embarrassment. Not only had I betrayed my people by talking about Crunamar City, but I'd also just told Lys he smelled *delicious.* But, damn, he did.

"You like the way I smell," Lys said, leaning in to sniff me. I threw my hands to the side as I pushed him back when his nose scraped across the ticklish skin of my neck. "That's the only thing I heard. I've gotta say, you smell pretty great, too. Sweet."

I smiled up at the ceiling as Lys rolled over and turned off the lights, feeling the ache in my cheeks. Aside from Ostara's abrupt appearance, tonight was the most fun I'd had in ages.

"Is she always like that?" I asked, letting my head fall to the side. Part of me was shocked that Lys was still on his side, facing me, but I was tipsy enough not to be self-conscious in the moment.

"Nat?"

"No, your mom."

Lys dropped back, his arms behind his head as he sighed. "Pretty much, yes. Is Ronan always intense like that with you?"

"Not always," I said, the ache I felt for my family resurfacing. "He loves hard. Both his people, and us. His decisions are always with our best interest at heart, but sometimes he oversteps."

"I'd say forcing you to marry Owen is a pretty big overstep," Lys said, his voice taking on an edge I'd never heard before.

I didn't have an answer for Lys, but it wasn't really a

question either. Silence lingered between us for several beats as we both stared into the darkness.

"Do you regret it?" Lys asked, his words almost a whisper.

I scooted across the bed, lifting my head until I rested it in the crook of his shoulder, hand resting easily on his chest. Why I felt the need for contact with him, here in the dark with no witnesses to fool, I didn't know. Or maybe I did know, and I just didn't want to admit it to myself. "Emotional Distress Clause," I whispered, and his chest rumbled under my cheek as his arm came down behind me, pulling me in tighter.

"I miss my family," I answered honestly. "I've never been away from my sisters for more than a few days, and this is hard on me in a way I imagined only in my worst nightmares." The words sounded harsh, but so was my punishment. And yet, I hadn't answered Lys's question, had I?

Did I regret agreeing to this arrangement that had led me here, to this bed, to the male who rubbed his thumb across my back almost… lovingly?

Before I had time to answer, loud squeaking sounded from the room next door and Lys's hand stilled. Just enough light leaked through the windows to his side for me to see the incredulous look on his face.

"Think they're fighting over the plaid suit again?" Lys asked with a chuckle.

"Maybe he asked her to arrange his underwear by color. That'd probably do it for her."

Lys laughed, shaking his head as something slammed hard against the wall, rattling the guitars, followed by a loud moan I'd never be able to unhear.

"Ok, well. Enough of *that*," Lys said, flicking his hand in the air in the same way he'd done earlier around the house. That same tingle crawled across my skin, feeling the magic Lys cast around us as silence descended.

I held my breath, afraid he'd hear how hard my heart slammed against my chest in the deafening silence of the room. While I under no circumstances wanted to listen to whatever Kymari and Dillon got up to, I couldn't help but feel the tension in the air.

My mind chose that moment to catalog each touch, each look, each word Lys had said all day, planting little seeds of hope that needed to be ripped out by the root.

No matter if Dillon and Kymari found something real in each other, what Lys and I had was *not*. I had until after the Summit was over with him, and then we'd be back to… well, whatever we were before this had all started.

Strangers, I guessed.

"Goodnight, Maze," Lys whispered as he rolled towards me, his other arm dropping over my side as he pulled me into his chest. I mumbled something he hopefully interpreted as a drowsy slur of an answer.

I didn't dare move, afraid any slight shift would make him open his arms to let go of me, and I didn't want that. Not even a little bit.

Shit, I had it bad.

Chapter Twenty-Three

LYSANDER

I WOKE up the next morning intertwined with Maisie. Her leg was between mine, hand draped over my chest as she slept peacefully, and my heart fluttered in my chest.

Goddess, I wanted to roll over, pin her to the bed, and show her how much her words in front of my mother had meant to me yesterday. But that's what the old Lys would have done, and I didn't want to lead with physicality. Well, I *wanted* to, but I wouldn't.

Rather than backing down from my mother's hateful words, Maisie had risen to the challenge, defending me, saying I'd changed. She thought the words were false, just to annoy my mother, but she wasn't wrong. With Maisie's head on my chest, her arms around me, I felt changed. I couldn't go back to the way I was before, mindlessly hopping from one fling to the next. Not when I knew what it felt like to be with her.

Shit, I had it bad.

Sliding carefully out of the bed, I moved to the bathroom and turned the shower on ice cold. I shivered as the water rained down on me, but it cleared my mind.

What had started out as a contract with Maisie two weeks ago felt very real to me now. I just had to figure out a way to get her to fall for me as bad as I was falling for her before our time was up. The thought of her marrying Owen made my hands clench, anger rising in me quickly.

I shut off the water, grabbed a towel, and dried my hair quickly before wrapping it around my waist. Without thinking, I opened the door back into my room, eyes drifting up in time to see Maisie's naked ass in nothing but a blue thong as she bent to pull up a pair of leggings.

I stared for several seconds before I realized what I was doing. She looked over her shoulder and saw me standing in the doorway, letting out a shriek as she yanked on the waistband, and lost her balance in the process crashing into a guitar stand that set off a chain reaction of twanging strings and crashing instruments.

"Shit, Maze, are you —" I ran over, sure she'd just cracked her skull open on my Fender, and forced myself not to focus on it until I knew she was okay.

A moan sounded from the other side of the bed, and I was just rounding it when a leg flailed out, catching my ankle at the perfect angle to bring me down as well.

I landed with an audible *oof*, a muffled yelp coming from underneath me as I sprawled over Maisie's half-naked body.

My own body, unfortunately, was now *fully* naked, my towel abandoning me for the guitar stand I'd hurried past on my way over.

"Oh, my gods!"

"Sorry! I wanted — are you okay? — Shit, you're bleeding —"

"You're *NAKED!*"

Don't get hard don't get hard don't get —

I scrambled onto my heels, praying to whatever forces of nature might be on my side that Maisie was too distracted or potentially concussed to look at my rolling stones, and snatched the towel off the guitar stand, wrapping it around my waist.

I took a deep breath before chancing a look back to Maisie, who was covering her eyes with her hand.

"Are you decent?" she asked as she peeked between her fingers.

I bit my lip, noticing the way her green eyes appraised me even through her slitted fingers. "Almost never, but I'm covered."

"Get up!" she said, removing her hand from her face as she waved me off. "You'll see my whole ass if I try to move first."

I cleared my throat as I tried to blink away the image unsuccessfully. But nothing short of death or an angel mind wipe could make me forget that sight. "Afraid that ship has sailed."

"Poseidon, I can't with you."

"Well, there's one sign against concussion. Give me another — how did we meet again?" Partially, it was to distract her from this awkwardness, but I really was worried about her head, itching to reach out with my magic to check her over but not wanting to weird her out even more right now. I expected her to shoot me some snarky comeback about the whole coin fiasco she'd concocted, but her words caught me off guard.

"You came into Scallywags a few weeks after I started working there," her voice had gone softer, her fingers toying with the hem of her shirt. "You and the band, I think you'd just come home from a tour. The others grabbed a booth, and you came up to order drinks from me." She glanced up at me, biting her bottom lip, and my fingers tingled to brush my thumb across it and pull it from between her teeth. "I asked what you were having, and you grinned at me and said, 'I'll take anything you're willing to give me, gorgeous.'"

I tried to huff a laugh, but it sounded false even to my own ears. I hated to admit to myself, and certainly wouldn't admit to her, that I had no memory of the exchange. And yet, somehow, the words I'd said to her then had started to feel all too true in the present.

"I think your head's just fine, then," I managed to stammer, leaning away from her even further. "I'll just go back in the bathroom. Give you some privacy."

Without waiting for her to answer, I stood, fist clenched tight around the knot in my towel this time, and all but ran back to the shower. I flicked it on cold again, *ice* cold, and gasped as I stepped back under the stream, praying it would be enough to cool my blood.

After I finally recovered, or as much as I could, I pulled the door open slowly, calling Maisie's name, but she wasn't here. With a sigh of relief, I moved to my dresser and snagged my clothes for the day, going back to the bathroom so we didn't have the same incident happen twice. If Maisie walked in on me naked, I wasn't sure I'd be able to hold myself back again.

Shorts and a tee on, I went out to the kitchen where Dillon stood at the stove looking smug in his madras plaid suit. I chuckled, shaking my head as I grabbed a coffee cup and snagged the pot, pouring myself a large cup.

"Where are the girls?" I asked, looking around the house but not seeing any sign of Maisie or Kymari.

"Maisie left for work, and Kymari tagged along with her."

I nodded, a sigh of relief leaving me even as disappointment settled in. Of course she had to work. It's not like Maisie could drop everything to be with me 24/7. I shook my head, trying to ignore the fact that I wanted that.

"So, you and Kymari?" I raised a brow in Dillon's direction as I sipped at my coffee.

"Holy shit, dude," Dillon said, sinking into the chair to my right. "I don't know how you keep up with these sea nymph girls. *Insatiable.*"

I laughed, aiming for commiseration, even though I only had my imagination to go off of.

"I really like her," Dillon said, and I glanced up in surprise.

"Kymari?"

"Well, her too. But I meant Maisie. I like the *you* you are around her. The real Lys. The good guy I've always known. I feel like you always get dismissed as the player, but seeing as I've been on the receiving end of your love for the last two decades, I know how great you are. How special she must be to make you fawn over her like you do."

"Don't you think that's a little heavy on the emotions

before I've finished my first cup of coffee?" I asked playfully, hoping I didn't show how much those words meant to me.

"Sorry," he laughed. "Kymari has me feeling all sorts of sentimental right now. Marathon sex brings it out in me, I guess. Maybe I'll write us some new bangers, pun intended."

I chuckled, then pushed the chair back and returned to my room, ready to tackle the day.

The next two days were more of the same, except Maisie and I walked on eggshells around each other when the doors were closed. Yet, every night, as we lay in bed talking in the dark, silence spell engaged to block out the sounds of our friends next door, one of us found a reason to bring up the Emotional Distress Clause.

Every night, she fell asleep wrapped in my arms, fully clothed and platonic, even if my feelings for her were anything but. And every night, the thought of letting her go weighed heavily on me.

Sunday morning came, and I woke up filled with dread. A buzzing from my right startled me, and I rolled to my side to check my phone.

ORION

All Citizens of Deadlights Cove: Report to the town square by 10 a.m. for town-wide cleanup. All able-bodied, adult residents expected to attend. Official Mayor of this Town, Orion.

I blinked at the screen, the text having come blaring in at 8 a.m., despite the fact my phone had been on silent.

Orion's angel magic must have circumvented the setting to ring out its obnoxious alert signal so no one could miss his summons.

A minute later, my phone buzzed again, and I sighed heavily when I saw my mother's name pop up, the reason dread had found me so quickly this morning.

> **OSTARA**
>
> Tea with Clara at 2 p.m. at Immortali-Tea. Don't be late.
>
> Freshen up after Orion's clean-up.

I rolled my eyes that she thought she needed to include that, and didn't bother to respond. She'd know I'd gotten the message when I showed up later.

Maisie shifted in the bed and I looked over to see her watching me, her eyes flicking between me and my phone. My breath caught in my throat at the sight of her, hair slightly mussed in a high bun on her head, face bearing creases from the pillow. *My* pillow. From sleeping in *my* bed.

Any other time I'd awoken to a woman in my bed, I could reach across and pull her to me, easing the ache that built with every passing second. And damn, I wanted to. Maybe more than I ever had.

But I couldn't reach across the bed this time. Couldn't kiss the living shit out of her. Couldn't make her drown in my affection. Not yet, anyway. Not until she wanted me as much as I wanted her.

Clearing my throat, I pulled up Orion's message again. "Did you get one of these?"

She held up her own phone, the same text showing on her screen. "Guess we'd better get ready?"

Dillon and Kymari followed us as Maisie and I walked through town, hand in hand, as if today was just a typical Sunday, and we were typical boyfriend and girlfriend. We'd all collectively decided to head to Scallywags for breakfast before we had to subject ourselves to Orion's demands for the day.

"Morning, lovebirds!" Val called from the coffee van parked in front of Scallywags. "Beautiful day today, isn't it?"

I looked up at the sky, seeing the storm clouds in the distance, then back to Val. "Kind of?"

"Any day with your lover at your side is a beautiful day, young Lysander," Caedmon said, planting a wet kiss on the nape of Val's neck. The sight was more than a little weird, but so were the two elderly supes.

"Can't argue with you there, boys," I said with a smile, squeezing Maisie's hand. "You want anything?"

I listened as Maisie ordered her lavender iced latte, watched the way she smiled easily, laughing at the guy's jokes. The breeze off the ocean had her hair lifting off her back, just like it had in her mer form.

"Lys," Maisie said, and I blinked, focusing on her.

"Hm?"

"They asked if you wanted anything."

"Oh," I said, turning back to the coffee van. "Just an iced coffee, thanks."

I handed over the cash for both of our drinks right as Caedmon leaned over and whispered, "He's got it *bad*."

Maisie looked at me, questions in her eyes, but I leaned

forward, kissing her forehead before I pushed her towards Scallywags.

We'd just settled in our booth when Orion came bustling into the bar, his eyes widening in something like frantic relief to see some of us up and ready.

"Excellent," he muttered, pulling a chair up to our booth, settling his wings over the chair back. "Lysander, you'll be with me, working to tighten up the glamour on the town. The last thing we need while everyone is here for the Summit is to have some hapless humans wandering in."

Petra dropped into the booth next to us with an iced coffee, Nimue and Kit joining her, then cleared her throat pointedly.

"Sorry." Orion shook his head. "About the hapless part, anyway. And yet, case in point, Petra. You shouldn't have been able to take the exit off the highway to get here. Clearly, the glamour has been flagging."

"Maybe she's just a special human, O," Blaze said, sliding a breakfast burrito in front of Petra with a wink. She rolled her eyes at him, and he planted a noisy kiss on her forehead before heading back behind the bar.

"Hey, make me one of those," Dev called back to him, pointing at Petra's burrito as she slid into the booth beside her.

Orion sat back, brow furrowing, and stared at Devanna. "*You* came?"

Dev glared at him, and held up her phone. "I can read, can't I?"

"Considering you have your hands full with the church, I figured there was no way you'd show up," Orion said as Blaze dropped a burrito in front of Kit, skirting Devanna's directions. Before Kit could take a bite, Devanna reached across the table and pulled it in front of her. "It's not like you'll finish renovating it in time anyway."

Devanna paused, the burrito halfway to her mouth, and I swore the entire room held their breath.

"You've really done it now, O," I laughed, wide eyes dancing between the look on Dev's face and Orion, meeting her deadly stare head on. I leaned back in my chair, desperate to see how this played out.

"You don't think I can do it?" she said, slightly tilting her head as her blue hair cascaded over her shoulder.

"In a week?" Orion gave a forced laugh, throwing his head back. "No. Not a chance."

"How much?" Dev asked.

Orion leaned forward, elbows on the table, his grey eyes sharpening. Maisie looked at me with the same shocked expression I was sure I also wore as we watched this exchange, wondering who would explode first.

"Dev," Nimue said, flipping around to peer over the booth. "I'll help."

"No, you won't," Orion said, shaking his head, but never looking away from where he held Dev's gaze. "You need to get the cottage ready for the Summit dinner. That's not an order."

Nimue muttered a quiet *"Kumquats,"* at Orion's intentional skirt around the demon's need to oppose direct orders.

"I don't need help," Dev said, pushing her burrito away from her as she stood. "I'll have the entire church renovated in the next 48 hours, better than you'd ever expect. It'll be so fucking shiny you'll need sunglasses to walk past it."

"Sure," Orion scoffed. "I'll save some glamour magic to cover it when *that* doesn't happen."

Dev grabbed her burrito off the table, took a savage bite of it, teeth clashing together loudly as she glared at Orion and turned to stomp out of the bar. As she passed behind Orion's back, he flinched, teeth baring, and I saw a feather clenched in Dev's hand as she made for the door. Right at the entrance, she dropped it, stomping it into the ground as she swung open the door and left.

"Childish," he muttered to himself, rustling his wings as though she hadn't just plucked out one of his feathers, and turned back to the rest of us, eyes sharp. Daring us to mention it. I might not have known a lot about angels — nobody did — but I did know they prized their wings above all. Feather-plucking seemed taboo, at best. Potentially illegal, at worst.

The door swung open again a moment later, Mo walking in with Ruby behind her. Mo turned to look back out the door, watching as Dev stomped her way past the window muttering to herself. As she swung back around, her eyes settled on Orion with a shit-eating grin.

"And the student becomes the teacher," she said, her hand coming to rest on Orion's shoulder. "You don't even need my help, do you, dear? Make her so mad she'll jump you out of spite. Good strategy."

I didn't think I'd ever seen anyone touch Orion, and the shocked look on his face said it had been a while. Mo patted his shoulder fondly, each subsequent *pat-pat* making his jaw twitch more and more fervently, until he finally jumped out of his seat, dislodging her hand.

Before he left, Orion dropped a paper on the table,

pointing at it. "Find your assignments and meet your team at the gazebo in ten minutes."

Mo snatched the paper off the table, squinting through her teal glasses as she eyed it. "Oh good! Lys, you and I are with Orion today. Ruby, you'll stay with us, of course."

She handed the paper to Nimue next. "Looks like the skulk is with me at the Cottage," she said with a smile, leaning into her husband as she kissed him. "I'm never going to say no to spending a day with you."

"You spend *every* day with him," Blaze said as he ripped the paper from his cousin's hand.

"Never enough," Kit growled low in his throat as his brown fingers tangled in Nimue's long hair, pulling her into a deeper kiss than the peck she'd offered him.

"Ah, love," Mo crooned with a happy sigh, her arms draping around me and Maisie both, pushing us slightly together until our shoulders bumped. "You can tell when it's *real*, you know?"

Maisie jerked slightly in Mo's hold, her face swinging to me with a startled expression. I glanced up at Mo, seeing the saccharine smile she offered. My face heated as I looked back to Maisie, feeling like I needed to do *something*.

Kiss her, every thought in my head screamed loudly as Maisie leaned towards me slightly.

But here? In front of everyone?

My knee bounced with every second that ticked by, indecision racking me. Sensing my hesitation, Maisie leaned her head on my shoulder.

"Wish I was paired with you today," she said, loud enough for the whole table to hear. My knee slammed into the table, rattling the dishes as I fought to recover from her words. Since when was *I* the awkward one?

"Yeah?"

Mo giggled, the sound filled with devious glee. "Ready to go, Lysander?" Mo said, patting my shoulder again.

I tugged Maisie into my side, squeezing her harder than I'd intended and slid from the booth.

Chapter Twenty-Four

LYSANDER

"YOU THREE WORK ON THE EXIT," Orion said, pointing towards the highway. "Morgaine, you take the north side, Lysander and Ruby, you head west, I'll take south and east. We want this glamour to be so unappealing, no human would dare think of stopping in Deadlights Cove."

"Bye, dears!" Mo waved as she hopped towards the north, far more sprightly than you'd expect from the elderly woman. I wasn't entirely sure of her age — witches, shifters, and nymphs aged much slower than humans, but weren't as long-lived as angels or demons — but was willing to bet she was over 400. "Lysander, make sure you go slow and show Ruby what you're doing."

I nodded at her words, happy to help the young witch.

"What about me?" someone called from behind us, and Ruby and I turned to see my neighbor, Mrs. Farrington, jogging down the road. Her black cat, Bagheera, was attached to a leash around her waist, aggressively pulling at the rope as he tugged the small witch to the side in his desperate desire to break free. "I'm here to help!"

Orion pinched the bridge of his nose, his eyes closed as he fought to breathe evenly. Mrs. Farrington hadn't been on the roster for job assignments, and Orion looked more than a little flustered with her presence.

"Why don't you work between Mo and us, making sure the glamour covers the seam?" I offered, not wanting to subject *any* of us to working with the crazy woman who dressed her cat in a damn raincoat. Bagheera thrashed from side to side, trying to bite at the yellow fabric on his back. I wasn't worried about Mo's and my magic meshing, so the assignment was a wash, but was nicer than whatever the mayor would say when he opened his mouth.

"Oh." Mrs. Farrington nodded, her whole body swaying as the cat jumped, willing to risk strangulation to get away from the woman. "Okay. Sure."

Trees rose on all sides around the road, casting the area in shadows even on sunny days. The sky was dark overhead as I walked through the tall grass towards the green exit sign that read *Deadlights Cove: No Attractions.* I'd lived here my whole life, and everytime I passed this sign it made me chuckle.

I couldn't count the number of times I'd thought about leaving the Cove behind, of moving on, of taking the risk and moving to Nashville to pursue my music, of abandoning all of my mother's expectations for my future in the Coven.

Today, staring at the highway leading away from town, I didn't feel that same desire. No, all I wanted to do was turn around and head right back into town, even with the giant mosquitos, rocky beaches, and my overbearing mother.

"Should we say it's haunted?" Ruby asked as she walked

up to my side, her dark eyebrows rising as she grinned at the thought. "I love ghost towns."

"You and every other paranormal thrill-seeker," Orion called from in front of us as he moved to the south. "Leave the ghost towns to Colorado. We don't need a potential tourist attraction. We want *no* attractions, like the sign says."

"Hmm, good point," Ruby said, biting her red nails that matched the ends of her hair.

"Are there ghosts in Colorado?" Mrs. Farrington asked as Ruby followed me to the treeline near the highway.

"Probably," Ruby said, hovering at my side. "Weird shit happens there a lot. But I'm not a Necromancer, so I can't see ghosts."

"Necromancy is very rare. There are only three I know of in the States," Mrs. Farrington said, and I frowned. Most Necromancers didn't advertise what they were, secretive on the whole. While she was old, Mrs. Farrington had lived in Deadlights Cove her entire life, and wasn't well connected outside of our Coven. She was a Green Witch, and not very powerful at that. How would she even come to know of *any* Necromancers?

"Can you, Lys?" Ruby asked. "See ghosts, I mean?"

"No," I chuckled. "Ostara tried to have me learn about necromancy, but that was the hard limit to my powers."

Mrs. Farrington and Bagheera drifted off as Ruby and I moved west along the forest edge.

"You really can do *everything* else?" Ruby said, her wide brown eyes focused heavily on me. With my magic at full power, I noticed her contrasting red and deep blue auras pulsing with excitement, then dwindling to a darker shade. She sighed heavily, fingers twitching at her side. "You and

Mo are both so powerful. I feel like I'll never learn how to use my magic. Owen was at Mo's a few days ago, and just watching how he and Blaze and Nimue can twitch a finger and *boom!* Magic. Demons are so cool. I wish it was like that for me. Even Mo doesn't cast many spells. It's all so effortless for her."

I wasn't sure what part of that monologue to focus on — that she'd noticed how different Mo's and my own magic was? Or that Owen was casually hanging out with everyone in town?

"No, I can't do *everything.* It wasn't always this easy for me either."

That was a lie, but hope bloomed in her face, and I was glad I'd said it. It would have been true for any *other* witch in our Coven, so she didn't need to know I'd somehow been born with easy access to my magic.

"What did you think of Owen?" I asked, not sure why I'd decided to torture myself like this.

"He's pretty nerdy," Ruby said, pursing her lips. "But like, a *hot* nerdy. Like, Jude Law as Dumbledore, nerdy. He got really excited when he was talking to Mo about some book he can't find, hoping maybe she had it. But he brought us blueberry muffins from some old family recipe, and they were to *die* for. I accidentally ate six."

"Hate when that happens." I forced a smile, but my stomach soured at the thought of Owen potentially plying Maisie with fresh baked goods to win her over. Sticking my hand in my pocket, I fiddled with my phone, wanting to text her. To pull her attention away from Owen and his magical muffins.

With a deep breath, I shifted my focus to the barrier

magic around the town. The spell shimmered like a bubble, casting a rainbow of colors in the air that would be invisible to most supes, and all humans. Anyone with supernatural blood wouldn't feel much of anything crossing the border into town, but for a human, the repelling magic could vary from anything to an impending sense of dread to a sudden memory of an iron left plugged in at home. If a human — like Petra — *did* make it past the barrier and into town, everything was spelled to look so dilapidated and unwelcoming it might as well be a ghost town.

Ruby drifted closer to the barrier, her aura still slipping in and out of the in-between, though it didn't seem to bother her.

I wasn't sure if she could see or sense the barrier, so I called out her name right as she was about to step across it, not wanting her to disrupt it any further.

"Oh, sorry," Ruby blinked, looking around the forest in a daze, then shook her head in a laugh. "I must have zoned out there for a minute."

I furrowed my brows in concern. "Everything all right?"

"Yeah, yeah. I just must not have slept well last night with all the hubbub. Can you show me what you're doing?" She asked, pointing at my hands in the air, feeling the magic around the town. "I don't know how to work glamours yet."

"Oh." I dropped my hands back down and turned to her. "Yeah. Why not?"

Stepping behind her, I positioned her feet just so. "Hands up," I coached, and as she did so, I pulled a small bag from my pocket containing pre-mixed ingredients I'd snagged from Dev before leaving town. Pouring a little of the ingredients into each of her outstretched palms, I showed her how to crush them between her fingers, rubbing it into an almost paste-like substance that smelled faintly of lavender.

"Breathe deeply," I said, mimicking the motions with her hands as I tried to follow my own instructions, clearing my head of all thoughts of stupid muffins. Ruby did as I said, and I nodded, watching as her aura switched to a brighter, more focused red than I'd seen it yet. "Good. Now, repeat after me."

"Bagheera!" Mrs. Farrington called as Ruby and I worked our way back to where we'd left her. "Bagheera!!"

"Everything okay?" I asked as we approached.

"Lysander!" Mrs. Farrington cried, voice full of panic. "He escaped! We have to catch him!"

I glanced at the forest, connecting into the National Park that spanned almost 50,000 acres. "He ran into the woods?"

"Yes, just right there. But Lysander, Bagheera's domesticated — he won't survive in the wild! He's not even wearing his raincoat!" She held up the little yellow coat then clutched it to her chest.

I wasn't sure I'd call Bagheera *domesticated* in any sense of the word — that cat was as feral as they came. I sighed, looking up at the dark clouds moving in from over the ocean, then back to the trees before turning to Ruby. "You stay with Mrs. Farrington and see if Bagheera comes back while I go look for him."

She nodded, and I turned to trudge off through the

forest, letting my magic open up as I searched for the damn cat.

"Bagheera!" I called, feeling like an idiot. There was a zero percent chance the cat would answer to his name, especially if he thought I was taking him back to Mrs. Farrington. I couldn't blame the guy — I'd run for the hills, too.

The sky grew darker by the minute, but I circled the area calling his name, hoping he hadn't gone far. I was about to give up when rustling sounded from my right. I stopped, casting my magic out as I searched for danger.

Magic pooled to my right, and I turned, squinting into the darkness. Massive antlers appeared a moment later, far above my head. I held my breath as the moose moved into the clearing towards me. Winston was a regular in Deadlights Cove, but I was still hyper-aware of the fact that the bull moose outweighed me by over 800 pounds.

His head swung, black eyes focused on me as I held my breath. Planted right between his massive antlers was a small black cat, a tiny paw resting on an antler as if he was steering the giant animal he rode on.

"You know what?" I whispered, backing away from the duo, "Live and let live, buddy."

The glamour was up and as strong as I could make it. My phone beeped in my pocket and I slid it free, seeing the time and the corresponding calendar invite.

Out of time, I went off to find Orion.

Chapter Twenty-Five

MAISIE

"BEACH CLEANUP," Kymari snorted as we headed down to the harbor. Dark clouds gathered over the water, headed our way, but the sun was shining and warm for the moment. "Of course."

"At least it'll be easy," I said, handing over one of the buckets we'd picked up at the gazebo to throw trash in. We kept our ocean clean around here, so there shouldn't be much to clean up other than the occasional litter from someone on land.

"Wait!"

We turned, and I shielded my eyes against the sun to see Owen jogging after us. Kymari shot me a look, eyebrows practically at her hair line, and took a dramatic step away as she kept walking, hopping over the stone wall onto the rocky beach right as Owen caught up to me.

"Orion didn't have a specific assignment for me, so I thought I'd join you, if that's all right?" Owen slid his hands into his pockets, ducking his head slightly to meet my eyes, and offered a tentative smile. Today he was wearing a hunter green short sleeve button down that was snug enough over his shoulders to show more muscles than I would have expected from an academic, and khaki colored pants with what I assumed were his best attempt at casual sneakers. All of it was stuffy in comparison to my pink tank top, ripped jeans, and sandals.

"Um, sure," I said, my mouth suddenly going dry. "Sorry I — I mean the other day, at the bar, I should have introduced myself once I realized who you were, but, well, I thought, here's my chance to —"

"To spy on me?" Owen grinned, brushing a hand through his dark blond waves, then took the bucket from my hands and jerked his head towards the beach. "I understand. Shall we?"

"Uh, wait —" I held my hand out to stop him, and he turned back to me with a hint of confusion. I cleared my throat, fixed my posture, wiped my palm on my pants, and held it out again. "Maisie Douglass," I said, and Owen took my hand in his warm one, shaking it. "Pleasure to meet you."

His black irises twinkled. "Owen Kinkaid. Pleasure's all mine, lass. Though, we've met before." He dropped my hand, and we stepped over the rock wall onto the beach together. "I think you were about yay-high, though," he held a hand up to his waist, chuckling, "So I understand if you don't remember."

We combed the beach, pebbles crunching under our shoes as waves gently lapped at the shore. The harbor bell buoy clanged melodically every few minutes with the current, and gulls called overhead, making me feel the most at home I had since I'd been banished.

"Can I ask you something?" I meandered closer to Owen after a few minutes of beachcombing.

"Anything."

"Why would you agree to this whole marriage thing? What's in it for you?"

I could have sworn a blush crept over the demon's cheeks as he darted a glance at me, the corners of his eyes crinkling in the smile he tried to keep off his lips.

"Well, there's a handful of reasons," he said, incinerating an old crumpled receipt with a snap of his fingers. "One, your mother's family is close with mine back home. Two, this magic — the linking magic, that is — is a new venture. It's new research. Well, I suppose technically it's very *old* research, in a way — the once and future magic, as it were." He chuckled at his own joke, though the reference went over my head. "Anyway, it has the potential to do a lot of good for our people — supernaturals in general, I mean — but we have to make sure we get it right. It seems fitting that I, as one of its principal researchers, should be one of the first to test it out."

"So, for science?" I said, genuinely curious. And honestly, for research made more sense than anything else he could have said even with the little I knew about the male.

He smiled again with a nod. "That was part of it, sure. I've also, uh —" he licked his lips, flicking his hand as he gathered a large clump of seaweed tangled on the rocks, burning it to ash without even looking at it. "Well, I've always loved sea nymph lore. Always wanted to see your cities, and the idea of having some of your magic?" His eyes widened, but he wasn't looking at me, focusing on the ocean behind me. "You know I've never even gone swimming?" He gave a sheepish, slightly self-conscious laugh, and I found myself warming to him instantly.

"Really?"

"Nope. Demons can't stand water — well, most of them. I've always loved it — at least, from a distance." Owen tore his eyes away from the water and back to me. "I hope you don't think that's terribly cold of me. I'm sure, in time, we can come to care for each other, too. You should have heard your mother talk about you, Maisie. I'll do my best to be a male you deserve, and teach you everything about my magic that I can to help your people."

His gaze met mine so earnestly, so hopefully, I started to feel myself falling under his spell. Had I been wrong to throw this whole idea in Ronan's face when he'd suggested it? I knew it was for practical reasons, for the protection of our city and our people, and yet, standing here on the beach with the smell of the ocean on one side and Owen's smoky scent on the other, his endearing smile and enthusiasm for his work, it wasn't such a bad prospect. Owen seemed sincere in his interest in our magic, in his desire to make it work for the best of both of us. And it hadn't escaped my notice that he used his magic so effortlessly, it was easy to tell how powerful he was.

I tried returning his smile, timidly at first, but when his own broke out into true happiness, I couldn't help but meet it with the same.

"What about you?" he asked, walking slightly ahead of me as he gave me space I desperately needed. "Why did you agree? Are you not romantically involved with Lysander?"

"Uh," I stopped, lead settling in my stomach. Had

Ronan not told him I'd been banished and the deal was off? Did Owen not know Saoirse was now set to be his bride?

Just then, my phone buzzed in my pocket, and I excused myself as I pulled it out, Owen continuing on the beach to give me privacy.

He really was incredibly considerate.

I clicked on my phone to find a text from Lys.

LYS

I can't wait until we're done here.

Wish we'd been paired together.

Ready to be near you again.

I blinked at my screen, then looked hurriedly around me to see if Kymari or Owen was nearby. They weren't, and I furrowed my brow.

Was someone reading *his* phone over his shoulder? Why would he text this, unless it was for show?

Unless… was it *not* for show? Did he actually just want to see me again?

I decided to play along, just in case someone was watching him text and expecting something flirty in return.

That was definitely why I texted back,

MAISIE

Oh yeah? What will you do then?

I held my breath waiting for his response. Would he be able to tell I was just playing along?

And yet, I did want to know what he would do. Part of me had wanted him to reach over and kiss me in Scallywags when Morgaine was teasing us.

242

LYS

So many ideas, so little time, princess.

Figured we could make beignets tonight.

I eyed my phone in confusion, not at all expecting him to discuss baked goods. The guys' house had barely any food in the cabinets, and nothing so far had led me to believe he even knew *how* to cook, so was this some sort of weird euphemism I was too naive to understand?

LYS

Sweet, like you.

Feeling like I needed to respond, but not knowing what to say, I simply wrote back,

MAISIE

Yum!

LYS

So good. Life changing. You'll see stars,
begging me for more.

Okay, now I was pretty positive this was a euphemism. Right? Glancing around the beach, I felt my cheeks flame, embarrassment flooding me. I was in uncharted waters, no idea how to be sexy back.

MAISIE

I like the sound of that.

LYS

You have no idea.

"Everything all right?" Owen asked.

"Huh?" I jumped, pulling my phone to my chest protectively as my heart slammed violently against my ribs.

Owen pointed at my phone, then picked up another piece of trash. "All good? No more emergencies?"

"Oh, this?" I said, glancing back down at my phone as another text lit up the screen.

LYS

So many things I want to try with you.

A nervous chuckle-snort erupted out of me, my mind imagining all sorts of things I wanted to try, none of which I would ever say aloud, especially not to the male standing in front of me. Sliding my phone back in my pocket, I nodded. "Yes. All good. Great, actually. Never been better. *Spectacular*, even. So good you wouldn't believe it."

Owen eyed me carefully, then smiled, the look so genuine and relaxed I forced my racing heart to slow the fuck down, willing it into obedience.

"Glad to hear it," Owen said and I forced myself to step back up to his side. "I have to say, I'm a little surprised to see you spend so much time ashore. That is unusual for your kind."

"Well," I drew the word out, trying to think through how much to tell him. "Kind of a funny story."

"I'd love to hear it. I'm quite eager to learn more about you, Maisie."

Did he have to be so nice? This would all be so much easier if he was some ugly toad with warts on his face and a surly disposition, not genuinely curious and open. My phone vibrated in my pocket, but I didn't pull it out again.

"How's it going over there?" Kymari asked, saving me from answering. "I've got the north side taken care of. Looks like there was a bonfire up near the lighthouse at some point, but otherwise it's pretty clear."

"Humans?" Owen said, brow scrunched as he looked to where Kymari walked towards us. "That's far too close to town. Maybe I should go take a look, just to be safe. Keep the glamour intact to discourage any who might think to return."

"*Great* idea," I said as my phone vibrated in my pocket again. "I'm sure Orion would appreciate that."

"Let's chat more later," Owen said as he turned to me, pressing a gentle palm to my shoulder as the wind ruffled his blond hair, the clouds moved closer to shore with the incoming storm. Aside from the handshake, it was the first physical contact we'd had, and it felt... nice. But also more platonic than anything exciting. "I'm dying to know more about you, Maisie."

I smiled, feeling too many teeth show as I nodded, then gave him a thumbs up just in case he hadn't understood the smiling and nodding for confirmation, like the absolute weirdo I was.

Owen flickered out, and Kymari approached me where I was bent over, hands on my knees as I fought to catch my breath.

"Poseidon, I can't do this," I said, unsure what part exactly I was referring to. Couldn't flirt with Lys? Couldn't remember it was fake and keep my emotions in check? Couldn't confess how awful I'd bungled things for Owen? Couldn't keep secrets from my best friend, standing right in front of me?

Yes. All of the above.

Kymari's hand pushed on my head, forcing it lower between my knees. "Breathe," she said, holding me down. "You're panicking."

I pushed at her hand, shoving it away from me even though I knew she was right. "I'm fine."

"Sure," Kymari said, falling to the rocky shore as she sat looking out at the waves, growing taller as the storm moved closer. "We're both fine, right?"

I lifted my head, eyeing my friend as a wave of guilt crashed over me. Dropping to her side, I leaned my head on her shoulder. "Have I told you how sorry I am yet?"

She tilted her head to cradle mine. "No."

I cringed. "I am, though. *Really* sorry. Even in all of my many worst case scenarios I didn't think you'd be banished, too. I never wanted this for you — that's why I kept so many secrets."

Kymari sighed, pulling off her shoes as she toed the water crashing on the shore. "I figured as much. I can't say it doesn't hurt though, Maisie. You have a whole life here, and I didn't know about any of it."

My phone buzzed a third time, but I ignored it, the pain in my friend's words cutting me deeply. "I really didn't mean for this to happen."

"It *did* though, Maisie," she said, pulling away from me slightly. "Whether you meant for it to happen or not, it *did* happen. I can't go home, and neither can you."

Tears gathered in my eyes right as the dark clouds above finally broke, rain falling steadily on the water in front of us. "I don't know how to fix it."

"I don't either, Maisie," Kymari sighed again, head tilted back in the drizzle.

I laid down on the beach, rocks digging into my back as I stared at the dark sky, feeling the water soak into my skin in a way it hadn't in days. Inching my hand across the rocks, I found Kymari's hand, lacing my fingers through hers.

"I'm so glad I have you," I said, the words almost whispered as I squeezed her hand. "I don't know how I'd do this without you."

Kymari turned, resting her chin on her shoulder as she smiled at me, but the look didn't meet her eyes. "You wouldn't."

I grinned, yanking on her arm as I pulled her down to her back at my side, then curled into her. "Love you. Mean it."

"I know."

Neither of us moved, not even as the storm worsened, our clothes soaked and cold against our skin. With the waves crashing at our feet, the rain falling from above, and my best friend at my side, this was the closest I could come to home, and I didn't want to let it go, not even when tears slid down my cheeks, blending in with the rain.

Chapter Twenty-Six

LYSANDER

BY THE TIME Orion was satisfied with the glamour, it was almost time to meet my mother and Clara at the tea shop. If I wasn't already irritable about *that* happening today and Orion being at his most nit-picky I'd ever seen him, the fact that Maisie had stopped responding to my texts would've set me off anyway.

Why had she stopped responding? Had I gone too far? Was she busy hanging out with *Owen?*

Could she tell that I wasn't playing? Because I'd meant every damn word I'd sent her.

I exhaled slowly as I strode back towards my house, trying to push all the images aside that were flooding my mind.

Visuals of all the things I wanted to *try* with Maisie.

I jogged up my front steps, unlocking the door with magic as I adjusted my pants. I'd make time for a quick shower — I'd worked up a sweat with all the magic today, after all — and then head over to Immortali-Tea.

Twenty minutes later, I was dressed and ready in a

black button down and dark jeans. I grabbed my phone off my dresser, but still no response from Maisie. With a disappointed shake of my head — both for her lack of response and my reaction to it — I slipped my phone in my pocket, and headed for the tea shop just around the corner.

Crossing the street, I saw Ostara already seated inside through the large windows that made up the front of the shop. I took a deep breath before pulling open the door.

"Ah, Lysander, perfect timing." She appraised my appearance with a glance as she held a hand out to indicate someone behind me. I turned to find a woman standing just behind me, and quickly moved to include her in our conversation. "This is Clara Barrett. Clara, this is my son, Lysander."

I offered her a polite smile — this wasn't her fault, after all — and extended my hand. "Nice to meet you, Clara."

Clara shook my hand, her brown eyes warm as she subtly looked me over, and smiled. "Nice to meet you, Lysander." Her light brown hair fell almost to her waist in loose waves, and, in her wedge sandals, she almost matched my height. Smoothing her sunflower yellow dress, she sat opposite my mother, and I took the last seat at the small, round table.

Ostara raised her eyebrows pointedly at me as Nadir came over and placed a tray down at our table, a pot of water and assorted teas and cakes arranged on it. I smothered my sigh and leaned forward, placing tea cups in front of each of us.

"So, Clara, my mother tells me you're from Vermont," I began, pouring water into each cup after we'd selected our teas. I hadn't even looked when I placed mine in, grabbing one at random.

"I am." Clara smiled. "I love it there. Hiking, breweries, kayaking on the lake with friends —"

"And you're prepared to leave all that? Your family, friends, your whole life?"

"*Lysander*," Ostara hissed, then offered Clara a sympathetic smile.

"What? *Won't* she be leaving all that behind?" I felt a little bad for being an asshole about it, but it was the truth. I turned to Clara, already done with this whole facade. "You can't possibly want this."

"I —" Clara stuttered, placing her tea cup down to buy herself a minute. She glanced between Ostara and me before leaning forward and lowering her voice, though I wasn't sure who she thought would care to overhear this conversation. Sure, Nadir was hanging on every fucking word from the counter, but with his fox ears, he'd be able to hear her regardless. "Could Lysander and I speak alone for a minute, Ms. Theroux?"

Ostara gave a clipped, "*Of course,*" before standing and moving several tables down to give us some privacy.

Clara scooted her chair closer to me and pursed her lips. "You don't want this alliance," she stated, but it was a question.

I didn't see any reason to beat around the bush. "I don't," I admitted. "It's nothing personal. Do *you* want it?"

"I'm…" she traced the lip of her tea cup with her finger, "Intrigued, I suppose, by the thought of gaining witch magic."

I tilted my head. "What would you do with it?"

"You know shifters are essentially the lowest type of magic," she said, and I nodded. "We all heard about what happened here last fall, with shifters stuck in their animal forms. If adding witch magic could help prevent that happening again — or at least, help us still have access to magic even if it did happen again — any of us would jump at that chance."

Remembering how frantic the shifters had been last fall, I could understand where she was coming from, to an extent. "There must be witches in Vermont, though. Ones you wouldn't have to give up your whole life to link with?"

Clara bit her lip. "Yes. But your mother mentioned you're a particularly strong Harmonic witch?" I conceded to that with a nod. "There's been some discontent within our den. Our old Alpha, my aunt, passed on, and several members of the den have been vying for the position ever since. My cousin, who should inherit the role by both birth and power, hoped some Harmonic magic could help everything settle down."

"I see."

"If she wasn't madly in love with her childhood sweetheart, I'm sure she'd be here herself arranging this alliance," Clara said, eyes dropping to the table.

And shit, that pulled at my heartstrings. Even though I didn't want this alliance in any way shape or form, I also didn't want Clara to walk away feeling like crap because I turned her down.

Reaching across the table, I grabbed her hand. "Hey. I promise my hesitation in this has nothing to do with you, no matter your position in the pack. I wouldn't be open to it even if it was your cousin here instead of you." Clara eyed me skeptically, so I went in for the kill. "I can't agree to this because I'm in love with someone else."

Clara blinked in surprise, slowly pulling her hand back from mine. Shock coursed through me at my choice of words. Why had I said *love?* Not just in a relationship?

Clara's lips moved, but I swallowed heavily, trying to pull myself back to the present. "Sorry, can you repeat that?"

Clara chuckled at my distracted moment. "I said I don't want to cause anyone problems. Why wouldn't your mother mention this when she agreed to our arrangement?"

I sighed, ignoring the scowl Ostara was shooting at me, her dark eyes mere slits. "She doesn't approve of my girl-friend. There's some old beef with Maisie's dad that I don't understand. I saw him a lot when I was a little kid, mostly when my aunt was around, but then he disappeared. Suddenly my aunt was sad, and my mom hated him. I don't know, though. Everything is a vague memory from the eyes of a six-year-old."

"So she agreed to an arranged marriage without your consent?" Clara said, her nose wrinkling in distaste. She leaned forward patting my hand. "I'm going to tell her I can't go through with this. You deserve to be happy with whoever you choose, even if your mother doesn't like her father. That's a stupid reason to keep two people in love apart."

I couldn't help the smile that stretched across my face, genuine and real as my heart lurched at her words. "Thank you, Clara. If you really need a Harmonic witch though, I'm happy to help. We don't need to link our powers for that."

Clara pulled her hand back, then tucked her hair behind

her ear. She was pretty, but didn't hold a candle to Maisie's stunning, natural beauty. "You seem like a great guy, Lysander. Maisie is lucky."

"Trust me," I laughed, leaning back in my chair as a huge weight was lifted off my shoulders. "I'm the lucky one."

"Regardless," Clara said, waving off my comment, "I'm glad you found someone you're happy with."

I watched as she pushed back from the table, moving over to sit with Ostara. The two women chatted briefly, then Clara stood, nodded at me, and grabbed her umbrella.

"You're making a mistake," my mother said as she took Clara's vacated seat, staring at me across the small tea table. She poured herself a new cup of tea, steam rising from the cup. "The Crunamars don't follow through on their promises, *ever.* You *think* Maisie is different from her father, but she's not. I saw her on the beach today with Owen Kinkaid. Isn't that who Ronan wanted to link your sweet little princess with?"

I crossed my arms, tongue running across my teeth as I contemplated her words. I didn't remember seeing Owen's name on the list of assigned responsibilities this morning, but that didn't mean he hadn't joined Maisie on the beach.

"She loves me," I said, hoping my voice gave confidence to the words I was sure weren't true. No way could Maisie love me. Not yet. Not even if I wanted her to.

"Yes, well, Ronan once said he loved Lyra, too," she said, her tea cup clattering on the saucer as she brought it down with force. "Right up until the day he left to marry Maisie's mother. A political alliance he couldn't say no to. Sounds familiar, doesn't it, Lysander?" She bared her teeth in a harsh smile, the look betraying 30 years of bitterness. "Don't say I didn't warn you when she chooses Owen without a backwards glance your way."

I stared at her, stunned by her words. "What do you mean? Ronan was with Lyra? I thought they were just friends?"

"Mm, yes, well. Rebelling against their parents must be a sea nymph trait. Ronan, much like his daughter, didn't particularly care for the strict rules his father implemented. Lyra came here with me when I moved to Deadlights Cove while I was pregnant with you, and the two met. I don't know the exact details, but they were together for six years, and then he disappeared. She never heard from him again."

"That" — I shook my head, trying to recall what I remembered of Ronan when I was a child — "that can't be true."

"Believe me or not, it doesn't matter," my mother said, leaning over the table. "Maisie *will* leave you. Do not be foolish enough to fall for her. She is a siren, luring you into this. You, my boy, are full of so much untapped potential, and I can't bear to lose you like I did Lyra. Don't get caught in their net."

"Lyra's death was an accident," I said, remembering the day Lyra hadn't come home eleven years ago. My aunt had always been the yin to my mother's yang, loving and kind in a way I wasn't sure my mother even knew how to be, even if Lyra had seemed to carry an ever-present sadness with her too.

How Lyra had ended up at the top of the lighthouse, I'd never understood. How she'd fallen, I still couldn't believe, not even after I'd cast the imprint reading myself, watching her body tumble off the roof by some invisible force as she was launched into the rocky sea below.

"Nothing about her death makes sense," my mother said, drawing me back to the present and away from that gruesome day, "except that she landed in the ocean, the one place Ronan controls above all others. If it had truly been an accident, he could have saved her. But he never even tried, never showed up, as if she meant nothing to him, and never had."

My mother stood, grabbed her belongings, and moved towards the door as I sat in shock, trying to understand her words. "Don't say I didn't warn you, Lysander. Leave that girl, and leave her now. For your own good."

She pushed through the door, not waiting for a response, and I watched her walk out into the rain.

"That was awkward for a multitude of reasons," Nadir commented as he cleared the tea tray from the table in front of me. "I'm headed to Scallywags to meet some of the boys tonight, and I'm going to go ahead and say you should join me. Not even really asking, man. You need it."

I nodded aimlessly, my mind still reeling over my mother's story. What other secrets had she kept from me?

Chapter Twenty-Seven

MAISIE

"OH, MY GODS, WHO IS *THAT*?" Kymari stopped in the middle of the street, pointing in through the glass front of Immortali-Tea.

I followed her line of sight to Lys seated at a tiny table inside, practically knee to knee with a woman with long, light brown hair, my gut twisting as I realized who it must be.

"That little shit is *cheating* on you?" Kymari seethed, already preparing to tie her braids back.

"Shh, it's not like that. Come here." I tugged her arm, pulling us out of sight of the tea shop, and leaned back against the brick wall of the building as I tried to figure out what to tell her.

I settled on some form of the truth. As quickly as I could, I relayed how, like Ronan wanted me to marry Owen, Ostara wanted Lys to link with Clara, who I assumed that must be.

"Oh, I see how it is," Kymari scoffed.

I bit my lip. "Do you?" Did *I*?

"Yeah. You spent the day with Owen, so now, Lys is trying to get back at you. Throwing *Clara* right in your face." She shook her head in disgust, and I tried not to laugh, though my heart warmed at my loyal friend.

"Right, I'm sure he assumed we'd walk by the shop right as he happened to be having tea with her," I said dryly, and she turned her scowl on me.

We peered around the corner again, Kymari practically steaming in righteous anger for me, and me, well… curious. Yeah, that was this feeling. Curiosity.

Curiosity twisted my stomach like a knife and choked my heart, practically suffocating me when I saw Clara place her hand on top of Lys's, and he smiled in return.

Okay, maybe it wasn't just idle curiosity I was feeling.

I swallowed heavily, and Kymari's gaze swung back on me.

Clara reached out again, placing her hand on Lys's forearm, and suddenly, the world was spinning. Bile crept up my throat as I broke out in a sweat, despite the chill from the rain that still drizzled around us.

"What's happening?" Kymari pressed the back of her hand to my forehead. "Are you — is this catching a cold? Poseidon, we are so unprepared for handling land-based water events."

"No, no, it's nothing like that, I just need a minute to —" I took a shuddering breath, not even sure how to end that sentence, but voices reached us coming around the corner of the building, so I didn't have to.

"I haven't found any evidence of that being possible in the literature," I recognized Petra's voice right before she rounded the corner with Morgaine and Nimue.

"But if you *did*, you would do it?" Nimue asked, sharing a mischievous smile with Morgaine behind Petra's back.

Petra tilted her head in thought. "Potentially."

"Ah, ladies," Morgaine said as she spotted us. "And who are we hiding from this afternoon?"

"No one," I said in the same breath as Kymari muttered, "Two-timing players," to which I shot her a sharp look.

Morgaine, Petra, and Nimue all looked past us to the tea shop window, the three females quickly putting the pieces together as their eyes widened, spying Lys inside with Clara.

"It's not what it looks like," I said hurriedly, choking over my own words. It was ridiculous of me to be getting so emotional, I knew that; but it did help our whole cover-story, so I went with it.

Morgaine's eyes softened, and she held a hand out to me. "Well, we're down a few people for movie night, if you two would like to join us?" She glanced back at Lys fleetingly, then to me. "Nothing like a good old-fashioned distraction sometimes, dear."

"Movie *night*?" Kymari asked, checking the time. "It's 3 in the afternoon."

"It's *Lord of the Rings* marathon day," Petra announced matter-of-factly, as though everyone should have known that. "We meant to start earlier, until Orion had the audacity to interrupt those plans."

Kymari's eyes lit up. "Well, why didn't you say so." She tugged my hand, and I felt myself giving in. Not that I had a good reason not to join them, anyway.

"All right, Aragorn it is." I smiled, and fell into step beside Morgaine as we crossed the street over to her magenta and teal house. "Thanks."

She linked her arm through mine, patting my hand. "It'll all work out, dear. Just wait and see."

"I'm not saying Faramir is *better* than Aragorn." Nimue waved a piece of popcorn emphatically, a few glasses of demon-wine and a movie-and-a-half later. "I'm just saying he's under-rated."

"If anyone is under-rated, it's Boromir," Petra cut in. "Faramir gets his redemption. He gets to live a happy life with Eowyn. Boromir has his death battle, and that's it. But he was carrying the weight of his father's expectations for *years*, and just doing his best for his people."

Kymari shot a look at me, and I sighed, taking a long sip of the stiffest paloma I'd ever had. Morgaine was known for her drinks, having taught Blaze everything he knew, but Poseidon, this drink had a lot of tequila in it.

Biting her lip, Kymari turned to Morgaine. "What do you think, Mo? If you had to choose — and Aragorn is off the table — who do you go for?"

"Oh, my dear," Morgaine chuckled lightly. "I *never* choose. This one time in Rio de Janeiro, I ended up with four—"

"*Mother,*" Nimue said as she choked on her popcorn, then shook her head. "I'll take Things I Don't Need to Know About My Mother for $500, Trebec."

"Need another, dear?" Morgaine asked, nodding to my glass, which I had apparently finished. However, with the way my head was already swimming, I thought I'd better take over my own drink making.

"I can grab it," I said, standing on slightly shaky feet. "Anyone else need a refill?"

Kymari's empty glass shot in the air, and Nimue held up the empty popcorn bowl.

"I'll help," Petra said, grabbing the bowl as I took Kymari's glass, and we made our way to the kitchen.

Petra threw a cup of kernels into Morgaine's old-fashioned popcorn maker like she did this all the time, and I watched her out of the corner of my eye as I made another round for Kymari and myself, my own drink light on the alcohol this round.

Crossing to the fridge, Petra helped herself to a cider, popping the tab and leaning back against the counter as she waited for the popcorn.

She seemed so at ease here. And yet, she was utterly new to the town — newer even than I was. But she'd been accepted, made a home here for herself — despite being a human.

"Out with it," she said, raising a red eyebrow at me as she took another sip of her drink.

"What?"

"I can hear you thinking from here. Whatever it is, just ask."

I blinked at her bluntness, and took a sip of my mostly-seltzer drink. "How was it for you — moving here, finding out about all this, getting involved with a —"

"— infuriating basket case?"

"— demon?"

She smirked, lifting a shoulder, as popcorn started pelting into the bowl, the smell filling the kitchen. "It was definitely the last thing I expected when I came up here. Not something I'd planned on at all, least of all falling for a guy — *male* — like Blaze."

"You guys are *nothing* alike," I blurted, the words gone before my brain had even considered them. I winced, but Petra chuckled.

"True." The popcorn slowed down, and she started scooping it into the bowl as it finished. "I think that's why it works, though. If I was with someone like myself, we'd probably kill each other. At least with Blaze, even if I try to kill him, he'll survive it."

I laughed, and her eyes crinkled in amusement, but I considered her words as we turned to head back to the living room.

I had to admit, if I was with someone too similar to myself, we probably would try to murder each other. Was that why Lys and I could work? Because we were so different?

I shook my head, feeling stupid for even thinking it. Despite his flirty texts today — *probably just a distraction from dealing with Orion* — none of this was real. I had to keep that in mind.

"What were you three talking about when you ran into us — what would you consider?" I asked, suddenly remembering the conversation that had been interrupted earlier.

"Oh, that. They want me to try linking magic with Blaze," she said nonchalantly, but I knew that tone well enough — recognized it as one I adopted regularly myself — to know she was trying to cover up stronger feelings. "But there's no evidence that trying to share magic with a human would work. Not yet, anyway."

We were passing Morgaines's back door on our way

back to the living room when it popped open, Devanna coming through under a black umbrella. She popped it into the coat rack by the door, stomping the water off her boots.

"You're joining for movie night?" Petra asked, as Dev spotted me behind her, hanging up her dripping coat.

"Hello, it's *Aragorn*," Dev scoffed, as though that answered everything. "I didn't miss it, did I? It took me forever to get that damn paint off my hands."

"*It?* No. Fear not," Petra laughed.

"Thank the Goddess." Dev brushed past me into the kitchen, presumably to get herself a drink, and I followed Petra back to the living room.

"*It?*" I asked, feeling stupid for not knowing what they were talking about.

Nimue and Kymari snickered as I took my seat up again.

"You'll know it when you see it," Nimue offered, eyes twinkling knowingly.

I turned to Kymari. "*You* know what it is?"

Kymari laughed. "Of course."

Dev joined us a minute later, offering a stiff greeting to Morgaine, and took a seat on the sofa, tucking her legs underneath her.

Ruby came down a little while later, saying she'd been on a video call with her sister back in Colorado, and helped herself to popcorn, sitting on a cushion on the floor.

Being surrounded by all these ladies made me feel both homesick for my sisters and strangely comforted. Even though I was only close with Kymari, Ruby reminded me so much of Riona, I knew they'd be fast friends. Nimue had never been anything but kind to me, and I'd gotten to know Petra a little from how much time she spent in the bar. Dev, despite being the least approachable, I knew was as loyal to her friends as I was, a quality I could respect. And being around Morgaine always felt like being around the mother I no longer had.

Taking a breath, I settled back into the couch, choosing to focus on comfort rather than stress for once. Maybe that was the tequila helping, too, but I leaned into it.

Towards the middle of the movie, Nimue, Dev, and Kymari were practically vibrating with anticipation, so I figured we were getting closer to whatever *it* was.

Morgaine's front door opened and closed softly, footsteps coming down the hall, and I turned to see Orion standing in the doorway, his wings filling the space and his expression only slightly surprised to see so many people crammed into the small living room.

"I came to bring your bracelet back. You dropped it while we were out reinforcing the glamour," he said by way of explanation, pulling it out of his pocket.

"Oh, how silly of me!" Morgaine exclaimed, popping up out of her seat to take it from him. "Yes, I was using the crystals in it to help power the spell work. Thank you so much for bringing it back."

I couldn't help but notice the way Dev turned her body, like she was actively *not* acknowledging Orion's presence, keeping her gaze locked on the tiny box screen.

Morgaine took her seat again as Orion cleared his throat. "I saw you made some progress out there, Devanna," he said.

She flapped her hand in his direction. "Shh, this is it. No speaking."

Orion snapped his mouth shut, his lips pressing into a thin line, as we all watched the screen.

With dramatic flourish, Viggo Mortensen pushed open the doors to Theoden's hall, sweaty hair swaying, swagger dripping off him in spades. Dev, Nimue, and Kymari all gave appreciative sounds, and Ruby and Petra chuckled at them.

The moment passed, and Dev sat back on her chair again. "Now *that* is a real male," she said, half to herself, but loud enough for everyone to hear. "A man not afraid to get a little dirty."

Kymari and Nimue *mhm*'ed in approval, and Orion looked like his jaw was about to crack with how tight he clenched it.

Without a word, he glanced at Morgaine, then hastily retreated through the house. Morgaine's gaze tried to bore a hole through the back of Dev's blue hair, but she paid her no mind.

Suddenly, I realized there was quite a lot going on abovewater I'd never noticed, despite how long I'd been working in the bar.

Between the *Two Towers* and *Return of the King*, Ruby took off, worn out from working her magic earlier, and headed to bed early. Morgaine and Petra popped into the kitchen to throw some pizzas in the oven, and Nimue and Dev turned their sights on me.

"So," said Nimue, drawing out the word. "Trying to hook Lysander?"

I groaned. "Not you too with the fish puns."

Kymari and Dev snickered.

"As long as you never mention his dick in any capacity," Dev said, leaning back in her chair, "He's practically a brother to me. Spill the deets. I need to know how this came about."

Heat flared in my cheeks as I covered my face in embarrassment, trying to think through the story Lys and I had told the others.

"She's had a crush on Lys for *at least* a decade," Kymari said, and my head shot up, mouth gaping in horror as I looked at my best friend.

Dev's eyes lit up as she leaned towards Kymari. "Go on."

"I don't know the whole story as she kept all of it a secret until a week ago," Kymari said, and hurt flashed through me once more, feeling the bitterness of her words even if she hadn't intended them. "But, I have to say, they *are* incredibly cute together. I've almost puked on multiple occasions."

"*You're* one to talk," I said, pointing a finger at her. "I heard exactly what happened last night."

"Wait, what happened last night?" Petra said as she came back in with a fresh bowl of popcorn. "What did I miss?"

"That you're six doors down from Pound Town, I guess," Dev said, grabbing a handful of popcorn. "These girls are gettin' it."

"What's Pound Town?" Morgaine asked as she pranced through the hallway right as the movie began. "And how do I get there? Sounds lovely."

"Mom," Nimue said, rubbing her forehead. "Please. No."

"What?" Morgaine said as she pulled her hot pink floral kimono around her. "Just because I'm old doesn't mean I don't have needs to be met, Nimue."

"I would rather die than have this conversation," Nimue said, to which Petra laughed. "Again."

"I'll send you some links, Mo," Dev offered casually, and Nimue choked again. "There's nothing a man can do that the right device can't do better."

"Please just start the movie so we can get to Mo's no talking rule," Nimue said, sliding down the couch and onto the floor as if she could disappear. "This might be worse than Romp 'n' Romance month."

"Mm, yes, *Her Five Mates*. What a delightful book that was. Gave me so many feelings" Morgaine said as the movie began. "Now girls, quiet. No more talking. Except you, Maisie. You can tell us all about Lysander. Such a lovely young man."

I shoveled popcorn in my mouth, pointing at the screen as an excuse to say nothing more even as Morgaine eyed me with a smile.

Chapter Twenty-Eight

LYSANDER

I STAYED while Nadir closed Immortali-Tea, following him to Scallywags. The sign said closed on the door, but I could see four tables full of patrons inside.

"Is there something going on tonight I didn't know about?" I asked Nadir as he pulled open the door to the bar. With my band's travel schedule, I didn't participate in a lot of events at Scallywags.

"Game night," Nadir said with a mischievous grin that told me there was more to it than a simple game night, but that was to be expected in Deadlights Cove.

"Gentlemen," Blaze said, scanning the group of mostly males congregated in the bar. "And lady. Sorry, Peg. Gentlepeople? What's the correct term for Guys' Night when it's not only guys?"

"Thursday?" Julian said, and the wolves around him laughed. I didn't know the local pack Second well, but Nadir pushed me towards where Kit sat at a table with Ryker. The dragon looked up as I pulled a seat back, his green eyes boring holes in my head. As always, the male was dressed in head-to-toe black, his blond hair grown back in and tied in a knot on the top of his head. Combined with the tattoos covering all available skin but his face and his imposing beard, Ryker looked every bit the Viking dragon shifter he was.

"Good to see you, Ryker." I smiled, resting my hands on the table. Ryker said nothing, only grunted in response. Looked like happily-in-love-with-Selene Ryker was just as surly as pre-Selene Ryker. To his left sat a male I didn't know with slightly shaggy dark brown hair and piercing hazel eyes, nearly as large as Ryker himself.

Kit pointed at the newcomer, then me. "West Larkin, wolf pack Alpha from Timber Creek, Colorado, meet Lysander Theroux, local witchboy extraordinaire."

"Timber Creek?" I repeated as I shook his hand, noticing the geometric pack tattoos on his forearms extended up beneath his dark green tee. Alpha power oozed off the man, the strongest blue aura I'd ever seen. A caretaker. I liked him already. "Do you know Ruby?"

"Of course," West nodded. "I sent her here to Morgaine."

"Oh, great," I said, pausing momentarily to wonder why a wolf Alpha was sending witches *anywhere*, but didn't have time to ask. As I took my seat, I noticed Dillon standing at the bar to my left, chatting with none other than Owen Kinkaid. I glared at the back of my friend's head, magic sizzling at my fingertips as I thought back over my mother's words from earlier.

Even if Owen *had* spent the day with Maisie, it didn't mean what my mother implied. My relationship with Maisie may have started out fake, but my meeting with Clara made me realize my feelings for Maisie weren't. Our contract extended until after the Summit, and then she could choose who she wanted — even Owen, if that's what she decided — but I wanted her to choose me.

As soon as the thought entered my brain, I squashed it.

Not Owen. *Anyone* but Owen.

I pulled my phone out under the table to check my messages. Still no word back from Maisie.

"Tonight we'll be playing Twisty Bobcat Pretzel," Blaze said, taking a sip out of his demon wine where he stood at the table on the right side of the room, and I tried not to bore a hole through the back of Owen's stupidly perfect blond hair.

"Twisty Bobcat Pretzel?" I whispered to Nadir, confused by the name, but he waved a hand to silence me.

"We have a few new faces here tonight, so here's my advice: Be like Lucy Kelson. Improvise, adapt, overcome." Blaze shrugged at our confusion. "The best way to learn it is to play. The only thing I can tell you is if you lose a point, you're subject to truth or dare by the person who catches you."

Caedmon chuckled, rubbing his hands together. "I've been dreaming of winning a secret from Orion for *years*. It's a shame he didn't show up."

"It's true," Val said at his side, leaning in and kissing his partner on the cheek. "So curious, my lover is. Always wanting to learn new things."

"Oh, what *kind* of things?" Peg asked from Caedmon's other side, the purple-haired ancient witch from the Historical Society clueless to the innuendo.

"Well, he's always wondered about the correlation between wingspan and—"

"*OH*-kay," Blaze said loudly over the crowd as every other patron in the bar looked anywhere but the quirky trio at the front of the room. "Have fun, gents, er, residents? No. I don't know. All of you. May the best supe win."

Suddenly, everyone in the room stood, so I followed suit. Most of the locals kept one hand on the table, so I did too, despite having no idea what was happening.

"Aaaaand three, two, one — GREEN!"

In a flurry of motion, everyone shot up from their seats, running around the bar in utter chaos, though to what end, I didn't know.

"Ha! Lysander's down a point already!" Peg shouted from where she stood on a booth in the corner, hand pressed to the green lampshade above her. "Truth or dare, Lys?"

Kit caught my eye from where he stood with a hand on West's green t-shirted shoulder, shaking his head in warning.

"Um — truth?"

"What position did you lose your virginity in?"

Ryker coughed where he stood to my right with his hand on a bottle of Tanqueray gin, and I turned wide eyes on Blaze, who shrugged. "Should have followed the rules. Now you have to answer."

"Or what?"

"Well, by participating, you agreed to a non-verbal contract. You have to abide by the truth or dare rules of the game. Anyone who doesn't forfeits their magical abilities for a week. Or you can kiss the person whose truth-or-dare you shirked, whichever you choose."

"What'll it be, Lysy darling?" Peg cooed from her corner, fluttering her eyelashes at me.

"Fucking hell," I muttered under my breath, earning chuckles from a few of the guys around me. "Fine. Reverse cowgirl."

Peg gave an *Ooooh* of intrigue, fanning herself, while several others called out, "Yeah right!" and "Fat chance, you liar."

"ALLEGATIONS!" Blaze shouted, and suddenly, everyone was leaping off the floor. Not wanting to be caught out again, I followed suit quickly, jumping onto a chair. "When someone's truth is under investigation, the floor is lava until the verdict. Good job this time, Lys."

"Not so good, West." Kit pointed at West's feet, clearly in the "lava," and West swore under his breath.

"One at a time, gents. And Peg. Back to Lys's so-called truth." Blaze pointed at me again with flourish.

I crossed my arms. "It's true."

"Oho, Lys, no no." Blaze reappeared on the chair right beside me, shocking me into nearly tumbling off my chair, and patted me on the shoulder. "Explain yourself. It's storytime."

Everyone stared at me, clearly waiting for the whole sordid tale. I rolled my eyes. "We were at a drive-in movie, all right?" I threw my hands up. "It was the best way for both of us to still see the screen and not alert everyone around us as to what we were doing."

"How charming," Owen said, and I ground my teeth together.

"Unfortunately, I can testify this is true," Dillon said

from where he stood on the bar behind me. "Lys wasn't as subtle as he thought he was."

The room collectively cringed, except Peg who stood on the chair across from me, biting her lower lip.

"Hmm." Blaze narrowed his eyes at me before flickering back to his previous spot across the room. "Well? All who believe this story to be true, say *Aye*." Everyone in the room spoke up even as several shook their heads, staring at me. "The Ayes have spoken. Or something like that. All right, now West! You have been weighed and found wanting. What'll it be? Truth or dare?"

"Truth."

"Most embarrassing shift," Kit supplied without missing a beat, and all the shifters in the room snickered. Apparently, a common question for them.

West sighed, raking fingers through his hair while he thought. "Well, like it probably was for most of you assholes, it was when I was out with a young lady a little too close to a full moon. I tried to climb through her window, caught a scent of her cucumber melon lotion or whatever it was, and fuck. Got way too excited. Wolfed out halfway through the window, she screamed, I got stuck. Her dad came charging in with a broom, then bashed me over the head. Fell backwards out the window — shifted *back*, now I was naked, obviously. At this point her entire cul-de-sac had woken up and watched me run into the woods, holding my junk." West cleared his throat and took a long swig of beer. "Needless to say, I never spoke to that girl again. Had to pretend I couldn't see her sitting next to me the whole rest of 8th grade."

"That was beautiful," Blaze grinned. "No challenges on that truth? Going once? Twice? Nope — THREE!"

All at once, everyone jumped down from their spots, rushing around the room. I had no idea what I was supposed to do, but grabbed the table in one hand, touching someone's beer glass as it sloshed over the lip, and a salt shaker in the other.

"Ryker!" Caedmon cried out, his whole body shaking with excitement like a chihuahua. "Truth or dare!"

I looked at the dragon shifter holding two limes, a deep set frown on his face. "Truth."

"Really? No more dares?" Julian said with a knowing smirk. "Last time was so fun."

"Ryker is banned from dares," Blaze said, chopping his hand through the air.

Caedmon's eyes bounced between Blaze and Ryker, and I was just as curious as him. "Okay, why are you banned from dares?"

Ryker raised a brow. "Is that your question?"

Caedmon nodded, then lifted his shoulders as he smiled.

"The last time I played this, Blaze dared me to shift and take him for a ride over the ocean, which I did."

"You carried me in your *talons*, repeatedly dunking me into the ocean like the worst parasailing experience known to mankind," Blaze said with a deadpan expression I'd never seen on the male.

"That's on you for not being more specific." Ryker shrugged.

Blaze sighed. "Moving on. SANDRA BULLOCK."

At this point, I was starting to catch on as I yelled out *"WHILE YOU WERE SLEEPING!"*

"Nox didn't have one!" Casey, one of the fox-shifters in Kit's skulk, called out, pointing at the young demon who glared back at him. "Truth or dare, Noxy?"

"Dare."

"Hmm." Casey tapped a finger against his chin, then beckoned Nox over to whisper something in his ear.

"You're trying to get me murdered, aren't you?" Nox muttered, a second before he flickered out.

Long moments passed while we all waited to see what would happen next, but Casey wasn't talking, merely looking deviously pleased with himself about whatever he'd dared Nox to do.

"What's that sound?" Kit asked after another minute, and eventually, I heard a deep roar coming closer.

Suddenly, Ryker's eyes turned to slits, shooting daggers first at Casey, who was outright cackling, then to the window.

I watched as Nox rode by on Ryker's motorcycle a minute later. Ryker tore out of the bar after him as Nox circled the square before parking in front of Scallywags.

"How the fuck did you get through my security? Into the garage?" Ryker growled at him, but we could all hear in the bar.

Nox shrugged. "Secrets of the —" but his words cut off with a yelp as Ryker lifted him by the front of his shirt.

"Oh Ryker!" Blaze sing-songed, magically pushing the front door open. Both males swung their gazes towards Blaze, even though Ryker didn't drop Nox. "You left the building. Truth or — well, truth! What movie last made you cry?"

Smoke curled as it left Ryker's nose, his green gaze

furious as he threw Nox back inside. "Why the fuck do I ever agree to play this game?"

"That's not a movie," Val said, then cowered as Ryker swung his attention to him on his way back inside.

"*How to Train Your Dragon*. Brought back a lot of memories. If I ever hear this repeated, I will char all of you so thoroughly, not even your teeth will remain to tell the tale of what happened."

"And the first bonus point goes to Casey for tricking Ryker through Nox's dare, which means —"

There was a chorus of "DRINK", and everyone started chugging whatever beverage was in their hand. I had a feeling I knew how this would end, so I made sure I was *not* the last to finish my beer.

"Sayana!" Several of the wolves pointed at Kit, who'd had to run around the table to make it back to his drink to down it, and had been the last to finish.

"Shit. Dare," he muttered, and the guys who had caught him huddled up to brainstorm their challenge. After a few moments, they turned on him with a smirk.

"We dare you," Julian began, "to steal Orion's Summit dinner seating chart."

Calls of *Ooooooh* rang around the bar, and a few of us glanced out the window to see if Orion's office light was still on, indicating he was still hard at work. Indeed, it was.

Kit shot Julian a dark look filled with the promise of retribution and started for the door, stripping out of his clothes on the way to whistles and catcalls, leaving his boxers on.

"Look away, Peg. I'm a married male," he called over his shoulder, and Peg tittered as he let the door swing shut behind him. Then a large red fox was shooting across the square, making for Town Hall.

"No way he gets it," Casey commented.

"Oh yeah? Ten bucks says he does," Nadir said, elbowing him.

Casey laughed and shook his head. "Keep your money, dude."

Everyone crowded the front window, holding our breaths as we watched a blur of red slip through the front doors of Town Hall.

Heartbeats later, Orion's office window slid open, nudged by a fox snout, and Kit shot out of his window, white paper unmistakably clenched between his teeth. A cheer went up in the bar as Kit raced across the square, then a crack of lightning and thunder boomed overhead.

"Oh, shit," Julian laughed as Orion flew out of his office window. "This is even better than I thought."

A streak of lightning shot across the square, followed by a strangled shriek as all Kit's fur stood on end, sending the paper flying out of his mouth. He collapsed to the ground in a smoking lump.

The wolves were laughing so hard they couldn't breathe, and Orion turned to the bar, immediately seeing us pressed up against the glass. He pointed an accusatory finger at all of us, as though to say *I see you and I know exactly what this is about and all of you will be held accountable*, before marching back into Town Hall.

"Someday," Caedmon murmured softly, watching Orion disappear back into the building. "Someday, we will blackmail him into playing this game."

Val patted his shoulder. "Of course we will, dear."

Kit slowly pushed himself up, still smoldering slightly, fur singed at the ends, and limped back to the bar. There was a pause when he made it just outside the door, and when he opened it, back in his boxers and in human form again, he still looked dazed, hair sticking up in all directions, blinking to try to focus his eyes.

"Fuck, Orion does not kid around about seating charts," he coughed, running a hand through his hair to try to get it to lay normally again, but it was a lost cause.

"BEANIE BABIES!"

I paused, my mind blank as people called out "Princess Diana!", "Patti!", "Seaweed!", and other words or names I had no idea what they meant.

"Lysander," Owen said with a cocky grin, and all eyes swung to me. "You didn't say the name of a Beanie Baby."

Anger seethed in my veins as I looked at the cocky son of a bitch with his stupid accent, hating that it was him who called me out for something so stupid. The room was silent as I fought to control my temper while Owen stood at the bar, tapping his fingers on the wood. "Do you love her?" he asked, and my blood ran cold.

"What?"

Owen's black eyes met mine. "I'm collecting my winnings, Lysander. Are you in love with Maisie?"

Dillon stared at me wide-eyed as I fought to breathe.

"He didn't choose a truth or dare," Dillon said, coming to my rescue. I'd always known Dillon was my best friend, but this moment solidified it.

"Yes," I nodded, struggling to hold in the relieved sigh. "I did. And I choose dare."

"Fine," Owen said, standing to put on his blazer, all

calm confidence while he rocked my world to its very core. The entire bar was silent as everyone watched our exchange, sensing the bigger meaning behind the words even if they didn't know the truth of it all. As far as I knew, no one else knew that Owen was to be engaged to Maisie. "I dare you to answer my question. Are you in love with Maisie, my betrothed?"

This time, when he asked, magic laced the question and I had no choice but to answer. My ears rang as blood raced through my body, overwhelmed by the *yes* that clambered through my brain.

And fuck, when had that happened?

But it had, hadn't it?

Somewhere along the line, probably about the time Maisie stood toe-to-toe with my mother, I'd fallen for her. And I'd fallen *hard*.

But even if I loved her, was choosing me truly what was best for Maisie? She missed her family desperately, and was born to be the leader and defender of her people. By choosing me, would she have to give that all up?

That wasn't the question Owen had asked though. He'd asked if I loved her, and the answer was yes.

I did.

I opened my mouth to answer as Ryker's phone buzzed on the table. He pulled it towards him when Blaze's went off too, then mine and everyone else's in the bar just as the regular buzzing turned into the *Emergency Alert* alarm instead.

I slipped my phone out of my pocket, expecting it to be a weather warning or an amber alert, but my eyebrows shot up when I read the screen.

PARANORMAL REGULATIONS AND
INTERSPECIES COUNCIL

EMERGENCY NOTICE: At 8:21 this evening,
8 inmates in the Iron Keep broke out of their
cells. They escaped to Earth and should be
considered a threat. If you see any of them,
report it immediately to your nearest
governing angel and vacate the area. Inmate
photos to follow.

"Holy shit," Blaze breathed.

Photos started coming in, and the entire bar seemed to hold its breath as we waited to see who had escaped, but there were only three names I recognized.

Errakal, demon-witch.

Nergal, demon.

Inessa, sea nymph.

"How," Blaze started, looking between his phone and Ryker in bewilderment. "How could this happen? Only —"

Ryker growled low in his throat. "Only angels can move between realms."

"There's an angel helping them, then," Owen said, and Ryker nodded.

"This has to be why Kal was so calm about getting arrested. He'd been planning this all along."

"Do you think they'll come here?" Kit asked, concern written all over his face, and for good reason. The last time Kal had showed his face in town, his sister Lily had been kidnapped.

Ryker looked around the room, tension ratcheting up by the second. "Until we know otherwise, anything is possible."

Ryker's phone rang and he stepped towards the door, phone to his ear. I sat, stunned by both my earth-shattering realization of moments before and the catastrophic news of the escaped prisoners.

"I'm going to find Petra," Blaze said, ushering everyone towards the door. "Out. Out!"

I grabbed my stuff, and rushed from the building with the others, everyone desperate to find our loved ones, and I wasn't even surprised to realize that for me, that now included Maisie.

Chapter Twenty-Nine

MAISIE

MY PHONE BUZZED in my pocket, but I ignored it like I had all day. As everyone else's went off, I looked to Kymari who pulled hers out.

"Maisie," she gasped, standing and moving to where I sat on the couch, popcorn in hand. With one look at Kymari's startled expression, I dropped the popcorn back in the bowl and wiped my hands on my jeans. Gasps and exclamations of shock came from the others as well as they read their messages.

"What's wrong?"

"Inessa escaped."

My stomach lurched, but I shook my head, wondering if I'd misheard her. "That's… that's not possible. She's been in the Iron Keep for a decade."

"Yeah, well, not anymore."

"Oh dear," Morgaine said, hand placed delicately on her chest. "Errakal and Nergal. Nimue, go find Blaze please. News of his father and brother on the loose is more than a little alarming."

Nimue flickered out of the room, gone in an instant as Dev and Morgaine spoke quietly.

"Who is Inessa?" Petra asked from my side as I pulled my phone out to read the alerts. Bile rose in my throat as I scrolled through the pictures of the escaped convicts. Rather than give in to panic, I stood, grabbed Kymari's arm, and moved to the door.

"Ladies, this has been a lovely night, but I have to go."

Someone said something in return, but I didn't hear it. It didn't matter anyway. I had bigger issues right now.

Kymari and I ran through the rain towards the pier, an unspoken draw to the ocean we were sworn to protect pulling us home.

Blaze's brother and father had just escaped the Iron Keep, and were now back out in the world. In human terms, considering them armed and dangerous would have been just the tip of the iceberg.

But I had to get home. *Immediately.*

It didn't matter that I had been banished. If Inessa was on the loose, she'd surely come for my father. Ronan needed to know about Inessa's breakout, and he needed to know *now.*

Ronan had a phone — Orion had insisted when he'd been installed in the Cove — but he rarely turned it on. Ronan didn't like to bother with abovewater business unless absolutely necessary.

Well, now it was damn well necessary.

"What's the plan?" Kymari said as we ran towards the water.

"We have to warn my family."

"But Ronan's magic," Kymari said as I stripped out of my clothes on the pier, throwing them to the dock. In a flash, I dove and shifted, kicking down to the city like my life depended on it despite Ronan's magic tugging me back towards the surface.

Like *all* our lives did.

The magic that had banished me from the sea ached, my chest too tight as I fought against it. Frustration warred in me as I shrieked, the sound nothing more than bubbles in the water, but magic exploded out from my skin in a pulse like I'd never felt before. Suddenly, the force pushing me back stopped, and I swam faster, not pausing long enough to wonder what had changed.

Crunamar City came into view ahead of me, soft light glowing inside the hundreds of glass bubbles hooked together to encase the many homes and buildings within. I bypassed the closest entrance, headed towards the center where the landing pad was for the royal household.

I burst through the magic into the landing pad, pulled on one of the robes kept there, Kymari at my heels as I ran barefoot through the tunnels to Ronan's office, ignoring anyone trying to get my attention.

His office door banged open as we rushed through it, scanning the space frantically, until I saw him in the back alcove. Ronan had a cut-out in the floor allowing access to the ocean, and he sat at the edge, feet dangling into the water, as he mended a net. It wasn't something he needed to do, of course — he had any number of people to do this kind of work for him — but it was a task that had been passed down through the royal family for generations, a therapeutic duty we did for our people. We could infuse them with stronger magic due to our lineage, so they would be stronger and increase their catch.

"Pearl?" His brows furrowed as he took me in, the wet footprints I left as I came forward. "How did you —"

"Dad," I choked, falling to my knees beside him. "She's out. Inessa is out. Do you have your phone? You need to check it. She escaped the Iron Keep and is loose. A whole bunch of them escaped in a big jailbreak. They must have an angel on the inside, because they made it out of the Keep and back to Earth."

Ronan set down the net, his expression troubled but not shifting to the frenzied alarm that it should have.

Did he not understand what I was saying?

Did he not believe me?

"How are you here after I banished you?" He stood, pulling me to my feet as well, then made his way over to his desk. In the second drawer, he shuffled things around until he found the phone, clicking to turn it on and then meeting my eyes again as he waited for it to start.

I swallowed. *That* was what he chose to focus on? "We'll talk about that later," I said. I winced at the immediate anger that rose to Ronan's face, but pushed on. "Just… just check your phone." I licked my lips, my hands still shaking. Had they ever stopped? "It's unheard of, right? How could they escape? How could *she* —"

Ronan held up a hand, his phone now fully on, as he read through the alerts that had come in, his features hardening further every minute. Tossing a glare my way that told me we weren't done with this conversation, he buzzed the intercom on his desk.

"Xuma, my office, now."

Ronan leaned over his desk, readying to turn his attention back on me, and tension coiled in the air as I braced for his temper.

"Explain to me how you two are here." His voice was low and deadly.

I took a step closer. "I saw the alert, and I couldn't think about anything but being here, protecting you. Protecting our people."

"Do you understand what you've done, Maisie?" Ronan said, crouching to drop a hand into the water behind him. He sighed heavily, his eyes closing as a look of defeat crashed down over him that I'd never seen before.

I shook my head, not understanding where he was going with this. "I was just—"

"You removed my magic from our city, Maisie." Ronan's jaw worked as he stood once more. "When it pushed you back, you shattered it."

"No," I shook my head, not believing the words he said. "No, I'm not powerful enough for that. I just needed to get here to warn you."

"Yes, Maisie," Ronan said, his dark blue eyes meeting mine. "You overpowered my magic, and blew it apart. We're now not only vulnerable to Inessa, but to *everyone*, humans included."

I sucked in a breath, stepping back until I bumped into Kymari.

"If you are here, then she is no longer banished from Crunamar City," Ronan said, his chin dipping slightly as resignation set in.

I opened my mouth, then closed it again, trying to think

of anything to say. Just then, the door to my father's office crashed open again and Xuma stormed in.

"Sir, the magic is down," Xuma said, his eyes flicking to where Kymari and I stood. "The city is in chaos."

I turned back to my father, wide-eyed. "I can fix it. I can—"

Ronan held up a hand, silencing me. "I think you've done enough. Leave my city, Maisie."

"But—"

"*I said go,*" Ronan said, his voice full of so much power, I couldn't believe I'd somehow overpowered his magical protection.

Kymari's hand settled on my elbow, pulling me back the way we'd come. "Let's go."

"I can't *leave* them," I said, grinding my teeth together, anger keeping the gut-wrenching heartache at bay. "We need to be here, to protect our people."

Saoirse turned the corner as Kymari dragged me backwards from my father's office, stopping suddenly when she saw us. "What's going on?"

I pulled my sister into my arms, squeezing her tight. "I fucked up so bad, Saoirse."

Her hands came up, touching down on my arms lightly as she pulled me away to see my face. "What did you do?"

"Inessa is out. Ronan isn't thinking straight. He never is when she's involved, not since she murdered Mom. I need to be here, to protect *you*, not back ashore. He says I overpowered his magic over the city and brought down the protections around the city. If that's true, then I need to be *here*, now more than ever."

Saoirse studied me, then looked to Kymari with a nod. "Go. I'll see what I can do. Keep your phone on."

Kymari and I surfaced back at the pier, pulled ourselves out of the water, and grabbed at the rain-soaked clothes we'd left behind.

"Talk to me, Maisie," Kymari said, her voice barely above a whisper as she pulled her wet braids out from the neck of her shirt. "You're hurting."

"I'm fine," I said, hearing how clipped the words were, not even a little convincing.

"She won't attack today," Kymari said as I stormed down the pier. "They have time to fix it, to prepare. Your father is an excellent ruler and has mine at his side. This is what he's good at."

"Right," I laughed bitterly. "Everyone is *much* better with him at the helm. All I do is mess shit up. That's what *I'm* good at. Maybe this banishment was a good idea. Maybe I'm better off far, far away from my people."

Kymari grabbed my arm, yanking me to a stop. "Stop it. Right now. You know that's not true."

"Let go, Kymari," I said through clenched teeth.

"Stop reacting emotionally and be a leader."

"I don't need your pep talk right now."

"Good, because I don't have a pep talk for you. You fucked up, big time. If you'd trusted me and told me about your life, maybe some of this could have been avoided. We could have figured some of this shit out together."

"I don't need you."

Instantly, Kymari's hand dropped from my arm as if I'd burned her with my words. "You're right. You don't need me."

Kymari stepped back, and I turned, watching as she moved back towards the water. "Kymari, wait."

"No, Maisie." Kymari shook her head. "You said it. You don't need me. I'm only here because I got caught helping *you* get out of trouble you brought on yourself. I thought we knew everything about each other, thought we had each other's backs all the time, but you have a whole life here I'm not a part of, that you *chose* not to share with me. *You* don't need me, but our people do. I'm better off with them, cleaning up your messes. After all, that's what I'm best at, right?"

Tears gathered in my eyes as she spun, turning her back on me. Without even shedding her clothes, Kymari dove into the water, a shark fin protruding the water seconds later, and then was gone.

"Maze?" Lys's voice cut through my haze, and I turned to see him walking towards me from Scallywags, umbrella held against the rain. He stepped up to my side until the umbrella covered me too, then noticed the tears that I refused to let fall. "What happened? Are you okay?"

Lys wrapped his free arm around me, pulling my face into his chest as his warmth surrounded me, not caring about my drenched clothes. I stood frozen, unable to function as I watched the waves crash against the pier, only the white crests visible in the dark.

"No, Lys," I said, letting my hands circle his waist as he kissed the top of my head and I closed my eyes. "I'm not okay."

He said nothing for several beats, hugging me to his chest. But the comfort his embrace offered me soaked into my skin, warming me despite the chill from the storm. Why did it feel so good to be in his arms? To feel safe, for just this moment, knowing Lys was on my side?

The sound of footsteps drawing near made me open my eyes.

"Owen," I said, dropping my hands from Lys's waist, but Lys didn't let go of me. Instead, he spun us slightly so he could see Owen as well.

"Lysander. Maisie," Owen said with a nod. "Everyone all right in light of the news?"

"Yeah," I answered, not exactly sure what else to say. Lys pulled his arms around me tighter, holding me to his chest. Though I hadn't answered Owen's question earlier today about Lys and I, the way his black eyes roved over us probably was enough of an answer. And yet, I didn't push Lys's arms off of me, even though I was positive he'd let go if I asked.

"Glad to hear it."

"Hey, Owen," Lys called as Owen turned to leave, hands in his pockets. Owen stopped, and turned back towards us, his head tilted slightly. "For the record? The answer is yes."

"I can see that." He nodded, mouth a grim line.

I looked at Lys, confusion clouding my mind as Owen walked away. "What was that about?"

"Don't worry about it," Lys said, kissing my forehead gently. "Let's go home."

With a silent nod, I let him take my hand in his, leading us down the dark streets and towards his house.

But this wasn't home.

My home was deep underwater, more vulnerable than ever. Everything I'd ever loved was now at risk, a huge target painted on the city, all because of me.

I was quiet most of the night and into the next morning, climbing in bed shortly after we made it back to Lys's house. He must have sensed I needed to be alone, and let me wallow in peace. My mind spun one wild scenario after another, imagining all of the worst possible things that could happen to my family. To my people.

Inessa, destroying our city.

Inessa, poisoning our sea.

Inessa, murdering my sisters like she'd murdered my mother.

And yet, here I was, curled into a ball as I huddled under the blankets. Useless.

The door opened and closed at some point the next day, and Lys perched on the edge of the bed. "I brought you some snacks."

I peeked over the blankets as my stomach grumbled, looking at the basket Lys had brought. An apple sat on top of several bags of chips, cookies, nuts, candy, and two bottles of water. Snatching a bag of Cheetos, I sat up to lean against the headboard, letting the blanket fall in my lap.

"Thank you," I said, licking the dust off my fingers after I'd eaten several. By the third finger, Lys finally pried his eyes from my hand, clearing his throat.

"Of course," he said, now staring intently at the guitars on the wall. "Anything else I can get you?"

"I mean, you've pretty much covered all of the bases here. This is a wide variety. Thanks for the apple."

"Yes, well. An apple a day keeps the anxiety away. Or maybe that's Oreos." He reached into the basket, grabbing the blue wrapper I'd recognize anywhere. "Definitely Oreos."

I chuckled, pulling the bag open and sliding a cookie free. Snapping a bite off, I offered him the other half, holding it in the air between us.

Lys met my eyes briefly before leaning forward and biting it, his lips touching down on my fingers for only a second before he pulled away, crunching down on the cookie.

My heart raced, the tension between us pulling taut. With every kind gesture, every sweet word, every joke used as a distraction, I had a harder time separating what was real and what was fake.

Because his sincerity, his kindness? Those weren't fake. No one was here to witness him taking care of me, and he was the same Lys he always was with me.

"Do you want to talk about what happened with Kymari?" Lys asked after several minutes of silence, aside from chewing, had passed.

"No," I answered immediately, then amended, "Yes?" I sighed, slumping back against the pillows. "Maybe."

Lys chuckled. "As long as you're sure."

"I feel like since the moment my dad mentioned Owen's name, I've been stuck in a riptide, fighting to find the surface before I get pulled under again."

"Shit has really hit the fan lately," Lys said as he moved to pull the chair from the corner and dropped into it, grabbing his guitar. "And I'm sorry about that. For any parts I've caused, or made worse."

I pointed an accusatory finger at him. "If you sing so much as *one* bar of *Yesterday*, we're done, witch boy."

Lys laughed, and started strumming something else I didn't recognize, but the sound was soothing as a backdrop to my rabid pre-hibernating-bear snack binge, so I allowed it.

"There's nothing to be done, and that's the most frustrating part," I said, lying back on my pillow as I shoveled gummy bears into my mouth. "Nobody can make Ronan do *anything*. He's the most stubborn male in existence. And he also happens to hold my entire future in his hands."

The strumming stopped, and I glanced over at Lys.

"Not your *entire* future."

Before I had time to process what he meant, the doorbell rang. Lys broke our stare-off, putting his guitar down to go answer it. A minute later, he returned with a delivery box.

"It's for you."

My dress for the Summit dinner. That Kymari had helped me pick out. My stomach turned over at the thought of seeing her, seeing my father and all my sisters, now that I'd been banished.

I pulled myself out of my pile of comfort food, dusted off my fingers, and perched on the edge of the bed to open it.

"I'll order us some food. Pizza?"

I nodded vaguely, and Lys left the room, sensing that I needed a moment alone.

At the first sight of the beautiful teal taffeta skirt and

matching top, the same color as my scales, my resolve started to shore up.

Lys was right. My father could banish me from the city, but that didn't mean he controlled my whole future. *I* had chosen to come here. I had overpowered his own magic to get back to my city. I was defying him, choosing *not* to go along with the arranged marriage.

Sure, everything was a total disaster at the moment, but it was *my* disaster. Of *my* making.

Nobody could take that from me.

Okay, I'll admit, as far as silver linings go, it's a bit flimsy. I turned over the skirt in my hands, admiring its shine in the light, like beams of sunlight through water. *But even the flimsiest one is still made of silver.*

Allowing myself one final sigh, I stood and walked to the kitchen, determination to fix my mess settling in with each step.

Chapter Thirty

LYSANDER

I PULLED at the collar of my shirt, the tie around my neck suffocating. Rarely did I wear full suits, but knowing the effort and time Maisie had spent on getting ready, I felt a little better about the situation. At least if I was suffering for the sake of vanity, so was everyone else.

Orion had transformed Blaze's backyard into a wonderland, tea lights twinkling in the trees, circular tables set up with eight chairs around each. I was willing to bet if I had a measuring tape, they were all spaced the exact same distance apart, but still, the mayor fiddled with the napkins on one table.

"Looking dapper, Mr. Mayor," I said with a smile as I walked up to him. "Everything looks great."

"These aren't the napkins I ordered, but I don't have time to fix them."

I glanced down at the crisp black cloth napkins under each silver charger, white china arranged perfectly. "I'm not sure how much my opinion matters, but I think it looks great."

Orion's grey eyes lifted up to mine, his mouth so straight I decided I was better off dropping it. Electricity crackled through the air, the line between him and tipping over the edge into insanity was so fine at this point, I did not want to be the one to push him over the edge.

"Do you have the music handled?" I asked instead, my hand lifting to rub across the back of my neck as a small jolt of electricity in the air sent every hair on my body upright.

"Clara will be playing the harp," Orion nodded. "I'm glad your mother suggested it."

Of course she had.

I breathed deeply, trying to will away the annoyance that my mother hadn't given up hope for Clara and I, but I could admit a harp would be perfect for this event. Just as pretentious as the wrong napkins under china I was afraid to touch.

Guests started trickling in and a strangled noise erupted from Orion right before he rushed past me towards where they entered the yard from the patio, having used the front door of the cottage rather than the illuminated walkway Orion had set up from the street to the venue.

Clara passed me with a smile in a fluttery light purple dress, her hair braided into a crown around her head, and took her seat on a stool next to a stunning harp. Effortlessly, she pulled it towards her and began to strum. The sound was as ethereal as the scenery around us, waves in the distance lapping on the shore, trees rustling softly in the summer breeze.

I turned towards the walkway right as Kymari stepped through an archway made of the brightest pink roses, entering into the space the way Orion had intended. Her pearl-white jumpsuit fluttered softly in the breeze, matching the barest hint of scales she wore across her forehead. I sucked in a breath at the obvious display of her sea nymph status, something I'd never seen done before. Her lithe frame moved towards me, arm in arm with Dillon, who was tugging at his collar uncomfortably in a suit and tie. His blond hair was tamed in a way I'd never seen in all our years together, and I fought a smile as my friend didn't even try to hide the way he ogled Kymari in her finery. She was regal, and it showed.

I approached them as Kymari dropped Dillon's arm and they separated. My feet stopped, unable to move another inch as my jaw all but unhinged at the sight of Maisie.

Head high, Maisie stood under the arch and surveyed the yard, more beautiful than I'd ever seen her. A full skirt of the deepest teal floated around her, pooling like water at her feet. A sliver of pale skin showed between the top of the skirt and the bottom of the lace top she wore, peeking out between the iridescent material. But it wasn't her outfit that caught my attention. Maisie wore her hair in loose curls, flowing down to her waist, topped by a flower crown intertwined with pearls. Just beneath it, in the same fashion Kymari had, Maisie's purple and teal scales showed across her brow and down onto her temple, framing those sea glass eyes I couldn't look away from.

Ronan may have renounced her as his heir, but tonight, Maisie was every bit of a sea nymph princess. And I couldn't breathe at the sight of her.

"Stunning," I managed to say as she looped her arm through mine. She offered me a small smile in return, placing her other hand on my elbow. I felt the way her hand trembled as she searched the crowd for her family, but I hadn't seen any of the other sea nymphs arrive yet.

Several angels I didn't know stood around Orion, speaking softly with the same no-nonsense expression Orion wore so often as the notes of Clara's harp wove through the space.

Despite the near heavenly view, I couldn't help but notice the stiff posture, the forced conversations, and the shifting eyes with each new guest that arrived. While it wasn't surprising given how the news of prisoners escaping the Iron Keep affected everyone here, I itched at the discomfort oozing off everyone.

"Look at them," scoffed a voice from beside us, and I half turned to find Devanna in a black leather dress. With long sleeves, it might have looked conservative, but the oval-shaped cut-out across her collarbones dispelled that notion, along with the way it only reached mid-thigh to meet the top of her six-inch heeled boots. "What a bunch of PRICs. Is it possible Orion is the *least* stuffy of them?"

"Careful, Dev, or they might combust at the sight of you," I flicked a gaze down to her again. "Or lock you in the Keep for treason."

"Please. As if that hunk of cardboard could hold me," she gave a devilish smirk, before turning more serious. "Or anyone, apparently."

"Did you get your house-church finished?"

"Of course."

I leveled a look at her, and she shrugged. "All right, well, the outside is done at least. And remember," — she pointed a threatening finger at both of us in turn — "snitches get stitches."

She glanced around the space before a disgusted sound came from the back of her throat, and she hurried away a moment before Orion took her place.

"Christ, Malachi is going to have a heart attack if he sees her dressed like that."

"Who?"

"Oh," Orion fiddled with his tie, almost seeming surprised to see us standing there next to him. "No one. I mean, the Premier. But he probably won't show up. If there's any mercy in the world, anyway. Especially now that they're saying it was Seraphina, his most trusted chief of staff, that was involved with the escape." He cleared his throat, then turned and placed a hand on my shoulder. "She was found dead at the Keep. Could you, um," his expression turned pained, and I sensed he was about to ask me for a favor. "Never mind."

I stared at him. Was he at a loss for words? Embarrassed? What was happening?

Another throat clearing. "The angels are a bit... unforgiving."

Narrowing my eyes, I tried to read between the giant gaps in the string of clues he was leaving. But, miraculously, Maisie read it better than I did. She leaned forward, lowering her voice, and told him, her breath coasting across my chest as she did so, "We'll keep Dev away from the angels here."

Orion pressed his lips together before giving Maisie the tiniest nod, then scurried off, likely to attend to something as equally as disastrous as the napkin situation.

"What was that?" I turned to Maisie, and she rolled her eyes.

"He's worried about Dev and them," she jerked her head towards the angels. "That she'll piss them off, I'd guess."

I nodded slowly as that sank in, then laughed. "She probably would. All right, let's go babysit the world's grumpiest witch and hope she doesn't notice when I start watering down her whiskeys."

As we meandered around, vaguely but also purposefully following Dev, we met all sorts of supernaturals. There were a handful of demons from a town near Las Vegas, a place almost exclusively inhabited with demons and what I could only assume must be a total shitshow. A delegation of sea nymphs from some islands off Hawaii. An eagle shifter from Alaska, who chatted familiarly with both West and Ryker. Two individuals from the Carpathian Mountains in Europe, whose aura was difficult to read and who wouldn't divulge what kind of supernatural they were, which suggested some kind of rare shifter who didn't want their weaknesses exposed.

I was curious to meet the two angels here — Ezra and Pascar, from what I'd gathered — but they were in deep discussion the whole time with various leaders from the other towns, so the opportunity didn't present itself.

"Petey would kill to be out here," Blaze sighed as we gathered another round of drinks from him at the bar. He was alternating between making drinks and trying to put out fires — luckily, metaphorical — that Orion's uptight grumpiness left in his wake.

"Where is she?" Maisie asked.

Blaze jerked his head behind him at the house, and we looked up just in time to see a flash of red disappear from one of the upper windows.

"Too risky with the PRICs here, which is a shame since it would really help her research project," he continued. "That one bastard would probably snuff her out on sight if he found out a *human* lived here." His eyes darkened as he said it, and I followed his gaze over to the meanest looking angel of the bunch, Ezra.

"Well, we'll relay any information to her later that might be helpful," Maisie offered, and Blaze perked up, beaming at her.

"Would you? She'd love that," he said, then snapped his fingers. "Actually — oh, shit." The tablecloth had sparked with the snap, and he hastily dropped an ice cube on it to put out the flames. "Do you have a tape recorder? That would be best. Petey *loves* getting recordings of things. She says it's the best way to make sure to get the most accurate —"

"We'll remember what we can. See you around," I cut him off, dragging Maisie away before he started asking us to take detailed notes for his girlfriend.

A screech pierced my eardrums, and my heart rate exploded in terror before Maisie peeled her arm out of my hand, practically leaping across the yard before colliding with half a dozen blondes in a rainbow of bright dresses.

"Must be the sisters," Dev mused from beside me, popping a grape in her mouth as I caught my breath.

I nodded, entranced by the joy that spread over Maisie's face as she chatted animatedly with her sisters, all of them talking over each other but somehow understanding each other all the same. Then she turned to me, waving me over and grinning ear to ear.

"Everyone, this is Lysander —"

Several of the sisters sang coy *Oooh* sounds at that, and Maisie flapped a hand at them to get them to knock it off.

"Hush. And Lys, this is Saoirse, Isla, Blaire, McKenna, Riona, and Corissa," she called out rapid-fire like an auction dealer, pointing to each one of her sisters in turn who eyed me with open curiosity.

"Pleased to finally meet you all Saoirse, Isla, Blaire, McKenna, Riona, and Corissa," I said, shaking each of their hands as I said their names.

Seven mouths dropped open that I got all their names right so quickly, and I smirked at Maisie, who slapped my chest.

"What was that, some witchy trick?" the youngest, Corissa, asked. I'd already known from having seen her unconscious a few months ago when Ronan came ashore begging for our help, but of course she wouldn't remember me.

I laughed, flashing a grin at her. "No, just a good ear for cadence and rhythm, and sharp eyes."

Her sisters moved off, and Maisie squeezed my hand, a glow of gratitude on her face that sparked an ember in my chest.

A moment later, her expression faltered, though, and she bit her lip. I could guess what that was about.

She heaved a sigh. "Ronan must be here, too, then."

I nodded. "Do you want to find him? Or avoid him?"

"Both. I want him not to be here so I don't have to make that choice. I want to strangle him and hide from him all at the same time. I want to beg him to unbanish me and also kick dirt in his face. That's reasonable, right?"

"Totally."

"Maybe we just shove Ronan and Ostara together and see what happens, then deal with whatever is leftover."

"Another great option."

She took a deep breath, exhaling it sharply. "Okay, no. I want to find him. I can't stand this hiding-in-the-shadows, peering-around-every-corner business. I'm not cut out for that. I'll turn into a puddle of vibrating goo from the stress, and it would mess up this outfit. Kymari's already not speaking to me. Ruining this dress might be the final straw for her."

"Good, because he's right behind you."

Maisie yelped, and spun around, face to face with Ronan, who was glaring at my hand on his daughter's lower back so fiercely, I had no doubt that were he a demon, I would have caught fire by now.

"Maisie."

She shifted her weight subtly, but it had the effect of cocooning her even more snugly against my side, and it took all my effort to smother the glint of satisfaction from showing on my face.

"Ronan." She inclined her head. "I see you *do* own a shirt."

I coughed to cover up my laugh, and the twitch in Maisie's cheek told me she was biting her tongue against the same. It was true that, while I hadn't seen Ronan on land many times before, this was the first time I'd ever seen him bother to put on a shirt — even if it was only a navy blue linen one, the buttons opened halfway down his chest.

If I wasn't mistaken, though, it seemed like Ronan was trying to quell a tiny smile of his own before he frowned at me.

"Well, I see nothing here has changed. I hope your life abovewater is everything you expected." With that, he turned on his heel and left.

Maisie blinked after him for a moment, her lower lip trembling, then looked upward, blinking again, and I knew she was suppressing tears.

I moved around in front of her, placed my hands on her shoulders, and squeezed, hating to see her like this from a few cold words.

"Hey." I kept my voice soft, and she took a breath again before meeting my eyes. "Not tonight, all right? He doesn't get to mess with your head tonight."

Maisie blinked, nodded slowly. "Not tonight."

Unable to help myself, I traced my thumb over the scales at her temple, trying to memorize the way the iridescence shimmered with the changing light, how cool they were compared to her skin. "Tonight, no matter what he says, you're a queen."

Her breath hitched as my hand dropped, and I put a step between us before I crashed my lips to hers like I desperately wanted to. I only hoped she believed my words, and realized the royalty she was, with or without her father's blessing.

"Residents of Deadlights Cove," Orion's voice boomed over the speakers as he spoke into the microphone on the deck after we'd all taken our seats at our tables. "We've gathered here for several reasons. Yes, tomorrow we will listen to some exciting new research about how we can all potentially share magic with each other, but we've also come together to meet and mingle. For a long time, all of our species lived very separate lives, only interacting under the direst of circumstances or when battling each other. Since the Paranormal Regulations and Interspecies Council formed 500 years ago, little has changed, other than that we agreed upon some common ground rules. Within the past few hundred years, we slowly started to come together in towns like this one as the best way to stay concealed from the humans, and to be able to live our lives with the least day-to-day secrecy.

"If the magical linking proves to be possible, we will live closer together than ever before. It's important that we learn to make the most of that situation, and to cooperate to the best of our abilities." His gaze flicked to the angels for a moment, but he didn't let it rest there. "While we have so many visitors in the area, I hope you all make the time to take this opportunity to speak with each other, to get to know each other, and form new friendships and alliances.

"We all know what happened two nights ago. Eight prisoners escaping the Iron Keep — and *any* number of escapees is unheard of." He took a breath. "None of them are safe to be loose in this world, and now, we can only wait to see what they'll do with their freedom. The Council is determined to recapture them, but we have to assume the convicts will try to work together, and we all know how difficult it was to capture them separately.

"We have a lot of hard work ahead of us to seize all of them back." His jaw worked before he looked directly at

Ezra. "Working *together* will be the only way for us to ensure they are brought to justice again." His gaze moved back around the room as Ezra shifted in his seat. "We need to trust each other. Whatever their motives for escape will not be good news. Some of them have been in the keep for centuries, and they didn't escape just to hide out and live their lives in peace. We have to expect violence in our future. And we have to be ready to meet it, and defeat it, together."

Without another word, Orion sat back down.

A few people coughed. Chairs creaked as people shifted, twisting around and looking at each other, trying to decide what to do with Orion's doom speech.

Under the table, Maisie squeezed my hand.

"On that charming note, let's eat!" Blaze offered. When Orion nodded stiffly, food appeared on everyone's tables by magic.

After a moment of tentative clinking of silverware and uncomfortable laughter, people finally started to awkwardly dig in.

It was going to be a long, strange night.

After dinner plates were cleared, people began to mill about the yard as they mingled and drank. Clara started up her harp again, a soothing tune that had me stifling a yawn.

"I'm bored," Dillon whispered, and I couldn't fight the smile that tugged at my lips as I draped my arm across the back of Maisie's chair. Kymari dropped into the empty chair at his right, pointedly avoiding Maisie.

"You look beautiful," Maisie said to Kymari, and my

heart squeezed, watching the two women closely. Maisie had told me about their falling out, and, for both of their sakes, I hoped it was a rift that could be easily mended. No matter what Kymari thought, Maisie *did* need her.

Kymari smiled stiffly, her eyes never rising to meet Maisie's, but hope wasn't lost as she said, "I'm glad I picked that color for you. It brings out your eyes."

"How," Maisie started, then glanced behind us to the table where her sisters sat. "How is everything in Crunamar City?"

Kymari sighed, closing her eyes as she shook her head slightly. "Let's not talk about it."

"Right," Maisie nodded, and I squeezed her leg under the table in support. "Sure."

Voices rose from behind us, and I turned to see Ronan, chest puffed as he spoke with Ryker. While I couldn't hear what they were talking about, anger was written on both of their faces. Selene stood between them, a hand on Ryker's chest as she pushed him away from Ronan. Maisie turned to watch the commotion as well, a deep frown on her face.

My knee bounced, uneasiness hitting me hard as I looked around the yard, noticing it wasn't just Ronan and Ryker about to throw down. Between Orion's uplifting words and the news of the impending threat, the air was heavy with stress and crackling with the static of coiled magic. It was unbearable — physically uncomfortable for me as a Harmonic witch attuned to these things. I hopped to my feet, rushing to Blaze's side.

"You still have that guitar I gave you?" I asked.

Blaze looked away from where he'd been staring at an

upstairs window, confusion written on his face. "Yeah, in the music room. Why?"

"Can I have it?" I asked, remembering to pose it as a question, not a demand when asking for something from a demon. Instantly, Blaze flickered out then back, guitar in hand as he passed it to me.

Not wasting another second, I hopped up onto the deck, grabbing the mic. "Sorry I'm late," I said, the sound of the mic cutting through the tension as every eye in the space turned to me. "It's kind of my thing. But who's ready to get this party started?"

Crickets chirped in the trees behind me.

A goat bleated in the distance.

Orion's wings fluttered, his eyes so wide I was momentarily afraid they might tumble to the ground and roll across the grass.

I forced a smile, hoping it looked convincing, as my gaze found Maisie the way it had all night. Her sister Riona had taken my seat at the table, and the two paused to watch me. Maisie cocked her head to the side, brow slightly creased, but I couldn't stand the strain in the air another second.

Without thinking, I began strumming, the chords for Goo Goo Dolls' *Iris* coming together as I found Maisie, unable to look away. I played, singing the tune I'd sung so often I didn't miss a beat, but felt the words in a way I never had before.

Like the lyrics said, I hid from the world, never revealing my true self, never feeling like I'd been understood at a deep level. Until her. I leaned into the mic as I sang, hoping she could tell I meant every word.

I wanted her to know me.

I wanted her to choose me.

I wanted to be worthy of the most beautiful and captivating woman I'd ever met.

I wanted her to be hopelessly in love with me like I was for her.

Maisie smiled softly, then pushed her chair back, grabbing Riona's hand as she moved to the small space in front of the deck, and began to sway with her sister. The two danced, not caring that they were the only ones in the center of the floor, a broad smile on Maisie's face as her gaze focused on the table to her right where the rest of her sisters sat.

Corissa, the youngest, hopped to her feet as she rushed to join them, hands in the air as she swayed. Maisie laughed, throwing her arms around her sister, the others joining in shortly after.

Sometime in the middle of the song, Dillon appeared on stage, Bodhi and Blaze flickering in with the rest of our instruments. By the time the song was over, the Lost Talisman had taken over as if this had always been the plan.

As the song ended, Dillon beat on the drums, effortlessly picking up the beat as he pushed us into *Gimme All Your Lovin'* by ZZ Top. Natalie strummed, moving to take over the mic as she and Dillon sang their favorite duet together. I stepped back with a grin, watching as several others joined the dancing sisters, the mood already lifting.

By the fifth song, the party had started, Mo dancing wildly with Nimue and Blaze at the center of the floor. The two angels stood at the back of the space, arms crossed, but they appeared to be the only ones not having fun. Even my mother was shifting slightly in her seat —

more than I'd ever hoped for. She'd never seen me play a show, and I was giddy knowing that she saw how much magic I could wield with my guitar, just as I could my spellwork.

The stiff party from before was gone, and I bit my lip with a smile as Maisie threw her arms around one of her sisters, shimmying to the beat as they laughed and hugged in turns. I knew she'd been dreading tonight, and my heart soared at the genuine happiness I saw there.

Just as the song ended, Dillon beat on the drums, signaling *I Love Rock 'N Roll*, and Natalie switched with him, catching on immediately as she picked up the beat. Just as I leaned into the mic to sing the opening lyrics, a man walked through the rose archway at the entrance, hands in his pockets. He looked around the yard casually, taking in the dancing with a smile when his eyes found Mo in the center.

"Lotty!" she yelled, her arms high above her head as she moved through the space to him. Lotty beamed, his smile broad as it filled his whole face, white teeth flashing, but I couldn't look away from him.

The shape of his face, the cut of his jaw, all of it was familiar, as if I'd seen it thousands of times before.

But his eyes… Pale green.

I furrowed my brow. *My* eyes.

My magic slipped free, showing me the rainbow of color as I looked around at the guests, seeing their auras. My breath caught in my throat as I looked at the man chatting with Mo.

Deep green splashed with indigo-blue. Just like mine.

Natalie started the intro again, giving me time to collect my thoughts, but I froze, my gaze finding my mother in the audience. Ostara sat still as a statue, eyes locked on Mo and Lotty, watching the way they embraced.

Words were lost to me, my mind spinning wildly as I looked between my mother and the man in the center of the floor, searching for answers I'd wanted my whole life.

Dillon hit the drums harder, Natalie starting over for the third time, but my heart raced in my chest like it never had before.

Chapter Thirty-One

MAISIE

NATALIE PLAYED the opening for *I Love Rock 'N Roll* for the second time, and I looked to Lys, wondering what the hangup was. Of the many times I'd seen him perform, he'd never forgotten the words. I watched the way his chest rose and fell quicker than normal, and turned to see what had caught his attention.

A man I didn't recognize stood at the back of the dance floor chatting with Morgaine and Blaze, hugging them in turns. I couldn't help but notice the many similarities between Morgaine and the newcomer, wondering if they were related.

And then I noticed how familiar his face looked: the bright smile and the slope of his jaw, but especially those pale green eyes, the exact shade and shape of Lys's.

I whipped my head back to the deck. Lys stood frozen on the stage as Dillon slammed harder on the drums, trying to catch his attention, but Lys didn't move.

Without thinking, I pushed through the crowd, jumped

on the deck, and grabbed the mic, ignoring the way my pulse started racing at what I was about to do.

Natalie shot me a confused look, but I smiled, hoping it didn't show how utterly terrified I was. By the time they played through the intro for the fourth time, I lifted the mic, and began to sing.

My voice, laced with all of my siren magic, worked perfectly for this song, but I couldn't help but notice the way my voice shook. By the time I got to the chorus, my sisters were belting the words along with me, and I smiled, their support giving me confidence.

Eventually, I got up the courage to look at Lys, who had finally started playing his portion of the song. His eyes locked onto mine, and I couldn't help but notice the intensity in his gaze.

Feeling the adrenaline rush that had led me up to this stage, I let my guard down, smiling as I sang, feeling the way the music called to me just as much as the ocean lapping on the shores in the distance. I refused to look at the back of the crowd where I was sure my father stood with a disapproving frown, but he'd already banished me. What worse could happen? I trip and fall off the deck?

I missed a note as panic seized me momentarily at the thought of catapulting the few feet to the ground in a way only I could. Right then, Lys leaned in and sang along with me, our faces mere inches from each other as we shared the mic.

My heart fluttered, noticing the softness in his eyes, whatever had caused him to panic earlier gone as he studied me, singing along. Lys leaned forward, grabbed the mic off the stand, and handed it to me with a wide grin. Heat flared in my body at the way he watched me sing.

Emotions flooded me, feeling anything but fake as he strummed his guitar and sang with me. Being the center of Lys's attention was overwhelming, a tide pulling me under, and one that I was losing the will to fight against. I wanted to drown in the way he made me feel, the confidence he instilled in me, the joy he brought to my life.

It was intoxicating, and I didn't want it to be a lie.

It wasn't fake anymore for me, and a spark lit in my chest as I hoped I was interpreting the way he stared at me correctly. That maybe, just maybe, it was real for him, too.

The audience clapped along as I sang the chorus over, moving towards the finale. The song ended, and my chest heaved with a swirl of emotions, but nothing mattered other than the way Lys swung his guitar around to hang behind him, his hand lacing around the back of my neck as he tugged me to him, his lips descending on mine fiercely.

My world exploded, body tingling in all the right ways as my chest heaved. Lys's kiss was consuming, full of more emotion than I could comprehend, even with how brief it was. He pulled away far too soon, but his hand still lingered on my neck as he tipped his forehead to mine.

"You and me," he murmured, his eyes closed as he pulled in a deep breath, magic coating my skin in a way I knew meant he had created a bubble of silence around us. My head turned slightly, eyes traveling over the large group standing before us, wondering what was happening, but Lys grabbed my chin, pulling my attention back to him. "We're the only ones here that matter. Not your father or my mother. Or, damn," he stuttered a laugh, "Pretty fucking positive that's *my* father here, too."

I nodded, my fingers gripping the lapel of his jacket as my knees weakened with each passing second in his embrace. "You okay? Do we need to leave?"

"No baby," Lys said, kissing me lightly, then again as if he couldn't stop himself now that he'd started. "I'm good now. With you at my side, nothing else matters."

"I'm pretty positive that anyone who didn't buy our dating before does now," I said with a weak smile, all too aware of the way my heart pounded in my chest at his words.

His fingers tightened on my neck, and his voice lowered when he said, "This isn't fake anymore. Not for me. Hasn't been for a while now, Maze."

I held my breath, tears stinging my eyes as his words sank in. Before I had a chance to respond to that, to tell him it was real now for me, too, Natalie nudged us with her guitar. Lys looked up, clearing his throat, and the magic on my skin fizzled out as he turned back to the mic.

"Wasn't my girl fantastic?" Lys said into the mic, his face tipped towards me so I could see his megawatt smile.

My girl. A blush crept over my skin as I hopped off the deck and moved to where Kymari stood slack-jawed with my sisters.

The intensity of the last few moments after the adrenaline rush of singing on stage for the first time came crashing down around me, and my knee twisted. Kymari grabbed my hand, keeping me from falling as we moved to a table nearby and sat down.

"I can't say I ever saw that coming," she said as Lys and

the band started their next song. If my heart hadn't been ready to explode at Lys's kisses, it was now as I squeezed my best friend's hand, hoping we were working our way towards forgiveness.

And I couldn't disagree with her, for a multitude of reasons.

This wasn't fake.

It hadn't been for a while.

And Lys was all mine.

Chapter Thirty-Two

LYSANDER

ALL I COULD THINK about through the rest of the songs was whether Maisie would have said it back if she'd had the chance.

Was this real for her now, too?

I thought I knew what I'd seen in her eyes the moment before Natalie had broken the spell, but I needed to hear it myself.

But first, we needed to wrap this up. While we'd been playing, Blaze had been setting up some other sound equipment in the background, and hopefully he'd be able to take over as DJ in a few more songs.

A few more songs. Then, I could grab Maisie and get out of here. I needed answers.

But the town needed this. The supernatural community gathered here needed a sense of normalcy, a sense of fun, and the longer we played, the lighter everyone's auras grew.

Even my mother's. She'd watched with an intrigued expression through our entire show, except for the glances she'd shot at *Lance*, my probable-father. Something I'd have to deal with *after* dealing with Maisie.

Maisie came first.

I stifled my chuckle at my choice of words into a smile as we switched songs. I gave the signal to the others that this would be the last one, and they each nodded.

"Deadlights Cove, always a pleasure to play for you," I called into the mic as our last song ended. "Thanks to Orion for letting us crash his shin-dig — if I go missing, you all know who to blame — and to Blaze for the Minuteman set up."

Dillon wrapped up the rest of our close-out speech for me, our audience clapping and cat-calling for us as Blaze switched on his music, keeping the atmosphere upbeat as we left the stage.

The minute we hopped down, I turned to Dillon. "I have to go. Can you guys —"

"We'll break it down, don't worry," he said, a knowing grin on his face. "Look at you, man."

"Yeah, shut up." I clapped him on the back, finishing with a shove that only made him laugh, but I was smiling. I scanned the faces in front of me, searching for the only one I wanted to see.

I found Maisie with her sisters, singing and dancing along to Blaze's music. Her face lit up when she saw me, and I stepped into her space so I was all she'd see.

"Come with me?" I grabbed her hand before she had a chance to nod, and the second she did, I tugged her away.

We passed around the edge of the house, the sounds and lights of the party fading. I knew down at the Cottage's private beach there was a boathouse that would give us some privacy.

"Wait —"

My heart leapt to my throat as Maisie pulled me to a stop. Was that it? Was she going to tell me this was all one-sided?

But she only bent down and slipped her wedge sandals off, holding them by the ankle straps. I inclined my head towards the boathouse, and I could have sworn, even in just the glittering moonlight, a blush rose on her cheeks.

As I followed a step behind her, I didn't bother to hide my grin.

Waves crashed onto the shore mere steps away as I flicked the boathouse lock open with magic, stepping into even deeper darkness. An inlet of water came through the center of the space, moonlight reflecting off it from outside and offering just enough light as our eyes adjusted.

A kayak hung on the wall, along with a few paddles and life jackets, but I couldn't have given less of a shit what else was in this space when Maisie was here, too.

"Maze, I have to know —" I turned to her once the door closed behind us, cradling her face in one hand, my other hand still gripping hers.

"Yes." Her hand closed over mine on her face as my heart stopped, scared to hope she meant what I thought.

"Yes, what?"

She pressed her forehead to mine, her voice barely more than a whisper as she said, "This is real. For me, too."

"Thank the Goddess."

I pulled her in, pressing my lips to hers, pressing every

curve of her body against every hard edge of mine. She let out a gasp, and I devoured the sound straight from her lips, walking us back until she bumped against a table, anchoring us. Her hands fisted in the lapels of my jacket only a breath before she started scrambling to pull it off, and I laughed as I moved only my torso back — our hips still firmly pressed together — to tug it off.

"Impatient," I commented, but then she dragged me back in by my tie, and I shuddered as I grew harder against her hip. *Finally*, I didn't have to fight that. "Fuck, Maze — no rush, you know?"

She pulled back, retreating, and felt like a total dick.

"Oh." Shit, she sounded so *small*. "Sorry, I thought —"

"I mean, I'm going to fuck you in this boathouse." I tilted her chin up. "But we're going to take our time. We have all the time we want, and I want to savor this."

She let out a squeak that I took as encouragement.

I pressed my lips into the soft skin of her neck, relishing the way she shivered in anticipation at the gentle touch, and moved my mouth just below her ear. "I've had to sleep with you in my bed, your scent invading every space in my house, unable to touch you, for weeks now, Maze. I've had a lot of time to think about all the things we could be doing." She shuddered, closing her eyes as I kissed down her chest, meeting the top of her crop top. "All the ways we could do them."

I found the zipper on the side of her top, and slowly started to work it down, letting the sound of the metal teeth unlinking fill the space along with Maisie's rapid breath.

"I've just only ever had quickies," she blurted as the

zipper opened completely, her top hanging open at the side. "Like, illicit, tell anyone and you're dead, or *I'm* dead, kind of quickies. And it was fine, I mean, it wasn't like I wanted anything more with him, he's my father's guard, and to be totally honest, Drew wasn't exactly the most *skilled* in the whole, ah —"

"Okay." I pressed a finger over her lips, and she clamped them shut. I went back to pulling her top off, trying not to groan at the lacy teal bralette she wore underneath. "I'm not a big rules guy, but I don't want to hear about the other dudes you've been with. Deal?"

"Dude."

"What?"

"One dude. Drew."

I grimaced. "Let's agree that's the last time you say his name when I'm undressing you." She nodded. "And, *one* dude? And he wasn't even good? Maze."

She shrugged sheepishly. "Who's got the time, am I right?" She gave a nervous laugh, and I furrowed my brow at her.

"Wait. Do you mean — have you never come with another person?"

Pink tinged her cheeks at my words, her gaze darting away, but I clamped her chin between my thumb and finger and made her look at me. "Well, you know what Dev says. There's nothing a man can do the right device can't do be—"

"Fucking hell, she's like my sister. Never repeat that to me again."

"She was sending Mo *links*. I'm sorry, you probably didn't want to know that part either?"

I narrowed my eyes. "Are you doing this on purpose now?"

She shrugged, wide-eyed innocence, then bit her lip. My jaw slackened.

"You are."

"I'll stop."

"Good." I breathed a long sigh through my nose to regroup. "All right. I take this as a challenge."

She tilted her head. "What?"

"You'll know it when it happens." I grinned.

Maisie's first sexual orgasm, coming right up.

I lifted her up, depositing her on the table, and picked up where we left off, taking her mouth again. A soft moan escaped her as I pressed my tongue against hers, tasting her like I'd been so desperate to do.

My hand drifted down, skating across her bare ribs, and I tugged her right to the edge of the table, my legs between hers, grinding into her, the friction tantalizing through so many layers of fabric.

"*Lys* —" she breathed into my mouth.

I chuckled, and reached to undo her bra, then slid it off. I couldn't resist the groan that escaped me, and quickly bent to suck her nipple into my mouth, first one, then the other, until she was panting.

"Lean back."

Her eyes were dark as she did as I asked, pressing her palms behind her, watching my every move as I slowly rolled up the sleeves of my dress shirt. With a smirk, I knelt between her legs, my hands tracing up her legs, pushing up her skirt. I found a lacy edge, and she lifted her hips so I could tug her thong down, tossing it beside her bra.

My hands pressed to the inside of her knees as I met her eyes, silently asking permission for this, for what I'd dreamed about for weeks, and she licked her lips before her legs relaxed, knees falling open.

322

Chapter Thirty-Three

MAISIE

THE MINUTE LYS knelt at the edge of the table, I knew what he was about to do, but I had no idea it would feel like *this*.

My knowledge of the devices Devanna had mentioned might have been limited, but I couldn't imagine *any* of them would be able to replicate what Lys was doing between my legs.

"Poseidon, that feels so good," I said, my voice raspier than usual.

"You taste just as fantastic as I knew you would," Lys said, biting my inner thigh as my legs shook. "Goddess, I've wanted to do this since you tripped in the bar that first night. Thought about dropping to my knees in Blaze's office and shoving you up against the door. Wanted to lick you from head to toe when I saw you in that tiny scrap of a thong."

I whimpered at his words, feeling the desire coating every one. His tongue was warm as he moved it rhythmically against me, and my head fell back as I was lost to the sensation. Drew had certainly never done *this*.

A tiny part of my mind was worried he was going to suffocate down there under my skirt, but the rest of me couldn't be bothered to care while his tongue and then — *oh, Poseidon, his fingers too* — were moving so expertly against me.

I tried to collapse gently onto my back on the table, but landed with a thud instead, my arms unable to hold myself up any longer. Lys chuckled against my skin, his breath tickling me gently. "That's right, baby. Squeeze my hand."

My body followed his directions, not needing any encouragement, even though I loved his dirty words.

I was a panting, writhing mess in no time. Was I humping his face? He didn't seem to mind. In fact, every time I couldn't control the movement of my hips, I heard a groan of approval coming from him.

"Yes, Maze. Use me. I wanna feel you shatter."

I bit my fist, trying to stifle my pathetic whimper, but Lys noted it right away and reached up, tearing my hand away from my mouth.

"Don't you fucking dare," he smirked. "I want to hear every sound you'll give me. You're the sexiest woman I've ever met."

He held my gaze as he lowered his head again, tongue pressed against me right as his fingers did something I knew I'd be begging him to repeat again soon, and I exploded.

"Fuck," Lys moaned, working me through it.

My mind went blank as my body lit up, pleasure like I'd never experienced before racking my every nerve, wrenching and releasing every muscle.

So this is what people mean when they talk about seeing stars.

That was my first thought, once I could actually think coherently again. I blinked my eyes open again slowly, staring at the dark ceiling as I fought for air.

"Holy kumquats, Lysander Theroux," I breathed. He laughed, flicking his eyebrows up as he met my gaze and got to his feet.

"Kumquats?"

I waved my hand in the air. "It's a Nimue thing. Good phrase, though."

"I'll take that as a mission accomplished, then," he said, pressing his hips against mine in a reminder that we were nowhere near finished yet. It didn't escape my notice how large the bulge in his pants was, and I ground down on it, needing more. "Ready for more?"

I licked my lips as I nodded, even though I'd barely got my breath back, and reached for his shirt. Passion burned in his eyes as he stared into mine, watching my every move as I undid each button, my hands moving over his tattooed chest as I pushed it down his arms.

"Are these witch symbols?" I asked, tracing a few. He grew impatient, tossing the shirt away, and took over unbuckling his own belt and shoving down his pants.

"Some of them. Some are spells, or Coven symbols. Some are for the band, or just for me." He stepped out of the last of his clothes and wrapped a hand around his thick girth. "But I don't want to talk about my tattoos when I have you splayed out before me looking so absolutely fuckable."

I swallowed, staring at how large he looked in his hand. "You sure that's going to fit?"

Lys smirked, his free hand tugging on the zipper for my

skirt, sliding it down. "I'll make sure your body is so desperate for mine, I'll slide right in."

I was already desperate. I pulled away from him only long enough to shimmy out of the skirt, and his gaze trailed down my entire body, his hands running along my sides from thigh to ribs.

"Do you trust me?" His hands stroked and caressed and kneaded my body before sliding back between my legs. He circled, spreading the wetness there, then pushed two fingers inside again, scissoring them. Before I had a chance to respond, his mouth devoured mine again, one hand tilting my head so he could deepen the kiss.

"You mean —"

"I assume you're clean," he said between kisses, his hand moving relentlessly.

"What about —"

"Spelled." He said it so nonchalantly, like it was common knowledge there was magical birth control. At least underwater, it was *not*. "It's not an issue. Now, do you trust me?"

Lys was practically vibrating with the restraint it took to hold himself back. But I knew, meeting his eyes, that if I said no, we'd stop. He'd either procure us a condom from somewhere or we'd postpone this until we could.

But, I did trust him. So I told him so.

"Thank the Goddess," he breathed, and lined himself up with me.

"I thought we were taking our time —" I gasped as he pushed into me. "Oh, fuck."

"Must have been an idiot who said that," he murmured, tilting my head up to kiss me again, waiting for my body to adjust to his size before he pulled his hips back, pushing in a little farther with each thrust.

"Mmhmm," I mumbled, feeling the delicious stretch as he moved inside me. "No argument here."

He gave my ass a playful slap and started moving. My breath caught as I moved with him, as much as I could on the table, meeting him thrust for thrust.

I clawed at his back, desperate for more, for him, for this.

"You are so fucking perfect," Lys said, kissing along my neck as my eyes rolled back in my head with each move he made, each frisson of friction we created. "How I've waited weeks for this is beyond me. But I'd happily wait a thousand more if it would make me worthy of you."

"No need to wait when you're wonderful, just as you are," I whispered, wanting him to feel the honesty in my words. "I wouldn't change one thing about you. You, Lysander Theroux, are everything I've always needed. I've always wanted."

His hand slid under my ass, lifting me slightly, and the change in angles was enough to send me flying over the edge, moaning his name.

"Fuck, Maisie," he said, lips crashing down on mine as his hips lost their smooth rhythm. With a low groan, his body shuddered, arms shaking as he held himself over me on the table.

My heart thudded in my chest as I lifted my hands, cupping his cheeks, and peppered him with kiss after kiss. "12/10. Excellent job."

Lys laughed, his chest rumbling against my skin as I smiled up at the roof. "Glad I could deliver."

"I'd give you a standing ovation if I trusted my legs not to immediately give out on me, but you only have yourself to blame for that."

Lys kissed me, this one longer, sweeter, full of unspoken emotion. "I aim to please."

I leaned forward to kiss him again but stopped abruptly, my attention snapping towards the door. The sound of voices rapidly approaching the boathouse overshadowed the music in the distance and my heart leapt to my throat.

Lys heard them a second after I did, but, true to form, he was more amused than panicked at the thought of someone walking in on us fully naked. But I was panicked enough for both of us.

"C'mon!" I said before I could think through my plan. I grabbed his hand and dove into the water, pulling him under with me and just to the outside of the boathouse, our backs pressed up against it when we surfaced.

"Maisie —" Lys hissed, wiping the water from his face and shaking his hair, but I brought a finger to my lips.

"I guess we weren't the first ones inspired tonight," someone said with a chuckle from inside the boathouse, no doubt finding our clothes piled on the floor in front of the table. I rolled my eyes when I recognized Dillon's voice, then Kymari's.

"Shut up and take your pants off, witch."

"Yes, ma'am."

Lys covered his mouth to smother his laughter, and I gestured for him to swim down the long side of the boathouse, away from our lascivious friends and further into the shadows.

"Now what?" Lys whispered when we were far enough

away not to get caught. "You have me in your sea, naked." He flashed a smirk. "You've already had your way with me. Now is when you drag me down to the depths, right?"

I bit my lip, looking at the shore in the distance with no clue how to get out of this one. Why hadn't I grabbed our clothes?

"It's cool." Lys shrugged. "I knew it would happen eventually."

I shoved him underwater, and he came up again laughing. How could he be so carefree all the time?

"Relax, Maze," he chuckled, and twined his fingers through mine. "Everyone is busy at the dinner right now. We'll have no problem streaking across town back to my house."

I gasped, heat rising to my cheeks at the image he painted. "Oh, my gods! I am not streaking anywhere!"

"Kidding." He grinned. "I can glamour us enough to get back unseen. You just have to keep your hand in mine so the magic covers you, too, and you'll be good."

A breath whooshed out of me in relief, and I tightened my grip on his hand. I had no intention of letting go anytime soon.

Chapter Thirty-Four

LYSANDER

"IF YOU LOOK at the date on this letter to Andras Propsero, a demon, dated 1642, he mentions a ceremony with his beloved wife Cordelia, a coven leader of a prominent witch family in New Orleans," Owen lectured from the front of the conference room in Town Hall. Orion had removed the large table, installing rows of chairs instead, and I sat towards the back between Dillon and Maisie.

An hour into the Summit the next morning, I was struggling to keep my eyes open. Listening to Owen's obnoxious voice with his terrible accent for an hour had not helped either. But knowing that Maisie was mine, really mine, and not his? That helped a lot.

Maisie and I had made our way back to my place after the boat house, but I gave her an encore performance, and then another this morning before we'd found our way here.

Dillon elbowed me in the side when my head started to tip forward — we hadn't gotten much sleep, after all — and I jerked upright, blinking myself awake.

"What's important about this letter is down here, in the

last paragraph, where Andras mentions his wife's powers expanding, requiring less spellwork than before."

At that, I jerked upright, leaning forward in my seat as I looked to where my mother sat in the front row, pen in hand. Three seats over was the male from last night — Lance, Mo's brother, I'd come to learn after asking several people this morning before the lecture began. Ostara still hadn't said anything to me, and I had yet to introduce myself to Lance, so I did what I did best when faced with unhappy feelings.

I avoided it.

Pulling my hood up over my head, I stared at their backs, trying to figure out this riddle with the little clues I had.

Ostara refused to make eye contact with Lance, but he didn't have the same problem, staring at her almost constantly with a small smile. Mo sat at his side, leaning in to whisper with him during the lecture, but never looked back to where I sat in the last row against the window.

If Lance really was who I thought he was, why wouldn't Ostara introduce us? Why wouldn't he introduce himself? It wasn't like I needed a father figure; I was 36. If anything, it would be more to settle my life-long, idle curiosity.

I squinted at him, and drew up my magic to get a better look at his aura, a deep green with streaks of indigo-blue. *If* this was my father — Goddess, even in my head, the word sounded strange — that could be where my Harmonic strengths came from. Green indicated good communicators, witches who had strength with forming connections between people and magic and objects, like Harmonizers. Goddess knew that wasn't my mother's strength.

And, I had to admit, his aura looked a lot like my own.

Fuck, I was going to have to confront him, wasn't I? Or her. Yeah, I should start with Ostara. See what she had to say for herself. I had lots of practice confronting *her*.

Rubbing a hand over my face, I blinked away from Lance and his many mysteries, my gaze drifting past my mother's red aura to land on Ruby.

Ruby, whose magic I thought I'd fixed weeks ago, and had worked fine when we'd worked together on the glamour. And yet, looking at her now, I could see it still didn't look quite right. My brows furrowed as I noted the way her mixed-color aura faded in and out of the in-between, trying to puzzle out what could still be going wrong with it, and why she hadn't mentioned it still being wonky. Had she not noticed it?

That seemed improbable. What about Morgaine? Surely she would have mentioned it still being off. I'd sensed there was more to Ruby than met the eye, my suspicions only growing when West Larkin had mentioned that he was the one who'd sent her out here to Mo, but I also knew none of them would tell me about it unless they wanted to.

I'd never encountered magic like Ruby's before. It almost bore a strange resemblance to demon magic, but she hadn't shown any signs of being a demon hybrid or being able to perform demon-style magic.

There were only a few witches I knew that could do anything remotely like demon magic, Mo and I being two of them.

Still, maybe a little research into demon-witch crossover magic couldn't hurt. After all, I'd never actually looked into my own magic much, how it was different than other witches' and what could have caused it.

Maybe Lance would know.

A lump formed in my throat just at the thought of confronting him, of confirming the truth that I felt with 99% certainty in my gut.

Research felt safer.

After what felt like hours, Orion finally announced we were breaking for lunch, and I breathed a sigh of relief. I hadn't spent this much time sitting in one place since school, and it was fucking terrible.

"Let's go." I grabbed Maisie's hand, tugging her into the hall with me, Dillon following along behind us, as I all but sprinted out of there and down the street to Scallywags.

I didn't want to risk running into anyone after the chat. Not yet, anyway.

"Sounds fascinating, doesn't it?" Maisie was saying as we settled into a booth. "I mean, if it's possible."

"Sure." Dillon nodded. "It's just weird that it has to be so intimate. It sounds like you essentially have to share your innate well of power with them."

"Power has to come from somewhere." I wrapped an arm around Maisie's shoulders, my chest warming when she melted into me, her head tilting to rest against my chest. It felt so good to be openly affectionate with her and have her return the embrace. I pressed my lips into her hair, inhaling her coconut and peaches scent like it would keep me alive.

Then her hand landed softly on my thigh, and my arm tightened around her.

Dillon noticed and deadpanned, "Should I find a new table?"

"Oh, don't be silly," Maisie said, and he took a deep breath right as Blaze showed up at our table.

"Food?" He flipped open a notepad, and it immediately caught on fire. "Ah, dammit. Third time that's happened. Anyway, your options are BLT, or if you're vegetarian, LT. I don't have time for anything fancy what with —" he gestured to the rest of the bar, where it seemed like the entire Summit delegation was here to find lunch in the interim.

Maisie sat forward, motioning for me to scooch out of the booth. "We'll help."

"Oh, I mean, it's your day off, and you're all cozy with —"

"Blaze. We're happy to help." She waved him off as she all but climbed over me out of the booth, then tugged me to my feet. Dillon too. "Aren't we?" She gave both of us a pointed look that had us agreeing, too. "I'll get some more hands for us. You two, start taking orders."

Just like that, Maisie moved off, tracking down Saoirse, Blaire, McKenna, and Isla to help as well, ushering them behind the bar and handing out aprons. Devanna was already stacking glasses of water, iced tea, and lemonades on trays, handing them off to Nadir and Emerson, and Nimue had a crate of wrapped silverware she passed around the dining room.

"I guess it's all hands on deck." Dillon and I divided up the dining room, and started taking lunch orders.

An hour later, everyone visiting for the Summit had been served and were starting to head back to Town Hall for the afternoon session. Those of us who had been corralled into waiting tables were just sitting down to stuff our faces.

"I owe you guys." Blaze was still cleaning up, wiping down tables and throwing dishes in the dishwasher. Every so often, a napkin or towel would go up in flames, and he'd curse and snuff it out.

"Truth, dare, or favor?" Dev asked.

"Sure, sure, whichever."

"How about money?" Maisie's sister McKenna called, and Dev chuckled.

"Or that. Invoice me." Blaze ducked back into the kitchen, with a tray of dishes.

"Good. I need new paints," McKenna nodded to herself as Petra peeked her head out of the kitchen door, checking for the all-clear. Yet another yelp sounded from the kitchen indicating another stray fire.

"Petra, is Blaze… all right?" Maisie asked.

Petra sighed, slumping into a booth with a sandwich in front of her, red ringlets across her brow from the sweat we'd all worked up over lunch. She hadn't left the kitchen so as not to run into any of the visitors in town but had worked just as hard as the rest of us. "He's getting excited preemptively."

Maisie and I exchanged a confused look, while Devanna narrowed her eyes, glancing down to Petra's stomach.

Petra scoffed. "Please. No."

Dev let out a shuddering breath of relief, hand over her heart. "Thank the ever-loving Goddess. Can you imagine a mini-Blaze on the loose?"

"He's excited about the magic-link," Petra continued, ignoring Dev and lowering her voice, glancing at the kitchen door. "In case it could work… with me. But there's still no evidence for that," she added hastily, then resumed eating her sandwich like nothing had been said as Blaze returned to the dining room.

"But there's no evidence against it, either, Petey," he said, like he'd been a part of this conversation the whole time, dropping into the booth next to her. His arm went around her shoulder effortlessly as he leaned forward, taking a bite from the sandwich in her hands.

"What's the worst that could happen?" Blaire asked.

"Probably death." Dev shrugged.

"Probably not *death*." Blaze leaned over to flick her shoulder. "And best case scenario…" He trailed off, uncharacteristic for him, as he and Petra met each other's gaze. His hand cupped her jaw, thumb tracing along her cheek. "If I could keep you with me forever, Petey?" He gave a shaky laugh. "Fuck, yeah, I'd do it."

Petra tilted her head, pressing her lips to his, and Blaze took full advantage, pulling her in for an entirely indecent kiss, given how many people were still in the room.

We laughed as Petra finally pulled back, blushing scarlet, and resumed her lunch, Blaze grinning beside her like the cat that got the canary.

But his words did make me think. If it was possible to link with humans in a way that could potentially give them magic or extend their lives, it could open up a whole realm of new possibilities for human-supernatural relations. Some of which might come to be dangerous.

We stood in the Town Hall lobby, staring into the conference room, and I grimaced, pulling Maisie to a stop before we re-entered.

"I can't do it," I whispered, feet frozen in place. The mere thought of sitting in those seats again for interminable hours made my skin crawl. "I can't sit through more of that."

Maisie rolled her eyes and laughed. "Come on. You can handle it."

"I'm just going to pop into the library, all right? There's something I want to look up."

"Aw, I didn't know you could read," Dev taunted, reaching up to pat my head as she pushed past us back into the conference room, and I gave her retreating back the finger. "Hey, I sensed that!" she called over her shoulder.

"I'll be in there in a bit," I said to Maisie, pressing a kiss to her forehead. Then, when her hand fisted my shirt, planted another kiss to her lips with a groan.

"Incoming," Saoirse muttered as she passed us. We jolted apart right in time for Ronan to pass through the lobby, his fist flexing at his side like he was thinking about knocking me out right here in front of the whole town and all the supernatural leaders from around the country.

I had no doubt that he would. With a last look to Maisie, I peeled off, heading into the library.

There had to be *something* in here that could tell me what was going on with Ruby's magic.

An hour later, I still had nothing to show about Ruby's magic for all my research. Kai, the librarian in town, had helped me find dozens of books on witch magic and hexes, but none of it fit the way Ruby's magic was moving into the in-between. I'd even broken into the *Rare Collections* section of the library, and, nothing.

For my own magic, well, that was another story. I'd found a dusty book hidden behind a row of other dusty books that detailed the history of one of the oldest witch Covens, who'd had magic that bridged the gap between demons and witches.

Witches that could wield magic without always needing to perform distinct spells, use charms or talismans, or recite specific texts. Witches with magic like mine, and Mo's.

And probably, her brother Lance's.

It is believed this line descended from one witch and one demon, whose offspring then carried abilities from both into their lineage. As demons were rare, no other crosses were made into the ancestry, and over time, the demon magic weakened. Eventually, the Coven's magic returned almost completely back to normal as the demon-magic was weeded out. However, among some of its members, it seems some demon abilities persist, like a recessive gene. The Coven kept those particular members under secrecy, to protect them from other Covens who may have wished to use their abilities for ill or to force heirs from them with stronger abilities. Many claim this Coven has died out, though occasionally rumors appear of witches with unusual powers. If the Coven does persist, they have not regis-tered with the Paranormal Regulations and Interspecies Coun-cil, as all official Covens are accounted for.

Was this the answer? I read over the several paragraphs of text about this mysterious Coven again, trying to parse out any information I might have missed about where it might have gone and where it had been located to begin with. I wasn't sure knowing any of that would confirm anything for me, since I didn't know where Mo was from, and my mother could have traveled to meet with Lance.

If he even was my father.

I sat back in the creaking wooden chair I'd found in the musty room of *Rare Collections*, debating going back to the lecture.

But even if this potentially offered some answers for my own magic, it still didn't solve anything for Ruby's. The way her magic slipped into the in-between was distinctive, and there were no similarities there with my magic or Mo's. Closing the text on the Coven, I sighed, and decided to take one more look for answers for Ruby. There was something niggling at my brain about it that I couldn't shake, some-thing decidedly *off*.

Chapter Thirty-Five

MAISIE

THE AFTERNOON LECTURE was filled with more theories, more research, more evidence. Owen finished up his passionate detailing of all his research into the topic, and eventually, the discussion broke out into questions from the audience.

Would magical linking be possible between *any* two species?

Could linking happen between *more* than two individuals?

What was the worst case scenario if the link didn't work? Would the individuals simply be unaffected, or would something happen to their magic?

All the research suggested the linked individuals would need to remain in close contact to recharge themselves and each other, but was there any data on exactly how much time they needed to spend together? Most of the case studies had a romantic relationship, but was that *necessary*, or simply convenient?

On and on it went, questions coming from all sides and

all species, with Owen doing his best to answer them, despite the limited data he had to pull from.

What it came down to, more or less, was that this was uncharted territory. There was some previous experience they could refer to, yes, but on the whole?

Even if links had happened before, most of them had been a long, long time ago. The research was spotty, at best, and subjective, possibly unreliable, at worst. There would be a great deal of risk for anyone who wanted to attempt the ritual, with no clear outcomes that could be guaranteed.

Yet.

"Part of the problem I have run into time and time again is the sparse amount of evidence from any demon side of this history," Owen said as Ostara asked if there were more accounts on the original couple from the letter. "Demons, as a whole, don't keep wonderful records, much to my chagrin. Almost all of the original sources are from a witch's perspective, and do not pinpoint the original source of the magic that allowed for the linking to happen."

"And you haven't found *any* sources for this?" Lance, the man next to Morgaine, said, leaning back in his chair with a leg crossed, the picture of ease.

Owen paused, turning to look at him as if seeing him for the first time. "No, I haven't. Do you know of a source I'm missing? And, I'm sorry, I didn't catch your name."

"Lance Morgaine, Brigid's brother," he said with a smile. "It's been centuries, but I swore my sister used to have a book of demon history, didn't you, Bridgie?"

"No one has called me that in well over a lifetime, Lotty," Mo said as she shifted in her seat, her lime green and teal mandala kimono fluttering as she tugged it over her shoulders. "Honestly, I can't remember, but I gave almost my entire collection to Orion when he opened the Rare Collections section of the library."

Owen shook his head, his frown taking over his whole face. "I've scoured the Rare Collections section already. That's why I arrived in town early. Although your library is fantastic for such a small town, I didn't see anything in the demon section that I haven't seen before."

Mo turned slowly in her chair, eyes drifting to where Blaze stood in the corner of the room. He looked to his left, then right, before pointing a finger at himself. "Me?"

"Dear," Mo said, lips pursed in thought. "You know how much I love you. But, I have to ask, have *you* been in the Rare Collections section recently?"

"Oh, sure," Blaze said, arms crossed over his white tee. "Something goes missing in town and *immediately* I get blamed. I thought you knew me better than that, Mo. I'm a changed male. Always wrongfully accused."

"Blaze was in the Rare Collections section several times last fall," Orion mused from his seat on the far right side of the room.

"Did you even slow the bus down before you threw me under it, O? Or do you just love the *thunk thunk* sound of squashing your dearest friend?"

Lance laughed, his smile as bright as Mo's when he meddled. "You *do* have it, don't you, Blaze?"

"You know, Lance," — he pointed — "you were my favorite uncle until right now."

"You don't have any other uncles that I'm aware of."

"Yes, well, now I just have one really rude one."

"I bet it's in his hidey-hole if he has it," Nimue added, and Blaze mimed pulling a knife from his chest.

"Does *no one* in this family value loyalty?"

"Let me guess," Lance said, green eyes alight with mischief, "it's under a loose board in your house. I showed you the hidden compartment in the floorboards of my house, and you copied it, didn't you?"

"Please," — Blaze waved a hand dismissively — "I'm far more creati—"

"It's under a board in his room," Nimue said, rising to her feet. "Like any good little sister, I found it snooping when I was ten."

"Sabazios," Orion said, standing in front of Blaze, and I couldn't look away, not with how power oozed off Orion, white wings lifting outwards slightly, making Orion seem to grow in size. "Did you take a book from Rare Collections when you were in there this fall?"

"Okay, it's a library." Blaze held up his hands. "You're *supposed* to take the books."

"Blaze," Mo intoned pointedly, not bothering to get up from her chair as she poured something out of a flask into her iced tea on the table in front of her. With one simple word, she could command an authority-immune demon.

"Fine! Fine. Son of a kumquat," Blaze muttered, pushing off the wall and flickering out of the room.

Chatter broke out, everyone whispering as we waited for the missing puzzle piece, but Owen lifted his hands in the air.

"I think now is as good a time as any to break for the day," he said, quieting the room. "I'll review this new source and share what I find in the morning."

Chairs creaked as we all stood, emptying out into the hall. As I moved to exit, following behind Dillon, I saw Lance approach Ostara.

"It's been a long time, my Star," he said, hands in his pockets as he smiled at her. I paused to eavesdrop, pretending to read the boards displayed around the room with Owen's research. "Looking as radiant as ever."

"I'm shocked to see you here," Ostara said, her voice sounding more uneven than it had the night she'd ambushed us at Lys's house.

"It was past time to check in on Brigid and the children, but of course, they've grown up without me."

I peered over my shoulder, wondering which children he meant. Had he known about Lys and just chosen never to visit? Or was the fact that Ostara had a son new information to him?

"That does happen when you wait over thirty years to visit."

Oh, yeah. Lots of bitterness in that comment.

"Imagine my surprise when I found out you were here all along, hiding in plain sight," Lance continued, seemingly unaffected by Ostara's attitude. "The secrecy spell on my sister was a bold move, but a smart one, I suppose. I've removed it, naturally. I can't help but wonder what it is you wanted to keep such a secret from me. Or perhaps, *who*."

My heart raced as I stared wide-eyed at the poster in front of me, a blown-up version of the letter Owen had referenced this morning. Part of me regretted the choice to stay and listen, but the rest of me was dying to hear how this played out.

Ostara said nothing, though, just grabbed her bags to leave.

"That musician last night," Lance said, and damn, I wished I could have made myself invisible. Maybe if I linked powers with Lys, that was a witchy thing I could learn to do. Then my heart stopped as I realized the thought I'd just had, zoning out slightly until Lance spoke again. "A witch of yours, I assume. His aura is different, but I guess you already know that, seeing as he's your son."

"I must be going," Ostara said, pulling on the lapels of her red blazer.

"Does he know I'm his father?"

"We cannot have this conversation right now, Lance," Ostara said, holding her hand out to stop his words. "And no, he knows nothing about you. Now is not the time."

"I'd say it's very *much* the time, seeing as he carries the same powers as Brigid and me," Lance said as he handed her a pad of paper she'd left on the table in front of her. "But again, you already knew that, didn't you?"

"Maisie," Ostara suddenly barked. I jerked, spinning on my heel and, of course, lost my balance. Before I could fall in a crumpled heap on the floor, Lance held a hand out, righting me as his son had done so many times before. "Please don't tell Lysander any of this."

My mouth opened to answer, to tell her what, I wasn't sure. Would I keep this secret for her? Sure, the information shouldn't come from me, but Lys deserved to know the truth about his family, whatever that truth was. "I won't lie to him if he asks. You don't do that to someone you love."

Lance smiled at me, that same grin I'd seen so many

times on Lys's face, then turned to leave. Ostara clenched her jaw, staring at the door then back at me.

"He deserves to know who his father is," I said after a moment of tense silence. "Don't keep that secret from him."

Ostara regarded me coolly before answering. "There's more to it than that, but perhaps you're right. The time for secrets is over."

I nodded, then turned towards the door.

"One more thing," Ostara said, and I paused. "If you leave my son for Owen, abandon him the way Ronan did my sister, nothing will stop my wrath. I love my son more than anything. That's why I've shielded him from this for so long. I will destroy everything you've ever loved if you hurt him. Do you understand?"

Shock coursed through me at the mention of my father. Ronan had left Ostara's sister? He'd dated a *witch*? How had I never heard of this? The rest of her words slowly trickled in, as did a fiery wrath all my own. "Do not even *begin* to question my undying loyalty to those I love. If you come for my family, I have no problem burying you in a watery grave, Ostara."

I met her stare, a long moment passing between us, before the corner of her mouth tilted up ever so slightly. "Good."

Lys had never returned to the lecture, but after seeing how he avoided his mother's gaze, I didn't blame him. Hell, I was tempted to skip with him tomorrow, but I needed to know more about linking magics in hope that maybe I could find out how to get more power to protect our city.

I found Lys at Scallywags later, and we stayed until almost everyone else had cleared out for the night. He was so preoccupied with the mystery of Ruby's magic that he never asked about his parents, and I didn't volunteer the information, hoping Ostara made good on her word to talk to him.

Lys hung around the bar, pestering Blaze with question after question about demon magic. Mostly, Blaze didn't answer them, either because he didn't know or some sort of spell prevented him from sharing demon secrets.

"It's just strange. I've never seen anything like Ruby's magic before," Lys said as we got ready for bed later that night, lost in his thoughts. "I hoped Blaze could help point me in the right direction. I can't stop thinking there's some sort of tie to demon magic with her, but he didn't give me anything new to go off."

"What do you think is causing it to be so different?" I asked as I pulled off my shoes, unbuttoning my jeans to shimmy out of them for the night.

"Have you ever noticed that Mo —" Lys looked up right as the jeans were halfway down my thighs, his words cutting off abruptly. I stilled my hands, waiting for the nervousness to return under his gaze, but instead I found a well of confidence I'd never felt, watching the way his eyes roamed over my skin hungrily. "Goddess, you're beautiful."

I smiled, pushed them the rest of the way off, and climbed into his bed, rolling to my side to listen to him if he still wanted to talk about Ruby.

Lys stripped out of his clothes, just his black boxer briefs remaining as he dove onto the bed, tackling me to the mattress, and began peppering me with kisses. "I'm still in disbelief that this is real. That you're mine. That I can kiss every inch of your smooth skin, can lavish you with attention so you'll be addicted to me the way I am you."

I tossed my head back, feeling the way his tongue licked across my skin followed by tender kisses that turned greedy quickly.

"It's real," I said, my voice already gone breathy, not sure whether I was answering him or telling myself. Thoughts of our parents, of escaped criminals, of magical linking ceremonies, of the entire world drifted away when I was in Lys's arms, feeling loved like I never had before.

Chapter Thirty-Six

LYSANDER

I WOKE before the sun the next morning, watching as Maisie slept peacefully at my side, her hand on my chest. My heart ached at the sight, fuller than it had ever been. How had I not realized what I was missing? The way I felt about Maisie was so much more than I'd ever felt about anything, except music. She was the air I breathed, the beat of my heart, the rhythm in my blood.

We'd only known each other for a matter of weeks, but already I couldn't imagine my life without her.

I rolled to my back, staring at the ceiling as I was lost to my thoughts, waxing poetic about how much I loved her. I couldn't imagine leaving her, which then somehow brought my mind to my mother. And then, *him*.

Did he even know I existed? Had my mother hid me from him intentionally? And, if so, why?

I shook myself, clearing my head of the past. I was a grown man. I didn't need a father, and whatever drama existed was between Ostara and Lance, not me. I needed a distraction, and Ruby's magic was the perfect excuse.

Quietly, so as not to wake Maisie, I slid from the bed, grabbed clean clothes and went into the bathroom, getting ready for the day.

No way was I planning on attending the Summit again. With both Ostara and Lance in the room, any ability I had to focus on whatever Owen said would be lost, and I knew Maisie would tell me what she learned later.

Exiting the house quietly, I turned right, headed towards Mo's house, hoping I could catch Ruby before they left for the Summit.

"Sorry, Lys," Ruby shrugged, her hands wrapped around mug of coffee in Morgaine's kitchen thirty minutes later. "As far as I can tell, everything is normal now."

"That's just not possible," I said, bewildered. I looked to Mo for help, who eyed Ruby curiously. "You can see it, can't you? Her aura is still all messed up."

Mo hummed in agreement. "It *is* strange," she admitted. "But if it's not doing any harm, I'm not sure what else there is to do. Your magic does seem much more controllable, dear," she added to Ruby, "and that's the most important thing for now."

"You haven't had any other strange occurrences?" I pressed, leaning forward, and Ruby shook her head. "Nothing with fire, or anything like demon magic? No bursts of magic, or any bizarre results from spells you're casting?"

"I mean, I think my spell casting is more powerful," Ruby offered, and Mo nodded in agreement. "But I'm pretty sure that's just because I can focus better now, without the hex. It's easier to harness my power."

Frustrated, and knowing there was more to this than met the eye, I left Morgaine's to head to Town Hall early. The Summit would reconvene later, but I wanted to check the library. Again.

When had I become such a bookworm?

Since magic stopped making sense, apparently.

Pulling my phone from my pocket, I shot off a quick text.

LYS

Good morning, princess. Headed to the library, but will meet you for lunch at Scallywags later.

Still staring at my phone, I contemplated adding an "I love you" on the end, but deleted it. The first time I said those three words to her, I'd say them to her face. Not watching where I was going, I ran right smack into someone on the sidewalk.

"Sorry." I slid my phone back in my pocket as I looked up with a smile. "Wasn't paying attention."

And then I realized who I'd run into.

"Not a problem, son," Lance said as he patted my arm. "Texting and walking is a dangerous combination."

The blood in my veins iced over at the word *son*. Sure, it wasn't an uncommon phrase, but had he meant it that way? Remembering my manners, I stuck out my hand for a shake.

"I don't think we've met yet." I offered a smile. "Lysander Theroux."

"The witch I've heard so much about lately." Lance

shook my hand. We were nearly eye to eye, and it was eerie to stare into a gaze that I'd only ever seen in a mirror before. "Lance Morgaine. Call me Lance."

I nodded, words lost to me. What did one say to their potential father? *Nice eyes. They look like mine. Is it your recessive gene that gave them to me?*

"Theroux," Lance said, dropping my hand. "I've known the Theroux family for quite some time. Care for a coffee? I swear I saw the van parked near the pier this morning."

Even though I was heading to the library, I couldn't say no. Holding my hand out, I pointed in the direction of the ocean, and Lance nodded, some sort of internal battle won.

"Your mother was a dear friend of mine some time ago," Lance said as he slid his hands in his pockets. I said nothing, hoping he'd keep talking, that he'd take care of this whole conversation for us. My heart slammed in my chest in anticipation. "I'd never seen such an inquisitive young witch as my Star. Her curiosity was enrapturing."

Okay, gross. That sounded like a pet name for my mother, and no one wanted to think of their mother as *enrapturing* anyone.

"Did you know your mother put a secrecy spell on Brigid?" Lance turned to see my reaction as we neared the beach. My brow dipped in confusion, not recognizing the name. "Sorry, I believe you call my sister by our surname, Morgaine. Or Mo, I believe."

"Oh." I nodded, my brain moving in a thousand directions at once. "And no, I didn't know that. Why would my mother put a secrecy spell on Mo?"

"A question I believe you should ask her yourself." Lance stopped in front of the aqua blue coffee van, then stepped back, eyes wide as he noticed the giant bull moose sitting only a few yards away on the beach, sunbathing on the rocks.

"That's just Winston." I gave a dismissive wave. "He loves to sunbathe. He won't bother you unless you walk down the beach with a frosted donut, then it's every man for himself. Nothing stands between Winston and his sweets."

"Noted," Lance chuckled. "It's becoming more and more evident why Bridgie likes this town. It's as strange as she is."

"Without a doubt."

"Good morning, oh —" Caedmon popped up on the inside of the coffee van, glancing between us with slightly widened eyes. "Lance, it's been ages! Val, Lance is here!" He looked around behind him. "Where'd he run off to?"

The back door of the van cracked open as Val slipped inside, dusting off his hands. He stopped in his tracks, looking up at Caedmon guiltily, and Caedmon made a choked noise as he whipped around, leaning out the open window of the van. I followed his line of sight to see Winston's long pink tongue licking his lips.

"Were you — did you just *give* Winston a donut?"

"No?"

"This is why he keeps pestering us! My husband is a sap!"

"He looked hungry!"

Caedmon shook his head as Val gave him a sheepish smile, then turned to us. He, too, looked between us curiously.

"Wow, you both have the *strangest* light green eyes I've ever seen, and green is already one of the rarest eye colors," he commented conversationally, like he hadn't just picked up the spoon to stir the biggest pot of drama in town at the moment. "Are those contacts?"

I pressed my lips together, rubbing the back of my neck as I shot a look at Lance, who cleared his throat and replied, "No, they're not contacts."

"Oh." Val nodded, oblivious to the tension he'd created. "What a weird coincidence, then!"

We ordered coffees, and I could sense Lance wanted to say more, but something was holding him back. Fearing what I'd say to fill the awkward silence, I bolted back towards the library after a brusque goodbye, leaving him by the pier.

I was climbing the steps to Town Hall when I spotted a woman approaching at the same time.

"Excuse me, could you point out the nearest coffee shop?" she said, pointing at my cup.

I didn't recognize her, but there were a lot of visitors in town for the Summit. She smiled brightly, pale skin almost the same color as her teeth contrasting heavily against her inky black hair. Her eyes had that same blue-green shade found on many sea nymphs, and something tugged at me, a feeling like I should know who she was, but I dismissed it. "I guess you haven't been to town before?"

"No, just here for the Summit," she said. "Why?"

"Well, I'm afraid we don't have a coffee shop." I moved down a step to join her on the sidewalk. "The coffee van is parked down by the pier today, or there's Immortali-Tea across the green." I pointed, and she turned to follow my arm.

"Oh, what an unusual bracelet!" she said, grabbing my

wrist to inspect it closer. I bristled slightly at her cold touch, but, for the sake of friendliness, allowed it. "Is that sea nymph twine?"

I tried to hide a smile as I examined the intricately knotted rope Maisie had given me. "It is. My girlfriend gave it to me." Damn, I still loved being able to say that and mean it, no pretense attached.

"And you're a witch?" she said, black eyebrows rising slightly in surprise. "You two must be thrilled at the idea of a linking ceremony, then."

I gave a non-committal, polite smile, pulling my wrist out of her grip.

"How sweet." She smiled, though it didn't quite meet her eyes. "Which nymph is your girlfriend? I met a few of them at the lecture yesterday — maybe I ran into her. I'd love one just like that for my, ah… niece."

"Maisie Douglass. She'll be around later, I'm sure she'd be happy to make more. What's your name and I'll tell her to look for you?"

"Ness. And you are?"

"Lysander. I'll pass along the message for you."

"How wonderful." She took a step back. "Well, don't let me keep you, Lysander. I'm sure we'll see each other around soon."

With one last wave, I started up the steps again, the woman turning to walk away.

I blinked, my vision going slightly hazy, and shook my head.

Then I missed a step, my knees crashing to the stone steps, and everything went dark.

Chapter Thirty-Seven

MAISIE

"MOST EXAMPLES OF LINKING MAGIC, while sparse and lacking in sufficient detail, are relatively positive," Owen said as the lecture continued the next day. It was an unseasonably warm day in the un-airconditioned conference room, and my giant iced tea from Immortali-Tea was already half-gone. Lys and I had been up half the night busy with… other activities, and I was already watching the clock for the next break. "However, there is one instance of an attempt going wrong that is important to study."

He clicked his remote, and the slide changed to a news article from thirty years ago, citing a rare tsunami off the coast of Maine.

Rogue wall of water plunders Old Orchard Beach; thousands of fish and other marine life wash up dead hours later.

"This event stemmed from a sea nymph attempting to harness witch magic for her own use," Owen continued. I blinked in surprise as I sought out the back of Ronan's head, several rows in front of me, but it was immovable. If he knew of this event — and how could he *not* — he gave no sign of it, and he'd certainly never mentioned it to me. "Some of you may have known Inessa before she was put into the Iron Keep. She fell in love with a human, and due to the laws of her people, decided she would give up her power altogether in order to be with him. Using witch spell-work, she attempted to purge herself of her nymph magic, though no one has confirmed what spell she attempted. Whatever it was, the combination of the spell and her own power backfired, corrupting the water around her, her magic, and some say, her mind as well." Owen paused, looking out into the audience, then stopped when he found Ronan. "Ronan, is there any more to that story you could add to help us?"

Ronan tilted his head back as he considered what else he was willing to share with the crowd. We all knew her name — it was hard to forget the name of the person who murdered your mother — but I hardly knew anything about her beyond that.

"The female Inessa became after that was not the friend I grew up with," he said finally, his voice tight. I exchanged a glance with Saoirse beside me. "The things she's done since that day... I only thank Poseidon her parents aren't still alive to see what she's become. I have no knowledge of the spell she tried to work, or what went wrong." His tone turned colder as he crossed his arms. "I do know, now, that supposedly angels have the ability to take power away, so if they'd been willing to help her, maybe some of this tragedy could have been avoided."

"Powers are only ever removed as punishment, and have only been taken permanently on a handful of occasions," Ezra, the Chancellor, answered the underlying accusation in

Ronan's tone. "Inessa didn't come to us, but even if she had, we would have denied her. It is unheard of for a supernatural to *ask* for their magic to be taken away. She would have been institutionalized first."

Ronan scoffed, not bothering to turn around to meet Ezra's eye. "Inessa knew her own mind, even if I never would have agreed with or supported her decision. And at least if you had institutionalized her, it might have avoided the aftermath."

"Did *you* know about any of this?" Blaire whispered, leaning forward to shoot accusatory looks at both Saoirse and myself, but we both shook our heads.

"Ronan's only mentioned her being a nymph turned evil, the worst of the worst," I whispered back. "I had no idea he actually *knew* her."

Saoirse nodded. "Remember he used to just call her Ursula when we were kids? She was like a cautionary tale."

We sat back, returning our attention to the discussion.

"It's possible her spell backfired because she was working alone, as far as we know," Owen said. "All the other recorded events included individuals working together. For instance, the witch and the demon who were able to share powers — *both* were present, and both contributed to the spell." Owen set his papers down on the podium, crossing one ankle over the other. "From here, it might be a game of trial and error."

A yelp erupted from the back of the room, and we all turned to see Blaze hastily trying to put out the fire he'd accidentally ignited — right in Peg Fernsby's coiffed purple hair.

Maybe we were all a little on edge.

When Lys didn't show for lunch at Scallywags, I wondered if he'd gotten lost in the library. Except that I knew for a fact our library had maybe ten rows of stacks, and was impossible to get lost in. Still, I didn't want to seem clingy on our second day of dating, so I tried to keep my text casual.

MAISIE

How's the research going?

I waited for a response while I sat in the booth with my sisters and had lunch.

I waited through the afternoon portion of the Summit. Still nothing.

MAISIE

Is everything all right?

That one might have held a hint of clinginess, but I was starting to get worried.

Then I waited through dinner with Dillon, when he also mentioned he hadn't heard from Lys all day.

I went to bed that night — Lys's bed — alone, and stared at the ceiling as I went through every single scenario that could have possibly happened.

With a gasp, I bolted upright. *Fucking hell. He's driven into a ditch somewhere and has been taken to a human hospital and they're going to ask him his blood type and he's not going to know it and he's going to die!*

Hand over my racing heart, I tried to quell the rising

nausea. How could he not know his blood type? I'd *known* something like this would happen!

No, he'd said they could easily do the test at the hospital and figure it out, if it was necessary. Besides, a hospital would have contacted next of kin by now, right?

Ostara would know?

And she would have told me. Wouldn't she?

I pulled Lys's pillow over my face and groaned into it, inhaling his citrus and vetiver scent as my only source of comfort. Then I spent the night tossing and turning, assuming the worst.

The next day, when I still hadn't heard from Lys, I was officially Concerned. With a capital C.

Back in the conference room, the seats had been rearranged to facilitate more discussion, now that the lecture portion of the Summit was concluded. From here, the leaders would discuss what to do next. Ideas for how to proceed, and who might want to be our magical guinea pigs.

I marched right up to Ostara the moment I entered the room.

"Have you heard from Lys?" I realized my voice was coming out too blunt, too bold, but it was better than shaky.

Ostara raised an austere brow, then sighed and reached for her phone. "Trouble in paradise already? Well, don't say you weren't warned that Lys isn't a *settling down* sort of boy."

I clenched my hands into fists at my sides, resisting the urge to slap her both for insinuating Lys was already done with me, and for calling him a *boy*. The male was 36, for Poseidon's sake!

Then Ostara's superior expression faltered, her brows furrowing. "He's not —" She looked around the room. "Was he outside? His phone shows he's in the building."

Of *course* she had a tap on his phone. Ignoring the righteous indignation on Lys's behalf about that, I peeked at her phone screen, and frowned at the blinking dot for Lys's phone that did, in fact, look to be right out front.

Relief whooshed through me , and I spun and rushed from the room, running down the stone steps outside Town Hall.

I twisted around, looking up and down the street, but saw only other people heading in for today's Summit. No Lysander.

"Ah, you must be Maisie," a melodic voice said behind me, and I turned. A woman with inky black hair and sea nymph green eyes stood before me in a loose-fitting black maxi dress that caught in the breeze.

"Do I know you?"

The woman clutched a phone in her hand. Was that —?

"Sadly, no," she pouted, but it felt like mockery. "Your stubborn father never wanted us to know each other. Isn't that tragic? You should have grown up practically a niece to me."

My breath caught, hardly recognizing this frail woman from the photos the PRICs had sent out after the prison break. "Inessa?"

"Oh, so you *have* heard of me." A laugh pealed out of her, one that might have sounded effervescent to a human, but I recognized the chime of siren magic within it, and my blood chilled. I fought not to take a step back, but she was holding Lys's phone, so I stood my ground. Her laugh petered out, her expression growing steel-cold. "Then maybe you also know what I'm capable of."

"Inessa."

Ronan's voice boomed across the town square as he strode over. He didn't look at me, but his hand came to rest firmly on my shoulder as he stepped in front of me, half-blocking me from her view.

"What are you doing here? What do you want?" He nodded towards the building behind her. "You know there are angels in there just waiting to re-arrest you."

"Oh, Ronan, don't you worry about little old me. I'll be long gone in a moment."

Kymari came out of the Hall with her father then, both stepping up to our sides. My hands shook with anxiety, an overwhelming sense of dread taking over as I stared at Inessa clutching Lys's phone. *Why did she have his phone?* Kymari's hand slipped into mine, squeezing tight as she nudged my shoulder, chin held high as she stared down the most wanted sea nymph in the world.

"Where is he?" My voice cracked, breaths coming in ragged gasps as I fought not to spiral out of control.

"Sweet boy you have," Inessa said with a shrug, looking down at his phone. "Imagine my surprise when I found out your daughter is in love with a *witch*, Ronan. I guess the apple doesn't fall far from the tree, does it?"

"Enough with the shit, Inessa," Ronan spat at her. "You've taken enough from our family, don't you think?"

The door behind us opened again, several more people filtering out as Inessa broke into a wide smile, her eyes scanning the faces there as a giddy laugh escaped her. "This is so fun. When Nergal told me the plan was to expose you all to the humans starting here in Deadlights Cove, I just *knew* I had to be involved."

"Where is Lysander?" Ronan took a step closer to her.

"What?" Ostara pushed forward, shock showing in her face. "Why are you talking about my son?"

"Funny thing about Deadlights Cove," Inessa said with a deep breath. "It's so *close* to the human world. Naive of you all to think this little town could stay hidden here when so many popular tourist destinations sit on either side."

"*Where is my son?*" Ostara said, her voice shaking as she pushed forward, magic sparking at her fingertips.

"Why, he's enjoying a day at the beach! I always forget, can witches breathe underwater?" Inessa said, right as a demon who looked eerily similar to Blaze flickered into the square behind her, hand resting on her hip. I'd only heard of Blaze's brother Errakal before, never seen him myself, but the resemblance was obvious enough. Same olive skin, same black eyes, only Errakal had messy, shoulder-length hair and gave off serious *Stay back, he bites* vibes. "I guess we'll all find out soon."

With a wave, the two disappeared, and chaos ensued.

Chapter Thirty-Eight

MAISIE

OSTARA SPUN ON RONAN, chest heaving. "What beach? Where is he?"

Ronan's jaw worked, teeth gnashing together in a way that was entirely more shark than human. "The only one that mattered to her. Old Orchard."

Orion moved to the front of the gathered crowd as my vision started to black out, panic consuming me. "That's a human beach. There is no way we can get in and out of there unseen."

"My magic doesn't extend that far," Ronan said grimly. "I can't hide us in those waters."

"We'll have to go in by boat then," Orion said, and I shook with anger, hands clenched tight as I spun, searching the crowd for Blaze.

"Maisie," Ronan called as I stormed off. "Don't do anything rash."

I turned on him, teeth bared as tears streamed down my face. "Don't you *dare* tell me what to do right now. You have no power over me, disowning me, banishing me from our people. And now you expect me to fall in line when you're talking about how to rescue the male I love? To take my time, when he's out there *drowning* because of *me*? No. I'll do what I have to do, and you can either help, or get out of my way."

"You can't do this on your own," Orion said after my father didn't answer. "It's too much ocean to search alone."

"She's not alone." Kymari moved to my side, followed by each of my six sisters, standing in a circle around me. "I'm going, too."

Ronan shook his head, his eyes wide at the eight of us standing against him, realizing this was a battle he couldn't win.

"I will never forgive you, Ronan, if you let my son die today," Ostara added, her eyes meeting mine briefly.

Ronan exhaled, resignation settling in, but he was already turning to the ocean beyond. "Xuma. Gather your guards. How many sharks will it take to clear the water near the beach?"

My body buzzed with energy as I whirled back around to Blaze at the back of the crowd. "Blaze, get me to a boat, *now*."

"A boat?" he asked, nose scrunched as he fought to follow my reasoning. "What kind of boat?"

"A boat as close to Old Orchard Beach as we can get."

Without missing a beat, Blaze hopped down the stairs, followed by Owen and Nimue. "Everybody grab on," Blaze said as he gripped my hand and Kymari's. My sisters each latched onto Nimue and Owen, holding on as we prepared to flicker out. "Nimmie, I'll text coordinates the second I have them. Captain Blaze Sparrow, comin' up, and — in two seconds when you start screaming — remember you asked for this."

Two seconds later, we screamed. We'd reappeared above the water, the ocean shining below us as far as the eye could see, and growing rapidly closer as we tumbled through the air.

"Not to worry, I see a boat! Once more —"

With another nauseating twist, Blaze flickered us again, and this time, we clunked down onto something solid.

"What the fuck?" an unknown voice shouted as my knees crashed to a slippery floor. I grabbed onto the side of the boat we'd crash-landed onto as it bobbed in the ocean waves. "Did you just fall outta the fuckin' sky?!"

"Uh" — Kymari and I exchanged a glance, but Blaze was texting away, and a minute later, reinforcements joined us in the form of Owen, Nimue, and my sisters. The man whose boat we'd commandeered went even wider-eyed than he'd been a moment before.

"Sincerest apologies," Owen said, his accent making the situation even more ridiculous. "We need to borrow your boat for a little while, lad."

I fought to keep my breakfast down, the world spinning from my first — and then second — experience flickering, as the man screamed at us, "Where the fuck did you come from?"

"Hell." Blaze stepped up to the man, pinched his neck lightly, and the human fisherman collapsed to the floor of the boat.

"Did you just kill him?" Isla gasped at my side.

"Nah." Blaze dragged the man up to the front of the boat, propping him against the side and out of our way. "He's just napping until I can have Orion wipe his memory later."

"Hell?" Nimue asked, a hint of laughter in her voice as she looked at Blaze. "That was dramatic, even for you."

"And appearing out of nowhere *isn't?*" Blaze scoffed, hands on his hips. "At least I didn't ask him why the rum was gone."

"Move," Kymari ordered, nudging the demons out of the way, getting behind the wheel, and turning over the engine. In seconds, we were roaring through the water, moving towards shore. As we neared, I saw hundreds of humans, playing in the water and on the beach in the distance. My heart raced as I patted Kymari's arm, and she killed the engine.

"Ready girls?" My voice shook as adrenaline coursed through my body. "Don't worry about the humans. Just find him."

"On it," Saoirse said as she stripped down, stepping onto the platform on the back of the boat, and dove into the water. An instant later, a shark fin split the water before diving deep. One after the next, my sisters did the same, some taking mer form, some sharks, and the twins as dolphins until it was only Kymari and me on the boat.

"We're gonna find him, okay?" she said, grim determination on her face.

I nodded, words lost to me as I pulled her into a hug. "Thank you for coming, for being here and trying to help —"

"You know I'll always have your back when it counts, M."

We broke apart, even my no-nonsense, tough best friend's eyes glistening, and together, we stripped and dove in.

Head towards shore, girls, I projected to all of them. *She wants us to accidentally reveal supes, so Lys must be somewhere that could happen.*

I swam, cutting through the water faster than I ever had, feeling the rush of my magic returning to me in spades as the water pulsed around me. I scanned the water as I rushed towards the shore, not even caring when I passed below surfers and swimmers.

Shit.

There were so many humans here, I didn't know how we'd ever get out of this, but right now, Lys was more important. Panic clawed at me with every passing moment, not knowing how long Lys had been down here, or how much time he had left. If he had *any.*

A choked sound escaped me at the thought, but I refused to give it even an inch of space in my mind as I kicked harder, swam faster.

Above the water, I heard screams, and I looked over my shoulder, seeking the cause of the commotion. Swimming towards me was my father in his Great White form, cutting through the water as swimmers fled back to land. And Ronan wasn't the only one here: Xuma's hammerhead form swam to my right, skimming the surface as his fin sliced through the waves, entirely too close to a surfer who paddled hard towards shore.

My heart surged, tears pricking my eyes as I noticed the sheer number of my people who had shown up to help. There was no way we were getting out of today without helicopters overhead documenting the unprecedented shark activity in the area, but I didn't care. And, apparently, neither did my father.

Try the pier, my father said. I nodded and turned, swimming hard, pushing through the water. I dodged anchored boats as I left the swimming area and moved closer to the pier as if my life depended on it. But it wasn't *my* life at stake.

I spotted the pilings jutting down into the water before I saw anything else, the dark churning water below cast in shadows. Weaving through the posts, I searching frantically, each second that ticked by dragging me down like lead weights.

Kymari stuck close to my side, her white scales glittering in the fractured sunlight as she searched the left side while I took the right, diving deeper, looking everywhere.

Be here, Lys, I thought to myself, the words a desperate plea. *Be alive.*

To your right! Kymari called, pointing behind me. I twisted around, sucking in a breath when I saw him. Lys was tied up inside a cage, the cage attached to a piling near the end of the pier. His head was bobbing half-submerged in the water, which crept up higher and higher with every wave as the tide came in. He was unconscious, his eyes closed as I swam to him. With a strangled cry, I went for the cage door, trying to focus on the fact that his chest was still moving, even if every other breath he tried to take was underwater, choking him as he coughed and sputtered in his sleep state.

The cage wasn't spelled, but Inessa hadn't skimped on the quality of the metal.

Maze!

Kymari's call cut through my panicked fumbling with the lock. I jerked my head up, cutting off a gasp as I saw floating around us hundreds of Portuguese Man o' Wars. They couldn't harm Kymari or myself — at most, it would feel like a bug bite — but Lys? Attacked by this many of them?

I groaned in frustration, forced to leave off the cage for now to deal with the venomous creatures.

On three?

Kymari nodded, and together, we pushed out with our magic, churning the sea around us to move the dangerous, drifting animals away.

The water covered Lys's nose.

Dad! Even in my head, my voice sounded choked, watching Lys's head submerge more and more with each moment we had to spend pulsing the water, clearing it of the animals. We wouldn't have a moment to lose to get him out of there once they were cleared.

A giant Great White shark stalked up out of the blue as the last of the creatures were cleared out, and without a word, Ronan knew what to do.

Lys was choking and coughing on the water, still knocked out, as the water reached his eyes. Another cry bubbled out of me.

Ronan's large jaws clamped onto the cage door, tearing through it with his increased magical strength. He tossed the door away, and I hurried in, ripping through the bonds that held him, pulling them free as fast as I could. Kymari appeared at his other side, working on his legs as I freed his upper body.

Get him back to the boat! Kymari said, but I ignored her, needing to breach the surface with him as soon as possible. I needed him to breathe. To be alive.

Surging up, we surfaced beside the pier. As my head cleared the waves, a human leaned over the railing, pointing at where I held Lys in my arms. "Get out of the water!! There are sharks everywhere!"

I looked up, and heard the click of a camera. "What's on her face?" someone said, then another click.

"Oh my God, is that a tail?" someone else pointed, but I tuned them out.

I needed Lys to take a breath. I shook him lightly, and sealed my mouth to his. I kissed him hard, infusing him with my magic, needing to dispel whatever Inessa had used on him to knock him out.

With a wheezing gasp, Lys came to, his eyes blowing wide as he choked and coughed up the water in his lungs. I let out a relieved exhale, wanting to pull him into my arms but not wanting to disrupt his breaths.

"Lys," I cried, his name a choked breath as I cupped his face. "Just breathe. Fuck, I thought you were dead."

"Hey," he said, shivers starting to rack his body as Inessa's spell left him. "Where are we?"

There was another camera flash, and Lys turned, finally noticing the humans on the pier above us and the misguided lifeguards racing towards us on jetskis.

"I'm so sorry," I said, the words clawing out of my throat as I thought through every possible way this could end between supes and humans. None of them were good. But Lys was in my arms, and he was breathing.

A startled cry caught my attention and I looked up to see several people pointing out to sea.

"What the fuck is that?!" someone called, and I swiveled to see where they pointed.

"Is that a *kraken?*" another answered, and my heart pounded in my chest. "Holy shit, that thing is huge, Jay."

"What are you doing, Ronan?" I muttered, trying to understand what I was seeing. A giant tentacle rose above the waves right as it curled around the jetski closest to us, snapping it in half as the lifeguard dove into the water off the side, swimming for shore like he'd been attacked by a mythical creature. Maybe because he had.

"Oh fuck," Lys said, eyes wide as he looked back at me.

"I think it's time to go." I shifted my hold around his waist, starting to swim through the water. Two dolphins appeared on either side of me — Blaire and Isla — bobbing in the water as I shifted Lys to their backs, showing him how to grab their dorsal fins.

"You idiot! Why are you swimming *away* from shore?" someone called from the pier.

"Ignore them. Ready for the ride of your life?" I said as Lys looked back at me. "Don't let go."

I ducked below the water as my sisters took off, carrying Lys away from shore and towards the boat Blaze still captained further out.

I realized I should be dreading the fallout of this, not knowing how anyone could explain away a commandeered boat, unusual shark activity, a mermaid, a kraken, and then random dolphins appearing out of nowhere to carry Lys *away* from shore as the icing to this chaotic cake. But Lys was alive, and, at the moment, nothing else mattered. Following my sisters, I surfaced as Blaze pulled Lys out of the water, and Selene was waiting there to help him.

"You're breathing, so that's the first step," she said with a nod, pulling free a stethoscope from her bag. "But I still want to give your heart and lungs a listen, and you've got a few nasty welts."

"Portuguese Man O' War in the water," I supplied, and Selene nodded. "They're not native to this area; Inessa must have brought them in to slow us down."

"Once we get back, Dev has a toxin-removing salve in her shop we can use that should help," Selene said.

"Yeah those sting like a bitch, but I'm fine," Lys said, pushing Selene's hands away as I pulled myself out of the water. Lys stood on shaky legs, stumbling towards me as I threw myself into his arms, kissing him passionately.

"I thought I was going to lose you," I whispered as he crushed me to his body, pulling us to the floor. A towel landed over my back, covering what I now realized was my entirely naked form, sprawled across Lys's lap.

"I'm right here." He smiled, kissing my forehead and soothing a hand down my back, as if *I* was the one who'd nearly died, not him. "You know, I don't think that lady really wanted my bracelet?"

"Why are you always so damn calm?" I slapped his wet chest. "You almost *died* at the hands of a psychopath, who is a known murderer. Don't you have any feelings about that?"

"Now, *she* was one of those sirens you're always warned about. And hey, maybe I could've died, but I didn't," Lys breathed against my forehead, his lips still resting there, like he couldn't stop kissing me. "You saved me, just like I knew you would."

The boat roared to life, engine rumbling under us as Kymari took over at the wheel, steering us back out into the ocean. "Where to?"

"Home," I said, tears pricking my eyes. "Get me away from here."

With a nod, Kymari pushed the boat into gear, cutting through the waves.

Chapter Thirty-Nine

LYSANDER

ONCE WE WERE FAR ENOUGH off-shore to avoid most of the camera crews and helicopters now swarming the beach, Blaze had Kymari stop the boat. As the engine stilled, Blaze flickered out, returning a moment later with Orion.

"He seems fine," Selene said from where she squatted in front of the human fisherman, checking his pulse. "Are you ready for me to wake him up?"

With a heavy sigh, Orion turned to the rest of us. "Time for you to get home," he said, eyes trained on the demons. "Owen and Nimue?"

Leaving the question blank, he skirted the demon's inability to comply with demands, but we all knew what he needed. "Meet you at Town Hall?" I asked, eyeing the mayor. His hair was more disheveled than I'd ever seen it, like he'd run his fingers through it a hundred times today. Even though he would have been wearing a suit for the Summit earlier, he was now only in a grey button down, no tie, sleeves rolled hastily to the elbow. Orion nodded, and I stood, Maisie, now dressed, at my side. Her sisters and

Kymari gathered around us, each grabbing onto Nimue and Owen.

In an instant, the boat disappeared, and our feet slammed down on the grass in front of the gazebo. My mother jumped up from where she sat, peeling away from Lance, who'd been holding her protectively.

"Lysander!" she cried as she pulled me to her.

I dropped Maisie's hand, hugging my mother tightly, feeling how she shook with emotion as she clung to me. When was the last time my mother hugged me? I couldn't remember. Certainly, I'd been shorter than her. Now, I could rest my chin on her head, and I let my magic loose, pooling in my fingertips as I'd watched Mo do so many times. As I smoothed my hand over her back, I pulled every calm thought I could to the surface, soothing her worries with my steady presence. "I'm fine, Mom."

"When she said she'd taken you, my heart stopped," Ostara said, her voice choking with sobs. Not once in all of my 36 years could I remember my mother crying, and it pricked tears of my own. I met Lance's eye where he'd hung back, watching us with a small smile.

"Maisie saved me," I said as I felt my other's breathing evening out. "And Ronan. Mom, he can be a *kraken*."

"I know." Ostara stepped back, wiping the last of the tears from her face as she chuckled, rolling her eyes. "The male is nothing if not dramatic."

Maisie laughed behind me, and I held my hand out to her, pulling her forward and into my arms.

"Thank you, Maisie." Ostara gave her the warmest smile she'd offered her yet. "I'll never forget this."

My heart swelled at my mother's words, leaning in to

kiss Maisie's head as she brought hand to my chest. "Good, because neither will I. I'll spend the rest of my life working to be worthy of her."

Maisie tilted her head up to mine, laying a soft kiss on my lips. "You already are."

My mother's eyes drifted between us, seeming to reassess the woman in my arms, but I was done sharing her for the day.

"We're going home. I want out of these clothes," I said, not waiting for anyone to answer as I dragged Maisie along with me. Luckily, everyone was smart enough to not follow us.

"You should clean those welts out right away."

"Definitely."

Yeah, right *after* I showed Maisie just how amazing I thought it was that she saved my life.

As we turned away from Town Hall, my mind flashed back to yesterday. Inessa must have knocked me out in town, because the next thing I knew, I was in a cage under the pier, tied up and locked in as the water rose at my feet, coming in with the tide.

"Nothing personal," Inessa had said, then cackled, the sound echoing off the pier above as she held me in place with her magic. "Well, not personal for *you*. Very personal for me. I do so love ruining Ronan's life any chance I can. Since I've already killed both his wife *and* Lyra, the love of his life — on the same day, no less — I figure starting on his daughters' lovers only makes sense now. I guess that makes it a little personal, doesn't it?"

Shock coursed through me at her admission, thinking of

Maisie's mom and my aunt Lyra, both murdered to hurt Ronan. No wonder he was so protective of his family.

The moment the lock had clicked in place, magic had coursed up through the water, around my feet, sucking any energy I had left from me. My eyes had closed while I fought against the bonds, the world fading as regret swallowed me along with the water. Regret that it had taken me so long to notice Maisie. Regret that I'd never told her how much I loved her. Regret that I couldn't have one last kiss.

When I'd woken to Maisie literally breathing life back into me, I thought I'd died and was dreaming. If there was an afterlife, an eternal bliss waiting for me, then she'd be there, guiding me home.

Then the flashes of human cameras had brought me back to Earth, and the rest of the pieces had fallen into place.

I hadn't died.

And now, with Maisie's hand in mine, I felt more alive than I ever had. I ripped open the front door, glad the house was so close to Town Hall. I needed her like I needed oxygen to breathe.

A feeling I was acutely familiar with today.

I kept my chuckle to myself as I pulled Maisie through my room, then into my bathroom. She had said I should clean off, after all.

"Are there some on your back you need help reaching?"

I laughed as I pulled the shirt off my head, throwing it down on the tile with a wet plop. "Probably."

I switched the shower on, then turned back to Maisie, her eyes darkening when she figured out what I wanted.

"Oh."

I nudged her back until her hips met the counter, then threaded one hand through her platinum waves, the other on her jaw, angling her face up to mine.

Steam fogged the mirror as my lips crashed down on hers, hands working up her side as I pulled her shirt over her head, needing to feel her skin. Sensing my desperation, she pulled at my jeans, unbuttoning them as I did the same, stripping each other down to nothing.

"You saved me." I kissed down her jaw, skimming her neck, and across her collar bone as I dug my fingers into her hips. Her hands lifted over my head, scratching through the back of my hair as she pulled me into her, head tipped back. Every touch, every sound she made, grounded me, reminded me how very alive I was.

Nearly dying would do that to you.

"Goddess, Maisie," I said as she leaned into my touch, my lips trailing down her body, worshiping her. "I never knew love could feel like this. So consuming. All I could think about as the world faded out was that I wanted to kiss you one more time. But it'll never be enough, will it?"

"Never," she agreed, reaching for a towel. "And I never want to be so afraid I'm losing you again."

She pushed me back a step, and dropped the towel at our feet, sinking to her knees on top of it.

"*Maze* —"

My breath stuttered as her fingers trailed up my thighs, her face inches from my hard length, her warm breath ghosting over me as she met my eyes. And wrapped a hand around me before pulling me into her mouth.

"*Fuck.*" The tight, wet heat of her mouth was perfection, and my hand threaded through her hair, tugging gently. There was no way she was fitting all of me into her mouth, but she took in as much as she could and kept a hand wrapped around me too, moving it in tandem with her mouth. It was all I could do to hold still, to let her set the pace, but I didn't want to push her too hard, too fast, knowing she was less experienced than me.

"You're so fucking beautiful," I managed between bobs of her head as I stroked her cheek. Her eyes flicked up to mine again, those seaglass green eyes heavily lidded as lust shone through, making me twitch in her mouth.

She pulled free with a wet *pop*, running her hands along my length as she licked the underside. My head tipped back as I held onto her, feeling her wet tongue lap along the underside of my shaft. "Shit, you're good at this."

She took me down again, setting a rhythmic pace that I couldn't help but match, and it didn't take long before I was on the brink, my entire body keyed up and ready. But I wasn't ready for this to be over.

"Maze, I need to be inside you," I tugged her head back, groaning as she licked the tip of me, then wiped her mouth. "I need to feel you come around me."

I pulled her back to her feet and kissed her, plundering her mouth, tasting myself on her tongue. Grabbing her hips, I lifted her high enough to wrap her legs around my waist as I backed her against the wall.

"I love you, Lys." Her breath was hot on my neck as she ground herself against me. "The thought of living a life without you wrecked me."

"Good thing you don't have to then," I said. "Though I do have plans to wreck you time and time again." I planted her against the wall and reached between us, a whimper escaping her as I teased her. "Fuck, Maze, you're so wet for me."

Unable to wait any longer, I lined myself up with her, and she moaned as I slid home, her head falling back to rest on the wall. My head dropped down to her chest, hearing the way her heart raced as I moved.

"You feel so good," I said, my voice choked as I fought back the need to pound into her, to make her feel as undone as she made me.

"More." The word was strangled as Maisie gripped my shoulders, her nails digging into my skin, moving her hips in time with me. "I need more. Need all of you. Don't hold back."

So I didn't.

"Hold onto me." She locked her ankles behind my waist, twined her arms around my shoulders, and I braced an arm on the wall behind her. Her hips dropped a fraction, seating herself even more deeply on me. My other hand gripped her ass as I held her pinned to the wall, picking up the pace, slamming into her at just the right angle until she couldn't stop the cries escaping her. She met me thrust for thrust, her nails digging deliciously into my back, my teeth scraping her collarbone. Both of us, uncontrollable.

The room was filled with steam, shower forgotten as we lost ourselves in each other, giving in to the all-consuming need until we crashed through the grand finale, shuddering together, panting and sweat-covered.

We breathed into each other for a long moment, then I kissed her again, more softly, and guided her legs back down.

We slid to the floor, still entangled in each other's arms, my heart threatening to break free from my chest. A laugh stuttered out of Maisie, and I looked at her questioningly.

"I'm sorry," she said, breaking into another laugh. Then another, ending in a snort.

"If you hadn't just squeezed me half to death, I might be offended by your laughter right now."

This only made her laugh harder.

The sound was so full of joy, of happiness, of *Maisie*, I couldn't help but chuckle, even without knowing what we were laughing at.

With a sigh, she stopped, her eyes settling on me as she ran her hands through my hair. "I have messed up so much in my life, Lys. And maybe nothing as epically as thinking I could ever not fall in love with you. You are my biggest fuck-up, and my best *everything*, all at once."

Placing another kiss on her lips, what was surely the thousandth of the day, I pulled her to her feet and into the shower, thankful the hot water was magical and hadn't run out. "I can live with that."

When we finally emerged from the water what felt like ages later, I wanted to collapse into bed and rest, my body and magic worn out from the events of the past 24 hours. But Maisie insisted on taking care of my welts, and luckily, Dev had left the salve on the front step.

As Maisie gently massaged the salve into every wound the venom had given me, easing the biting sting one spot at a time, I hoped I'd have a lifetime to show Maisie how much she meant to me, not just for rescuing me at my darkest hour, but for believing I was worth rescuing in the first place.

Chapter Forty

MAISIE

THE NEXT MORNING AT SCALLYWAGS, Blaze had the news playing on the TV for the first time since I'd ever ventured abovewater. All of the visitors here for the Summit had left, heading home to their own people. Half the town was gathered in the bar, barely making a sound as everyone watched what was happening.

"Sightings of what can only be described as monsters have cropped up all over the globe," the news anchor said as images and videos flashed behind her, showing all manner of shifters, including one familiar-looking kraken. "Many claim these videos to be the work of pranksters; however, there are hundreds if not thousands of eye-witnesses reporting they've seen these creatures. The evidence is stacking up to prove that what we all thought were merely myths might actually exist. Heading to Maine, of all places, for more on this story."

The screen flicked to a sandy beach, another news anchor strolling along the pier.

"It started just like any other day," he said, "when

suddenly, people fell from the sky. Then the water became infested with what people *thought* were just sharks."

"I saw a mermaid." The clip cut to a local, speaking with the news anchor. "I know that sounds insane, but hand to God, I saw a mermaid."

More images and videos flashed on the screen, showing footage from the rescue yesterday, and when I grimaced, Lys squeezed my hand.

Shifters were all over the news. And not just from our rescue. Blaze flipped through the channels, and it seemed like Inessa's operation had been just one of many that took place yesterday to force supernaturals to be revealed to humans in one way or another, in big enough numbers that it would be impossible for people to brush it under the rug as a hoax or doctored footage.

"Will the Council be able to cover this up?" Petra asked from where she stood between Blaze's legs, leaning back against him seated on a stool in front of the TV.

"They'd never be able to alter memories on this kind of scale," Ryker murmured, arms crossed where he sat next to Selene. "A handful, sure. But shifters have been seen all over the country at this point — different shifters, different sources and events. Probably internationally, too. There's no stopping the images and videos that have gotten out, either." He locked eyes with Orion. "Cat's out of the bag."

"Shit." A few people said it all at the same time, all of us on the same page.

"What do we do?"

"What happens now?"

"This is all Nergal's doing?"

"What has the Council said?"

"What's the plan?"

"Have they caught any of the prisoners?"

"Humans haven't harmed any of the shifters, right?"

Orion stood amidst the muttering, holding up a hand to get everyone to quiet down. It looked like he hadn't slept in days, dark circles under his eyes, his shirt wrinkled like it was the same one he'd worn yesterday.

"The Council is convening as we speak," he said, voice rough from exhaustion. "They'll send out their directions as soon as possible. For now, they've advised that we all lie low, and stick together. Shifters in particular should not go out anywhere alone, especially into any human-populated areas." He took a breath as a heavy silence fell over the room, all of us letting that sink in. "It's very possible our entire way of life is about to change. We might… It depends on how the humans react to this. It's a waiting game at this point."

"It's more important than ever that we learn how to link and increase our power, then," Julian said, and there were several hums of agreement.

"Especially shifters," Nimue agreed, squeezing Kit's arm beside her. "If there's any possibility they might be targeted by humans."

"Are you two volunteering to go first?" Owen asked, raising an eyebrow. Curious, but not pushing them.

Nimue and Kit exchanged a look, but before they had a chance to respond, Lys spoke up.

"I should go first," he said, and all heads in the room swung to look at him. "The most detailed account that we have was about a witch, right? So, a witch needs to go first.

And of all the witches in town, my magic is the most adaptable to others' through my Harmonic powers."

I met his eyes, and he swallowed before continuing. "I wouldn't force you to Link with me if you don't want to, because Goddess knows, it might not work. It might not be safe. We hardly know anything about this. But if given the choice, I wouldn't want to share magic with anyone else, Maze."

"Are we sure that's a good idea?" A voice called out from the back. "The only sea nymph story we have is that she went insane."

Lys's thumb traced across the back of my hand where he held it, his eyes never leaving mine while he answered. "Inessa worked alone, and had no idea what she was doing. She was also trying to rid herself of magic, not share it." He lowered his voice, speaking just to me. "I believe we can do this, Maze. It'll work." Pressing his forehead to mine, his words dropped to a whisper. "Let me share my magic with you. Let me offer you any measure of protection and power that I can. Just in case shit is about to go sideways."

"It could backfire," I reminded him, hating to burst his optimistic bubble. But actions sometimes had consequences that couldn't be reversed. Was that really a risk we wanted to take?

"It won't. I won't let it."

"You don't know that for sure. We'd be leaping into the unknown."

He grinned. "So leap with me."

I couldn't even help myself from mirroring his smile, his energy so contagious it was a current, pulling me along before I knew it.

"Do you trust me?" He cocked his head, repeating the words he'd said to me a few nights ago.

I licked my lips, my heart rate increasing as I took a breath. Because I did. Of course I did.

"Let's leap."

Three days later, Lys and Ostara, Morgaine and Lance, Owen, Blaze and Petra, and Ronan and I all met in the Town Hall conference room again to perform the very first Linking.

Petra had insisted on being there to observe and take notes. Before we'd arrived, she'd set up both an audio recording device and a video camera, and was ready on her laptop to record whatever other observations she deemed necessary. She and Owen had consulted extensively with each other, Ostara, and the Morgaine siblings on the best course of action.

Lys, as usual, was perfectly at ease, still confident that this would go off without a hitch. I, on the other hand, was already on my third shirt of the day, having sweat straight through the first two.

"It'll either work, or it won't," Lys offered helpfully, and I narrowed my eyes at him.

"You should be a motivational speaker."

"I basically am. What do you think music does for people?"

"If this renders us insane, I'm going to follow you around the psych ward for the rest of our days with a bubble gun laced with Man o' War toxin. Everytime they pop on your skin, you'll get zapped."

"If we both go insane, you won't remember to do that."

"Well, I'll text Kymari to do it then."

He shook his head, laughing softly, and squeezed my hand.

"You two ready?" Owen called over, and Lys stood, pulling me to my feet. We walked to the center of the room, which had been cleared out of chairs to make enough space for all of us to stand there together.

"Are you sure about this, Pearl?" Ronan's hand curled softly around my shoulder as he ducked his head to meet my eyes, his own filled with an unfamiliar concern.

I nodded, half to myself, and gave a bracing smile. "Yeah. We need this magic now more than ever, Dad." I looked up at Lys, his eyes soft as they met mine and there were no questions in my mind. Lys made me feel seen in a way I never had, and the thought of living my life anywhere but at his side was unimaginable. "And I want to share power with Lys. To share forever."

Lys beamed, dimples flashing as he leaned forward to kiss me lightly, showing me just how much my words meant to him. We'd talked a lot over the last three days, making sure this was what we both wanted, but I was prone to changing my mind. Not on this though.

"And Lysander?" Ostara quirked a brow at her son. "You know there are no guarantees here, don't you?"

"Well, seeing as he's my son, and Brigid and I are from the Coven of witches who completed the first Linking, his chances are better than anyone else in the room," Lance said, and the room went dead silent.

I wasn't even sure what part to focus on, staring wide-eyed at Lys, whose jaw came unhinged at this revelation.

"You figured it out though, didn't you Ostara?" Lance said, turning to Ostara at his side. "That's why you ran from me, but ended up here, with my sister, in case you were right."

"I wasn't sure," Ostara's voice cracked, her words whispered as she stared at Lys, not daring to look at Lance. "I was afraid you'd take him from me if you knew."

"Your magic is different, isn't it, Lysander?" Lance said, not addressing Ostara's comments as he stared at his son.

"He's one of us," Mo said with a bright smile as she wrapped an arm through Lance's, squeezing him to her side. "Even diluted, the demon blood is there."

"This explains *so* much about you, Mo," Blaze said with a shake of his head. "How anyone didn't automatically assume you were part demon is beyond me."

"Yes, well, I was well-equipped to be the Mother of Hellions."

"I have so many questions for all of you," Petra said from the side, eyes wide with excitement.

"Should we try it, then?" Owen said, his expression no less exuberant than Petra's.

Lys turned back to me, hands cupping my jaw as he smiled. "I'm ready to dive in."

I laughed, seeing the mischief that danced in his eyes at his fish joke. "There's no one I'd rather go crazy with."

Lys leaned in to kiss me again as Owen stepped forward. "No hard feelings, right Owen?" he said, his lips hovering just over mine.

"I wouldn't dare stand in the way of true love," Owen

answered, and I looked to the side, seeing the small smile he offered me. "That is a magic all its own."

"Excellent." Lys pulled my face back to his. "You're all mine."

My heart fluttered with anticipation as I listened to Owen's instructions, hearing the spell that Lys would cast over us to begin the Linking, but I couldn't concentrate on the words.

"Are you ready?" Lys said, holding his hands out for mine.

I laughed, a high, manic-sounding one even to my own ears. "Beyond ready. So ready it's crazy. No one has ever been more ready than me. You know me, when you hear 'crazy-dangerous-unprecedented-magic', you hear 'Maisie'."

Lys chuckled, his eyes shining as I touched my hands down to his, feeling the pulse of magic that hummed in his veins. "Close your eyes," he said, his voice low, a deep harmony meant only for me.

I did as he said, focusing on the way his power felt, feeling the expanse of it. As it soaked into my skin, colors exploded in my mind's eye, painting the room in a rainbow of shades, even with my eyes closed. I sucked in a breath, watching the magic move around me.

"Is this how your magic works? You can see it like this?" I said as I opened my eyes. Lys shone with a bright green and indigo glow, like looking at the ocean waves. I looked down at my own hands, a vibrant yellow, lacing through his.

"I can," he said, and nodded towards where his mother and Lance stood side by side. "And it sounds like I have even more to learn about my powers."

Lance smiled, placing an arm around Ostara's shoulders. She flinched at the touch, nearly jumping away from him before he dropped his hand back to his side.

"Okay, ready for mine?" I asked.

"Bubbling with excitement."

I laughed, then closed my eyes once more, reaching into my well of power, and bringing it to the surface. It moved through me in a wave, a tide called out to sea as it pushed through my hands and into Lys, mingling there.

"I can feel it," Lys said, his voice filled with awe. "Holy shit, this is insane."

I opened my eyes, seeing the way his aura now was a mixture of yellow and indigo, the colors swirling together, just as they did in me. My chest tightened as emotions overcame me, understanding what we'd just done. I wasn't fakedating Lys, or even *real* dating him anymore. We were Linked, tied together magically in a bond that would last forever. The thought of spending the rest of my days at his side brought happy tears to my eyes.

"Do you think it worked?" I asked, my voice barely above a whisper.

"I know the perfect way to find out," Lys said, bending at the waist as he picked me up and carried me out of the room on his shoulder.

"Put me down!" I called as he hopped down the steps and walked through the square, headed straight for the pier. I squirmed, trying to break free of his hold, my long hair practically trailing the ground as he walked.

A slap landed on my ass and I jerked up. "Quit squirming. I'd hate to drop you."

"Why are you carrying me?" I said as he stepped onto the pier.

"You're my buoy. Just in case this didn't work and I sink like a rock." As he said it, he stepped right off the edge of the pier, dropping us both into the water below.

Water closed over our heads, and I spun towards him, watching as his eyes blew wide with shock, then his mouth opened in excitement.

I'm breathing! Lys said, his mouth moving even though he didn't need to anymore.

Pulling him to me, I latched my lips onto his, kissing him deeply.

Then I pulled back enough to meet his gaze. *Want to see something cool?*

He nodded, bubbles tickling past both our faces, and I smiled.

Take me down to the Paradise City.

I rolled my eyes, but he was right. That was exactly where we were going.

The End

BLAZE

Epilogue

"BLAZE," Petra whispered, squeezing my hand, and I shook myself again, the flames at my fingertips flickering out. I'd been doing that so often this week, I probably looked like a dog with fleas. In a way, I was — only instead of insects shaking loose, it was sparks of my magic.

"Oops," I shot back, flashing her a grin.

It had been a week since Lysander and Maisie had Linked their magics and all hell had broken loose in the magical world. My brother Errakal and father Nergal had joined forces with not only Inessa, but rogue supernaturals all over the world, causing mayhem of all kinds.

Humans were reacting as everyone would expect — pointing fingers at enemies, and threatening the next witch trials. History sure did love to repeat itself.

Meanwhile, here in Deadlights Cove, Petra and Owen had poured over the recordings of the Linking ceremony and the book I'd turned over from my safekeeping, testing Lysander and Maisie to within an inch of their life.

"Are you all right over there?" Nimue called over to me

from where she and Kit stood on the steps of Town Hall, and I waved.

"All good! Carry on, Nimmie."

Petra and I — well, I, and then Petra, like the decent human being she was, had joined me — had been asked to step back a couple dozen steps from the proceedings. Due to my excessive spark production.

We were outside in the town square for that reason, a safe distance from the gazebo. There was currently a ring of scorched earth around me that might have looked ominous to an observer who didn't know any better.

But I couldn't help it. My energy and my magic was zip-zapping through me and it was all I could do to stop myself from flickering all over the place to dispel it.

I gave my hands another shake, and tried to focus on the sight in front of me, a grin spreading over my face as I did.

Nimmie, my Nimue, my favorite sister-cousin, was about to Link her magic with Kit's, her husband and mate.

Kit, for his part, looked decidedly more nervous, though he was doing his damnedest — which, honestly, wasn't that much — to be cool about it. He was right to be a bit nervous — demon magic was nothing to joke about, and he was about to go through all sorts of weird demon-puberty fails as he tried to get the hang of it.

It was going to be hilarious.

Morgaine, Lysander, Mo's brother Lance, and Owen were conducting the Linking, guiding them through the magical steps that would tie their powers together.

"Do you think his tattoos will burn off?"

I turned to Emerson, Kit's younger brother, who stood a

few feet away from the ceremony with several others from the skulk, his arms crossed.

"Hundred bucks says he burns the treehouse down," Nadir commented, eyebrows flashing, and Kit shot him a look that silenced the other members of his skulk.

"The spell doesn't turn him into a demon, so the tattoos should be fine," Lance explained, and a fleeting look of relief swept over Kit's face. The tattoos were symbolic to the skulk, and an important part of their shifter culture. "He won't have demon fire running through his veins, merely the ability to access Nimue's magic and thus have access to all of her abilities. It's an open pathway, not a new set of DNA."

Emerson still didn't look convinced, but they continued with the spell.

What felt like ages and also only minutes later, Kit's eyes went wide.

"Breathe," Nimue murmured, grasping his hands, which had begun sparking immediately and incessantly. He flinched, and Nimue laughed — the demon magic flowing through him balking at the direct order.

"Now do you see how hard it is to be told what to do?" Nimue smirked, and his eyes flashed yellow for a moment, though he was still working on breathing through the rush of new magic.

Finally, he wrestled control of the flames, the sparks tapering off until they were gone. He pulled Nimue in for a kiss before wrapping his arms around her, hers going around his waist, and those of us with superior hearing tuned out their moment of sweet nothings.

"Shift!" The heckling came from the skulk again, the tender moment over.

"Can she shift?" Kit asked the witches and Owen, pulling back from his wife but keeping an arm around her.

"Shifting is rooted in your magic, so I would think so, though it might not come as naturally as the flames," Owen offered with a shrug. "But, with practice —"

Kit had already stopped listening, his eyes gone molten amber as he met Nimue's.

"Do you want to try?" his voice was low, but I heard him all the same.

She murmured something in return, nodding. Kit pulled her close again, whispering something in her ear that brought a vibrant blush to her cheeks, and then —

With a flash, Nimue shifted, a jet-black fox standing in the puddle of clothes she'd been wearing, and Kit was right behind her. Whoops and cheers went up from the skulk as the rest of them shed their clothes too to join them in the shift.

A shower of sparks flew from Nimue's black paws as she and Kit danced around each other, fox-Kit over the freaking moon.

"Pokemon status achieved!" Akil, Kit's other younger brother, shouted in glee as he shed his shirt. "Fuck yes!" A blink later and he was a fox, bounding forward with the others.

All that excitement proved too much to contain and Kit once again lost control of his flames. The unfortunate victim was the gazebo.

"Oh, no — Blaze, dear?" Mo called over to me, then

decided against my help as her gaze trailed over my scorched earth ring, turning to Owen instead.

"Not a problem, Ms. Morgaine," Owen assured her. He pulled the magic out of the gazebo with ease, leaving only charred marks behind.

"Orion's not going to be thrilled about that," Petra muttered, and I shrugged.

"Nothing a little paint can't fix."

The foxes all greeted Nimue, fluffy tails thumping wildly at their official new member, though Nimue had been part of the family long before. Then, they were off — scampering out of the square and into the woods, heading onto skulk lands.

"Should we keep an eye over there for smoke trails?" Lysander asked the rest of us.

There were sooty paw prints all the way out of the square, and I wasn't sure who'd caused them.

Lance and Mo hummed and shrugged — their expressions so similar, it was easy to see the family resemblance.

"There are enough shifters with them. If anything gets out of control, they'll let us know," Mo said, then turned back to the rest of us.

"Next up?" Lance clapped his hands together, and I opened my mouth, about to volunteer Petra and myself, but the rumble of a motorcycle cut me off, drowning out all living beings within a five-mile radius.

Ryker pulled right up onto the sidewalk next to the gazebo, dropping the kickstand of his precious Harley into the flowerbed there since parking was a rare commodity in town today. I had to admire his chaotic thinking.

Selene unbuckled her helmet, slipping off the back of

his bike as she stood next to it, gazing up at the giant blond Viking dragon-shifter still sitting astride the bike.

"You ready for this?" Selene asked with a bright smile on her face. "Ready to let me annoy you forever?"

Ryker seemed to pale at her words, but grunted and hopped off his bike, taking her small brown hand in his giant tattooed one.

"We're next!" Selene called, waving her free hand in the air as they moved towards where Owen and Mo stood together.

"This is such a good day," Mo grinned, her eyes shining with tears brimming. "All of my babies, growing up."

"Pretty sure Ryker is twice your age, Mo," I said, trying and failing to picture Ryker as a child.

"Once I've had to offload bad investments for someone, I'm free to call them whatever I want," she answered. Ryker shot her a fierce look that only seemed to make Mo grin wider.

"The dragon shifter, right?" Owen said, staring up at Ryker as they stopped in front of him at the foot of the steps to Town Hall. "Well, this is exciting."

Selene scrunched her brow, turning slightly towards Owen as she studied him. "Any particular reason?"

"Well," Owen paused, heat rising in his cheeks as he looked away from the couple, staring over Selene's shoulder to avoid making eye contact. "It's just that, um…"

"Spit it out," Ryker growled, annoyance evident in his tone.

Sparks licked at my fingers again, and I shook them free. It was too much fun to witness someone on the receiving end of Ryker's aggression.

Owen cleared his throat, then looked at Selene. "As a physician and a fellow scientist, you should know that, when Linked, the chances of the two of you creating as close to a full-blooded dragon shifter as possible is something the supernatural world hasn't seen in almost six-hundred years. Now, it's not impossible that two of the remaining five dragons left in the world couldn't decide to mate and try for a full-blooded dragon shifter. But their reproductive cycles are much slower than yours as a witch, Selene, so your chances of getting pregnant and carrying to term are much higher."

Selene chuckled nervously, and Ryker's eyes flashed to his dragon's green, slitted pupils as smoke curled out from his nostrils.

"Oh, look!" Mo said, clapping her hands together happily as she leaned into Lance, "Ryker's just discovered he has a latent breeding kink. Grandma Mo is ready."

I suppressed a shudder before leaning down to whisper to Petra, "It's disturbing my mother knows what that is."

"You sure about this?" Selene said, facing Ryker again. "We don't have to. If you need more time to think about this, or even if you never want to do this, I can learn to —"

"We're ready," Ryker cut her off, nodding stiffly as he pulled Selene closer to him. "Now."

Owen stepped up, his face giddy as he neared the pair. "To be a part of history like this... Astounding. I've never actually met a dragon before and —"

"What part of now did you misunderstand?"

"Right, right." Owen nodded then began the same speech he'd given Kit and Nimue.

I bounced on my toes, clenching my fists to maintain the

loose hold on my flames as we watched, not daring to look at Petra for fear of burning the whole town down.

The moment Selene's brown eyes flashed to a neon purple with slitted pupils, Ryker slammed his mouth down on hers, lifted her high in the air until she wrapped her legs around his waist, and carried her off into the woods. Wings beat minutes later, a large black dragon rising above the town followed by a much smaller one with iridescent scales that shimmered a rainbow of colors in the sunlight.

Selene swooped low, and if it was possible for a dragon to look gleeful, she would have in that moment.

She opened her jaws, and a billow of smoke plumed out of her before a jet of fire followed it. Unfortunately, given her newly shifted status, her aim left a little to be desired, and —

"Oh, dear." Mo tutted as the gazebo, once again, burst into flames.

"Hmm," Owen murmured in agreement. "Afraid I can't do much with dragon fire."

"Well, with any luck, Orion won't have seen —"

"What is it with everyone in this town trying to sabotage the gazebo?" Orion boomed, swooping out from town hall, white wings bristling with rage.

"You've got to admit, it's a bit of a rite of passage, O," I said, then yelped as a zap of angel lightning got me.

A moment later, the dragon fire died out with a whomp, which meant Orion had doused its magic. As the smoke drifted away, Orion let out an exasperated sigh at the sight of the gazebo — its original white paint now thoroughly charred, the wood splintering in multiple places and half the roof drooping as the dragon fire had melted through it.

"Petra?" Owen said, and flames licked across my whole body, like a living bonfire.

"Sorry."

"Are you two ready?"

I tried to press my lips together to contain the manic — possibly maniac — grin that threatened to erupt over my face, but it was hopeless. I grasped Petra's hands in my sparking ones, letting go to shake them out every few seconds, but Petra didn't seem to mind.

"You really want to do this?" I asked. I could feel how much she wanted this, but I needed to be sure. Needed to hear her say it, again and again. I knew how much she could get into her own head, and I didn't want her to wake up in a week, a year, ten years, and have regrets. "No take-backs."

Her ocean blue eyes met mine, her cheeks already dusted in freckles even though it was only June. Fuck, how had it not even been a year since I met this woman? How had I ever lived without her?

"Hmm, let me check." Completely poker-faced, Petra reached into the pocket of her skirt and pulled out a scrap of paper. "Pro — will never need a lighter again. Con — will have to listen to Blaze rant about Eleanor for eternity —"

"Okay, well, that one is also a pro, so keep going, professor."

"Pro, can flicker home to see my parents whenever I want, then leave Indiana so fast it'll be like I was never there. Con —" Petra swallowed, and I could tell what had started as a joke had turned more serious. She went to stuff the list back in her pocket, but I stilled her hand, reading the words she had next.

"Con, will outlive" — I flicked my eyes up to her — "my parents, and everyone else."

"Well, I was probably always going to outlive my parents," she reasoned, trying to brush it off.

I raised a brow. "Not like this."

She nodded. "Not like this."

I looked down at the paper, ready to read the next one, but Petra said the words first. "Pro, maybe won't throw up every time we flicker. Pro, can make Blaze keep his promise to flicker me to every library in the world. Pro, will spend the rest of my life with the male I love."

Mo sniffed loudly behind us, but I could hardly hear anything from how loud my pulse thrummed. "That's a lot of pros, Petey."

"Owen, I think we're ready," she said, but her blue eyes never left mine.

"Did it work?"

I licked my lips, excitement buzzing within me, and while I thought I detected stronger demon magic now, I couldn't be sure. Maybe it was just my own, all amped up.

"Lys? Can you tell? Did her aura change?"

Lys let out a long whistle. "Hell yeah it did. Bright, fiery red."

"Fuck, okay." I squeezed her hands, then dropped them, hopping back. "Okay, just try to — I mean, can you feel the tingly zings? No, that's not what I mean. I mean, not those tingly — okay, in your fingertips! Yes, focus there, and think of fire — how can you not? So hot, so beautiful, like you, babe —"

"I think what Sabazios is attempting to say" — Owen cut in smoothly as I continued bouncing on the balls of my feet, my own fire a lost fucking cause at this point, sparks shooting out of my hands every which way — "is to focus your attention on your hands, and see if you can feel power flowing through you. Focus on that feeling and channel it to your palms."

"That's what I said!" Okay, maybe not exactly what I said.

But Petra nodded, determination creasing her brow adorably, and held her hands out. My own itched to reach for hers, to help her with this, but only she could draw out her own magic for the first time — fuck, my human had magic and we were going to —

"Blaze, for the love of God, the grass." Orion pinched his nose, and I blinked back to awareness to see my own fire devouring the town square.

"My bad, O."

I extinguished it with considerable effort, the grass scorched beyond repair, and shot Orion an apologetic look. Though, if I was being totally honest, I wasn't sorry at all. Nothing could ruin this day for me.

"Oh my God."

Flames lit in Petra's palms, her jaw dropping open as she stared at them.

"I didn't — I didn't think it would really —"

In a blink, I'd flickered to her side. In another, we were gone, reappearing at the top of the lighthouse.

"Okay, well, so much for that getting better," Petra muttered as I set her down on the gallery, clutching the railing to steady herself. "What are we doing here?"

"We need to be away from most flammable objects."

"We do?"

I wrapped my arms around her, turning her so I could press her against the side of the lighthouse. "We do. Can't have you setting the whole town on fire in a couple minutes."

I pushed my knee between her legs, my need overwhelming me from the second I saw those flames in her palms.

"Oh yeah?" She arched her back, understanding dawning on what I intended. "And what exactly do you think is going to happen in a couple minutes?"

Unable to hold myself back any longer, I crushed my lips to hers, feeling her magic rise up to meet mine. "Well, once in a couple minutes," I breathed, trailing my lips down her neck, feeling her shiver at the ghost of feeling. "And then again a little while after that—" I found the hem of her skirt, drawing it up her thigh. "And maybe again —"

"Ambitious," she chuckled, fingers trailing over my chest, and I groaned at the scorch marks she drew.

"Magic," I countered, grinning as she rolled her eyes at me, and pulled her mouth back to mine.

Later, a long, long while later, we lay on the gallery, watching the stars come out as we had so many months ago. Petra rested her head on my chest, her hand over my heart.

"I still can't believe you did this," I said, soothing a hand over her hair.

"Me? I get magical powers and eternal life," she chuckled. "What do you get out of it? Nothing."

I frowned, tilting her face up to mine. "Are you serious? I got you." Pink tinted her cheeks at my words, my cue to keep going. "And I get to keep you forever." I dropped my voice an octave, and the rose turned deeper hued. "And fuck if that isn't the best exchange in the whole damn world, Petey."

LYSANDER

Bonus Epilogue

One Year Later

"YOU OKAY, MAZE?" I asked as I took her hand, helping her down the narrow steps from the tiny airplane. "You're looking a little green around the gills."

"No fish jokes," she groaned, hand over her mouth as we stepped onto the tarmac, her legs a little shaky. "Not right now."

Chilly mountain air whipped around us, the first snow dotting the trees in November. When Lance had invited us out to Timber Creek for Thanksgiving, I couldn't find it in me to say no. We still had a long way to go in getting to know each other, but he'd made a solid effort over the last year and a half, and I was curious enough about my father to take him up on the offer.

"I thought flying on a plane for the first time would be exciting," Maisie shuddered, closing her eyes. "Instead, I'm ready to recreate our meet-cute, puking corn dogs all over the place."

"Okay, except let's all remember that didn't actually happen." I shook my head at the memory of the wild story she'd concocted on the spot.

Her sea green gaze looked up at me, a hint of amusement there. "I'm not correcting the story for anyone, so yes it did."

I smiled as I pulled her into my chest, hugging her tight. "You're good for my ego, you know that?" She laughed, fingers curling into my shirt. "Breathe, and I'll help you dispel the motion sickness."

She did, and I sent a wave of magic through her. Now that I knew I came from the original line of linked demons and witches, I didn't have to hide how easily I could wield my magic. "Better?"

She nodded, stepping away from me, but I reached forward and grabbed her hand, not ready to let go of her completely. She squeezed my hand. "Are you nervous?"

I shrugged, trying to play it cool, but she knew me better than that.

"Don't worry." She gave a slow grin, her eyes twinkling in her tell-tale sign of mischief. "I'm ready to come to your rescue when things get awkward."

"That actually makes me more nervous."

"As it should. You never know what's going to come out of my mouth. I don't even know until it's too late to stop it."

Having stalled long enough, I took our suitcases from the attendant, and together we walked towards the small hangar where an SUV waited.

A lanky teenager in a Timber Creek logo hoodie jumped out of the passenger side door, golden blond hair disarray. "Lysander, right?" he asked, holding his hand out. "I'm Leif.

Lance sent us to pick you guys up since he got delayed behind a snow plow coming back from the store."

I shook his hand as someone emerged from the driver's side, and nodded when I recognized West Larkin. West was more or less the leader of Timber Creek, and the Alpha to the wolf pack here. "Great to meet you, Leif." Putting an arm behind Maisie, I urged her towards the open car door. "This is Maisie, my partner. Maisie, you remember West?"

Maisie waved, offering Leif a warm smile before climbing inside, and nodded at West. They'd only met in passing over a year ago at the Summit, but West was a difficult male to forget.

"Wow, we get a ride from the Alpha himself?" Maisie laughed, shaking West's hand. "We must be either important, or trouble."

West chuckled. "Lance is a good friend of the family, basically an uncle to us."

Once we were seated in the back with our luggage stored in the trunk, West climbed behind the wheel, and put it in gear.

Snow crunched under the tires as we pulled away from the landing strip onto a tree-lined road. I craned my neck, looking out the window at the winter wonderland around us. While Deadlights Cove was tucked into the national park in Maine and had plenty of both trees and snow, everything about the Colorado scenery felt more vast.

"How far are we from Timber Creek?" I asked, looking for any hint of the town my father called home.

"About 20 minutes," Leif answered. "Everyone's so excited to meet you."

"Everyone?" I asked, confused. When Lance had invited

me to Thanksgiving, he hadn't mentioned anyone else was coming. Did I have family other than him and his sister, Morgaine?

West laughed. "He didn't tell you about our Thanksgiving tradition, did he?"

I exchanged a nervous glance with Maisie. "No, he didn't tell me much of anything."

"Well, I hope you like big family gatherings," Leif said. "Lance has hosted our whole family for the last decade. Thanksgiving is loud."

***

It turned out loud was an understatement for pandemonium.

In addition to Lance, Leif, and West, there were West's four siblings, his two-year-old niece, his dad Heath, who was Lance's best friend, and a demon.

How we all fit into Lance's little mountain cabin was a mystery, but somehow he made it work, stuffing us into his dining room around a raw-edge dining table.

"So, you're the whizz kid," Heath stated, scooping out a giant spoonful of mashed potatoes, then passing it to his daughter Aspen.

Lance's ears went red, and I glanced between them.

"Lance here's always boasting you're a magical genius, how you can do all the types of spellwork," Heath clarified.

I shrugged, trying to ignore the intense stares of a roomful of wolf shifters. And, apparently, one adopted mountain lion. "More or less."

"He's amazing," Maisie piped up. "He's going to be taking over as Head of Coven soon, and that's on top of his super successful band and the camps he runs to help young witches get in touch with their powers."

I squeezed Maisie's leg under the table, shooting her a smile.

"Band?" Heath cocked his head, then reached over and clapped West on the shoulder. "Hey, we should have them do the festival some time."

West nodded. "Done."

"Oh!" the demon, Cruz, snapped his fingers, a flash of flame erupting between them before it quickly disappeared. "That's how I know you. Did your band play at Super-palooza a few years ago?"

I opened my mouth to confirm that we had played the supernatural music festival, but the family was already talking over each other.

"Is it true you're a princess?" came from the younger sister, Summer.

"Incoming!" warned West's brother Terran right before his daughter threw a glob of mashed potatoes across the table, giggling maniacally. It landed with a splat on Cooper's face, the lion shifter giving his niece a resigned stare while the tiny girl chanted "'Tato Cat! 'Tato Cat!" at him.

"I think it's an improvement, Tato," Cruz commented, grinning at the stone-faced Cooper, whose stare promised cold-blooded revenge.

"Yes," Maisie answered Summer, while Terran struggled to wrangle his daughter from throwing more food, her 'Tato Cat chants rising to a shriek as he tickled her. "My father Ronan is king of the North Atlantic sea nymphs."

"Wow," Summer sighed wistfully. "That's so amazing. You must have the most incredible wardrobe in the world. Is it like Cher's in Clueless, where you can push a button and it'll show you different outfits?"

Maisie frowned. "Um —"

"Ignore her," Aspen cut in, waving a hand towards Summer. "She thinks everything is a Hallmark movie."

"Truly, the dream," Summer nodded.

"I heard you two were a part of the Linking trials," West interrupted, glancing between us with curiosity.

"We were," I confirmed. "Though I'm still getting the hang of shifting."

Maisie snorted. "The first day he tried it, he just kept flashing between a dozen forms, but couldn't hold any one of them longer than a few seconds. It was hilarious. My friend Kymari kept snapping at him every time he was something smaller than a turtle."

The Larkins chuckled, but West only nodded. Clearly, he had more questions for another time.

"I think if I Linked with anyone, I'd want to be able to fly," Summer mused. "Or maybe flicker. It'd just be cool to be able to have that much freedom."

"It'd be way more practical to have witch powers," Aspen said.

A collective groan swept through the siblings, and Aspen threw her hands up. "It's true."

"You're right, sweetheart," Heath said, patting her hand.

"God forbid anyone have fun with their magic," Terran scoffed, meeting Summer's eye conspiratorially.

"It might be practical, but it's not simple," Maisie cut in, easily fitting in with this boisterous family. She scrunched her nose. "I've been working with a few witches for a while now, and I still struggle. But it can also be fun — Mo taught me her special hangover remedy."

Appreciative ooohs went through the room at that, even Cooper offering Maisie a nod of respect.

I gaped at her. "She never taught me that recipe."

Maisie shot me a coy look, fluttering her eyelashes. "I know."

Cruz and Terran chuckled. "Burn, man," Terran shook his head.

"Teach me," I demanded.

Dropping a hand to her chest, Maisie widened her eyes. "I'm sworn to secrecy."

"You're a Morgaine now, son," Lance said with a glass raised towards me. My heart stuttered a beat at that turn of phrase, but it was great to hear. "I'll teach you, same as I taught my sister."

Maisie bumped my shoulder, and I looked down at her, realizing just how much love in my life I had to be thankful for this year.

***

Long after dark, the Larkin clan left, leaving us alone with Lance. Maisie excused herself to go to bed, tired as it was already late back East, but I decided to stay up. The house was quiet, feeling the absence of everyone here, but today had been fun. So different than dinner alone with my mother, as I'd spent so many years.

Lance pulled a beer from the fridge, holding it up in inquiry. When I nodded, he grabbed a second one, popping the caps before handing one to me and joining me in the living room.

"Sorry if that was a bit much with everyone," he said

with a grimace. "The Larkins are family. And ever since Heath's mate passed, I do what I can to be there for him, for them."

A twinge rippled through my heart at that, but I shoved it aside. It wasn't Lance's fault he hadn't known about me, that we hadn't had a chance for any of this before. That he had this whole crazy big family, had had them, for all these years.

For the last year, he'd done his best to get to know me, and day by day, I was getting used to the idea of him in my life, letting go of the resentment for all the years we'd missed together. My emotions must have shown on my face more than I'd intended.

"Ostara was doing what she thought was best," he said, then took a long pull of his beer. "And we can't change the past." He raised his bottle. "To the future?"

I smiled at his words, his attitude so much more like my own than my mother's had ever been, and raised my beer to clink against his. "To the future, and many more chaotic holidays to come."

Want more Deadlights Cove?

There's more to come in our little paranormal universe! Join Aimee's newsletter at aimeevancebooks.com to be the first to know!

Deadlights Cove

Smoke Show

Deja Brew

A Very Merry Christmoose (Novella)

Wing and a Miss

Pier Pressure

Karma is a Witch

Foxing Day (Novella)

Timber Creek

Wild Wild Wolf

Love Bites

ALSO BY AIMEE VANCE

Mayhem Hockey Club

Moms of Mayhem

Call of the Norns: A Viking Time Travel Fantasy Trilogy

Fates Illuminated

Fates Promised

Fates Defied

Acknowledgments

When we started writing *Smoke Show,* the idea was to create a chaotic supernatural town where everyone could fit in. Along the way, we have truly fallen in love with this world and these characters.

To everyone who has ever picked up one of our books, thank you for reading and diving into this universe we've made. It's been so fun to share it with you! We have so many more stories to tell, and we hope you'll stick around!

To our DC Team — Amy, Brit, and Elle: We're not sure what we did to get so lucky to have you as friends and supporters. Thank you for being our biggest champions.

From B: To J, thank you for all your support.

From Aimee: To Chris and the girls, I can't even begin to explain how much I love you.

And to Dani, Your friendship on this indie author journey has meant the world to me. I'm going to bug you relentlessly until you read this book to see your name printed back. I'm serious when I say I'm never gonna give you up, never gonna let you down, never gonna run around and desert you. Yep. I just Rick-Rolled you on paper.

About B. Perkins

B. has been making up stories about magic since she learned how to write words on paper. When not immersed in fictional worlds, she enjoys spending time in nature. She has several degrees in various things, and if all they're good for is to provide background in creating fantasy worlds and systems, then maybe they were worth it.

instagram.com/b.p.writes

About Aimee Vance

Fueled by peach tea and chaos, Aimee Vance writes heartwarming and laugh-out-loud romance stories. She holds a B.S. in Public Relations from Texas Christian University and has always been an avid fantasy reader.

Residing in Texas with her husband, two young daughters, and Labrador Retriever, Aimee loves to transport readers to worlds hidden between the pages where magic and love intertwine. She prefers sassy heroines, grumpy heroes, and enough humor to keep you chuckling with every page.

facebook.com/aimeevancebooks

instagram.com/aimeevancebooks

goodreads.com/aimeevancebooks

amazon.com/author/aimeevancebooks

bookbub.com/authors/aimee-vance

www.ingramcontent.com/pod-product-compliance
Lightning Source LLC
Chambersburg PA
CBHW030055310726
48970CB00004B/1020